SIR JEAN OF ACRE

Helena P. Schrader

MINERVA PRESS
MONTREUX LONDON WASHINGTON

SIR JEAN OF ACRE
Copyright © Helena P. Schrader 1997

All Rights Reserved

No part of this book may be reproduced in any form,
by photocopying or by any electronic or mechanical means,
including information storage or retrieval systems,
without permission in writing from both the copyright owner
and the publisher of this book.

ISBN 1 86106 109 9

First Published 1997 by
MINERVA PRESS
195 Knightsbridge
London SW7 1RE

Printed in Great Britain by
Antony Rowe Ltd, Chippenham, Wiltshire

SIR JEAN OF ACRE

*To Frank & Elizabeth
with thanks for countless,
stimulating discussions & travels
which are the source of my
writings.
Love
Helena*

Contents

Najac — April 1278	7
Peyroles — June 1283	34
Cahors — June 1283	43
Acre — October 1283	55
Acre — 1287	71
County of Tripoli — April 1289	91
Nazareth — March 1290	108
Acre — August 1290	181
Acre — September 1290	189
Acre — April 1291	203
Acre — May 4, 1291	219
Acre — May 16, 1291	227
Acre — May 18, 1291	242
Acre — May 19, 1291	258
Acre — May 25, 1291	275
Najac — June 1291	292
Marseilles — July 1291	308

Limassol — August 1291	312
Kolossi — August 1291	324
Limassol — August 1291	331
Cyprus — October 1291	347
Paphos — October 1291	356

Najac
April 1278

The sun flooded the tower chamber the moment the shutters were flung open, and Eleanor, pausing to consider the countryside awakening to spring which was spread out before her in the valley, smiled unconsciously. "You have a splendid day for your wedding, Alice," she told her eldest daughter without turning her head. Her gaze swept across the landscape delighting in the shimmering sun on the river as it coiled around the foot of the hill, the bursts of forsythia on the bank beyond and the haze of green that announced the budding of the trees.

"May it be a good omen for my married life," Alice replied eagerly, and Eleanor turned from the window to her daughter.

Alice stood stark naked before the fireplace, letting her maid dry her from her bath. With straight, dark eyebrows, a well formed nose between prominent cheekbones, and a long, regal neck, she was an attractive young woman. Her hair, black when wet, as now, hung to her thighs. Her breasts were large for a maiden of eighteen and her belly and thighs well rounded. Alice was smiling with confidence and delight.

'And why shouldn't she?' her mother thought indulgently. 'She is much prettier than I was at her age, and her bridegroom is a young man she has known all her life and with whom she is head over heels in love.' "I'm sure it is a good omen, child," she lied. She did not believe in such omens, considering her own wedding day had been wet and gloomy. She stepped down from the window. "I must see to our guests and household, but I'll be back before we proceed to the church."

Eleanor de Najac was forty-seven years old. Her dark hair was streaked with strands of grey, and her skin had lost its resilience, but she was still a handsome woman. She was tall, slender and held herself very straight, despite the shattered thigh that gave her an awkward limp when she moved. Her brow, like her daughter's, was high above a straight nose and prominent cheekbones. The lines carved into her skin were benevolent, reflecting the emotions which had formed them.

She navigated the narrow, spiral stairs of the tower with agility despite her handicap, her left foot leading on each step. As she reached the landing giving access to the great hall, she was assaulted by a flustered steward. The Comte de Foix had arrived the previous day with a far larger escort than anticipated and now Philippe de Grailly had been announced with his wife, daughters and twelve attendants. The arrangements for the accommodation of the guests were no longer adequate.

Eleanor calmed the elderly official. Mentally, she registered it was past time to find him an energetic and able assistant, but the old man resisted and alienated the clerks put under his direction. Only her son Jean seemed to have a way with the irascible old man, she reflected, and wondered where Jean was. There was no time to enquire. She discussed the alternatives for the accommodation of the noble Philippe de Grailly and together with the steward found a suitable solution.

Meanwhile the kitchen clerk had come in search of Madame.

The cook had discovered that half the oranges imported at such expense were already rotten. The purveyor responsible ought to be dismissed or charged the cost of the losses! For the feast, however, some other delicacy would have to be hastily made, and the cook requested her decision. Eleanor went with the clerk down to the ground floor kitchens. Here a dozen boys, many come from the village for the days of the wedding festivities, kept the fires going, turned the spits, pounded almonds, chopped onions and parsley, beat eggs, ground pepper and performed various other tasks. Between the high-pitched chatter of the boys and the shouts and swearing of the cook and his assistants, the kitchen seemed like bedlam, and the heat was oppressive.

The cook was an officious man fully aware of his importance. He was nearing fifty, burly of build and greying of hair, and he commanded his kitchen staff like a sergeant. It was rare for mishaps to mar the results. Now he blustered and raged against the purveyor, feeling his entire reputation was in jeopardy – and that with half of Languedoc assembled and the Comte de Foix himself present. Eleanor let him rage, and then assured him that she had the utmost confidence in his ability to salvage the situation. "Your Lombard slices are greatly praised whenever they are served."

"Lombard slices!" The cook humphed. "Much too ordinary for a wedding!"

"And pine nut candy?"

"Fried fig pastries would be far more appropriate, m'lady, but we need another ten pounds of figs."

Eleanor calculated. It would take a squire on a fast horse more than two hours to reach Cordes, where figs could be obtained. That meant it would be five hours or more before he was back, assuming no mishaps, and with the horse all but foundered. That was too little time and not worth the expense or the risk.

"No, make pine nut candy for the lower tables, and fig pastries with the figs you have for the upper tables."

The cook frowned, but he did not contradict her.

Emerging from the kitchens into the sun-soaked inner ward, Eleanor was almost run down by her son Louis. Louis was her second son, but, as his elder brother Geoffrey had died at the age of three, Louis was now her heir. He was twenty-two years of age, and of all her children he resembled his father most closely, with reddish brown hair and a stocky figure. He wore his hair long and his face clean-shaven except for a moustache, a fashion his mother found somewhat affected and foppish. Louis was in fact a very serious and dutiful youth whom she could not fault with the slightest frivolity or irresponsibility. It was as if he affected the appearance of a dandy to make up for his overly sober nature.

"Mother! Where have you been? Philippe de Grailly has arrived with his lady and daughters. Papá has been asking for you."

"Then we shall go up to him. Do I look all right?" Eleanor paused to let her son inspect her, fearing her morning activities had left her skirts soiled or her veils in disarray.

Louis gave her a conscientious inspection, as she knew he would. He pulled the collar of her gown straight where it had slipped lopsidedly under her surcoat, tightened the laces of her surcoat under her right arm where they had become loose, and told her to rewind her wimple. Louis insisted on things being picture-perfect. Eleanor did his bidding, vaguely bemused by the thought that he would make a demanding husband, whereas Geoffrey took little interest in details of dress, much less disarray, because he insisted she was beautiful as long as she was happy.

Louis officiously took her arm and escorted her through the great hall to the great chamber where the guests of importance were already starting to assemble. This square high-ceilinged room occupied the entire first floor of the eleventh-century keep. In addition to the newly arrived De Grailly with his family, the Comte de Foix, the Sire d'Albret and the lords of Lavaur and Argentat were present with their ladies and older children. The most prominent merchants from Cordes had also been invited and attended in strength, honoured and eager for the opportunity to mingle with the nobility.

The commander of the Knights Templar at Cahors was also among the guests, Eleanor noted with mixed feelings. Pierre de Bourgneuf was a congenial, balding man in his mid-fifties who had made a career in the Templars because of his remarkable administrative abilities. He was largely credited with building up an efficient network for providing the Templars in the Holy Land with well-trained, quality remounts. This was an astonishing feat if one considered the rate at which the Templars 'consumed' horses in desert warfare and escort duties, despite the shrinking size of the kingdom of Jerusalem.

But for all Bourgneuf's positive personal qualities, Eleanor would have preferred it if her husband did not retain such cordial relations with him. She had nearly lost Geoffrey to the Templars a quarter of a century earlier, and he still possessed a letter from the late Master De Sonnac which would secure him readmittance to the order at will. The very sight of the white surcoat and red cross made her stomach tighten with latent resentment.

Louis guided her across the room to where Geoffrey was standing with de Grailly. De Grailly's wife and daughters were still changing out of their travelling clothes and he was alone at the moment, chatting to his host and the Comte and Comtesse de Foix. The invitation of De Grailly had been a somewhat risky decision on Geoffrey's part, for De Grailly was one of the wealthiest and most powerful Gascon vassals of the English king. But the kings of England and France were on relatively amicable terms at the moment, and De Grailly and the Comte de Foix were bound by a mutual hatred of the Comte d'Armagnac.

As she approached them from across the room, Eleanor felt a surge of pride at the sight of her husband. No one would have guessed that he was nearing fifty for he had the hard, athletic figure of a much younger man. He still wore his hair trimmed short and his beard full – remnants of his novitiate with the Templars, and both beard and hair were only lightly salted with white hairs. As the father of the bride, he was dressed with exceptional elegance – for him. He was wearing a knee-length surcoat of embroidered blue silk, open at the sides to reveal the amber velvet tunic beneath. His hose was blue and his shoes a natural, brown leather. Compared with the Comte de Foix in his patterned hose and cloth-of-gold surcoat with jewelled buttons, Geoffrey looked humble. But that was appropriate for the son of a landless crusading knight and a Cypriot peasant woman. Anything more showy might have provoked animosity.

Geoffrey caught sight of his wife and smiled at once. As she joined the group she dipped her knee to the Comte and Comtesse of Foix, but De Grailly bowed low over her hand. "Madame, if your daughter is graced with your beauty she will be a beautiful bride indeed."

"Alice is far prettier than I ever was, *Monsieur*," Eleanor replied proudly. "We are deeply honoured that you made the long journey from Bordeaux to be with us today."

"I combined the visit with business in Toulouse and Albi," De Grailly admitted, "but I am delighted to be here."

They exchanged various pleasantries, until the arrival of the bridegroom and his family distracted the company. Antoine de Montfranc was an elegant young man with fine, blond hair and a clean-shaven, boyish face. Many maids, including Alice, found him irresistible and, unfortunately, he was aware of the fact. Eleanor considered him somewhat superficial and unsteady but hoped he would improve with marriage and age. Geoffrey considered him a spoilt, self-centred youth of limited intelligence and inferior education. But Alice had her heart set on the match, and Antoine was heir to an established and respected noble family with substantial holdings. It was very much to Geoffrey's credit that the Montfrancs considered Alice a fit bride for their heir – even if the dowry they expected had depleted Geoffrey's reserves entirely.

The Montfrancs at once joined the circle around the Comte de Foix, and Eleanor, conscious of the hour set for the wedding approaching, asked Louis where his younger brothers were. Neither Jean nor William were anywhere in sight.

Louis lowered his voice and turned his head away from the assembled company so his words would be heard by his mother only. Gaston de Foix, the Count's eldest son, had apparently 'insisted on taking Antoine to the brothels of Cordes last night. Jean went with them, and no doubt he is still trying to make up for the lack of sleep and excess of wine.' Louis's tone was contemptuous, and Eleanor sighed inwardly. She did not like the way Louis seemed to relish every fault in his younger brother Jean. Jean was barely a year younger than he was, and from the time they had been little boys, Louis had made a point of telling her about each and every one of Jean's frequent misdemeanours. Transparent and understandable as the jealousy had been when he was a child, Eleanor felt that he should have outgrown it by now. It should have been perfectly obvious to Louis that she would prefer not to know that Jean and the bridegroom had spent the night at a brothel. Protecting her feelings should have been more important than the opportunity to make Jean look bad. But this was not the place or time to reprove Louis. "And William?"

"William rode out with the other youths at dawn, but they swore they would be back long before noon." Louis was more lenient towards his youngest brother. William would be turning fifteen in the summer and, as it happened, half-a-dozen of the guests had brought youths of roughly that age with them. Like William himself, the bulk of them were serving as squires in some other noble household and this wedding was a splendid holiday from their alternately taxing and dreary duties. It was only natural that they would band together and think up any number of activities, but Eleanor doubted if they would make much of an effort to attend the wedding mass. More likely they would arrive, sweating and starving, just in time for the feast. 'Well, it is the nature of youth,' she decided with an indulgent shake of her head.

Pages were offering the assembled guests spiced wine and wafers and, since everything was functioning smoothly, Eleanor begged to be excused. It was time to return to Alice.

*

Jean had gone to help organise the stabling of the horses after Philippe de Grailly arrived. The castle stables were completely inadequate for the nearly two hundred horses now collected. Jean ordered the household draught horses and hacks transferred to the paddocks, and insisted that the horses of the visiting grooms and servants be stabled in the cattle barn, empty since the cattle had been put out to pasture earlier in the week.

It was while he was here that William's stallion had slunk in, matted with mud and sweat, rider missing. There was a great gash, bloody and swollen, along the off hind cannon bone. Jean questioned the grooms and learned that his brother had set off shortly after dawn in the company of Robert, the younger son of the Count de Foix, Olivier d'Albret, Pierre de Montfranc and Jacques Cardunier. They had been armed with crossbows and short swords.

Jean sighed and ordered his stallion to be saddled. His younger brother was one of those boys who always needed the company of other boys for his own happiness. He was simply incapable of amusing himself. He, furthermore, was the kind of youth who lived for the praise of his peers. Worst of all, he had a *penchant* for daredevilry and, if egged on by others, he knew no bounds because he confused common sense with cowardice. Jean could not know the exact nature of what had occurred, but he could guess the outlines of it. In some self-set test of skill and courage, Will had got the worst of it. With luck he'd only been humiliated by a fall and the flight of his stallion. If he was not lucky he was injured, possibly seriously. Jean avoiding thinking about the fact that he might even be dead. A bad fall could break a man's neck or spine, and a crossbow triggered accidentally would kill a man more surely than a boar.

*

As Eleanor entered Alice's chamber, her youngest daughter Eloise jumped up from the bed at the sight of her mother. "Mamá, help me with my hair. It's such a mess!"

"And whose fault is that?" her mother reproved her gently.

Eloise was twelve, plump and short-sighted. She had been a whiny child and showed every indication of growing into a nagging woman. She pouted and protested now. "It's not my fault! My hair is snarly by nature."

"Well, Eleni will have to help you. Your sister has first claim on my attention today."

Eleni was the Cypriot serving woman Eleanor had brought with her from that distant Mediterranean island after her marriage twenty-six years earlier. Sometimes Eleni admitted to homesickness for the olive and almond groves, the dry, hot summers and the fresh oranges, but on the whole she was content to be in service to the Lady Eleanor. Service to the Lady Eloise was another matter and she made a sour face behind Eleanor's back.

Alice's maid had rubbed her entire body with lavender-scented oil and then dressed her in fresh cotton drawers, corset and shift. She had slipped the sheerest of silk stockings on to her legs and fastened them with embroidered garters above the knee. As Eleanor arrived, she was just slipping the lilac coloured gown over the bride's head. The gown was closely fitted over the bodice and fastened up the back with buttons. It had a high collar, a modest train and long tight sleeves closed with amethyst buttons. The only other adornment was purple cording at neck and hemline. Over the gown, Alice wore a loose sleeveless surcoat that ended mid-calf. This was of purple velvet and had a broad band of golden embroidery from the hem to knee. Dressed in this finery, Alice sat down before her mirror and her mother took up her comb to brush out her hair, which the bride would wear free and uncovered as a symbol of her maidenhood.

Alice was as eager and elated as a bride ought to be and it made her mother angry and embarrassed to think that Antoine had spent the night before the wedding at a brothel. Admittedly, it was hardly reasonable or normal for a young nobleman to come to his bride a virgin. Ironically, she admitted, she had the hated Temple to thank for the fact that Geoffrey had been as virgin as she had been herself. But there was a world of difference between the conquests of curious and virile youth and the act of visiting a brothel on the eve of one's marriage.

"Is something the matter, Mamá?" Alice had seen her face in the mirror.

"No, Alice dear, I was just remembering what a miserable and rainy day my own wedding was."

"But you were a beautiful bride and given away by a king!" Eleni spoke up loyally.

"I'd rather be given away by Papá than any king," Alice declared proudly, and her mother patted her shoulder.

From the open window came the first clang of the church bells on the extreme point of the ridge below the castle. The villagers would be closing their doors and toiling up the narrow, cobbled street to line the path from the castle to the church.

*

In the village, they had been able to tell Jean that his brother and his companions had ridden north, and at the mill the information was confirmed. After that, tracking five well-shod stallions in the moist spring earth proved relatively easy even after they left the road beyond the river and cut across the fields. When the tracks entered the woods on the ridge beyond, Jean had to slow his pace considerably. The youths had spread out some, and it took more concentration to find the tell-tale signs of broken twigs, hoof-marks and horse droppings.

Jean now regretted that he had not brought a hunting horn with which he might have tried to make contact. Then he urged his stallion forward, leaning over his pommel to avoid low-hanging branches, and to track better.

*

The villagers and serfs, wearing their modest finery, lined the path below the castle leading to the church. They were clearly enjoying the holiday. Of course they had grumbled at the feudal fee owed to the lord for the marriage of his eldest daughter, but it was paid now and they had the day off and would have their share in the great feast. They enjoyed too the spectacle of the guests in their velvets, furs and cloth of gold, and they chattered loudly, comparing the dresses of the ladies and the outlandish elegance of the squires and knights. For Eleanor they raised a cheer as she was escorted by Louis to the portal of the massive basilica. But the biggest cheer was reserved for the bride and her father. Then the villagers crowded after the bride, following her, calling out their good wishes. Alice blushed in pleasure on her father's arm while Geoffrey put aside his own ambivalence about the wedding and smiled for his daughter.

The guests were clustered at the side portal of the basilica. The villagers had been forced to build this oversized stone monument as penance for their Cathar leanings in the first half of the century. To this day, the priests appointed were warned to watch for any signs of heresy among their flock and report it at once to the bishop. As a result, the basilica sat on its rock over the steep valley, an outsider, unloved by the people. But to have scorned the basilica for the wedding would have been to arouse suspicion, and Eleanor would not risk it.

In the open, before the church, Alice's hand was placed in Antoine's and the marriage vows exchanged. Then the bridal couple led the way into the church for mass. Though the sun shone with unseasonable warmth outside, the church was still gripped in the chills of winter, and Eleanor shivered. Geoffrey at once put his arm around her waist and his warmth comforted her. She leaned against his firm, muscular chest and basked in the security he offered her. Geoffrey dropped a kiss on the top of her head.

*

As he crested the next ridge, Jean was beginning to question the sense of continuing his search. The trail seemed to have disappeared, so he would have to retrace his steps until he picked it up again. Alone, such a search could take all day. He could hear the church bells clanging incessantly, and, looking back, the basilica stood out like a white scar upon the grey-green landscape below the crowning splendour of Najac castle. Alice was now Antoine's wife, he reflected sadly, wondering how Alice could be so taken with an ass like Antoine. He had tried to discuss it with her, but she had become irrational and angry. Now he shrugged, admitting his inability to fathom the female mind, and redirected his attention to his search. Since he had missed the wedding in any case, he might as well continue.

It took him a quarter of an hour to pick up the trail again, and he had not gone very far when his stallion abruptly baulked, then threw up his head with quivering nostrils and whinnied shrilly. From below came an answering whinny, and then a thin, young voice. "Hello! Hello! Who goes there?"

Jean did not recognise the voice, but it sounded young and frightened.

"Jean de Preuthune!" he answered, holding his fidgeting stallion to listen for the exact location of the voice which answered.

"Thank God! Sir Jean! Your brother's hurt! Come quickly!" the young voice shouted.

Jean followed the voice, calling out periodically for directions, and he soon met Jacques Cardunier riding towards him. The son of a wealthy Cordes merchant, Jacques knew the area better than the others, which was why they had sent him back for help. He explained this somewhat breathlessly as he turned his horse around and fell in beside Jean, indicating the direction to take.

Jacques led the way to an abandoned quarry, where they found the others. Three stallions were hobbled at the surface, and the boys were crouching in the bottom of the quarry beside Will. Jean dismounted and made his way down into the quarry. Pierre de Montfranc was just thirteen and looked pale and frightened while he crouched beside his injured friend. Robert de Foix and Olivier d'Albret both jumped up at the sight of Jean and hastened toward him, flushed, nervous, agitated. "We made a stretcher," Olivier pointed, "but we can't get up the slope of the quarry with it."

Jean glanced around at the walls of the quarry and nodded. One would need to use one's hands to scramble back up to the top.

"And neither of us can carry Will alone," Robert de Foix pointed out. Though already fifteen, Robert de Foix was small and slight of build, whereas Will was tall for his age and still somewhat pudgy. Again Jean nodded, advancing toward his brother.

Will lay on the quarry floor trembling with shock and cold and pain. His face was grey and contorted, he had bitten his lip until it was bloody and tear-streaks on his dirty face betrayed the fact that he had cried. He seemed more child than youth under the circumstances, his roundish face still soft and beardless, his body limp. His left shin was snapped in two, the bone sticking out of his skin and the blood soaking his hose all the way to his ankle-high boots. An improvised splint lay ready beside the leg, but apparently none of the boys had had the courage to fit it.

"Don't you have a blanket or cloak, anything to wrap him in?" Jean asked sharply.

The boys shook their heads, Robert adding feebly, "Only up by the horses—"

"Fetch it, damn it!" Jean ordered angrily, and then knelt down beside his brother as Olivier started scrambling towards the rim of the quarry. "Will? Are you hurt anywhere other than your leg?"

Will shook his head without opening his eyes.

"You're sure?"

Will nodded, and fresh tears started oozing out of his eyes.

"Good. Then I can carry you out of here on my back."

This was, of course, easier said than done. Any movement of the leg caused Will to cry out and, while Jean splinted the leg, Will cried out and sobbed with pain. Scaling the walls of the quarry perilously overburdened, Jean could not avoid knocking the wounded leg against the walls now and again, and each time Will howled with outraged agony. But at last they reached the surface.

Here they faced the dilemma of how to hoist Will on to a horse. Robert suggested they make a sledge of some kind, but Jean dismissed the idea. Mounting the smallest of the stallions, in this case Pierre's, Jean leaned down while Olivier and Jacques held Will upright. He took him under the arms and hauled him up across his lap. Will screamed and then fainted away, which was a relief. Pierre, however, could not handle Jean's highly-strung stallion, so Olivier mounted Jean's stallion and Pierre rode Olivier's. At last they could begin the return journey. It was now mid-afternoon.

*

Mass was followed by the wedding banquet, and the high table of the great hall was crowded with guests – the Comte de Foix and his Comtesse, Philippe de Grailly and his lady, the priest and Commander Bourgneuf, not to mention the bridegroom's parents and the bridal pair themselves set in the place of honour in the middle. Preoccupied with her functions as hostess and particularly with her dinner partner the Comte de Foix, Eleanor had no opportunity to enquire after her younger sons, but as time passed she grew increasingly uneasy.

Some time after the second course, she observed the flushed and bedraggled figures of Robert de Foix, Olivier d'Albret, Pierre de Montfranc and Jacques Cardunier slipping into the hall and waylaying the servants carrying in the trays of food. Then the young men squeezed on to the benches and avidly helped themselves to meat and drink without regard for the fundamentals of good manners. Frowning, she looked for Will, but could not find him.

To her astonishment, she discovered instead that Jean was standing behind the high table and leaning over Commander Bourgneuf, who at once pushed back his chair and excused himself. "Jean!" Eleanor called. Geoffrey shook his head at her behind the backs of the bride and groom and indicated that she should ignore what had transpired. With an effort, she did as her husband wished, knowing that he would have his reasons. Besides, this was Alice's day, she reminded herself, and refocused her attention on the bride.

Alice and Antoine were cuddling together, feeding each other titbits of food like a couple of turtledoves. The sight was curiously alienating. She and Geoffrey had sat stiffly side by side at their wedding feast, barely talking, afraid of any display of affection before the hostile, black-robed crowd around them.

As the wine flowed, the jokes were becoming more *risqué*, the musicians were moving from romantic songs to tunes with more explicit lyrics and the laughter was becoming louder. The light was fading from the day outside while the sweets were cleared away, and the tables dismantled to make room for dancing. At last, as Antoine led Alice to the first carol, Eleanor found Geoffrey beside her.

"What did Jean want with Bourgneuf in the middle of the meal? Where was he during the wedding? Where's Will?"

"All three essential questions without even stopping for breath." Geoffrey observed with a faint smile of approval lighting his eyes. "Will managed to break his leg in some daredevilry this morning. Jean, thank God, had gone looking for him. He found him and brought him home. He asked Bourgneuf to look at the leg."

Eleanor digested this calmly, but she had never been able to walk properly since the shipwreck which had shattered her thigh at the age of sixteen. She was not someone to take a broken leg lightly. She thought of Will, so full of energy and so utterly unsuited to any kind of scholarly activity, and shuddered. If he were too badly crippled to be able to ride or fight, he would die as certainly as a caged wild bird. Geoffrey read the worry in her eyes even before she asked anxiously, "Is it a bad break?"

"I can't say, I haven't seen it – but Jean seemed to think Will got off lightly."

"Oh, what does Jean know!" Eleanor blurted out, her worry overpowering her sense.

"Jean is the only one who has seen Will and I think he has a good head on his shoulders. Let's not ruin Alice's day."

Eleanor acceded, but she was relieved when shortly thereafter Bourgneuf reported to her: although Will had suffered a compound fracture of his right leg, he saw no reason why the youth should not recover completely and be none the worse for it. Eleanor thanked the Templar with the first sparks of sincere affection and inner guilt for ever having resented his presence. There was no question that the Templars had a better grasp of medicine than most French doctors because they were constantly observing and adopting the medical practices of their Islamic enemies. In a rush of gratitude, Eleanor took the balding knight's hand between her own and thanked him warmly. Bourgneuf blushed like a callow youth and Geoffrey leaned over to whisper in his wife's ear, "You shouldn't torture Bourgneuf, my dear, he still has a vow of chastity to maintain." But Geoffrey was teasing her.

Jean was next seen sitting beside the dark and beautiful Nicole Noyon. The Noyons were spice merchants in Cordes. Fabulously wealthy, they lived in one of the most impressive of the towering, stone townhouses with a battery of triple, trefoiled, arched windows on the second and third storeys over the arcades of the shop on the ground floor. The sight of Jean sitting astride the bench and flirting openly with the precocious beauty reminded Eleanor of what his elder brother had said about his escapades of the night before. Eleanor felt a rush of exasperation at this wayward middle son. One minute he was rescuing his younger brother from a serious mishap and the next he was seducing an honest maiden.

Nicole's father was a respected and respectable man of considerable influence. Geoffrey valued his friendship enough to favour him openly, and he would have much to lose if Jean seduced Nicole, because a man like Noyon would never forgive the insult. A merchant, after all, if he was striving toward acceptance among the gentry and nobility had to be even more jealous of his honour than a man of an established family.

'Poor Master Noyon', Eleanor reflected, 'will have his hands full with the flirtatious and wilful Nicole.' She looked once more to Alice, grateful that her elder daughter had been a modest and biddable maiden. It was a relief to have her honourably married to a young man who, whatever his faults, would provide her with status and financial security as long as she lived. That was worth much.

'Eloise would be much more troublesome,' Eleanor reflected, searching the room for her younger daughter, finding her slouched against a pillar licking honey from her fingers. Her gown was askew and so looked too tight for her shapeless body. There was still hope, of course, that as Eloise grew up she might develop a certain rounded beauty, but if she did not learn to stop pouting and whining she was not likely to attract many suitors for her own sake - and Geoffrey had endowed Alice with all that he could spare in land and goods. It would take years to collect a dowry for Eloise. Then again, she was only twelve and in six to ten years, with luck, they might have saved a dowry after all. Eleanor was determined to be optimistic today.

Jean rose and led Nicole to the dancing. Following him with her eyes, Eleanor saw that Louis was dancing with Isabelle d'Albret. Isabelle was not really beautiful, but she had a certain appeal - not to mention the fact that she was a niece of the Sire d'Albret and heiress to her father's lands. Louis was aiming too high by paying attention with Isabelle d'Albret, Eleanor calculated. The Albrets were immeasurably proud and had intermarried with royalty from time to time. They might let Will serve as a squire in their household, but it was out of the question that they would let one of their heiresses marry a Preuthune. De Grailly was more liberal, and he would value the fact that Geoffrey's father had been one of the Lionheart's knights. He had also brought two of his daughters with him, and they were not unattractive. Eleanor resolved to redirect Louis's attention towards the De Grailly maidens.

Some of the guests were starting to get rowdy, calling alternately for more wine or for the bedding rituals. Even as Eleanor watched, however, Jean, Louis and Geoffrey converged on the troublemakers from three directions and they were soon silenced. Geoffrey then had a word with his master sergeant, an Englishman who had once served as his squire in the Holy Land but was now married to a local girl and captain of his guard. The household guard discreetly took up strategic positions around the hall, ready to expel anyone who threatened the peace. Jean, meanwhile, had joined the troublemakers and was throwing dice with them.

Eleanor decided it was time that she went upstairs and looked in on Will, but she had no sooner risen than Alice signalled her over urgently. It was Antoine who spoke, his face flushed with wine and his eyes still bloodshot from the effects of the night before.

"Mamá," he addressed her with a teasing smile, "don't you think my friends were right? It is certainly time to retire – at least for some of us." His arm was around Alice's waist and his hand caressed her thigh as he spoke.

Eleanor repressed her irritation and glanced at Alice. She nodded her assent vigorously. "All right," she agreed.

Taking Alice by the hand, Eleanor raised her up. People started clapping and cheering from around the hall. The musicians struck up an appropriate tune and many joined in, singing the lewd chorus. The other ladies left their activities to crowd around Alice and her mother as they left the hall to make their way to the bridal chamber. Like a train of gabbling hens they wound their way up the stairs to the waiting chamber where they clucked and fluttered, and then passed around a cup of wine among them, giggling and telling stories of their own weddings and the misadventures of brides until finally the deep murmur of male voices announced the arrival of the bridegroom and his escort.

One of the ladies shot the bolt and giggled when the door was tried. Antoine roared to be let in. There followed an exchange of challenges and banter between the men and the women, until Antoine threatened to break the door down. Eleanor decided that things had gone on long enough and at her nod the door was opened – just as Antoine made a running lunge at it. He came hurling into the chamber, overbalanced and stumbled forward. Just as he lost his footing, he grasped the bedpost and, making a virtue of necessity, clambered up on to the bed. The men had crowded in after him, and then Antoine, kneeling astride his bride, started to strip off his clothes while Alice giggled almost hysterically and the audience cheered.

Eleanor exchanged a look with Geoffrey across the room and then found Louis and Jean. Both her sons shoved their way forward through the crowd, getting in a position to drive back the people. Then, nodding to Eleni on the far side of the bed, Eleanor grasped the heavy damask curtains and briskly closed them on her side while Eleni did the same on the far side. The crowd protested vocally, but the Comte de Foix and his lady, De Grailly and a number of the other more sober guests joined the family of the bride in starting the movement out of the chamber. Although some of the younger men resisted the flow and had to be persuaded by Louis or Jean that it was time to go, things went relatively smoothly. With relief, Eleanor closed the chamber door behind her and hobbled, left foot first, down the stairs after her guests.

Louis, directly before her on the stairs, offered her his arm. "You look tired, Mamá," he observed solicitously.

"I am, my dear. And I want to check on Will. You heard that he broke his leg?" Together they went to comfort the patient while Geoffrey and Jean were left to oversee the remainder of the feast.

*

The church bells were ringing for matins when the last of the guests finally withdrew from the hall – or were carried out by the watch. Geoffrey nodded good night and dismissal to the master sergeant, and with a yawn started to draw himself to his feet. Jean put out a hand and stopped him. "There's something I want to discuss with you, Father."

Geoffrey looked down at his son with disbelief, but the question why this couldn't wait till morning died in his throat. Of his surviving sons, Jean had always been the most independent. From the time they were children, Louis had anxiously consulted him about everything, seeking advice and reassurance, while Will was in constant search of praise and approval. But Jean had gone his own way, almost secretively at times. If he wanted to talk, then he had the right to be heard, regardless of what day or time it was. Leaning wearily back into his chair, Geoffrey waited.

"I've decided to join the Temple," Jean announced.

Geoffrey started bolt upright. "You what?"

"I'm going to return with Commander Bourgneuf tomorrow and join the Temple at Cahors."

"Are you mad? Last night one whore wasn't enough for you – you had to have two – and tomorrow you are going to take a vow of chastity?"

Jean reddened. He had not expected or intended his father to hear about his carousing in Cordes. It was not that he was ashamed of what he'd done. Society excused the sexual adventures of young noblemen as something inevitable, normal, even half-admirable. Certainly the demonstration of one's manhood was necessary for acceptance by one's peers, and sexual rivalry among youths was so fundamental an instinct that it seemed ridiculous to condemn it. Most fathers, remembering their own youth, were indulgent if not actually proud of their son's virility. But Geoffrey was one of those rare men who had lived by a different code, and Jean respected his father too deeply to wish to offend him.

Having been discovered, however, Jean replied steadily, "It is because I plan to join the Temple that I indulged in a last extravagant fling. That was my farewell to women."

Geoffrey was scowling. In his opinion, Jean was talking utter nonsense. He felt certain that he would never have been able to keep his own vow of chastity for six long years if he had not been virgin. Jean, by virtue of his considerable experience with women, would find himself suffering from a sense of deprivation the then inexperienced Geoffrey had never felt. Furthermore, for the bulk of Geoffrey's novitiate he had been virtually cut off from all temptation. The Templar Commandery at Cahors was in no way comparable to that at Limassol, Cyprus. Access to French women was far easier, and the rule kept much more leniently.

But Geoffrey was determined not to try to impose his perspective on his son. Already their sexual experiences were too divergent to make any comparison useful. Geoffrey had not only been a virgin on his wedding night, he had never once been unfaithful to Eleanor since. In his forty-eight years of life he had known only one woman sexually – and Jean at twenty-one had probably had dozens already. Instead of pursuing the fruitless topic of the viability of Jean's future vow of chastity, he asked simply, "Why? Why should you want to join the Temple?"

Jean had expected his father, the former Templar novice, to approve and support him. Having to defend his decision, he found himself starting rather hotly. "Because I have no future here—"

"Of course you do—"

"Oh, Father! Don't treat me like a child! I'm a younger son, and I know what that means! Louis inherits everything—"

"Louis inherits his mother's estate. Whatever I can purchase I can dispose of as I please. Do you think I'm not concerned about seeing you provided for? Alice had to come first—"

"And there's Eloise and Will..." Jean reminded him. He grasped his father's hand and squeezed it, pleading softly but intently for understanding. "Listen to me. I can remember how hard you and Mother worked to salvage her inheritance from total ruin. I remember when lightning burnt down the barns at Chanac and you lost the entire harvest. I remember the flooding that washed away the mill at Villeneuve. I know you borrowed from the Jews and from Noyon. It's taken you twenty-five years to secure the prosperity we have, and Alice's dowry has cost you every *sou* you put aside. You'll be lucky to put together a dowry for Eloise in time. Will and I have to make our own way in the world. That is our fate. And I can live with it. You didn't do so badly as a younger son of a younger son." He smiled.

"I married an heiress – something you cannot do as a Templar. Which reminds me, Master Noyon remarked that you and his daughter Nicole seem fond of one another. It was a cautious preliminary, but I'm sure we could pursue it..."

Jean was shaking his head. "Nicole is lovely and she will make someone a delightful – and difficult – wife, but can you honestly see me as a spice merchant?"

"There are worse fates. You have a head for figures..." Geoffrey broke off.

Jean was steadily shaking his head and he was right. He might have the intelligence required to run a merchant empire, but he did not have the temperament. Jean was spontaneous, energetic and generous. He did not have the patience and diligence to deal with the day-to-day running of a business, and his generosity could be disastrous in a merciless business.

Instead, Geoffrey asked more explicitly, "Why the Knights Templar? You could take service with the Comte de Foix, I'm certain, or if you prefer I could write to the king – he knows I was with his father and elder brother in the Holy Land."

"I have better chances of advancement with the Templars," Jean replied directly. "King Philip does not favour obscure outsiders."

"You may not have *any* chance of advancement in the Temple," Geoffrey warned ominously.

"Why not? Most of the knights are younger sons to start with and all have to renounce their property. The masters themselves have often come from obscure families."

"That's not what I meant. You don't know the whole of what happened at Mansourah." Geoffrey was speaking under his breath, not meeting his son's eyes.

For the first time since the conversation had started, Jean felt unsure of himself. "What do you mean? What is there to know?"

"Just a small matter of heresy."

"What are you talking about?" Jean asked with alarm. "Mother was released by the Inquisition—"

"I'm not talking about your mother. I myself made heretical statements – to the master of the Temple himself."

"De Sonnac? But I thought you saved his life?" Jean was confused. He had been raised on the stories of his father's heroics during the Seventh Crusade – stories his former squire loved to tell, though Geoffrey himself declined to discuss it.

"It's a long story and I'm too tired to go into it, but I'm not sure you would even be admitted to the order. De Sonnac sent some instructions concerning me to the seneschal of the Temple at Acre just before his death."

"But Commander Bourgneuf has encouraged me from the start. He assured me of acceptance."

"Commander Bourgneuf cannot accept you. Only the grand chapter can do that," Geoffrey reminded his son, continuing, "It's possible that Bourgneuf does not know what was in De Sonnac's dispatch to Acre, but your acceptance into the order is always provisional and subject to confirmation by the master. In Acre – where the contents of De Sonnac's letter are known – they might not confirm your admittance."

Jean considered this only briefly. Then he shrugged. "It's a chance I have to take. If Bourgneuf backs me, then surely that is more important than something you said over a quarter of a century ago to a dead master."

"Possibly..." Geoffrey conceded. The Temple was, after all, desperate for recruits, considering the nearly disastrous situation in the Holy Land. The Christian kingdom of Jerusalem had been reduced to a strip of coastline stretching from Acre to Tripoli. "But if Bourgneuf is willing to support you in more than a perfunctory way, then it will be because he's perfectly aware that you are an excellent rider and wants you to back his colts."

Jean grinned, proud of his riding ability and flattered by his father's compliment. His father was one of the most exceptional horsemen Jean had ever seen. Furthermore, the few horses Bourgneuf sold rather than sending to the Holy Land brought the highest prices. It was a great compliment to think that Bourgneuf would want him to train his famous remounts.

"You've missed the point, Jean." His father slapped his hand on the table top to draw his son's attention back to reality. "Do you want to join the Templars so you can spend the rest of your life training colts for other knights to ride?"

Jean flushed. "Of course not!"

"But that is very well what could happen," Geoffrey insisted calmly and with a hardness in his face and eyes which his son could not remember ever having seen before. "You vow absolute obedience to your superiors when you enter the order. If Bourgneuf wants to keep you here until the day you die, he can."

Jean swallowed in discomfort. "He wouldn't do that. He knows I want to go to the Holy Land. He knows knights are needed there."

"So are remounts."

"It wouldn't be fair to keep me back – for a couple of years, for my novitiate, of course, but not indefinitely."

"It doesn't have to be indefinitely. How much longer do you think there will *be* a Christian kingdom of Jerusalem?"

Jean stared at his father in disbelief, but his idealistic young heart refused to accept what his father implied. He shook his head. "There have been crises before. And always in times of crisis God sends someone or something to avert the final destruction of the kingdom. It is time to fight back with all our faith. I believe that, Father, don't you? In your heart?"

Geoffrey avoided the question. "And you see yourself freeing Jerusalem. Chasing the Muslim hordes back into the desert, and carving a new kingdom out of the rocky sands of Palestine." It was not said sarcastically or contemptuously. Such dreams were common in Cyprus where Geoffrey had grown up, son of one of Richard the Lionheart's knights. There too no one believed that the Pope and Western Christendom would really abandon the Christian kingdoms in the Holy Land. And all the young men who came, whether as crusaders or pilgrims or recruits for the orders of the Temple and Hospital of St John, believed that they would be the ones to turn the tide against the encroachments of Islam. Geoffrey had been no different when he followed King Louis IX to the disaster at Mansourah.

Jean blushed because his father made his dream seem naive and theatrical, but he insisted with conviction, "I don't believe I alone will change anything, but I think I can be a part of a new resurgence of Christian power in the east. Baibars is dead at last."

"I know."

Baibars had defeated Louis IX at Mansourah – and then proceeded to sweep his Islamic rivals from the board, crown himself sultan, and then, town for town, and fortress for fortress, reduce the Christian territories to their present precarious state. He had done so with a barbarism that would have shamed the great Saladin – whose descendants he had murdered. He had negotiated the free passage of all Templars from Beaufort in exchange for the surrender of the fortress – and then sold the knights into slavery. He had surrounded the fortress of Safed with the heads of the Christians he had slain in defiance of his own word. Baibars was dead, but his successor was one of his emirs with a no less gruesome reputation.

Geoffrey leaned forward. "You may be right about the Holy Land. God alone knows if it can be rescued, but you forget that you vow poverty, chastity and obedience – absolute obedience, and no one cares if the order is fair. For an intelligent man – and you are that – the obedience is by far the hardest part because so many commands seem stupid or unnecessary. And the saddest part is that many of them *are*."

"No one said being a Templar was easy. It isn't meant to be easy. I don't want it to be easy. It's because only the best can become Templars that it is a worthy goal. Certainly better than counting Louis's sheep the rest of my life!" Jean's resentment of his elder brother blazed briefly.

"Do you know what they do to a knight who has infringed upon the rule in some minor way? Say for failing to confess your misdemeanours, or pocketing a gift or failing to deliver a letter unread to the commander? The punishment is having a collar put around your neck, attached to a leash fastened to a ring and then being made to eat off the floor with the dogs."

Jean paled slightly and licked his lips. "If you endured it, so can I – or do you think I'm so much less worthy than you?"

In fact, Geoffrey had never endured that particular punishment, but Raoul once had – on account of a letter from his mother he had read in private instead of surrendering it sealed to the master to be read aloud to the assembled company. Geoffrey hated the thought of Jean being humiliated in such a manner, maybe on account of a letter from Eleanor. But nor could he deny him the respect he was demanding now. Slowly and deliberately, to lend his words the weight they deserved, he answered, "No, Jean, you are every bit as worthy as I. Very likely you will make a better Templar than I would have made. But remember you can change your mind at the end of your novitiate and before you take the final vows."

Jean smiled at that. "How could I forget – with your example the basis of my very existence? But women like Mother are not born every day."

Geoffrey shook his head. All the children assumed that Eleanor was the reason he had refused to take final vows. But that was only half the story. He had never told his children about Mansourah – except vaguely that he'd saved De Sonnac's life and been knighted by King Louis. "We both need some sleep. It will be morning far too soon." Geoffrey stood slowly, feeling utterly exhausted.

"Father, I won't change my mind overnight," Jean warned him earnestly, his face stubborn with determination. "I've given this a lot of thought. In fact, I've been thinking about it on and off for years, ever since I was a boy, but I decided definitely around Christmas. I stayed only for Alice's wedding."

Geoffrey considered his son carefully. For all that Louis had his looks and his apparent soberness, he saw more of himself in Jean. Jean had the inner strength to go his own way regardless of what the world thought of him, while Louis and Will were always looking over their shoulders, desperately anxious to conform. And while all his children were conventionally intelligent and Louis was an accomplished scholar, it was Jean who demonstrated flashes of insight which suggested a profounder analytical ability than all the others put together. Jean too would question things.

But sometimes – carrying his younger brother in his arms, poulticing the leg of a lame horse, wiping Alice's tears away after some childhood tragedy – Jean reminded his father of Raoul. The Muslims had mutilated and tortured Raoul at Mansourah – and Geoffrey himself had killed him. In the dim hall, the torches extinguished and the fire dying, he saw Raoul look out of his son's eyes and the hair stood up on the back of his neck. "Christ," he murmured under his breath. Raoul too had joined the order out of ambition rather than calling, and Raoul had from the start taken a more lax attitude toward the rule. Raoul had had the same ability to laugh and to comfort others.

"What is it? Why are you staring at me like that?" The façade of confidence had shattered and Jean was looking up at his father with anguish in his eyes. "Don't you understand at all?" This once he too desperately wanted his father's approval.

"Yes" Geoffrey admitted. The shudder that racked his body was visible, and the pounding of his heart was deafening. But he managed to nod and say, "Yes, Jean, I understand. It will be as God wills it."

*

Eleanor let Geoffrey sleep late, going to attend to her departing guests on her own. Most of the guests had some distance to travel and were anxious to get on the road after a cold, standing breakfast. Eleanor thanked them for coming and bade them godspeed in a steady stream.

Quite late, Alice and Antoine emerged to the good-humoured commentary of those still present. Alice blushed and lowered her eyes, while Antoine grinned and swaggered. His parents, however, were anxious to depart and slightly annoyed that the bridal couple had taken so long to rise. Alice, in a show of flustered obedience, started darting about, 'helping' her mother-in-law, while Antoine lounged at the table gulping ale and expounding to his friends on the incomparable thrill of deflowering a virgin. "God's nails, it's like an explosion!"

Eleanor was compelled to admit to herself that she hated her son-in-law. Capturing Alice as she scuttled to collect her cloak in preparation for departure, she put her arm around her daughter and hugged her. "Are you all right, Alice?"

"Of course, Mamá." Alice forced a smile, but her eyes were veiled. "I've never been happier."

Alice was lying. And she would go on lying to protect her own pride. Eleanor swallowed, gave her daughter a last hug, and then released her, knowing there was nothing more she could do for her but pray. "Oh, Mother" – Eleanor always prayed to her own mother rather than the Virgin Mary – "please help Alice to find the strength she needs." Then she sent a page for Geoffrey. He would not want to miss saying goodbye to his daughter.

Eleanor and Geoffrey went as far as the outer gate and waved goodbye as long as the Montfranc party was in sight, trotting down the street toward the gate of the little bastide. As the last Montfranc groom leading the pack horses passed through the gate, Geoffrey laid his arm on Eleanor's shoulder and walked with her back into the ward. At this worst possible of moments, Eleanor caught sight of Jean tacking up his stallion.

"Jean! Where are you going?" She could see the heavy saddle bags slung over his shoulder.

Jean looked up, startled. "Didn't Father tell you?"

Eleanor turned to Geoffrey. "Tell me what?" Eleanor was intuitive. Something told her this was no ordinary trip. Something made her blood run cold.

"Jean only told me last night after the feast. I tried to talk him out of it, but..." Geoffrey shrugged helplessly. It was an incongruous gesture in a man who had shaped his own destiny with so much determination over the years.

"What?" Eleanor demanded. The more evasive they were the more alarmed she became.

"Mother, I know I should have said something sooner, but with all the plans for the wedding I didn't want to distract you. It's something I've been meaning to do for some time. In fact, I only stayed because of the wedding, to see Alice settled. But it is time for me to take my future into my own hands. I'm of age and I've been knighted."

"You're leaving." Eleanor stated the obvious. It was not unexpected. Jean was an ambitious young man. He had to seek his fortune somewhere else. "But why does it have to be today?"

"Bourgneuf and I can travel together—"

"What does Bourgneuf have to do with this?" Her intuition knew even as her reason resisted, and the sharpness of her voice warned Geoffrey that one of Eleanor's extremely rare rages was about to burst.

"I'm going to apply to the Temple at Cahors, Mother. Commander Bourgneuf—"

"No!" She was shaking her head, and the look in her eyes was alien to Jean – furious and hate-filled and desperate. "Not the Temple! I would rather you were dead! You can't do this! Geoffrey, you can't let him do this!"

"Eleanor, please..." He tried to calm her, but Eleanor saw instead the white and red ghost that years ago had often hovered near Geoffrey, clutching at his heart, tearing him in two.

"NOOO!" She shrieked so loudly that grooms and servants stopped in their tasks to see what was happening. Geoffrey caught her in his arms and held her fast.

"Eleanor!"

First she struggled, then, capitulating to his greater strength, she went limp, shaking her head and whispering over and over again, "No, Geoffrey, no. Don't do this to me. Please."

"Father has nothing to do with this," Jean insisted with youthful pride. "It was my decision. He tried to talk me out of it. He paraded every argument against it, but I've not taken this decision lightly. I beg you to respect it, Mother—"

"Respect it? Why should I respect you for rejecting me?" Eleanor's fury flared up again. "If your father had rejected me that was his right, but you are my own son, my flesh and blood! I nearly died to give you life, I've nursed you, raised you, nurtured you, taught you! How can you toss me out like worthless rubbish!"

Jean looked at his father helplessly. "But, Mother, this has nothing to do with rejecting you—"

"You think I don't know the rule? You can never kiss me again, never receive or send a letter to me that is not shared with all your brothers first—"

Geoffrey saw Bourgneuf approaching, ignorant of what was transpiring, and he squeezed Eleanor violently with his powerful hands. "Don't do this to us, Eleanor, please."

Bourgneuf came up smiling and bowed low to Eleanor. "Good morning, Madame. I hope you had a good night's rest. The bride is happily on her way?"

"You are a traitor, *Monsieur*." Eleanor spat at him. Her eyes blurred with tears, she did not see his benign features or his indulged body. She saw only the blur of white and red, the cross like a stain of blood upon the mantle. "You took my hospitality with a smile and all the while you were planning to stab me in the heart, to steal my son away from me! You are not welcome here, *Monsieur*, ever again!"

Bourgneuf didn't know what had hit him, and his mouth dropped in astonishment. Eleanor broke free of Geoffrey's embrace and took one step away from them. She was trembling. "Jean! If you take the mantle of the Temple I will never speak to you again. Do you understand? You are dead to me." She turned on her heel and, limping, lurching and sobbing, she walked away from the three Templars.

Peyroles
June 1283

The bells were ringing for vespers, and in the narrow terraced fields on the banks of the Gardon de St Jean the serfs and brothers shouldered their scythes and rakes and started back for the village. The weather was fine and clear; there was no reason to fear that the harvest of hay would suffer during the night. The older women, their skirts hitched up in front, gossiped together in a group. A couple of the maidens, their hair looped up but not covered, walked with the men, and their high-pitched laughter carried far in the still evening air. Apart from the villagers, the brown-clad lay brothers murmured in lower voices. Their shaved heads were red and peeling from the intense June sun and their bare feet were stained green from the hay.

Passing over a stone bridge that arched over the raging and icy waters of the Gardon, the hay-harvesters entered the tiny walled community. Here nearly fifty dwellings were crammed close together. Most of the houses were stone, with tile roofs which nearly touched above the alleyways. External staircases led to the second storey of each house, and walled-in kitchen gardens provided the residents with fresh onions, cabbages, carrots, peas and leeks. Smoke rose in leisurely clouds from the piles of stone topped with a slab of slate that marked the vent for the hearth, and the smell of boiled carrots and cabbage hung in the narrow streets.

The main street paralleled the Gardon, for the valley floor was narrow and the village clung along the river. One street led uphill towards the squat church and beyond that to the Temple. In Peyroles, the Temple was no more than a walled-in manor house with attendant outbuildings to the north of the village.

The lay brothers passed under the arched gateway with the splayed cross chiselled into the keystone and painted red in contrast to the thin white washing that covered the walls and the buildings. The yard was plain dirt, and chickens scratched and strutted contentedly.

The lay brothers entered the shed nearest the gate to lean their scythes and rakes against the rough walls. At the stone trough before the stables, they stopped to dip their hands into the cool water and rub their faces clean of sweat. Directly opposite the stables, the round Templar church waited with open doors to receive them, the hoarse bell clanging insistently.

From the hall of the main house, the sergeant-commander in his black mantle emerged and descended the exterior stairs. He was accompanied by the sergeant-secretary. These two Templar sergeants and the priest were the only monks at Peyroles. Peyroles was a property bequeathed to the Temple over a hundred years earlier, and its sole purpose was to provide revenue for the order. With two sergeants, a priest and two dozen lay brothers, the 'house' at Peyroles performed its service for the Temple while living like any minor religious community, cut off from the world beyond.

The sergeant-commander had reached the foot of the stairs and just started for the church when the gateway darkened and three horsemen clattered into the yard to the alarmed squawking of chickens. The horses that came to an abrupt halt inside the gate were massive destriers, bred to carry a fully armed knight, and two of the men astride them wore the white mantles of knights.

The sergeant-commander changed his direction at once, the secretary hastening in his wake, while the lay brothers gaped open-mouthed from around the water trough. Several of the younger brothers, newcomers to the community, had never in their lives seen one of the legendary Knights Templar in the flesh. It was as if the Archangel Gabriel or St George had suddenly descended from heaven, and one of the youths fell on his knees in awestruck wonder.

The two knights were accompanied by a squire, also wearing a white mantle, with a smaller cross to indicate a novice, and all three men were dismounting and stripping off their leather gauntlets. On closer inspection, one could see the sweat caked with dust on their mounts and they moved with the characteristic stiffness of men who had spent long hours in the saddle.

The sergeant-commander bowed to his superiors, his face a mixture of surprise and unease, covered by a smile of welcome. Brother Roger had been born in bondage. His father, a wealthy man for his estate, had sent his son to learn his letters in a parish school, and the priest had recruited him for the Church. In exchange for a fee, his lord had set him free that he might serve God. After taking lower orders with the Franciscans, Brother Roger had transferred to the Temple, attracted by the wealth of the order and the unique opportunities it offered to a man of his birth. In no other order could he have lived as he did now – like a lord. Since the noblemen who joined the Temple became knights, were sent to the Holy Land, and died in hordes, the mundane duties of husbandry and estate management were left to the more humble. Brother Roger liked things that way, and he was happiest when it seemed as if the order had forgotten about Peyroles.

Unfortunately, the order did not forget about any of its properties. There were routine inspections and annual meetings and biannual payments to be made – payments that were more likely to reflect the demands of Acre than the capacity of Peyroles. The order's wealth was not left at the mercy of the consumption of its obscure members, and the standard of living at Peyroles was spartan. But the routine contacts with the order were things for which Brother Roger had time to prepare. He did not welcome unexpected and unannounced visits such as this and he feared it did not bode well.

"Just in time for vespers, Brothers." Brother Roger might be socially and militarily inferior in rank to the knights but as a monk he was also their equal. With smiling lips, he studied his visitors with alert, critical eyes. It was rapidly clear to him that of the three men only one was of consequence: the novice and one of the knights were very young men – still innocents. The other knight was also young, no more than twenty-five or twenty-six, but he exuded authority. He was a man of average height and build with exceptional red streaks in his curly, light brown hair, and grey eyes that saw too much.

This knight nodded absent-mindedly with a glance at the church, and then, speaking over his shoulder to the squire, he ordered special care for the horses.

"The stable boys can see to the horses – the brother novice is weary," the sergeant-commander offered at once.

"No, Brother Gilbert will see to our horses," the knight insisted in a tone that brooked no contradiction. The novice nodded agreement, as if he were anxious to affirm that he wanted the duties. Then the senior knight introduced himself and his companion as Brothers Jean and Alfonse from the commandery at Cahors.

Peyroles was a dependent house of the commandery of Alès, not Cahors and that did much to reduce Brother Roger's unease. Maybe the knights were just travelling through – any traveller could expect hospitality at a Templar house and the Brothers were required to seek accommodation with their brethren unless there was no house within reasonable distance.

"You will be spending the night with us?" Brother Roger enquired, as he indicated that they should proceed to the church.

Jean nodded. "We are on our way to Aigues-Mortes where a convoy for Acre is collecting. I have instructions for you from the grand preceptor."

"For me? From the grand preceptor?" Brother Roger could hardly believe such an honour. But they had reached the church portal, and one after another the monks entered the church, uncovering their tonsured heads and touching a knee to the floor as they crossed themselves.

The priest too was made nervous by the unexpected presence of knights. He did not speak Latin and so recited the service entirely by rote. This evening, he heard more than one muttered correction from the senior of the two knights, and this flustered him. He had hardly finished the service before the knight was rising and leading the way out of the church, his white mantle filling out and billowing behind him.

"Brother Roger," Jean addressed the sergeant-commander as he passed. "If you would be so kind. We have a great deal to attend to before compline."

"But surely there is time for supper first," the sergeant-commander urged.

"It wouldn't hurt," Brother Alfonse remarked with a smile to Jean, and Jean gave in. Slowing his pace, he let the sergeant-commander lead them to the refectory.

The refectory at Peyroles was a barrel-vaulted stone hall thirty feet long. To the sergeant-commander and the lay brothers, born in the mud hovels of serfs, it was a grand and dignified hall. To the knights, born to castles and accustomed to the refectories of great abbeys, it was a dingy chamber, bare of decoration.

The sergeant-commander apologised in advance for the food, conscious that his cook – one of the lay brothers – could not compete with those employed at the more important houses. He and his brothers were content that the food was always plentiful and the diet more varied than for the average peasant, but knights, of course, expected spices and meat and other delicacies.

Jean nodded absently. He had not expected anything better.

"We had not heard anything about a convoy at Aigues-Mortes," the sergeant-commander opened the conversation, impervious to the bad impression his ignorance made.

"No? It has been planned for months. The grand preceptor has ordered over a hundred knights from France to the Holy Land – and in addition to serving in the Holy Land they are to guard the shipment of arms, remounts, supplies and monies which will also be sent."

"Are there new developments in the Holy Land?"

Jean shook his head. "No. The situation is as precarious and threatening as ever." 'In five years,' he thought bitterly, 'nothing has changed at all.' Bourgneuf had raised him from novice to knight in less than a year. He had increased his responsibilities, entrusted him with ever more important duties, showered him with indications of his trust and respect – but he was still expected to stand on the quay and watch the others sail to the Holy Land. Jean resented it, and the more he resented it the more he compensated for his own sense of frustration with arrogance. "The grand preceptor," he indicated with a touch of his hand the letter he carried next to his breast, "has ordered a special tithe to support our brethren in Palestine—"

"But what else do we do? What else have we done since we were founded?" Brother Roger protested. With a gesture of his hand he indicated the naked walls, the barefoot lay brothers, the salted herring on their trenchers and the ale. "We live in poverty so that our brethren in Palestine may defend the Christian Kingdom – though when one sees how much revenue flows year after year to the Holy Land and yet how the Christian Kingdom shrinks ever smaller, one is compelled to wonder if the money is well spent, is one not?" Brother Roger had not risen from serf to sergeant-commander in the Temple because he was simple.

"Do you know the value of the horse I ride? Have you ever priced a coat of mail or a sword of Damascus steel? Do you know what it costs to hire a single galleon from Genoa or Venice, or what it costs to repair the damage done by catapults to a fortress tower? If I remember correctly, the annual revenues of this house amount to roughly fifteen gold florins – in a good year."

"Twelve, sir. Fifteen is very exceptional indeed."

"With twelve florins I can't outfit a single knight. Not one. The worse the situation in the Holy Land the more expensive it is to maintain even the *status quo*."

Brother Roger was impressed despite himself. He had never given any thought to the expenses that accompanied the profession of arms because he had never had anything to do with it. But whatever the costs of a knight, his modest house could not pay more than it earned. "When we have given all we have what more can we give?" he asked, opening his hands.

"Brother Alfonse and I will take a look at your accounts and inventory. Do you have need of all the grain stored? Surely some of it could be sold off." Jean was speaking from experience. He had been making tours of this nature for several months now and he had learned of a variety of ways in which the local commanders tried to keep revenues in their own hands. It was rarely a matter of outright corruption. Almost none of the houses he had visited exhibited undue luxury, but there was a natural – even prudent – tendency for each commander to keep some reserves at his disposal. The commander hoped to meet unexpected expenses or fulfil some humble dream of self-improvement without having to refer to his superiors. Jean knew that he would act no differently if entrusted with responsibility for a house.

"The winters are unpredictable here. Sometimes we have snow as early as October and don't see the last of it till May. For such years we must have sufficient grain in storage," Brother Roger pointed out.

Jean nodded. "After supper we will make an inspection and then consider your accounts. Do you wish to see the letter from the grand preceptor?" He removed the parchment from inside his surcoat and offered it to Brother Roger.

The sergeant-commander looked at the heavy red seal showing two knights mounted upon a single horse. No one had ever bothered to explain to him the significance of the image. The founders of the order had called themselves the 'poor knights' of the Temple of Solomon. Perhaps they had not been able to afford more than one horse for every two knights; or was the second knight supposed to be

Christ-Militant riding with every brother? He pushed the letter back to Jean. Reading was a laborious exercise for him and often he did not understand the words employed by such lofty persons as the grand preceptor. "That is not necessary. Your word is enough."

Jean returned the letter to his pocket, perfectly aware of the sergeant-commander's motives for leaving it unopened. This happened all too frequently as well. Jean reflected cynically that he could have claimed almost anything was in the letter and enriched himself endlessly – for a short time. In any hierarchical institution there were opportunities for corruption, but unless the institution itself was corrupt there were also sufficient mechanisms to discover the misdeeds of all its members eventually.

*

Three days later Jean and his two companions reached Aigues-Mortes. The great port built by King Louis was bustling. Inside the great golden walls, the shops lining the street offered their wares on tables set up directly beside the thoroughfare. The bright colours of the fruits, vegetables and textiles were vivid in the Mediterranean sun. Citizens and garrison soldiers, sailors, merchants, whores and friars mingled in the marketplace, their various robes fluttering in the stiff sea breeze.

Beyond the city walls, to seaward, the harbour was crammed with ships, only half of which were chartered by the Temple for the convoy to Acre. Several of the chartered ships lay alongside and were being loaded to the usual shouting and cursing of longshoremen and sailors. In the livestock pen beyond the estuary over three hundred Templar horses were milling about unhappily and uneasily, unused to such demeaning accommodation.

Here they had neither roof nor straw, but the sea voyage that awaited them would be even worse, Jean thought with compassion as he recognised several of the colts he had trained.

"There's Brother Gerard." Alfonse pointed to the seneschal of Cahors, in earnest conversation with an Italian shipmaster on the quay.

Jean trotted over and jumped down, waiting respectfully on one side while the seneschal finished his heated discussion with the Italian. The seneschal turned to see who had arrived, and his worried face relaxed somewhat. "Brother Jean! Good that you made it. How much were you able to collect? No - tell me later!" He glanced over his shoulder toward the shipmaster, who was now consulting one of his officers. "These fucking Pisans can't ever keep a bargain! There are extra fees for every damned thing! Wait and see if they don't try to charge us for the very air our men and horses breathe! Ah, Brothers Alfonse and Gilbert! You don't know your good fortune yet! Brothers Henri and Charles came down with some illness just as we left Cahors, so you two are to take their places."

Alfonse cheered and Gilbert asked with youthful earnestness, "As a squire still?"

"No, you'll be knighted before you embark - tomorrow should do." Gilbert's look of wonder was so undisguised that the seneschal laughed openly and clapped him on the shoulder. "Return to the Temple and prepare for your night of vigil. Alfonse, you'll want to take that horse with you, no doubt, so see that he is put with the others as we'll start embarking the horses tomorrow - we want to take advantage of the fair weather." He glanced at the sky, which gave no sign of rain or storm in any direction.

Alfonse, grinning still, started to turn his stallion about.

"And what about me?" Jean asked tightly.

"What about you?" the seneschal asked blankly.

"I'm supposed to return to Cahors?"

"Of course. We can go up and do an accounting immediately, if you like."

"Why Alfonse and not me? Why, in God's name, an innocent like Gilbert and not me?" Jean demanded without budging. He could still hardly believe that they had done this to him again. Never had he felt so humiliated and insulted. Both Alfonse and Gilbert had joined the order after him. Alfonse had been his squire until he took his final vows, just as Gilbert now was. He had trained them both.

"De Bourgneuf gave the orders, you'll have to ask him," the seneschal replied with a shrug.

"As if you didn't know what goes on in his mind!" Jean scoffed. Bourgneuf was no dictator; he took virtually no decision without consulting his council of officers. The seneschal, his deputy, was the most important member of that council and the most pedantic. If anyone opposed his wish to go to the Holy Land, then it was this brother, or so Jean suspected. "Why won't you send me to Acre? I've earned it a hundred times more than Alfonse—"

"Silence! You have your orders. You have no right to question them. No right to an explanation of any kind!"

"You entrust me with a fortune, but won't trust me with information that concerns me more intimately than any other! I want to know how much longer you intend to keep me here in France, playing tax-collector to illiterate—"

"Silence, or - I warn you - you will have to pay penance for disobedience and insubordination! You have your orders. Your duty is to say 'In God's name, sir, I will do this!'"

Jean spat.

The seneschal went livid with outrage. In twenty years with the Templars no knight had ever acted with comparable effrontery. "Confess your insubordination to the chapter or I will have to report you myself!" The punishment was always worse if a knight did not confess his own faults.

Jean collected his reins and vaulted into the saddle of his stallion. Glaring down on the seneschal, he untied his purse from his belt and dropped it at the seneschal's feet. It landed with the loud, distinctive chink of heavy coins. "That is every extra *sou* I could wring from the designated houses," he announced, adding, "I'm returning to Cahors, since those are your orders. Anything else?"

The seneschal sputtered. He liked Jean and he had always considered him a sensible and reliable member of the chapter. It unnerved him to have Jean abruptly and incomprehensibly turn troublesome. "No. Return to Cahors - and think how you have offended against the rule!" he admonished like a schoolmaster.

"In God's name!" Jean made it sound like an insult as he spurred his stallion from the quay, the weary horse slipping and floundering on the cobbles.

Cahors

June 1283

Entering his cell, his saddlebag over his shoulder, Jean was startled to find a man kneeling in prayer before the crucifix hanging on the wall between the narrow beds. He came to an abrupt halt, his spurs scraped on the tiles, and the heel of his boot made a loud clunking noise. The man – youth really – hastily crossed himself and drew himself to his feet as he turned around.

He had wispy brown hair surrounding a freshly shaved tonsure. Big ears stuck out from his head, framing a long, acne-marred face. Prominent, hazel eyes gazed nervously but openly at Jean. Then the youth mustered a lop-sided smile while smoothing his newly issued white novice's surcoat. "Brother Jean?" he enquired.

Jean dumped the saddlebags on the floor, his blood rising in fury. They had given him the latest recruit to mother, train, school and prepare for the Holy Land. Until his departure for Aigues-Mortes, Gilbert had shared this cell with him, and before that it had been Alfonse, before that...

"My name is Lucien," the youngster offered eagerly. "I was accepted by the chapter three days ago and was told to bed here. I hope you don't mind?"

"Mind? A Templar is not supposed to have his own mind. I must report to the commander." He turned on his heel and stomped out, leaving a discomfited youth behind him.

Bourgneuf had heard that Jean was back and he rose to welcome him as he entered. In five years Bourgneuf had grown stouter. His jowls sagged more, and he moved more slowly. "Ah, Jean, good to see you safely home." He offered his hand.

Jean bowed over it perfunctorily. "You've put a new recruit in my cell." He opened without preliminaries.

"Yes, do you mind?" Bourgneuf was genuinely surprised by the apparent anger simmering in Jean's voice and heightening the colour in his face. He indicated that Jean should sit opposite him, and sank down behind his desk. "With Gilbert gone, the bed was free and you have a way with awkward youths no less than awkward colts. Lucien is rather delicate for the Temple, and if we weren't so hard up for recruits I would not have accepted him. Even now I have my doubts, but if anyone can bring the best out of him, you can."

"I'm sick of training others so they can leave me standing on the quay! Why wasn't I sent to Outremer in place of an innocent like Gilbert? What made him more worthy?"

"Worthy?" Bourgneuf asked, blinking in bafflement. "Gilbert isn't worthier than you in any way. You know that."

"Then why did you prefer him to me? Why send him to the Holy Land when it could just as easily have been me?"

Bourgneuf sat very still, staring at the raging young man before him. He saw the boy of fourteen who had hung about the gates of the Temple just to catch a glimpse of the knights as they rode in and out. He saw the young man who had defied the curses of his own mother to join the order. He saw the novice who with laughing ease had mastered every skill, every trick, every test they had put to him. And he saw the young man who had time and again effortlessly restored the courage, hope and will of young men weaker than himself. He was a natural athlete with a gift for leading others. And he was not a fool. "You must know the answer," he stated softly.

"No, I don't. I've spent the last five days trying to find it, and my thoughts always end in the same place: you think Gilbert and Alfonse and all the others better Templars than I." Although Jean did not for a moment think that the others were better knights than he, it had occurred to him that if Bourgneuf knew that he had now and again broken his vow of chastity, he might be favouring the others as a mark of subtle disapproval. But Jean wanted it out in the open.

Bourgneuf shook his head sadly. "You know that's not true. You know it is the very opposite."

"Then why?" Jean insisted, his voice strained with tension.

"Do you really expect me to say it out loud?" Bourgneuf asked, the lines of his face vivid, his eyes dark with sorrow.

"Please!" Jean leaned across the table, his eyes fixed on his commander, demanding and anguished.

"Because I value you too much to send you to a senseless death." Bourgneuf did not dare speak these words too loud; he whispered them.

The shock that went through Jean was violent enough to be seen. It was the one answer he had not expected. He, who did not doubt that the Holy Land would be saved, had not dreamt that a Templar commander could have already despaired.

"My God," he whispered.

Bourgneuf sighed and heaved himself to his feet. "And now I have something else for you," he announced wearily. "A letter arrived in your absence."

Jean, still disorientated, lifted his head. "A letter?"

"From your father." Bourgneuf took a key from the ring hanging at his belt and opened a small cabinet, carved directly out of the thick stone wall. Here various documents were kept safe. He removed a parchment and handed it to Jean. The seal was broken. All mail went first to the commander, who read it before it was delivered to the addressee.

Jean took the letter as he got to his feet. He did not attempt to read it at once. That could wait. "Forgive me, sir, I... I had simply never... I should not have questioned you." He squared his shoulders. "I will accept whatever penance you impose, but please take into account that I want to go to the Holy Land. Now more than ever. I must go to Acre." He did not know himself why he felt this.

Bourgneuf's eyes were on the letter in his hand. "Read your letter first, Jean."

"The letter?" Jean looked down at it as if he had forgotten it was there. "What does—"

"Read it!"

Jean obediently unfolded the letter. He scanned it impatiently, but almost at once his heart started pounding, his pulse racing. His father regretted... his father wished he was more skilled with words... his father knew there had been a special bond between them... he hoped that Jean would have the faith to deal with the loss... that he would not blame himself for not having been near.

Will was not a boy any longer and no older brother could rescue him from his folly any more. This time it had killed him.

Jean looked up at Bourgneuf in a state of complete shock, and then he looked back at the letter. His little brother – freshly knighted –

couldn't really be dead. He read it again. *This time it has killed him.* Will had dismounted to finish off a wild boar he had wounded with a spear, and the boar had charged him. One of his companions had tried to save him by firing a crossbow, but the bolt had grazed the back of the boar and lodged instead in Will's hip. As he went down under the bolt, the boar had gored him fatally. He had died before they could get him back to Najac. Jean looked up at Bourgneuf. Will had been twenty years old.

"Go home, Jean. Go home and comfort your parents. When you return we can discuss Acre."

*

When Geoffrey woke he knew that Eleanor was weeping. She wept silently these days, with no sobbing or gasping, yet the tension of her body as it lay curled in his arms betrayed her. He lifted the hand that covered hers and brushed the back of it across her cheek to be sure. It came away wet, and now, knowing he was awake, she allowed herself a single gasping breath.

Geoffrey raised himself enough to place a kiss upon her head, and stroked her cheek. Eleanor turned and buried her face in his naked chest, clinging to him. He held her – it was the only comfort he could offer. From the open window came the sounds of the castle coming to life.

They had buried four of their children. Two daughters had died as infants, his namesake had died at the age of three and now they had buried Will. By far this was the hardest. Not only were they no longer of an age to have more children, but Will had been a part of their lives for twenty years.

"It's easier for you," Eleanor decided without reproach. "You can get more sons, while I will never bear another..."

Geoffrey pulled away from her and gripped her shoulders so he could look at her. Her hair was free, a tangled mess of brown and grey around her shoulders and her still full breasts. He remembered the wonder with which he had gazed upon them for the first time on their wedding night. He had never seen a woman's naked breasts before – not within reach, not presented to him. He had trembled to touch them, and she had received him, for all his clumsiness, with patience and timid joy. Her body had aged, thickened and become familiar, but he still felt a kind of wonder to see it lying before him, her breasts peering through the strands of hair. For thirty years this body had belonged to him, and if it was the worse for wear then he had to answer for it – for the eight children it had been stretched to carry and nurse, for the fatigue of a life not always easy.

"To get other sons, I would have to take another woman to my bed."

Eleanor nodded wearily. "I would understand."

Geoffrey was aware of anger even though he wanted to be gentle and understanding. "Does it matter so little to you that I have been faithful? Would you rather I had taken mistresses and spared you the burden of sharing my bed?"

"Don't be angry, Geoffrey." She reached out a finger and ran it down the side of his face. At once his eyes softened. "I would die if you ever left me – even for a single night – but I would understand. You are still a young and vigorous man." Her eyes lingered lovingly upon his body; it too was thicker now and marked with the passage of time. The hair on his chest was greying. But it was the body of a active, healthy man for all that. "You could sire a new family."

"Why should I? I like the one I've got. Alice has two fine children and will soon give us a third grandchild, and Louis's Marie is carrying after just five months of matrimony. Most important, the sons we have are both sons to be proud of."

"Ah, I forgot. You still have two sons, while I have only one."

"Oh, Eleanor! How can you say that?" It was an old wound, a perpetual point of friction in an otherwise harmonious relationship. Neither of them let the issue destroy or even cast a shadow on the remainder of their lives, but sometimes the issue bubbled up and confronted them. "Jean is your son, if you'd only—"

"Jean is dead." Eleanor dragged herself from the bed, her hair tumbling down over her naked buttocks as she walked away from her husband.

Geoffrey sighed, and turning over, rolled out of the other side of the bed. He did not want to fight with her.

They attended to their respective duties. Geoffrey went through the correspondence he had dictated the day before and signed it before he and Louis both consulted with the steward about the management of their extensive estates. It had been over a month since either of them had inspected the outlying properties. It was time that one of them made a tour of the other estates to hold the manorial court and check things generally. They agreed that Geoffrey should assume this task and Eleanor should be persuaded to accompany him; it might help distract her from her loss.

Eleanor checked the kitchen and wardrobe accounts, giving her approval to the requested new purchases and authorising the respective clerks to draw the designated sum from the household treasury. She then made her daily round of the castle, seeing that the routine tasks were being efficiently carried out, reproving, directing, praising as she felt necessary. As she followed in her mother's footsteps, limping where her mother had strode with unbounded vigour, she reminded herself that her mother had buried six children and her husband – before Montségur. She lost her last son at Montsègur. And it had never bent her down. Eleanor longed for her mother's strength, her mother's faith – the certain belief that death was freedom.

Not necessarily freedom, she reflected, descending the stairs one at a time to the protected corner of the garden where the medicinal herbs were neatly planted. Betony and vervain, cumin, fennel, dill and parsley were carefully cultivated here, and the gardener bowed and smiled to Eleanor as she appeared.

According to her mother's faith, death might be merely a passage to rebirth, an interlude between life and life, Eleanor reminded herself. Her mother's faith had been Cathar, and she had been burned at the stake for it. Yet she had been extremely reluctant to discuss her beliefs with her daughter. While Eleanor was still a small child it had become too obvious that the Pope's legions and the Inquisition would crush the Cathars. To protect her youngest child she had insisted that Eleanor go to Mass and obey the priest. Only occasionally, unintentionally or out of compassion, she had shared with her daughter fragments of her own beliefs.

Eleanor knew, therefore, that her mother believed in reincarnation, but she had never learned how it was supposed to function. When did the soul find a new body? Instantly upon death, or might it hang in suspense for years? And did the soul have any choice about its new habitat? Certainly the living could not conjure up the dead they wished, Eleanor reflected with a wan, inward smile. She had named her youngest daughter for her mother with a secret hope that her mother would be pleased to reside there – and Eloise, of all her children, was least like her namesake. Eloise had, as Eleanor's mother would have said, an 'immature soul', a soul not reborn often enough to have advanced very far towards wisdom and perfection.

But, if the mere wish did not guarantee the rebirth of a departed and desired soul, that did not preclude the rebirth of someone beloved in the circle of the bereaved, did it? Were souls never reborn into their own families? she wondered. Did they change sex? Nationality? Race? Religion? Eleanor sat on the garden steps and, propping her elbow on her knee, rested her chin on her fist, completely absorbed in contemplation. Wasn't it possible that Will's soul would pass into Alice's quickening womb? Or that of her daughter-in-law? Would she recognise him if it did? Would it still be Will?

"Mamá!" Behind her, the door to the castle ward had opened and her daughter-in-law stepped over the door frame and started down the stairs. "What are you doing here?"

Eleanor sighed inwardly. Louis had managed to marry an Albret after all, though his Marie was not an heiress and her dowry was modest. She had a certain doll-like prettiness: smooth, rounded features that would blur into blandness in a few years' time. And she was fair-haired, which was much admired in the Languedoc. She was seventeen, spoilt, smug, absolutely certain of herself and her future. At seventeen Eleanor had already spent two years in the hands of the Inquisition, been shipwrecked, crippled and virtually imprisoned in servitude to the Dowager Queen of Cyprus. She had to fight down an irritation undoubtedly rooted in jealousy whenever she dealt with the wife of her heir.

"It is my duty to see that the herbs are properly tended," she answered Marie's question. "Imagine if someone was ill and we discovered too late that a vital ingredient had not been planted or had withered or been choked with weeds."

"My mother always sends her almoner to see to such things. After all, he makes the purchases at the apothecary too," Marie replied breezily. She resented her mother-in-law's constant attempts to point out her duties to her. As if she, an Albret, didn't know what a châtelaine had to do to run her estates!

Of course, Madame d'Albret would never lower herself to looking in on a gardener, Eleanor noted sourly. "And what brings you here?" she asked, pulling herself to her feet. She felt weary though she had risen only three hours earlier and the day was young.

"I have such a craving for strawberries, and I wanted to see how they grew." There were strawberry plants in the garden beyond the herb plot. Marie stood cupping her lower belly in her hand. It was a pose many pregnant women struck, though Eleanor had always thought it vulgar. Seeing her mother-in-law's gaze, Marie smiled, "See how he grows! You will soon have a healthy boy to replace foolish Will!" Louis had always referred to his youngest brother affectionately as 'foolish Will' and the words slipped out now without thought.

Eleanor, however, was raw with grief and her response was sharper than it might otherwise have been. "No one can replace a lost child – as you will undoubtedly have opportunity to learn! And let us see how wise your babe is before you call mine foolish!" She grasped a handful of surcoat and gown in her fist and, pushing past her daughter-in-law, ascended the stairs to return to the outer ward, slamming the door behind her. Marie was left indignantly gasping for words, while the gardener bent over his weeding, shaking his head. Who did this wisp of a girl think she was to insult the mistress and Master Will?

She had other duties, but Eleanor did not feel up to them after this exchange. She already felt guilty for her response even as she rationalised it to herself. Besides, her contemplation had been rudely interrupted, and she wanted to resume it. She wanted time by herself. She wanted time to commune with her dead. She abruptly changed the direction of her steps and went through the outer gate with a nod to the porter. Then she turned right to cross the drawbridge and descend into the outer ward. Passing through the outer gate, she could see that the village of Najac sank to her left and then rose on the back of the spur and to her right the path fell down toward the brooding basilica. Every time she saw it, she resented it and longed for the little, somewhat dilapidated church of her childhood. But such wishes were useless. In this cold basilica all her deceased children were buried. Poor children.

She made her way down the well-worn path toward the basilica, the light breeze lifting her black veil away from her face and neck and catching at her light weight surcoat so it fluttered around her, despite the laces at her sides. They had not buried her mother. They had scattered her ashes in contempt. Somehow that was more comforting than being imprisoned in a frowning, dreary prison-like basilica. But her children were there and she needed to visit them.

She passed from the sunlight into the shadow, and the chill brought goosebumps to her arms. Then she froze. Beside Will's tomb, still raw and unadorned, a white figure loomed in the half-light. Like an angel, like a ghost, blood on his breast like the gouge of the boar which had laid open Will's lungs. She caught the back of the pew to support herself. Her 'dead' son raised his head and approached her cautiously. His white mantle billowed out behind him. His white surcoat, slit up the front, rippled around his booted knees. He stopped before her.

"Mother, I'm so sorry. I didn't get word until Monday. I came at once."

She turned her head away and closed her eyes.

Jean reached for her hand. She yanked it away. Squeezing her eyes shut but feeling with her hands the end of the pew, she made her way cautiously like a blind woman and sank down on to the seat.

"If you won't look at me, at least listen. You can't close your ears." His voice was close, warm-timbred and yet familiar. "I love you. You and Father mean more to me than any other living souls. If there is ever anything I can do for you, you need only tell me. If you ever want to see me or talk to me, for whatever reason, you have only to send word."

"Yes, and they'll read it out loud in the refectory and shake their heads at a woman's foolishness and then deny you permission to come!" She spat it out, her head still turned away, her eyes closed tightly. "I won't ever write. I will not beg for permission to see my own son!"

He bent over her, and she could feel it with every nerve of her trembling body. She felt his breath and then his lips, dry and warm and gentle, on her forehead. She drew her head back. "That's against the rule! You're breaking your vows!"

"I do it frequently enough and in far more serious ways." Jean thought of the women he had bedded. Kissing his mother was objectively less offensive, and yet by his own reasoning far more dangerous. She, not his casual bedmates, could claim a loyalty which ought to belong to the order alone.

"You take your vows so casually?" Eleanor asked, disapproval patent in her voice. Geoffrey's earnest attitude to his vows had nearly denied him to her, but she respected him all the more for it. More than that, she was intensely proud of his unequivocal adherence to his word once it was given.

"I'm not Father – though there is no one who respects him more than I." That, Eleanor knew, was too true. Both Louis and Will had been more concerned with title and wealth and each in their way had been slightly ashamed of their *parvenu* father. They had taken greater pride in their Najac heritage, and at times Louis – and certainly Marie – offered her more deference than they did Geoffrey. Jean, in contrast, had idolised his father as a boy, and even as he grew to manhood he had frequently shrugged his indifference towards men of higher rank and title, asking rhetorically, "Were they with King Louis at Mansourah?"

Damn him! Eleanor pressed her eyes yet tighter together, and the tears squeezed out and surged down her face to drip off her chin, cold and uncomfortable. She hastily brushed them away with a trembling hand. It was because he had idolised his father, his heroic crusading father, that he had joined the damned Temple!

"Your father had the sense not to take his final vows!" she told her son bitterly.

"He had good reasons not to. What reason did I have? What option did I have? No king had knighted me and offered me his favour. No heiress was prepared to take me as I was."

"How do you know? You gave none a chance to know you."

This dialogue was pointless and they both knew it. There was no going back, no reversing the decision that had been made five years ago.

Jean took a deep breath. "Can't you forgive me, Mother? Try to understand and accept me as I am."

"I do understand. You are fulfilling your father's untaken vow for him."

Jean did not see it that way. From his earliest memories the very mention of the Temple had filled him with a kind of thrill and ambition he could not explain. The sight of the proud white knights had filled him with longing akin to homesickness. He felt that he belonged with the Knights Templar, and in his dreams he had seen himself riding with them in the blazing desert sun, the sand stretching out to infinity. These secret feelings had nothing to do with his father's rejection of the Temple long before his birth. "You can't believe Father asked this of me."

"No, I know he didn't. I know he tried to stop you. But secretly I think he is not so unhappy with your decision. He has been to visit you in Cahors, hasn't he?"

"Yes. Regularly. A quarter rarely passes that we do not see each other."

Eleanor had suspected as much because Geoffrey occasionally let slip information about Jean which could only have come from him. She always pretended she had not heard and she never asked questions, but she was glad that the contact was maintained.

"Mother, look at me," Jean urged, sensing her hostility had softened. He went down on his heels before her and took her hands in his. She let him, thinking how long ago Geoffrey had walked back into her life after she thought he had abandoned her. That too had been a rebirth.

She took a deep breath, turned her head to the sound of Jean's voice and opened her eyes. His face lit up before her. She felt her heart racing to be looking at him after so long, and her eyes devoured his beloved features. He had changed, of course; there were lines at the corners of his eyes and he wore a full beard – rich and curly with red highlights. The tonsure gave him a high forehead over his penetrating eyes. It was a kindly face, a gentle face, a wise face.

"Oh Jean, promise me just one thing," she urged, squeezing his warm, capable hands in hers. "Promise me you will stay here – don't go chasing after holy grails and empty tombs in Outremer!"

Jean's features turned to stone. The light went out of his eyes. "Mother, don't." He begged it under his breath.

Eleanor understood instantly. He would not promise even this. Slowly but resolutely, she removed her hands. Her lips were pressed together harshly. Her eyes blazed with bitterness. "You insist upon crusading for a lost and corrupt cause?"

"Don't say that, Mother. The corruption of mere men does not make the Holy Land less holy. It is nevertheless the site of Christ's Passion and his resurrection."

The look in Eleanor's eyes was contemptuous and it wounded Jean. He retaliated. "Would you have me think you are a heretic?"

"Better a heretic than a fool. We thought Will was foolish! Trying to kill a wounded boar on foot is at least theoretically possible. Saving the Christian kingdom of Jerusalem is not!"

"I must go to Acre."

"Why?"

"I can't answer that."

"No, of course not." Her voice was laden with sarcasm. "The Temple does not reveal its secrets to mere women—"

"To *any* outsiders," Jean corrected.

"And what becomes of the Temple and all its secrets when the Holy Land is irrevocably lost? Your bones will bleach in the desert sun and the sands will bury you, your secrets and all memory of you! The mighty Order of the Knights Templar will turn to dust!"

Jean rose from his heels, his face flushed with emotion but the features no longer expressive. His body was rigid, straight, proud. "No doubt you are right, Madame. Now, if you will forgive me, I wish to speak with my father." He turned his back on her and his spurs made a clicking sound as each stride took him away from her. Briefly his white mantle was turned to translucent grey as he was silhouetted against the stronger light outside the basilica and then even the shadow of man and cloak were gone.

"Jean!" She pulled herself up out of the pew and called after him, but it was too late.

Acre

October 1283

As soon as the shout went up that land was in sight, the passengers crowded the deck, getting underfoot and reaping a harvest of abuse from the sailors. Eventually, all but the more important passengers were chased below deck again, and a frenzy of packing ensued – accompanied by squabbling, accusations of thieving, and half-hearted brawling.

Jean had not been chased below decks but stood under the canopy behind the wheel with the small, select cluster of important passengers, including two Hospitallers. Although the rivalry between the Temple and Hospital had been bitter and violent at times, Jean and the two Hospitallers had maintained cordial relations throughout the voyage. Jean found Jules de Villaret a particularly intelligent and congenial companion, a man of wit and understanding. The rivalry between the two militant orders seemed both childish and destructive in the intimate atmosphere of a ship bound for the threatened Christian territories in Outremer.

The Hospitallers were convinced, and seemed to have reason for their conviction, that the new Sultan, Kalaoun, was an even more fanatical opponent of Christendom than his predecessor Baibars – the implacable opponent of King Louis of France and Edward of England. Kalaoun, they insisted, would not hesitate to break the truce if he were sufficiently confident of success. And why shouldn't he be? Edward of England seemed more concerned with conquering Wales than saving the Holy Land and Philip of France was not in the least inclined to follow in his father's footsteps and die on crusade. The Spaniards and Portuguese always felt that the Moors at home were challenge enough, and the Germans and Italians... the Hospitallers shrugged. Though their own master was German, they wrote off any assistance from the Holy Roman Empire as hopeless.

A fleet of fishing boats danced off to the south in the glittering water. The wind smelt of land, that indefinable mixture of seaweed, mudflats, dried salt and fish landlubbers associate with the sea. It was now possible to make out the city of Acre, whitewashed and cream-coloured buildings clustered within massive fortifications. Church towers and minarets rose above the fig and date trees. Jean looked questioningly at Jules de Villaret. "There are mosques in Acre?"

"Of course. The king of Jerusalem signed a treaty guaranteeing freedom of worship in Acre in exchange for free access for pilgrims to Jerusalem. There is a large Muslim merchant community in Acre."

Jean tried not to look shocked; he could sense that the Knights of St John were amused by his naiveté.

The sails were furled upon the huge lateen booms and, as the long snout of the bow veered steadily from due east to north, the oarsmen took up the duty of manoeuvring the ship toward the harbour entrance. From the oar-deck came the steady dull thud of the muffled drum and the answering grunt of the galley slaves. Leaning over the rail, Jean watched in unending fascination as the twenty-six pairs of oars swung in near perfect unison. Like a giant centipede the ship crawled across the sparkling waters, spume catching the sunlight as the oars smashed into waves.

Jean's heart was beating with the drum now. The coastline, which from a distance appeared straight, broke suddenly, forming a promontory where the coast ran east to west for a short stretch before resuming its usual north–south course. A long sandy beach stretched southwards, but on the short stretch of east–west coastline a mole curved out into the calmer waters, enclosing a harbour crammed with shipping. The narrow entrance was guarded by towers perched on the mole itself and De Villaret informed him that chains could be drawn across the gap to close off the narrow passage to shipping altogether. To the left of the mole, on the very tip of the promontory jutting into the Mediterranean, a massive castle reared up behind the sea walls and fortifications. From a flagstaff perched upon the tallest of the towers, like a jewel set in the scalloped crown of ramparts, fluttered the Baucent – the black and white banner of the Templars.

Jean's rapture must have been evident on his face because De Villaret clapped him on the arm and distracted him with a friendly but insistent sentence. "And there," he pointed, "is the church of St Jean d'Acre," the Hospitallers' greatest church. The church, as the house of God, deserved the greater honour, but Jean's heart beat for the power represented by the mighty castle dominating the harbour.

They pulled alongside the quay on sheer momentum, the oars on the port side raised to the vertical like an opening fan. With a lurch that nearly knocked Jean down, the ship met the shore. Bare-legged sailors leapt deftly overboard with the hawsers and, creaking in protest down her whole length, the ship was made fast. Jean looked up from the quay to the jumble of warehouses, customs and shipping offices, taverns and chandlers shops.

Acre. Before his eyes, Turkish sailors naked to the waist were scrambling aloft to do some repairs in the rigging of a ship, glittering with Arabic lettering along its squarish stern. Two turbaned merchants with long white beards stood directly beside the ship on the sagging quay. African slaves were struggling to offload some cargo in barrels, their black skin shimmering with sweat. A woman, completely draped in a shapeless black garment, a veil across her nose and mouth and a pottery jug on her head, slunk along the side of a warehouse.

Around him the other passengers were taking their leave of the captain and one another, ducking back down into the stern accommodation to collect something or descending to the main deck, where the gangplank was being run out.

Jules de Villaret came to bid farewell to Jean. "I don't expect we'll see much of one another here. Master Lorgne disapproves of any contact with the 'enemy.'" He smiled to make it a joke, but there was a sadness about his eyes which suggested that there was more truth to his words than he would have liked. "Of course, we could meet privately now and again – in civilian clothes, you understand. If you send a native boy around to our commandery with a message, I will be glad of it." He held out his hand.

"I'll do that," Jean assured him and took the offered hand.

Then De Villaret and his companion descended to the main deck and pushed their way forward to the gangplank. Jean watched them go, and wondered why he felt so paralysed. He could hardly breathe and it took an effort to force himself to turn and focus on what needed to be done.

Sailors were already de-caulking a large rectangular cut in the hull which came just level with the quay. The horses had been loaded through this hole and then the planking replaced and caulked. Now the sailors were hastening to undo the process and below deck they were fixing a ramp from the horse deck to the deck above, where the planking was being removed. Fascinated by the speed and efficiency of this procedure, Jean remained on the poop, watching until he saw his two companions, his squire/novice Lucien, and the serving brother, Paul, suddenly emerge on the quay with two sorry-looking horses apiece.

With a start, he gave himself a mental kick and made his way to the gangway. Lucien caught sight of him and waved, grinning widely as he took the step across the gunnel. "They look miserable indeed, but we haven't far to go." He gestured behind him to the castle rearing up over them.

Lucien, grinning almost idiotically, nodded happily. "I saw the Baucent! Shall I fetch our bags or will they send someone for them?"

"No one is expecting us."

Bourgneuf had given Jean permission to sail for Acre and join the Templars already there. He had acceded to Lucien's wish to accompany him on the condition that Lucien remained a novice/squire for at least one full year after arrival. This meant that he would not be allowed to take part in any combat whatsoever. Paul had volunteered to accompany them because his brother had sailed for the Holy Land as a pilgrim four years earlier and never returned. Being illiterate, Paul had no other way of knowing what had become of him.

"I'll fetch yours and Brother Lucien's saddles. You can ride ahead and send a couple of serving brothers back to help me with the gear and the remounts," Paul suggested.

Paul arrived with the saddles, and Jean at once took a hand in tacking the healthiest of his stallions, Lionheart. The horses were no less interested in their strange surroundings than their masters. The strange smells caused their nostrils to flare with alarm. The bright colours and the sun made them uncomfortable after the dark of the hold. Their ears flicked backwards and forward and they moved uneasily, but they were too weak to prance skittishly. Even the weight of the saddle made the stallion wince and brace himself. Jean spoke to him gently and then he collected the reins in his left hand and held the stirrup in his right to mount. He felt the nine weeks at sea in his legs and wondered at how rapidly a body loses its fitness.

Lucien mounted, and, with a nod and promise to send someone to Paul promptly, Jean nudged the stallion forward. Lionheart responded unsteadily at first, and with a distinct stiffness. Then he seemed to regain confidence and walked forward on a long rein, swinging his head from side to side and peering at the world around him with open curiosity.

The castle of the Templars towered above the houses and shops of the town around the port, yet there appeared to be no street leading directly to it. Jean chose the nearest street and headed down it between the dilapidated warehouses with unpainted shutters hanging from rusty hinges. A gully ran down the street, dry now, but littered with refuse which had been flushed down it during the last rain, and a rat strolled nonchalantly across their path. Jean registered a certain disappointment that ports of the Holy Land were no cleaner than those in other parts of the world.

The street they were following bent more and more to the east, away from the Templar Castle, and so Jean looked for the first alley leading back to the west. They had already left the warehouses behind and now there were small shops, taverns and houses mingled together. His stomach was cramping curiously, and he admonished it in irritation. On account of the dry heat, the stench here was actually less than in many a crowded European town. His hands clutched unnecessarily at the reins and with an effort he forced them to relax. He was sweating profusely though it was in fact no more than pleasantly warm and the air was cooled by a light breeze.

At last a street led off to the left. Jean indicated it to Lucien and gently directed his stallion that way. They turned into the alley. The houses loomed up on either side so close that there was no room for two horses to ride abreast. The narrow balconies hung precariously on crude wooden supports and the roofs were balustraded. Jean looked up at the blue sky framed between the toothed edges of the roofs and the terror that seized him made him sway in the saddle.

From the clear sky, oil, bricks and stones were raining down upon him. Arrows clattered and ricocheted on the sides of the alley. The screaming deafened him – the incantations of the Saracens, the death squeals of his horse, his father's raw-throated, high-pitched voice shouting: "Back! Back! It's a trap!"

Jean hauled so violently on the reins while digging his heels into his horse's flanks that the weakened stallion lost his footing and scrambled, confused and helpless, his haunches suddenly giving way. Jean felt himself falling, and the stones pelted his head, shoulders and back. With his arm he tried to protect his face. An arrow caught him on the breast, ripping through his mail and cracking a rib. And then they were clubbing him to death. The clubs were parts of balconies and even rakes and other household implements. Then a pain shot through his genitals that made him crumple up and scream.

Lucien was standing over him. "What is it? Sir Jean! What's happened?"

He opened his eyes. He was lying on his back in an alley. Overhead the sky was blue between the tooth-edged skyline of Arab dwellings. The air was still in the late afternoon. The dust hung like listless smoke. It was Lucien who hung over him with a concerned, frightened but familiar face.

Jean drew a deep breath. He was unhurt except for the bruise on his right shoulder from falling off the horse. He sat up and looked around. Lionheart stood in the middle of the alley, his head down and his weight distributed on three feet. They were alone.

"What happened?" Lucien asked again anxiously.

"Nothing. Lionheart lost his footing unexpectedly and I fell off." He smiled. "You see, it can happen to anyone, if they don't pay attention."

"But you suddenly tried to back up."

Jean looked hard at Lucien. "I thought I saw something. I was mistaken." He hauled himself to his feet and walked over to inspect the unnerved stallion. As he approached, Lionheart raised his head, quivering and questioning. Jean patted his neck and reassured him automatically. He bent down and studied the favoured leg, but it seemed undamaged. In his mind he was seeing the attack again. He knew that he had either just been warned of what was to come – or he had remembered it.

He collected the reins and went to mount again, then stopped, one foot in the stirrup and the other still on the ground. Mansourah. He shook his head in irritation and heaved himself into the saddle. But as his seat touched the saddle he looked about with dawning comprehension. He had never been here before but it reminded him of some place – of Mansourah. 'Yes,' he acknowledged nodding mentally, 'I was with my father at Mansourah. He survived and I didn't.' Somehow this thought gave him a sense of calm. He drew a deep breath, and then hastily remembered to cross himself. It was heresy to believe in reincarnation. He clicked sharply with his tongue and sent his stallion forward with the pressure of his heels.

*

Although there were still Templar castles and garrisons in Tripoli, Beirut, Sidon, Tyre, Tortosa, Haifa, and Castle Pilgrim, Acre had the largest garrison in what was left of the Christian-held Holy Land. Here the master of the Temple maintained his permanent headquarters and over a hundred knights were stationed along with some four hundred sergeants and several hundred serving brothers.

Despite its location inside a great, prosperous city, the 'Temple' at Acre, like all Templar fortresses, was intended to be as self-sufficient as possible. The castle offered not only accommodation for man and horse with its own independent water supply and access to the sea, it had its own storehouses, mill, brewery, bakery, cooperage, smithy and armoury.

Skilled serving brothers, including entire teams of skilled masons, were a vital aspect of the Templar organisation and one of the least noted yet most important factors in their success as a military force. Since only their own brothers, volunteers who had taken simple monastic vows, were employed to build and service their fortresses, the chances of betrayal were reduced to a minimum. The Templar masons especially formed a closed guild within the order, who kept the secrets of their trade – and the fortresses they built – very much to themselves. Although Jean had known this, it was only as he passed into the ward of the Templar castle at Acre that he began to grasp the significance.

This castle was like none he had ever seen before. It had, of course, the traditional features of yard-thick walls pierced only by well-placed arrow-loops to ensure overlapping fields of fire. It had its towers with machicolations, merlons and embrasures, and a brooding barbican fitted with portcullis and murder-holes. But it had more. Drawing rein in the ward and looking up at the walls and towers which pressed in around him, Jean sensed that this was a fortress that a very few men could hold against an army.

In Europe the serving brothers were like the simple men of Peyroles, sons of serfs and impoverished peasants happy to exchange vows for lifelong security. They lived out their lives in the protection of the wealthy and powerful Temple, certain of food, shelter, clothing and spiritual comfort in exchange for the labour they would have given a secular lord in any case. Here, the tanned man in the brown habit of a serving brother who came to take his horse exuded self-confidence and competence. "Just arrived from the West, sir?"

"Is it that obvious?" Jean replied with a sheepish smile as he jumped down.

The serving brother assessed him with a glance and then admitted with an answering smile. "Yes, sir – and of course the horses betray you as well."

Jean laughed.

"You'll want to report to the commander of Acre. Go through that door there and up the staircase to your right. It's the second door on the left after that."

"Thank you. Brother Paul is still on the quay with the other horses and our gear. Could you see that someone goes to give him a hand as soon as possible?"

"Certainly, sir." The serving brother agreed cooperatively. It had not escaped his notice that Jean made it a question whereas most newly arrived European knights gave curt orders.

"Are you English?" Jean asked, thinking he detected an accent.

"Scottish, sir, Brother Ian of the clan MacDonald."

Somehow it was the last thing Jean had expected. He thought of the Highland Scots as barbarians, more Viking than Christian. The fact that the first Templar to greet him in the Holy Land should come from the Scottish Highlands made him want to laugh, but Jean thought better of it. It might offend the Scot. He introduced himself instead. "Jean de Preuthune."

"Welcome to Acre, sir. I hope you'll be staying with us."

"As long as Acre is Christian," Jean answered flippantly. Turning to Lucien, who had dismounted and now waited eagerly beside him, he instructed, "Help Brother Ian. I'll be back as soon as I've reported."

Lucien looked disappointed, but Jean was uneasy about the reception he would get and did not want any witnesses.

Jean made his way up the dark, windowless stairway and along an equally gloomy corridor, as Brother Ian had instructed, to knock on a heavy, iron-reinforced door. Entering, he found himself in a large, vaulted chamber with a startling vista of the turquoise Mediterranean through three large, double-arched windows. The open windows let in the sea breeze and the cawing of gulls. Against the brilliant light pouring through the windows and spilling upon the glazed tile floor, Jean could make out three knights in conversation with a sergeant by one of the windows. In the foreground were two large tables laden with parchment, inkpots, sand, quills, ledgers and sealing wax. A clerk in the white robes of a Templar priest was seated behind one of the tables working an abacus with dexterity before entering the results of his calculations on a wax tablet. Behind the other table two black-robed clerks were studiously copying.

When Jean entered, the sergeant by the window left his conversation and stepped down into the room. He was a tall, broad-shouldered man with a fringe of thick grey hair framing his tanned tonsure and a stiff white beard. He had bushy white eyebrows over deep-set blue-grey eyes and his face was leathery and etched with an extensive network of deep-cut wrinkles. Jean knew that the post of commander of the City of Acre was one of several senior positions in the hierarchy of the order reserved for sergeants. One look at the rugged, intelligent face studying him with open enquiry convinced him that this man was the commander of Acre.

"Commander, my name is Jean de Preuthune, from the commandery of Cahors. I've just arrived with my squire and a serving brother."

"Do you have dispatches from France?" the commander of Acre asked with a glance over his shoulder at the three knights still in conversation by the window.

"No, Commander, I... we... have come to serve here in Acre – in the Holy Land," he corrected; it was for the master to decide where in the Holy Land he would be stationed – or if he were to be sent back to France. Jean felt the sergeant's scrutiny and then felt naked and inadequate. It was as if the weathered veteran could read his very soul and was assessing his motives and his worth. "I have a letter from Commander Bourgneuf," Jean said to distract the sergeant-commander, reaching inside his surcoat for the letter.

The commander took the letter and broke the seal. One of the knights left the group in the background and made for the door. Jean stepped aside and opened the door for him. The knight nodded acknowledgement curtly and then stopped. "What is that for a sword?" he asked sharply, his finger pointing accusingly at the hilt of Jean's sword.

Jean flushed instantly, guiltily. "Sir?" he asked, pretending he did not know the cause of offence. The weapons of a Templar, like his armour, clothes and bedding, belonged to the order and were issued to each knight by his commander. Though they varied in size to suit the knights who had to wield them effectively, they were standardised. Knights were not allowed to adorn themselves with individual weapons. But Jean was wearing his father's sword, a parting gift when he left Aigues-Mortes nine weeks earlier.

"Give me your sword!" the knight ordered sternly. The knight wore no insignia of office or rank, but he too was a weathered veteran with a beard hanging to the middle of his chest. He appeared to be a good ten to fifteen years older than Jean and his tone of voice implied absolute certainty of authority.

The sergeant-commander had ceased reading the letter from Bourgneuf and was following the exchange at the door. The clerks too looked up and even from the window the remaining knights glanced over curiously.

Jean swallowed but had no choice. He withdrew his sword, holding the flat of the blade carefully on his open palm and extending the hilt to the knight who had demanded it.

Although the circular pommel of the sword was the standard Templar pommel of white enamel set with a red enamel cross, the hilt itself was crystal and contained the finger bones of St John the Baptist. "Is that a finger encased in crystal?" the knight enquired, holding up the sword so that all the others could see as well. "Rather like a reliquary?"

"Yes."

"Well, is it?"

"It is said to be the finger of St John the Baptist." Jean was fully aware that such a relic usually belonged only to kings and popes. He rather hoped that he would not be believed.

The priest at the abacus dropped it and stared at the sword with awe, while the two knights at the window slowly descended into the room and moved closer.

"Oh, really? A priceless reliquary – if it were true. How did you come by it?"

"It was my father's." There was no harm in admitting this. Secular knights, even married secular knights, could join the Templars for a limited time and enjoy an associate status. They took lesser vows, served their term and then returned to secular life where they could – without reproach – sire sons. It also lent credibility to the authenticity of the relic since a very wealthy nobleman might indeed have acquired such a relic.

"And he gave it to you?" the knight asked pointedly, his eyebrows raised in anticipation. This was the crux of the matter. A Templar was not allowed to keep the gifts he received. He was required to turn them over to his commander, who disposed of them as he pleased.

"Yes."

"And you kept it?"

"I was boarding ship at Aigues-Mortes. My commander was still in Cahors and no other Templar was aboard the vessel except my own squire and a serving brother."

"I see." The knight seemed somewhat mollified. "Then naturally you intended to surrender it to Commander Thibald – now," he concluded, handing the sword on to the sergeant-commander, who accepted it with a certain hesitation.

Jean watched his father's sword pass into strange hands with so much rage that it came close to choking him. Not a half hour earlier he had come to believe that he had been with his father at Mansourah. This sword was a bond between them greater than the usual gift from father to son. And these strangers would give it to someone else – someone who knew nothing of its past or his father, nothing of Mansourah.

"What's your name?" The man who asked was one of the knights who had been by the window and now stood directly behind the commander. He was studying Jean with penetrating brown eyes, and he asked the question with a slow intensity that suggested more than curiosity. He was a strikingly handsome man in his mid-fifties, with the kind of regular features in a broad, forceful face which adorned the statues of St George or the Archangel Michael in cathedrals – except that he wore a clipped beard. With a sense of doom, Jean noted that he also wore the insignia of the master. Commander Thibald turned to look at the master with a eyebrow raised in question.

"Jean de Preuthune," Jean answered steadily. His anger was forgotten in the realisation that his first encounter with the master of the Temple, William de Beaujeu, was this humiliating affair which imputed disobedience, greed and vanity to him. No one in the room believed that he had really intended to hand over the sword, and indeed he had not.

De Beaujeu's eyes lit up and a faint smile lifted his lips. "Then it *is* John the Baptist's finger," he declared to the astonished exclamation of the priest behind him and a protesting, "Why should you think that?" from the knight who had first noted the sword.

De Beaujeu ignored the others and held Jean's gaze with a magnetism that made it impossible for Jean to break free. "And it is De Sonnac's sword," he added.

This time it was the knight beside him who exclaimed. "Baucent! Are you sure?"

De Beaujeu did not let his eyes waver from Jean's, but he gestured for the man beside him to look at the sword more closely. "You are Geoffrey de Preuthune's son," he declared.

Jean nodded steadily. His father had reminded him in Aigues-Mortes that De Sonnac had sent a dispatch from Mansourah to Acre. He had been concerned that its contents could damage Jean's future in the order. He had warned him to be prepared. Now Jean waited with a certain fatalism for the results.

De Beaujeu nodded as if satisfied. "Welcome to Acre." He smiled and nodded again before he at last broke eye contact. "Thibald, it is your decision, but I would be in favour of giving Brother Jean his father's sword."

Without hesitation Commander Thibald returned the sword to Jean hilt first. But the knight who had first noted the unusual weapon broke in: "Sir, I must protest. If that is the late Master De Sonnac's sword, who met a martyr's death on the Seventh Crusade before the gates of Mansourah, then only you yourself should have the privilege of wearing it."

De Beaujeu considered the knight earnestly, and then replied with deliberate calm. "De Sonnac himself gave this sword to Brother Jean's father – for the small service of saving his life. De Sonnac hoped Geoffrey de Preuthune would bring the sword back to the order by taking our vows. But it seems he has sent his son instead. I am content to let the son who has taken his father's place and vow wear the mark of his father's service."

"Have you considered that it could engender jealousy for a mere knight to wear such a unique and valuable sword?"

"No, De Molay, it never occurred to me that any knight serving here at Acre could be so petty," De Beaujeu declared in a relaxed, even tone.

Jean sensed it was a quality very much the opposite of naivety which prompted the reply. He noted too that De Beaujeu had referred to the knight by his family rather than his Christian name – a mark of displeasure.

De Molay's ears reddened slightly. "And what will you say to the next knight who appears with an extravagant sword someone has 'given' him? If you allow one exception, soon it will be two and then a dozen until we all strut about in gaudy, bejewelled weapons like Mameluke emirs!" His eyes burned with genuine zealotry.

"Not all of us, I'm sure," De Beaujeu insisted in the same almost casual tone, which clearly infuriated the dogmatic De Molay. "You, for one, would never succumb to such nonsense, nor good Thibald, nor Peter here." He indicated the man beside him, who wore the insignia of the marshal of the Temple.

De Molay pressed his lips together and cut off the reply that apparently leapt to mind. "If you will excuse me, I have matters to attend to." He bowed his head curtly to the dignitaries of the order and withdrew with quick, decisive strides. Only then did Jean, with a tentative glance at De Beaujeu, risk returning the offending sword into its scabbard. He then went down on one knee and bowed his head before the master.

"There is no place for such formalities here," De Beaujeu informed him, indicating he should rise. "I must say it is a surprise to see you. I had long since given up hope that Brother Geoffrey would appear – it never occurred to me he would send a son."

"Did you know my father, my lord?"

"Yes, I was one of the two knights De Sonnac sent to carry dispatches from Mansourah to the seneschal here at Acre. I was not actually present in King Louis's tent when De Sonnac gave his sword to your father, but I learned of it the same night. And we travelled in company as far as Haifa where your father sailed for Cyprus."

"There was... forgive me."

"No, go on. Or rather come and sit with us in the window seat." De Beaujeu indicated the benches carved into the walls on either side of the central window. He led the way across the golden light spread upon the green and blue tiles and up to the window seat, mildly requesting one of the clerks to send for wine and wafers to greet their guest as he passed.

Jean knew he was being honoured beyond the ordinary and it embarrassed him – except that he realised it was a tribute to his father. This in turn made him intensely curious about what had been in the dispatch to De Sonnac's deputy. "My lord—"

"Please, 'sir' is adequate."

"My father warned me that I might not be received with any kind of favour. He... he said some dispatch had been sent by Master De Sonnac to his deputy..."

De Beaujeu considered Jean with a serious face and amused eyes. "Yes, there is a dispatch concerning your father addressed to the master of the Templars and their deputies, and still in our archives. I carried it to Acre after Mansourah, but I did not read it until I was myself elected master just over ten years ago." Jean understood: De Beaujeu had no intention of telling him what had been in the dispatch. He had to be content with the fact that De Beaujeu had read it and still welcomed him – warmly. "Did you know that your father was the only Templar I have ever known who could argue with De Sonnac over the correct translation – *ergo* interpretation – of the Scriptures?" Jean blushed, and De Beaujeu laughed delightedly. "Your father had read them in the original Greek – which put him at a distinct advantage over we common Franks who can only read Latin. Did he teach you Greek?"

"My older brother" – favoured, first-born Louis! – "can read Greek, but not I."

"A pity, but then we have enough work for us here without scholarly exercise. We are technically at peace, of course, but it is an illusion. Kalaoun would be happy to destroy us, and as soon as it is convenient he will try. In the meantime, he is not above harassing us deviously. He encourages Bedouins, pirates and common bands of robbers to attack the pilgrims who still – to the glory of God – seek to visit Jerusalem, Bethlehem and other holy sites. Kalaoun thereby pretends to respect the terms of the truce while in fact flouting its intention. Furthermore his surreptitious activities threaten our lines of communication from Haifa to Tripoli. Without a new crusade with thousands of knights and tens of thousands of settlers, we cannot hope to regain what has been lost. So we must be content to do what our order was founded to do: protect the Christians who are here. If we can hold on to these coastal cities, retain the right of access to the sites of Our Lord's Passion, and protect the Christians who live and visit, we will have done our duty to God. The days for slaughtering the infidel are gone."

Jean suspected he had made this speech to many eager newcomers before, and he heard a certain defensiveness in De Beaujeu's voice. Yet Jean found that the words inspired rather than discouraged him. Wasn't protection a far more admirable and Christian task than slaughter? Had the blood of non-combatants with which the first crusaders had flooded Jerusalem pleased an all-merciful Christ? Jean doubted it profoundly – or they might still be in possession of Jerusalem.

"I did not come here to slaughter anyone," Jean answered simply. "And I consider it an honour to follow in the footsteps of Hugh de Payens."

De Beaujeu smiled and nodded, evidently pleased by the response. "A pity De Molay doesn't share your point of view in this regard."

"Who is De Molay?" Jean ventured.

"He is a brave, competent, ambitious, opinionated knight, who thinks he could do my job better than I am doing it," De Beaujeu retorted with sudden strain in his voice and on his face.

"Come, William," the marshal tried to mollify De Beaujeu. "It is only natural that there are differences of opinions about the running of any institution. The pope himself is not free of criticism. You shouldn't take it personally."

De Beaujeu gave Marshal De Sevrey an unreadable look, and clearly decided that this was not a topic to discuss in front of a new recruit. Turning pointedly to Jean, he informed him in an almost exaggeratedly cheerful tone, "Your brothers from Cahors were sent to the garrison at Tripoli, but if you have no objections I would like to keep you here in Acre."

"Thank you!" Jean's relief and response were so obviously heartfelt that De Beaujeu had to laugh.

"You do me good, Brother Jean. Peter, to which troop should we assign this young man? He is not so very young, I think, that he needs coddling." He gave Jean another assessing glance.

"Brother Odo could use a strong young knight," the marshal suggested with a glance at Thibald, who nodded assent.

De Beaujeu laughed happily and, seeing the wine arriving at last, leapt down from the window to take the tray from the serving brother. He poured wine for himself and the others into silver chalices, and then raised his glass to Jean. "Welcome home!"

Acre
1287

As the little troop passed under the city gate, its duties officially ended. The heterogeneous band of nearly a hundred pilgrims, whether elated or disappointed by what they had seen, eager or reluctant to get home, dispersed according to their plans and their purses. Some made for the expensive lodgings of the Italian merchants, anxious to purge themselves of accumulated dust, sweat and weariness. Others hastened piously and frugally towards one of several hospices maintained by religious houses and still others were in a hurry to reach the brothels near the port. Their escort of eight knights Templar, eight squires and twenty sergeants turned for the Templar castle in a disciplined troop, riding in pairs.

Jean led the troop and his thoughts were on a bath. Since leaving Bethlehem he had not bathed, and sand had found its way through every crevice and every link of his chainmail to lodge itself under his swordbelt, down his back and even between his toes. 'A bath,' he thought contentedly, letting his weary, dusty stallion amble on a long rein, 'and then oranges followed by a glass of chilled wine.'

His eyes noted a scrawny girl coming toward him, bent under a basket, and he recognised her as the daughter of the Jewish shopkeeper from whom the Templars purchased the bulk of their fresh fruit. Distracted, he called out, "Rachel?"

The girl looked up with a startled, nervous gesture, but her thin, triangular face broke into a smile at the sight of Jean. Dumping the burdensome basket on the ground, she stood upright and waved. "Hello, *Monsieur* Jean!" When she smiled, she had a contagious mirth, though not even a smile could disguise her cleft lip.

"What are you doing so far from home?" Jean drew abreast of her and enquired in a stern, paternal tone which did not in the least impress the girl. Her real father was a harsh, unsmiling man of whom she was genuinely afraid. Sir Jean was someone who had given her a doll and later a puppy, and he never failed to smile.

"I've been sent to deliver these things to Madame d'Ibelin." The girl gestured to the basket covered with a checked linen cloth.

Jean frowned. Not only was the basket clearly too heavy for the skinny ten year old, but by the time Rachel had managed to drag her basket to the palazzo of the noblewoman near the royal castle it would be dark. Although Rachel was only a shopkeeper's daughter, the thought of her at the mercy of Acre's night population did not sit well with Jean. He made a decision. "Come here, Rachel. I'll bring you and your wares to Madame d'Ibelin."

He had not finished speaking, and already his squire, Pierre, was jumping down and collecting the basket. Lucien had been knighted, and Jean was now served by a young Gascon Lucien had befriended on the ship from Aigues-Mortes. Pierre had run away from his brutal service to Sir Baldwin de Montfort, and begged for a position with the Temple. He had explicitly rejected the idea of taking vows, however, even minor ones, hoping apparently that one day he could find the means to go home. Meanwhile, he served as a civilian for the standard annuity, and had been assigned to Sir Jean.

Pierre collected the basket and the knight riding next to Jean offered to take it on his saddle, while Rachel herself, with a smile that seemed to split her marred face in two, ran and grabbed Jean's stirrup. He reached down to help her up before his saddle, and was astonished by the strength in her wiry, thin arms as she clasped his leg and pulled herself upwards.

Jean turned back to the troop behind him. "No need for all of you to accompany us."

Relieved, they made no protest but laughed or joked as they pushed past him. Only the knight with the basket and Pierre remained with him. They turned their horses around in the narrow alley, and started back across the town.

Rachel was chattering happily in his lap. Jean understood only half of what she said because their common language was Arabic, a language he had far from mastered. But, like the chatter of most ten year olds, most of what she said had only limited interest for him. As they passed one great, Arab mansion with a tiled entrance way, Rachel informed him that this was the house of the slave trader who had bought all the captured slaves.

Curiosity half aroused, Jean enquired which captured slaves.

"The ones your brothers took from the pirate ship!" Rachel told him as if this should have been self-evident, and, seeing his surprise, she elaborated. "But you must know! Everyone has been talking about it for days. A big" – she stretched her arms as far as she was able – "hundred-oar galley!" Although Rachel could count well enough to make change for her father's customers, Jean knew this 'hundred' was figurative. "The pirates pretended to be in distress and sinking to attract the assistance of your ship" – all the Templars' ships belonged to Jean as far as Rachel was concerned – "and then when your brothers came to help them they attacked. But your brothers were much quicker and stronger and braver, and all the pirates were killed – well, some had their heads cut off in Justice Square later. Everybody in Acre went to see it, but my father wouldn't let me go. They say one of the pirates kept praying even after his head was cut off! The Arabs said it was a miracle from Allah, but my father says that it happens all the time, just like chickens flapping their wings after they've had their heads knocked off."

Jean nodded agreement. "How long ago was that?"

"Oh, the executions were just the day before yesterday."

"And the attack on the ship?"

"I don't know. They towed the captured galley into the harbour the day before the executions. It's still there!" she added excitedly.

Unfortunately, they had reached the Ibelin palazzo. The façade to the street was austere and forbidding, with iron grilling guarding the windows, and an armed guard at the gate. Jean lifted Rachel to the ground and his companion handed down the basket to her. Rachel went to the guard, let him inspect her basket and was admitted through the gate.

The forbidding house offered an enchanting interior, including a carefully cultivated garden with fountains and fish ponds strategically located among flowers and shaded by fruit trees. The hall was paved with marble. Jean knew because the knights of the militant orders were welcome guests in Acre's patrician society, and he had been entertained by the Ibelins more than once.

Jean's stallion stamped impatiently, then stretched out his foreleg to scratch the side of his face. From the city came the wailing of the mullahs, calling the faithful to prayer. 'Odd,' Jean thought, 'how familiar the sound has become.' He thought he would even miss it if ever he went home.

The gate of the Ibelin palazzo creaked and released Rachel. She skipped happily to the waiting horses, swinging her empty basket. When she reached Jean, she hung her basket over her neck, and reached up her hands to be hauled up as if it were her right. The knight beside Jean raised his eyebrows in disapproval and wondered aloud what the master would think if he could see Jean now. Jean shrugged and helped Rachel up.

"We could ride down to the harbour and look at the pirate ship," Rachel suggested eagerly.

"No," Jean told her firmly, and, collecting his reins, they started back whence they had come.

Feeling rebuffed, Rachel was less communicative now, and Jean too was almost regretting his spontaneous generosity. But the shadows were long, darkening the alleys. Women were nowhere in sight; they were locked firmly inside the safety of their houses. The honest tradesmen, workmen, shopkeepers and merchants had settled into their ordered domestic lives after their evening prayers. The figures that lingered in the alleys or squatted together carrying on unintelligible, guttural conversations were not men Jean trusted. Hardly a week went by without the body of some hapless pilgrim, sailor or citizen turning up in a back alley or floating by the quay. Rachel was carrying the price of her father's fruit in a little cloth sack tied at her waist on the inside of her gown. If Jean could see it there, then so could every thief in Acre.

Before they had reached her father's house, Rachel roused herself from her reverie and tugged insistently at Jean's arm. "Let me down, Sir Jean! Let me down here. If my father sees me with you he will beat me black and blue!"

Jean halted the horse as much from shock as in response, and Rachel at once swung her leg over the neck and slid down to the ground. She started to run away, then stopped to wave goodbye, before continuing with a determined urgency that spoke of genuine fear. Jean was left to ponder the absurdity of the situation. What in the name of any God was wrong with him befriending a scrawny ten year old child who appeared to have no other friends? Now he felt guilty for not taking her down to see the pirate ship. What would it have cost him? Another half hour and another raised eyebrow from

Brother André? He could have survived both. Rachel, however, had nothing but work. Her parents were poor – despite the Templar patronage – and her mother crippled. Her older sister cooked, kept the house and tended the crippled mother and Rachel helped in the shop. She was illiterate, with no prospects of marriage – and she was a Jew. Jean sighed.

They passed through the portal into the castle, as the sun sank below the horizon. Overhead the sky was already a luminous, sapphire blue and the evening star was vivid against the backdrop. The watch had been awaiting them, and the portcullis rattled down to fall into place with a decisive crunching thud as they drew rein in the ward. Knights, sergeants and serving brothers were streaming from the chapel as vespers ended, on their way to the spacious refectory for the evening meal.

André jumped down and, tossing his reins to a lay brother, joined the migration to the refectory. As he swung his leg over the cantle, Jean realised how dead-tired he really was. Every muscle ached, the sand chafed, he stank, his scalp itched, his eyes burned. Gratefully he turned his stallion over to the serving brother, and, disdaining the prospect of a silent meal in company, made for the baths with Pierre shadowing him.

The Templars had spent nearly two hundred years in the Holy Land and they had been quick to adapt to conditions there. While their knowledge of the terrain, enemy weaponry, tactics and leadership had enabled them to become the most effective opponents of the Saracens, they did not scorn those features of Arab culture that were compatible with Christianity and practical for life in the desert climate. Thus the Templar castle at Acre was provided with an extensive bath complex. A series of tiled rooms housed pools heated to different temperatures. The pools were fed, drained and heated using the same engineering techniques the Romans had employed a thousand years earlier and which the Templar masons had mastered completely.

As Jean entered the baths, he unbuckled his sword and laid it at the foot of one of the benches lining the wall. Then, resting one foot after the other on the edge of the bench, he undid his spurs and the garters holding up his chainmail leggings before pulling the dust-laden surcoat over his head and tossing it to the floor. At once Pierre sprang forward to help him remove his heavy hauberk with its attached coif, but Jean waved him aside. It was, to be sure, one of the principal tasks of any civilian squire to help his knight arm and disarm, but the Templar rule required every knight to dress and undress himself. The links of the chainmail harboured countless particles of sand which now cascaded on to the tiled floor. Likewise, Jean's chainmail hose rained sand upon the tiles as he untied the cord of his braes and let them sink to the floor. He stepped out of them then rolled down his cotton hose and threw them to join his surcoat. His sweat-soaked gambeson, soiled with the dirt that had worked its way through the mail and streaks of rust from the chainmail itself, looked utterly ruined. Either the labour of the native washerwomen, who collected and returned the Templar laundry, would restore it, or the Temple would provide him with a new one. His stinking shirt and braes joined the other cloth garments in the heap. All clothing was communal property and, because these garments were identical except for size, they were interchangeable. Pierre, in contrast, carefully piled his clothing in a heap to be collected later.

Naked, they descended the steps into the coolish water, taking soap from the shallow gutter around the pool. "Let me, sir," Pierre begged. Jean did not resist. He returned the soap, and hooking his elbows through the hand bar, lazily floated with eyes closed. He listened to the lapping of the wavelets against the pool, and relished the sheer luxury of being bathed. Pierre was gentle and thorough, massaging as he cleansed, starting at the feet. He carefully cleaned between the toes, and then massaged Jean's aching calves, his saddle-hardened thighs. Almost like a woman. Jean kicked abruptly and violently and fought to bring himself upright. He stared at Pierre. The youth blushed.

"Don't! Don't even think it!" Jean's voice was harsh.

"I... I... but..."

"There are no 'buts'! If you ever do that again – ever give me reason to suspect – I'll throw you out. Do you understand? The order does not tolerate any man who..." He could not get himself to state it explicitly.

Pierre was redder than a boiled crab. He did not meet Jean's eye. "I only..."

Jean turned his back on him, took soap and started vigorously washing himself. When he was scrubbed clean, he climbed out of the pool and without a glance or a remark to the miserable squire moved on into the next chamber with the hot, steaming bath. Pierre did not follow him.

Sweating in the steam, Jean calmed himself gradually. As he sweated out the ingrained dirt of two weeks on the road, he convinced himself he had overreacted. Pierre was only trying to do his best. He felt he had to prove he was worth something after having failed to please Sir Baldwin. De Molay had questioned whether the order should even accept a runaway squire who, from De Molay's point of view, had evidently proved unsatisfactory and probably deserved the harsh punishments Sir Baldwin imposed.

But that made the situation all the more delicate. Jean had vouched for Pierre and pledged his own word that Pierre would not prove unsatisfactory. And Pierre was diligent, eager and almost embarrassingly devoted. But what if his devotion was not mere gratitude and conscientiousness? If Pierre proved to be a sodomite... Jean sank under the water and ran his hands through his hair and beard briskly. Then he surfaced and, blocking his thoughts, made for the final chamber with the largest, moderately heated pool. Here several of the members of his troop still sat on the benches or were paddling about in the pool, relaxing.

They greeted him cheerfully. "Did you hear? Jacques de Molay took a pirate ship." Henri always liked to be first with news.

Grateful for the distraction, Jean responded readily. "That much I heard. Do you know the details?"

"Brother Jacques had been sent to deliver dispatches to Tortosa and Tripoli." This was routinely done by ship and the Templars maintained a small fleet of galleys for the purpose. "He was off Tyre on the return trip when he sighted a Cypriot ship, apparently dismasted and signalling for assistance. Although there had been some heavy wind, there was nothing like enough to dismast a ship, so Brother Jacques was suspicious and went alongside with the entire company at ready but hidden."

One of the younger knights, Bertram, eagerly added, "On closer approach they could see that of the sixteen pairs of oars only four were working so that the ship was barely making headway in the choppy seas."

Henri, irritated by the interruption, continued forcefully. "The pseudo Cypriot captain explained that he'd lost half his crew to fever and that was why he'd been unable to hand sail in time, causing the dismasting. He requested a tow to port. Brother Jacques willingly agreed – not giving the slightest indication that he was suspicious. When he manoeuvred close enough to pass the towlines, pirates swarmed aboard, thinking they could capture the apparently lightly manned ship. Instead they were cut down or captured and then – before those still aboard could cut free – Brother Jacques boarded and captured their ship."

"Aboard were not only the galley slaves for the full sixteen oars, but packed into cages nearly a hundred other captives as well," Bertram added with the kind of breathless relish only a youth newly arrived from the West could manage.

"Did we have casualties?" Jean asked, climbing out of the bath and taking a clean towel from the waiting rack to rub himself dry.

"Two sailors, Sergeants Baecker, Fuentes, Damme and Herriot, and Sir Godfrey were killed or died of their injuries. The other wounds were not fatal, though Sergeant Bouchet may lose his hand, which was crushed between the ships while he was boarding."

"And Sergeant Pirenne is under arrest and in the dungeon," Bertram added importantly.

"Why?" Jean started. Sergeant Pirenne was a man he knew quite well. Until recently, he had served in Jean's own company.

"He murdered someone," Bertram informed him.

Jean looked from one to the other in disbelief. Pirenne was an exceptionally tall, burly man of great strength and great courage. He loved a fight and was always in the forefront of any skirmish. But Jean could not imagine him committing cold-blooded murder. He was a jovial man, quick to temper but equally quick to forgive.

"It has nothing to do with the pirates," Henri concluded.

"Well, he was aboard the ship and they brought him back in chains," Bertram insisted.

"For killing a pirate?" Henri scoffed.

"No, of course, not. For killing one of the slaves. I think I heard that the slave was a Templar knight."

"They don't enslave Templar knights – they kill us," Henri informed the relative newcomer with pride.

"They sold Templar knights in Damascus after the fall of Beaufort in '68," Jean reminded them both in a low penetrating voice that gave them both pause.

"That's almost twenty years ago. None of them could have survived so long."

Jean did not answer. He finished drying himself, left the towel in the basket by the door and took a clean, striped caftan from a pile. Thus dressed, he returned to the first chamber to collect sword and armour. He noted that Pierre's clothes were gone; apparently he had not wished to join the company in the last chamber.

Carrying his armour, Jean proceeded to his cell. André was still in the refectory for the evening meal. It was a welcome relief from the rigidity of the rule at Cahors that here a brother returning from legitimate duty could expect a meal whenever he arrived. Without hurry, therefore, Jean changed into clean undergarments, gambeson and surcoat, leaving his chainmail to be thoroughly cleaned by Pierre.

"Sir Jean?"

Jean jumped in surprise. Commander Gaudin filled the entrance to the cell. The cell and the hall beyond were almost totally dark, but the last fading glow of the western sky above the Mediterranean cast Gaudin's worried features into relief above his black surcoat. The red cross of the Temple faded into the surrounding shadow, but the beard hanging well down his chest seemed all the more impressive. 'He looks a hundred years old,' Jean thought in awe and humility as he straightened and greeted his visitor. "Commander."

"When I saw members of your troop at dinner I realised you were back. There is something I wish to discuss with you."

A Templar cell did not offer comfort and Jean could only indicate the bed opposite his own, at once uneasy and curious about such an unusual visit.

The commander of Acre was a tall man; he pulled in his head as he passed under the doorway into the cell and sat down. The cells had no doors. Sergeant Gaudin sat down on the bed carefully – as if his joints ached or he were lost in thought – or both. Then he faced Jean and indicated that he too should sit.

"Have you heard about Sergeant Pirenne?" he opened simply.

"I was told he has been arrested for murder – something I find extremely hard to credit."

Commander Gaudin's expression seemed to relax just a fraction, as if one small load had been lifted. "Sergeant Pirenne accompanied Sir Jacques de Molay on his mission to Tripoli and was with him when they were attacked by a pirate ship. With God's help, our brothers were able to overpower the pirates and board their ship in turn." The sergeant-commander spoke with the abject humility of a man who did not doubt that all his successes were God's work and all his failures his own. "Sergeant Pirenne, as is his nature, was one of the first to board and one of the first to go below deck. He found cages built into the ship for the purpose of transporting slaves. These cages were filled to overflowing with the hapless victims of the pirates – very many once honourable and free citizens of all ages, race, sex and faith. Sergeant Pirenne broke the locks holding the cages with his sword – one after another. The freed captives flooded out, many gleeful for revenge upon their captors. They rushed upward toward the deck for fresh air or revenge – it is of no matter. But one man remained behind. As he bent over the man Sergeant Pirenne saw that he was legless – wooden pegs were attached to both knees and his thighs were wrapped in filthy, bloody rags. Sergeant Pirenne offered to help him to his feet and the man begged instead for Sergeant Pirenne to kill him."

Jean felt the cold sweat which always presaged an unholy memory of that which he could not possibly remember. He pressed his lips together and swallowed his fear. He knew he had nothing to fear – and yet the supernatural always induces fear.

"He begged – in French, you understand. He identified himself as a knight Templar, one of those captured at Beaufort, and he begged Pirenne to kill him."

Jean waited without moving or breathing, aware only that he could understand that desire without being able to explain it.

"Sergeant Pirenne naturally hesitated," Commander Gaudin told Jean, and Jean glanced up with a jolt. The inflection and intensity of Gaudin's voice had subtly changed. Commander Gaudin abruptly sought to avoid direct eye contact. "Seeing Pirenne's hesitation, the man – I should say our brother – seized Pirenne's dagger and turned it upon himself. To prevent this poor knight from committing a mortal sin that would damn his soul for eternity, Pirenne took the heavy burden upon himself and killed him first."

Jean looked hard at the commander. "Pirenne said that?" Jean asked with open scepticism, but it was not necessary. They both knew that Gaudin was lying – and they knew why.

"Brother Jacques has demanded that Pirenne be confined to the 'hermitage' for life."

"What?"

The 'hermitage' was a windowless cell, four foot by four, built into the thickness of the walls behind the chapel. A single inch-wide peephole allowed the prisoner to hear mass. Water was provided by a pipeline into a stone bowl, and a corner hole and drain functioned as a latrine. Food was provided through a trapdoor. The chamber had never been used in De Beaujeu's time, and the rumours had it that the longest anyone had been confined there was a month – for fleeing in the face of the enemy.

"Brother Jacques says it is an insult to claim that any Templar would ask for death – much less try to kill himself."

Jean felt the cramping of his chest muscles and the queasiness of his stomach as he shuddered. He knew what it was to want to die, but Commander Gaudin could not know that he would react like this, empathising with the mutilated knight. "Why did you come to me, Commander? I was not there. I cannot judge Sergeant Pirenne."

"But you must and shall. In chapter. There you and your fellow knights will pass judgement and sentence upon him."

"This hasn't been put to the chapter yet? I thought—"

"There wasn't a quorum until you returned with your troop."

"I have only one vote, Commander, among nearly a hundred."

"You have a voice that others listen to. The master will ask your opinion."

Jean tensed, acutely aware of the honour De Beaujeu did him. He was barely thirty years old and had been in the Holy Land less than four years. That they had entrusted him with a troop of his own seemed honour enough, and he was himself astonished by how rapidly his little band had moulded together into an efficient team, cohesive, at ease with one another, and bluntly loyal to him. He was proud of his troop and he could count on their support in anything – even such a delicate issue as this. But Gaudin seemed to imply that he might be expected to influence others as well.

Gaudin had risen to his feet and, overcoming physical weariness with discipline, he squared his shoulders. "Good night, Sir Jean. May you rest well after your trials."

"May I speak with Sergeant Pirenne?"

"No. He is confined to the dungeon and no one but Father Etienne is allowed near him. He is chained."

"Chained?"

"Brother Jacques insisted he might otherwise overpower his guards. He is a big man, stronger than most of us."

"Does Brother Jacques de Molay give the orders here?" Jean retorted in irritation.

"Well you might ask," came the discouraged reply, and then the commander faded into the shadows, leaving Jean to shiver in the wind blowing in off the sea.

*

The Chapter House of the Templars at Acre had been built for better times, when as many three hundred knights might travel from dozens of garrisons throughout the Holy Land and from the West for sessions of the grand chapter. Once even the chapter at Acre itself had numbered roughly two hundred knights. But one by one the cities of the Holy Land and the Templar castles – Baghras and Gastun, the twin Castels Rouge and Blanc, Beaufort, Safita and Safed – had fallen to the Turks. The garrisons that had manned them were slaughtered or captured. Despite frantic pleas for recruits and a continuing trickle of new arrivals, the Templar presence had shrunk to no more than four hundred knights throughout the Holy Land. At Acre, the quorum was met with just sixty-three knights.

These knights, dressed in pristine white cowled habits with red trim and crosses, filled only half the rows of carved masonry benches in the hexagonal chapter house. De Beaujeu, flanked by Father Etienne, the senior Templar chaplain, and Peter de Sevrey, sat upon the three chairs on the one wall without banks of seats. The seneschal, who ranked above the marshal and would normally have sat in De Sevrey's place, was in the West, tasked with inspection and recruitment. Over these three chairs, gilded masonry emphasised the dignity of the occupants. The other senior officials of the Temple, the commanders of the city of Jerusalem, the commander of the kingdom of Jerusalem, the commander of Acre, the turcopolier, the draper and the standard bearer sat in the first row. Conspicuously absent were the commanders of the cities of Tripoli and Antioch. No one had been granted the title of commander of Antioch since the city's fall, and the commander of Tripoli left his post only when specifically ordered to attend the chapter in Acre by the master. Behind them, in the second row, sat the commanders of the five companies stationed at Acre with their troop leaders, and then the deacons of the chapel.

Jean thus found himself in the second row, directly beside his company commander, Brother Odo. His troop filled most of the rows behind him, as everywhere, the knights were seated in precedence before the more numerous sergeants. André and Lucien were seated directly behind him, while De Molay sat directly opposite, backed by his company with his troop leaders beside him.

Brother Odo was a man now approaching sixty-five, hard of hearing, stubborn and reclusive. He was completely bald and wore the scars of countless battles on his desert-hardened skin. His scalp was roughly divided in two by one puckered scar which recorded the blow that had left him unconscious and presumed dead at Castel Rouge. He had lost an eye at Safita. He had seen with his remaining eye the heads of his brothers held high on Saracen stakes, when Baibar's army threatened Acre in '66. Odo was an uncompromising, unsmiling man, who lived within himself without revealing his thoughts or his feelings to others. Jean served him gladly, nevertheless, because he gave his troop leaders maximum freedom as long as things went smoothly, and he could be counted on to respond professionally in a crisis. What he thought of the case at hand, Jean had no way of knowing.

Father Etienne rose and took a step forward. The brothers rose to their feet and silence echoed in the soaring arches of the chamber. Father Etienne led them in prayer. Then he stepped back, and De Beaujeu replaced him, signalling for the knights to sit. He outlined the facts of the case before them, and then ordered the sergeants at the door to bring in the prisoner.

Pirenne was escorted by two sergeants. He was a good head taller than his two guards, and he had been given a clean surcoat. Even so he seemed like a broken man as they led him in, his legs chained together. De Beaujeu addressed him sternly but calmly, telling him that he was charged with murdering Brother Maurice d'Arbois, knight Templar of the commandery of Beaufort. He asked the sergeant to relate what had transpired on the pirate galley.

Sergeant Pirenne spoke so softly that most of the brothers could not hear clearly and shifted irritably in their seats. De Beaujeu had to ask Pirenne to speak up. The sergeant lifted his head slightly and collected his breath. He spoke in a monotone. Jean noted that his lips were crusted with sores – like a man who had been sunburned. 'He is a simple man,' Jean registered, 'who does not understand what has happened to him.'

Pirenne reached the climax of his narrative without evidence of emotion. "Then Sir... Sir Maurice grabbed my dagger and tried to turn it against himself..." The sergeant looked straight at De Beaujeu as he said this and Jean thought he saw the master nod.

'Christ,' he thought, 'It is not just Gaudin has put this story into his mouth, but De Beaujeu himself who is behind it!'

"This is preposterous!" De Molay protested.

"Don't interrupt the witness," De Beaujeu ordered, raising his hand with cool dignity. He nodded to Pirenne openly.

"He grabbed my dagger and tried to turn it against himself. When I realised what he intended I killed him to prevent him committing a mortal sin."

"This is preposterous!" De Molay repeated, half rising from his seat. "A legless man, enslaved for twenty years, would never be strong enough to wrench a dagger from Sergeant Pirenne—"

"You have not been recognised, Brother Jacques," De Beaujeu told him sharply.

"A question, sire!" This came from a younger troop leader, Fulk van der Burg, a Flemish knight. De Beaujeu gave him the floor. "Why didn't Sergeant Pirenne simply knock the dagger out of Sir Maurice's hand? There was no need to kill him!"

Pirenne looked helplessly toward De Beaujeu before stammering, "There wasn't time. He'd already started to draw blood."

"There was only one wound on his chest," Deacon de Fleury reported, shouting to be heard over the protest that had erupted from De Molay and Van der Burg – both loudly supported by their troops.

Lucien leaned down and whispered in Jean's ear, "I can't believe Pirenne did this! Did we know him so little?" His face was worried and confused.

Jean looked from him to the others. Only André looked cool and detached. The others were whispering among themselves and flushed with emotion.

De Molay had jumped to his feet. "Sire!"

De Beaujeu took his staff and called for order. Gradually the confusion dissipated and the chatter died down. All turned their attention expectantly toward De Beaujeu. "You requested the floor, Brother Jacques."

"It is even more ridiculous to believe Brother Maurice – God have mercy on his soul – tried to kill himself than to believe he begged for death—"

"He did!" Pirenne burst out with the first flare of raw emotion he had shown. "He begged me to kill him! He ordered me to kill him! If you had seen—"

"I did!" De Molay cut him off sharply with his ice-cold voice and eyes. The room went deathly still. "I saw you kill him."

Deacon de Fleury took up the accusation. "Put yourselves in the shoes of our Brother Maurice – tortured for twenty years by the indignity and brutality of slavery to Saracen pirates. Then against all hopes you hear the ship boarded, the sound of battle overhead, the cries of 'Vive Dieu St Amour!' that can only come from your brothers. You see one cage after another opened, the slaves liberated. You anticipate your own emancipation with the elation of a man seeing salvation on earth. The cage is opened, the other slaves flood out, and you see before you a Christian wearing the mantle and surcoat you so dearly love. He comes toward you and lifts his naked sword – you think to free you of your chains – but instead he plunges his sword into your belly and robs you of your life in the instant it has become worth living."

There was a shocked, numbed silence. They could all too easily picture themselves in Brother Maurice's shoes.

"He ordered me to kill him!" Pirenne repeated doggedly, lifting his voice in desperation so that it echoed off the converging fingers of masonry overhead.

"That is slander against a noble knight and slander against the order itself! No Knight of the Temple of Solomon would ever beg for death!"

There was a chorus of approval for Jacques de Molay's words, and Jean sensed that it was a larger chorus than had first supported De Molay. It was as if you could see the disease spreading from De Molay's own company to infect the men beside them. He glanced back at De Beaujeu and saw that he looked grey and haggard.

'This is nothing to do with Pirenne,' Jean recognised with unease. 'This is an attack on De Beaujeu himself.'

Jean felt as if he had to say something, but he did not know what. He could hardly stand up and announce that he believed, in a previous life, he had experienced something similar to Brother Maurice. They would lock him in the 'hermitage' for heresy! And yet he believed that Pirenne was telling the truth. He stood up, hot with nervousness, and waited for De Beaujeu to call for order and give him the floor.

"Brothers!" Jean's voice was weak and thin; he swallowed and took a deep breath. "You have been asked to imagine what it was like for Brother Maurice in the moment when Pirenne found him. I beg you to focus on what went before. A knight of the Temple, you wear the white mantle with pride – even if such pride is against the rule." He smiled apologetically toward De Beaujeu, but De Beaujeu had closed his eyes and appeared to be praying. "You love your order and your brothers with all your heart, and you fight with all your strength and skill at Beaufort. But your situation is utterly hopeless. You are outnumbered, cut off from all relief, your supplies running low. Though you are prepared to die for God, your superiors decide it is better to surrender and retire to Acre – there to strengthen the garrison, there to prepare to fight again. You follow orders. You have vowed to do so and to do otherwise would be a disgrace and damnation.

"But the enemy is not the Sultan Salah ah Din, but the Sultan Baibars. He does not keep his word. He does not let you return to Acre: he binds you like a beast, a rope around your neck, your feet hobbled, and he drags you across the desert, parading you in every village and every town. Your feet blister, putrefy and bleed. You are forced to crawl when you can no longer walk, and everywhere you are spat upon, pissed upon, deluged with refuse and abuse. You see your weaker brothers die, but you – God knows why – survive. You are taken to market. The customers inspect you – every part of you – your teeth, your eyes, your genitals. You've seen how it's done!" Jean challenged the embarrassed knights sitting opposite him in the sanctified atmosphere of the Chapter House. "You've idled on the edge of the slave market here in Acre or Beirut or Tripoli, hoping that they'll bring the girls out and some customer will insist on inspecting her most intimate features—"

"Are you going to allow such talk, my lord?" Deacon de Fleury demanded of De Beaujeu in outrage.

"Certainly. He is only speaking the truth," De Beaujeu responded calmly.

"Truth?! He's talking irrelevant nonsense!" Van der Burg announced with a show of contempt.

"Let him finish!" Odo's voice was a baritone which sounded as if it would bring the roof down and it made Jean start no less than the others in the room. Jean looked at his superior, but Odo did not deign to return the look, staring stolidly ahead.

Jean had no choice but to resume his hypothetical narrative. "You are sold first to one master and then the next. Some are better than others. Some kinder, some crueller, some fair, some arbitrary. But for all you are a slave. You have no rights. You have no Christian name, have the benefit of neither mass nor confession—"

"God himself hears the confession of prisoners in the hands of heathens!" Deacon de Fleury announced with passion.

"Undoubtedly, but the absolution he gives we cannot hear," Jean answered, and De Fleury was silenced through sheer astonishment. "We cannot know what Brother Maurice endured in twenty years of slavery. He was, I am told, roughly forty when he died. Was he a pretty youth at twenty who served masters for their sodomy—"

"How dare you!" De Molay jumped to his feet.

"Arrest Preuthune!" Van der Burg demanded. "He insults the honour of us all."

"By saying that Muslim slave owners could force a Christian youth into sodomy?" Jean yelled back abruptly, furious. "Rape is rape whether women or youths are the victims! Do you impute guilt to the victim?"

"This is not to the point," Gaudin pointed out wearily, while Pirenne looked confusedly about the room.

"Get to the point, sir," De Beaujeu urged with an intense look at Jean.

"But this is to the point. Don't you see? If you had gone through that and lost your legs... How do you think Brother Maurice lost his legs? Both of them cut off below the knee? An accident perhaps – or was it sheer sadism? Or did some master try to convert him forcibly to Islam by cutting off first one toe and then the next and the next – it's been done! Damn you all!" Jean was furious beyond all imagination, trembling with terror as he remembered. "It's been done! Toe for toe, finger for finger! And what if you succumbed?"

he demanded in an anguished tone that silenced even his opponents. "What if you accepted Allah to save your knees – and then saw your Christian brothers coming through the door?"

The silence was so intense that Jean heard only his own breathing. He sank back into his seat, breathing heavily and sweating so heavily that he smelt his own stench. He did not know Brother Maurice. He did not know what had motivated him. He knew only that it was possible to want to die.

Odo stood. "Brother Jean is right. There are circumstances that can make any man – even you, Jacques de Molay – wish he were dead. I vote for acquittal." He sat down as abruptly as he had stood.

"I would indeed rather die for my faith than succumb to such torture," Jacques de Molay replied with dignity. "Any man who had survived so much deserved to be taken into our care with love and respect – not brutally murdered. I believe that even if, in a moment of confused madness, Brother Maurice begged for death, Sergeant Pirenne should have known better than to accede to such a blasphemous wish."

"Sergeant Pirenne has taken a vow of obedience," Commander Gaudin pointed out. "A knight gave him an order."

A wave of protest rose from the ranks of the opposition. Jean estimated that a good third of the knights and sergeants were firmly in De Molay's camp. A third tended to sympathise with Pirenne, and the remainder were ambivalent.

Peter de Sevrey, the marshal, asked for the floor and received it. The opposition quietened down gradually. They respected De Sevrey as a distinguished commander and brilliant tactician. He had extricated his command from Haifa when the city fell and with hardly a single casualty had brought it intact through Saracen-held territory. But De Sevrey was also De Beaujeu's deputy, his friend. "No one denies that Sergeant Pirenne killed Brother Maurice. No one suggests this was right. Sergeant Pirenne has committed a grave sin, and for his sin he will have to beg God's forgiveness and do great penance. Only God can forgive him – and God knows if Brother Maurice tried to kill himself or merely asked to be killed and what his motives might have been. We do not sit in judgement on Sergeant Pirenne's soul. We are here to decide his fate as a brother—"

"I do not call a murderer 'Brother!'" Fulk van der Burg shouted vehemently, to scattered applause.

"Murder is against the rule and reason for expulsion from the order," De Molay declared sanctimoniously.

Jean glanced toward Gaudin. Was the story about the 'hermitage' a fabrication, like the attempted suicide? Something intended to win his support? If so, Jean resented the fact that De Beaujeu felt he could be manipulated – or that he needed to be.

"It is grounds for expulsion," De Sevrey replied to De Molay, ignoring Van der Burg. "We are not required to expel him. The punishment or penance we select is our choice."

"I must object," Deacon de Fleury croaked in a high-pitched voice that matched his crow-like appearance. "It is unthinkable that we should simply expel a murderer and let him loose on civilian society. Sergeant Pirenne must be rendered harmless for the rest of his life. The most merciful punishment would be confinement – in chains – for the rest of his life."

"No!" Sergeant Pirenne objected. "I'd rather you killed me!"

The words rang through the room and Jean looked from Pirenne to De Beaujeu and then to Gaudin and back to Pirenne. Had they planned this as well? Or was the outburst genuine? He couldn't tell.

In the ensuing silence, De Beaujeu announced in a slightly unsteady but studiously calm voice, "I cannot – we cannot – afford to do without Sergeant Pirenne in our present situation. We need every trained fighting man we have and more."

"Correct!" Brother Odo seconded the master without bothering to rise from his seat.

"You would let the murderer of one of our brothers go unpunished?" De Molay asked, and his outrage was not theatrics.

"No. Of course he must be punished. But there are many punishments that we can ordain – Sergeant Pirenne can be degraded to serving brother, detailed to the most unpleasant tasks, fed with the dogs or sent to sleep with the horses – but I want him here, armed and fit, when Kalaoun attacks Acre." De Beaujeu had roused himself to the first half-impassioned speech Jean had ever seen him make. And at once he seemed afraid of his own courage, and glanced at De Sevrey and Gaudin.

Jean leaned back. "André? Would you sleep comfortably with Sergeant Pirenne on guard?"

"More so than with three-quarters of the knights here," came the arrogant reply he had come to expect from this companion-in-arms.

"All right, then back me on this." Jean stood and was recognised. "I would be happy to take Sergeant Pirenne back into my troop and to offer security for his behaviour in future."

"What security?" De Fleury scoffed.

"If he commits a new crime, I stand accused with him."

"Brilliant!" Brother Odo barked sarcastically. "Then we lose two Templars at once. You're better than the Saracen! Sit down and shut up."

Jean obeyed instantly, flushed with shame. But Odo had heaved himself to his feet and announced, "This has gone on long enough. You heard the master. We cannot afford to do without Sergeant Pirenne. The circumstances that led Pirenne to manslaughter – and that is the only charge you can raise here, not murder" – his look of disgust made even De Molay quail – "are unlikely to occur again. If some of you are too fine to call this honest man 'brother'" – he spat the words at Van der Burg – "then let him serve in my company. Punishment, as the master says, can be found without robbing the order of Pirenne's sword." He sat down as abruptly as he'd risen.

Otto was practically illiterate, but no one – neither De Beaujeu nor De Molay – was willing to contradict him.

County of Tripoli
April 1289

The chilling rain cascaded from the unremitting cloud cover in sheets. No wind interfered with the deluge, and it fell upon a leaden sea leaving pockmarks on the waveless surface and closing down visibility to less than a mile. The sails of the galley sagged under the weight of the water, saturated and dripping on to the soaked decks and the equally sodden Soldiers of Christ waiting tensely in the waist of the ship.

The wind had died during the night, and the galley crawled forward under tired oars. The captain paced nervously along the poop, straining his eyes and casting the lead, uncertain if they had reached the appointed rendezvous or not.

Odo, cursing under his breath, left his company in the waist and clattered up the ladder to the poop to consult the captain. Jean glanced at the men around him. Their coifs were pulled over their heads and their cervellières - the close-fitting, rounded, open-faced helmets - affixed. Their chainmail mittens encased their hands and they wore their shields strapped on their backs. Their faces were grey, sober and weary from a sleepless night.

All of them, with the exception of the newcomers Robert and George, an English knight, had had their occasional skirmish with pirates, Bedouins or robbers, but this was the first time they were facing the prospect of battle with Mameluke regulars. The previous month, Kalaoun had laid siege to Tripoli, exploiting the inevitable confusion and rivalry which had followed the death of the Count Behemond VII without sons. There had been an attempt by the Genoese to establish a self-governing commune, but the nobility and the other Italian merchant communities favoured Behemond's legal heir, his sister Lucia. When Lucia shrewdly promised to grant the

Commune of Tripoli wide-ranging autonomy, she was acclaimed Countess and at last moved into the city – only to find herself subject to the Sultan's siege.

The Christians in the Holy Land rallied to her cause. The king of Cyprus sent his brother Almarac with a force of Cypriot knights and soldiers. The Hospitallers sent their marshal with a large contingent, and even the Templars, despite a history of tension with the lady's late brother, sent their seneschal, Geoffrey de Vendac, from Sidon with a substantial number of Templars.

Countess Lucia's husband, however, had been in Italy when the siege opened. Hastening back with some four hundred Italian mercenaries, he insisted on attempting to relieve the siege from the landward side. Goaded by the willingness of the Hospitallers to support the enterprise and aware that the situation in Tripoli was becoming increasingly untenable, De Beaujeu had agreed, against his better judgement, to provide the count with one hundred Templars (twenty knights with their squires and sixty sergeants). They were to rendezvous near Jubayl, where the Beirut–Tripoli road came nearly to the shore.

Odo stomped back into their midst. "We'll put ashore here and ride to the rendezvous," he announced; already the bow of the galley was nosing landwards cautiously. The captain, more nervous than ever, shouted his orders through the pipe to the oar-deck below. Odo gave the order to bring the horses on deck and prepare to disembark them.

As the shore drew nearer now, the captain ordered the oars to work at double time and then shouted for all hands to brace themselves. From the oar-deck came a last, drawn-out shout and then with a crunch and tearing sound the galley smashed on to the beach and ran part-way up on to the sand. Several of the horses shrieked and then broke loose. But they were rapidly recaptured and held firm while the first of the gangplanks were run out from the deck.

These tilted down steeply to wet sands below, and the horses baulked and sidled on deck, refusing the descent. Odo ordered his men to collect their own horses and lead them down personally – starting with the most docile. Three of the stallions still refused, becoming ever more nervous with each new attempt. Sweating and snorting, they plunged about, damaging the deck and endangering all within range. Odo made a quick count, and announced that they would leave the three troublesome stallions behind. Three knights would have to do without remounts.

On the beach, the serving brothers were helping to tack the horses and load the provisions and reserve equipment on to the pack horses. Most of the serving brothers would remain with the ship. Only a dozen and a priest would accompany the fighting men to attend to the remounts, pack horses and – in the case of the priest – their souls and wounds. Jean mounted rapidly and retightened his girth; the rain would stretch the leather, making it loose all too soon. Then he rode among the disordered men, collecting his troop and forming them up into a column.

Odo drew up beside him, looming over him on a gigantic bay stallion. He had donned his helm and the inhuman metal box announced that they were several miles from the rendezvous and behind schedule. Jean nodded without comment.

From behind him, he heard Sir George curse in English, "This bloody rain!"

"You should be used to rain, Englishman," Jean teased, proud that he had picked up some English from his father and the captain of the guard at Najac.

"I thought the Holy Land was a desert and that I would die of heat and thirst," Sir George replied, undaunted. "Nobody said it rained here worse than in England!"

With a command, Odo trotted forward and the first troop, led by Sir Thomas, fell in behind him. Then came the pack horses and squires, and then Jean's troop. They left the beach and scaled the escarpment to the plain behind. Muddy villages with shabby minarets could be seen north and south of them, and soggy, rocky fields lay between the villages. The road ran roughly parallel to the shore and was empty. Not so much as a mule or a camel could be seen in either direction.

Roughly a half hour later, they were hailed by a sodden squire in the Count of Tripoli's livery. He had been detailed to await the Templars at the appointed rendezvous, and announced that the Count had proceeded without waiting for them. One hundred and eighty Hospitallers had joined him the day before and with them and his mercenary force he had advanced. Grimly, but without altering their pace, they continued north. The rain at last started to ease up, giving way to a drizzle and then sudden and brief flashes of sun.

Two hours later they encountered an armed man galloping toward them on a near winded horse. He did not stop, but drew off the road and rode past them, crumpled forward in his saddle, horse and surcoat smeared with blood. "Deserter," someone commented.

"Then the count has engaged," someone else observed.

Jean glanced toward Odo, but he rode forward at the same stolid trot without shifting his iron-encased head to either side.

In the next village, they observed at least a dozen spent and bloody horses listlessly standing near the village trough. Men in blood-encrusted aketons leaned against the well or huddled against the buildings, eating or tending their wounds.

After that, they rode against a steady stream of disorganised men, some mounted and many more on foot. All swung wide of the advancing Templars, making no effort to communicate with the Soldiers of Christ. Since Odo ignored them as if they did not exist, the other Templars followed his example and rode in complete disciplined silence.

When they came up to an orchard, Odo abruptly called a halt, ordered men and horses to relieve themselves if necessary and drink deeply. Then they were ordered to don their great-helms, bring their shields to ready and take up their lances.

Jean felt nervousness almost overpower him while he fastened the padded, arming hood over his coif and cervellière. His fingers were trembling so much that he could hardly tie the laces at the neck. Then, as he drew the heavy helmet over his head, he got hold of himself again. He took the lance Pierre offered him and propped the butt on his right stirrup. A narrow, triangular white pennon with a red cross identified him as a troop leader of the Templars.

Serving brothers and squires were ordered to dismount and wait at the edge of the orchard with the pack horses, remounts and the priest. The squires' duty was to defend the others if necessary. Then the knights and sergeants formed into a more compact formation, four abreast, the knights in each troop leading the sergeants, so that blocks of white surcoated and trappinged riders were followed by blocks of black riders, the red crosses unifying them. They took up a trot again. Their plain white or black shields formed a neat, clean wall along their left side, reminiscent of the Baucent, the Templar battle standard.

Before they left the orchard, they started to encounter a veritable flood of fleeing troops, and now there were occasional knights among the refugees as well as sergeants and infantry. One knight drew up and shouted that all was lost. "They've taken the count captive!"

"Maintain formation!" Odo ordered unnecessarily. None of the Templars would have dreamt of fleeing before the enemy was even sighted. And yet, though they were now within earshot of the battle, they could not rightly see it. The chaos simply engulfed them. Not only were men fleeing, but some were fighting and some pursuing. With a sense of unreality, Jean registered that the horsemen pouring toward him from the right wore the silk robes and white turbans of Mameluke archers. The Arab horses, fleet and agile, leapt over the corpses of several dead knights and horses, and the riders raised a shout of triumph or challenge before lifting their bows and firing without even slowing their horses down.

An arrow clanged against Jean's helm, another pricked his thigh and two embedded themselves into the heavily-padded trapper of his stallion, but none of them did the least damage. A second shower of arrows clattered around him and someone let out a stifled cry, but the Templars were well armoured. Jean's stallion, smelling blood and unnerved by the corpses of man and horses littering the ground around them, started to fidget and snort. Jean automatically calmed him, and concentrated on the battle ahead. He searched for the banner of the count of Tripoli, which would mark the count's position. As long as it was flying, the count had not been killed or taken captive.

He found it at last, far away. Like an island in a stream, it waved above perhaps three score knights, predominantly Hospitallers in a sea of Saracens. Between that tight formation around the count and the Templars, there was a heaving, writhing turmoil of combat in which the bright silk, turbans and Damascene steel of the Mamelukes predominated. Automatically Jean guessed at the odds and concluded that they were somewhere between ten to one and fifteen to one.

Odo ordered Jean to bring his troop abreast of the leading troop and then gave the order to charge. With a ragged but rousing shout of *"Baucent à la recourse!"* they lowered their lances and spurred their stallions into a gallop. It was almost too late, but they managed to achieve some momentum before crashing into the main crush of battle.

The shock of a compact body of armoured knights upon the massed forces of the enemy was dramatic – greater than Jean had imagined, despite all he had heard. They seemed to cut right through the Mamelukes, toppling riders from their stallions with their lances and then trampling man and horse underfoot. Even as his lance broke and he drew his broadsword, Jean was astonished, almost elated, at the ease with which the heavy European weapon sliced through the limbs and deflected the weapons raised against him. He was aware of severed limbs spinning through the air, blood splattering his helm, and spraying his white surcoat. His sword bled and bit, effortlessly decapitating a turbaned attacker, while his own armour absorbed and broke the blows that reached him.

A sense of immortality swept over him as he hacked and hewed his way forward, though out of the corner of his eye-slit he saw Henri tumble backwards out of his saddle, blood gushing from his punctured throat. On his other side, Lucien's grey stallion collapsed abruptly, apparently cut down by the Mamelukes. The Mamelukes directed almost as much effort to killing the horses as the riders and Jean fought for his horse's life as viciously as for his own. Dismounted, he would have no hope against these odds.

They had no hope in any case, Jean registered with detachment. They had almost penetrated the enemy to join forces with the count of Tripoli, but the relief of the city of Tripoli was utterly hopeless. The relief force had disintegrated, most of it apparently abandoning their count as he valiantly pressed forward. Those few knights and sergeants who had not been killed or routed were clustered here, about to be slaughtered from all sides, while countless numbers of Mamelukes blocked the road north.

The Hospitallers around the count launched a sally toward the Templars and the unfortunate Mamelukes caught between the military orders were crushed and trampled. A cheer of welcome greeted the Templars as they were absorbed into the middle of the Franks. Odo rode straight for the count, identifiable by his heraldic surcoat and an extravagant Italian helm with magnificent brass fittings upon the steel. The count was surrounded by his household but the blood on his surcoat, shield and sword were evidence that he had been in the thick of the fighting. It made no difference that Odo was the illiterate son of an obscure Burgundian knight without a drop of royal blood. By virtue of his position as a Templar commander, he felt no undue awe of the count of Tripoli – certainly not one who had acquired the title by marriage. Odo did not waste time on courtesies. "We'll cover your withdrawal as best we can. Beyond the orchard you'll find our supplies and squires. A Templar galley will be waiting at Beirut."

The count pointed to the north. "They are burning Tripoli!"

Odo did not even look, but Jean turned his head in the direction the count pointed. With a sense of horror he saw the heavy, black clouds of smoke smudging the horizon. This could only mean that the walls had been breached and the fight was being conducted within the city itself. Given the overwhelming superiority of numbers on the Saracen side, it was utterly impossible for the Christians to triumph.

"Whether you choose to die here or not, Tripoli will burn," Odo told the count bluntly.

Without bothering to answer, the count hauled his horse around and headed back south, his knights closing around him while Odo swung his company of Templars to the north, to hold off the Mamelukes who would shortly recognise what was happening.

No manoeuvre is more difficult than covering a mounted retreat. The Templars no longer had the advantage of momentum, nor could they keep their attention fully focused on the enemy. They had to follow the progress of the count or risk being cut off and forfeiting their utility. Backing spirited stallions across a mile of corpse and equipment-littered battlefield is virtually impossible. They had to take a stand and then disengage and withdraw to make a new stand, one troop standing while the other withdrew, thus leapfrogging backwards. The manoeuvre had been practised, of course, on the fields outside Acre, and it was this training, based on the experience of seasoned veterans, which enabled them to make even a semblance of an effort. But the toll was appalling.

Dressed in identical equipment, their faces encased in the standard Templar helms, it was not even possible in the confusion and tension to know who was cleaved to the waist, whose intestines spilled on to his saddle, who was trampled underfoot. Jean could make out Sergeant Pirenne by his sheer size, and of course Odo was unmistakable – a ox of a man on a giant horse hacking and battering his foes, using his shield as much as his sword to force the enemy out of the saddle. One of his enemies took advantage of that fact and brought his sword upward under the shield as it was raised to strike a blow. The Mameluke sword penetrated the chainmail and the padded gambeson and blood gushed out in a burst that stained the white surcoat scarlet and drenched the saddle before splattering on the ground. Odo roared, his sword sliced down on to the back of his murderer and then fell uselessly to the ground as his hand went limp. "Form at... the orchard. Keep... them in for... mation! Jean! In form..." He toppled from his stallion and was lost.

Jean cast a look around for Sir Thomas who was senior to him, but the order had been so explicitly directed to him that he suspected Sir Thomas was already killed.

The knight with the company banner pressed his horse next to Jean's, acknowledging and proclaiming that he was in command of what was left of them. 'Christ Jésu, merciful God in Heaven!' Jean cast a glance over his shoulder and was astonished to see the line of trees, and the count disappearing into it. He made a decision to dash for it, and roared so loudly and violently that he felt as if he was tearing his throat apart. "Reform! At the orchard!"

Wrenching his stallion around, he broke off so abruptly that he caught his opponents by surprise, and the ferocity of his use of the spurs brought a startled protest even from his weary and wounded stallion. Jean was obsessed with one thing: getting to the orchard first and turning back to face the enemy so pointedly that no one could mistake the withdrawal for a full-blown retreat. When he reached the line of trees, he was astonished and moved to sudden tears by the sight of a half dozen Hospitallers already forming in the gap of the road.

As he turned to fall in beside them, a familiar voice shouted, "We've signalled for crossbowmen and there appear to be a couple of dozen still sound enough to take up positions in the trees."

"De Villaret?"

"Yes. Who are you?"

"Preuthune."

There was time for no more. When his knights and sergeants reached him, Jean distributed them along the road, sending a handful who were too severely wounded to fight on to the squires. Of the eighty Templars who had ridden on to the field an hour earlier, there were nineteen of them still mounted and able to fight – five knights, thirteen sergeants and himself. But this task, holding a set position, was much easier than the withdrawal, and they were stiffened by the Hospitallers and supported – miracles still happened in the Holy Land! – by some two dozen mercenary crossbowmen.

It was, in fact, the crossbowmen who brought the joyously pursuing enemy to an abrupt halt with a single well-aimed and well-timed volley. The first wave of Mamelukes suddenly tumbled forward as their horses crumpled under them, and, though some of the riders survived, they were scrambling for their lives while their comrades rushed the Frankish line.

The Templars and Hospitallers formed a solid barrier across the road, swords glinting in the sun, shields no longer pristine white or black or red but scratched and bloody. Casting a glance down the line to left and right of him, Jean felt a shudder of horror go through him. The helms that rendered them faceless made them seem inhuman as well. No one could see the pain, terror, sadness or hatred that must distort the faces beneath the iron masks. Jean could not even recognise his brothers – although he recognised André's favourite black stallion standing miserably upon three sound legs with an ear missing. It did not completely surprise him when he noted a certain hesitation in the enemy line before they finally closed and clashed swords with the Franks.

The relentless determination seemed to have gone out of the enemy. The Mamelukes wore open helmets, and though their faces were contorted with their yells and their curses their eyes were wary and nervous. It was an immense advantage for a knight to be able to see his opponent's eyes and facial expression while his own remained hidden. The enemy's eyes betrayed the direction they intended to attack even before they swung their swords. Jean, like all Templars, had been trained to respond to the movement of an opponent's eyes, and the training was paying off blow for blow.

The peaked helms of the Mameluke horsemen gleamed as the clouds abruptly rent and let the sun spill down upon the mud- and blood-soaked field. For a moment, Jean let himself look away from the men immediately opposite him and hastily scan the entire panorama. A man with the golden insets on his upper sleeves indicating an emir had ridden up on a magnificent white Arab stallion. He seemed to be assessing the situation and giving an order. To Jean's amazement, the order was to disengage and withdraw. Five minutes later, the Mamelukes were just a mass of horsemen withdrawing beyond the human, animal and material rubbish littered across the field.

Slowly Jean resheathed his sword, his hand trembling from exhaustion. His men followed his example, still sitting on their horses, facing implacably north.

De Villaret rode over to Jean. "How far back are your remounts?"

"At the start of the orchard." At a glance he guessed that they had hardly a sound stallion or gelding among them, and the Hospitallers were no better off. They would sorely miss the three stallions left on board ship. "Can we risk withdrawing so soon?" he asked the more experienced Hospitaller, indifferent to the fact that he wore the habit of a different order.

"That emir was a senior commander and he rebuked the *askari* for wasting time on us. They won't be coming back."

Jean nodded. It was over. This pathetic skirmish, which had lasted less than two hours, and would surely find no mention in the chronicles, had cost him nearly all his friends and comrades. Turning their stallions around, they abandoned their position and started through the orchard. De Villaret spoke to the captain of the crossbowmen, and then rejoined Jean. They rode side by side in silence.

As the small band emerged out of the other side of the orchard, the Templar squires and serving brothers let out a rousing cheer – which died in their throats as they registered the number of the survivors. Jean turned off the road and his eyes scanned the upturned faces of the men waiting with the rested horses. They gaped back at the blood-soaked apparitions before them, and the horror was plain to read.

Then Pierre broke from their ranks and rushed forward. "Sir Jean! You're wounded!" Pierre was at his bridle, holding up his arms. But the others too had pressed forward, asking after Odo and Sir Thomas and their individual knights.

"The Mamelukes are withdrawing north to finish off and sack Tripoli. We can search the field for survivors in another hour or two," Jean told them. "First let us drink and see to the wounded." The non-combatants were hushed in shame.

Jean went to dismount and discovered that his right thigh was pinned to his saddle by an arrow that had pierced his chainmail obliquely, grazed his thigh and embedded itself in the saddle. Reaching to yank the arrow free, he felt something tearing at his back, and Pierre, in a frenzy of concern, ordered him to sit still. De Villaret pressed his horse closer and yanked the arrow cleanly out of his back, showing it to Jean before tossing it to the ground, adding, "Sit still and let me get the one out of your helm as well."

An arrow had wedged itself between the sheet iron and the reinforcing band around the eye-slit. "I must look like a pincushion," Jean remarked.

"It contributed to your effectiveness," De Villaret noted dryly. "The Mamelukes are intimidated when a knight, apparently pierced by three arrows, continues to fight as you did."

Jean swung his leg over the cantle, feeling now the stinging of his thigh wound and the piercing pain in his back. He slid to the ground and stood for a moment holding his stirrup; then Pierre was offering him his arm. He shook his head, and stopped abruptly as he noted that Pierre had a bloody blow on his head and his chainmail hauberk was torn on his left shoulder. "What happened to you?"

"Deserters. They attacked us to try to get the horses – but we fought them off," Pierre declared proudly.

Jean turned to scan the other non-combatants, and the helm suddenly seemed to weigh a ton. His head was throbbing violently. He reached up and lifted it from his head, gasping at the rush of fresh air. Many of the other non-combatants helping the remaining knights and sergeants to dismount were indeed wounded themselves. He took a ragged breath. Somehow they had to get stock of their casualties, bind their wounds as best as possible, select which stallions could be saved and which had to be put down immediately. Then the fresh stallions had to be assigned – two men to a horse if necessary. Or they could abandon some of their equipment and ride the pack horses. If the Mamelukes really withdrew entirely, they should try to collect and bury their dead. Someone had to organise all that. He had to organise all that.

He looked over at the other survivors as they too removed their helms. Pirenne was still with him, along with seven other sergeants of his troop and six from Sir Thomas's troop. To his surprise he discovered that the knight who had fought directly beside him during the later phases was George, the Englishman, who seemed relatively unharmed. The standard bearer and another knight, both from Sir Thomas's troop, were also only lightly wounded, but to Jean's sorrow the knight riding André's horse proved to be a virtual stranger from

Sir Thomas's troop – and he was now collapsing. Two of the serving brothers caught him as he fell, and they carried him back toward the line of pack horses.

Here the other wounded were laid in a row, and Jean went to see who and how they were. Two knights, five sergeants, a squire and two lay brothers were lying side by side. He recognised the young freckled face of Bertram from his troop, and at once went down on his knee beside him. "Bertram!" He fumbled irritably with his chainmail mittens to free his hands, and then pressed his palm to the sweating forehead of the young man.

Bertram opened his eyes. "I'm sorry, sir. I know we're supposed to be able to fight with our left arm as well as our right but—"

Jean put his fingers to his lips and looked down at Bertram's right arm, which lay across his breast, almost severed in two. The bone was cleanly sliced, the hand hideously swollen and discoloured. Jean glanced back at De Villaret who had followed him, shadowed by the other five Hospitallers.

De Villaret in turn looked at one of the sergeants with him, who knelt down and gingerly fingered the hand. Jean felt his stomach turn over and looked in the other direction. He found that a serving brother was hovering uncertainly nearby. "Is someone seeing to watering the horses?" Jean asked, consciously countering the appalling lameness that seemed to surround him. "And bring us watered wine as well." The man hastened away, calling to one of his comrades.

The Templar surgeon, the priest, came hurriedly along the line of wounded and gave the Hospitaller a hostile look, his professional competence apparently challenged. "I am a trained surgeon," he announced pointedly.

The hostility between the militant orders erupted instantly as the Hospitaller sergeant looked up at him contemptuously and opened his mouth to reply. De Villaret put his hand on the man's shoulder and silenced him.

Jean answered for the Hospitallers. "We need all the help we can get, Father Hubért. There is more to do than you alone can handle." Vaguely he gestured down the line of wounded and then at the untended wounds of the men hovering around him – Pierre and De Villaret and all the others.

"Where is Brother Odo? Brother Thomas?" The priest openly challenged Jean's authority. Jean pointed vaguely to the north. "Go and look for them, Father. Commander Odo needs a Christian burial, and perhaps Sir Thomas can use the last rites as well." Though they had all been confessed during the night on the galley, no Templar would scorn the last rites if he had the chance.

Only then did the priest, who had been busy with the wounded, seem to recognise the magnitude of their losses. He swallowed, looked from Jean to the Hospitallers and then at the knights and sergeants who were dropping to the ground, stripping off their chainmail mittens, and inspecting the bloody gashes in their hauberks and hose. The blood drained from Father Hubért's face.

Jean pushed past him to the next wounded man, and, recognising the sergeant, went down on his knee and took his hand. "Brother Norbert, thank God you survived."

The man's eyes flickered open. "Sir Jean? You made it? How many—"

"Enough. The Count is safe. The Mamelukes have withdrawn north. We'll have you in Beirut by tomorrow."

He moved on to the next man and the next and the man after that. For each he found some word of comfort or praise. One of the two wounded serving brothers proved to be the Scotsman who had greeted Jean on his first day in Acre. "Ian MacDonald! What happened to you?"

MacDonald propped himself on his elbows and let out a stream of curses against the mercenaries who had attacked them to steal the horses. One had used a pike against him, piercing his thigh clean through. The head of the pike was still embedded in his leg muscle, and MacDonald was trembling with fever and glistening with sweat. Jean removed his mantle and tucked it around MacDonald, astonished to see a large bloody splotch upon it which could only have come from his own wound.

"I've brought some extra medical personnel," Jean made the effort to joke. "A genuine Hospitaller—"

"God damn the buggers!" Fortunately, MacDonald swore in Celtic, and even Jean did not understand him.

Jean continued in his casual tone, "Beggars can't be choosers – or would you rather I took hold of this pike and yanked it out?"

MacDonald shook his head. "I don't give a bloody damn who or how you get the thing out, just get it out of there. It's killing me."

Jean looked up at De Villaret, who nodded and signalled to a serving brother hovering nearby. "Can you boil water?"

"Sir?" The lay brother looked to Jean.

"Do whatever Sir Jules says without question," Jean insisted pointedly in irritation. He stood up.

"You should have your own wounds cleaned and bound," De Villaret advised.

Jean nodded but there was so much else to do first. Turning to the confused squires who hovered around him, evidently frightened and lamed by the sudden obliteration of their company, he ordered several of them to fetch and distribute bread and wine to the wounded and others to untack the warhorses, select those which could be saved and to put down the others.

"But what criteria do we use?" one of the young men protested in evident alarm.

"If a horse can ever be sound again and is capable of making it back to Beirut, save it; if not, cut its throat as quickly and cleanly as possible."

Jean then selected two of the elder squires to take fresh horses and ride through the orchard to keep watch. "There could be any number of wounded mercenaries who would willingly kill you for your horses, so for Christ's sake watch out. Do not venture beyond the trees – not even to help a wounded brother who is approaching. Do you understand?" They nodded and departed.

Pierre was beside him. "Please let me see to your wounds, sir," he pleaded.

Jean looked around. The sun was streaming from a blue heaven and the leaves of the olive trees shimmered cheerfully in a light breeze. It was a beautiful, warm afternoon – but for the faint smell of smoke brought by the breeze. Tripoli was burning. Of the great cities that once had been the seats of Christian power in the Holy Land – Edessa, Jerusalem, Antioch and Tripoli – not one was left.

And there was still so much to do. They had to see if they could find their dead and bury them and get the wounded to Beirut. Jean wondered if the galley would wait for them or assume they were all dead. Maybe the Hospitallers had a ship at Beirut. Or they could ride all the way to Acre – no, the wounded couldn't make it that far. Jean sank down on to the grass and started to fumble with the laces of his padded arming hood, aware only now of how sweaty he was and how uncomfortably the chainmail of his coif pressed into his neck. He knocked cervellière and coif from his head and removed his cloth cap underneath to let the sun and breeze dry and cool his head. It was several days since he had shaved and fuzzy hair was already reconquering his tonsure.

Pierre knelt behind him and unbuckled Jean's sword. Then he lifted surcoat and hauberk over Jean's head at the same time, loosed the laces of Jean's gambeson under his arms and pulled it off with his shirt, exposing the back wound to the light and air. Pierre drew in his breath and touched it gently with his finger. It occurred to Jean that Pierre had no training in medicine at all, and he would rather one of the Hospitallers or Father Hubért tended to him. "Pierre, go and see if Sir Jules can come and take a look at the wound."

He was answered by an anguished cry. "Do you hate me that much? Don't you care for me at all?"

Jean looked around so sharply that his wound sent a vicious pain right through to his chest. Pierre choked on his own breath and bit down on his lip, his chest heaving with stifled sobs.

"Pierre!" Jean could not bear the sight of him. He pulled him into his arms, held him on his breast and let him cry. Pierre sank into his lap, exhausted, frightened and ashamed. Stroking his hair, Jean's hand came away bloody, and he registered that the blow to Pierre's head was swollen to the size of a fig. "I love you, Pierre," Jean murmured to him, acknowledging this fact with a vague sense of tragedy. He loved all the men of his troop and the lay brothers who so selflessly served them. He loved Odo – had loved Odo, he corrected, wondering why love should suddenly be put into the past tense merely because the object of one's affections had passed on. 'My love,' he thought defiantly, 'is no less than it was an hour ago – maybe even greater.'

But in his lap Pierre shuddered and tried to lift himself, and Jean held him down gently. "No, not like that," he corrected, anxious not to awaken false hopes. "I cannot love you as a lover, but you are as much my brother as my father's other sons – or all the Templars. I love you. Don't ever doubt it. More – if I am to be honest – than any number of Templars like Van der Burg or De Molay with their self-righteousness and their cold virtue. I love you, but I cannot give you physical love."

It was a fact, but Jean felt an oppressive sadness as he acknowledged it. Pierre was not some kind of contemptible pervert: he was a young man cut off from home and family, too poor to marry and found a family, and desperately in need of affection. The chaste, cold affection of his employer was hardly sufficient.

'Men need love,' Jean reflected, 'and most men need to express and receive love physically. If they cannot have it from parents, wives or children, then it is only natural that some men will seek it from each other.' Not that he knew of any other specific cases in the order, but he knew that more than one of the brothers managed to visit the brothels of Acre or Jerusalem, Bethlehem or Tyre. And others, he reflected with a wry smile, indulged themselves by lavishing love upon their stallions or adopting children like Rachel. The rule had been made for saints or men incapable of love – and what sort of Christians were the latter?

Pierre had calmed himself, and, sitting upright, he murmured an apology.

"What for?" Jean countered. "For reminding me of what I owe you? Or for crying? I wish that I could cry – for Lucien, Odo, André, Henri, Robert... Not to forget my brothers from Cahors who were all in Tripoli. Do you think one of them will survive? Or even want to survive in slavery? They are burning Tripoli."

A shadow fell over them and they looked up. De Villaret, his red mantle billowing in the breeze, stood over them. He handed Jean a silver goblet filled with watered wine and a heel of bread. "Shall I look at that wound?" He did not wait for an answer. Bending over Jean, he studied the wound and then sent Pierre for cotton wool, wine and bandages. Then he sat down beside Jean. "It's not serious."

"I know. Why else do you think I kept ignoring it?" Jean asked with a wry smile.

"I thought you might be a misguided hero."

"No."

After a moment's silence, De Villaret opened again. "Do you know what this is?"

"What?"

De Villaret gestured vaguely toward the battlefield beyond the peaceful olive orchard. "The beginning of the end. Kalaoun has broken the truce. He won't stop at Tripoli."

Jean looked up at the cloudless sky. His mind was blank. "No, I suppose he won't."

"We can't hold the Holy Land with the men we have left."

Jean heard him, understood him, acknowledged he was right and still did not believe him.

When he did not answer, De Villaret continued. "De Villiers, the new master of the Hospital, is not the bigot Lorgne was. He would meet with De Beaujeu – if De Beaujeu asked him to."

Jean wondered why De Villiers couldn't simply invite De Beaujeu to meet with him, but somehow it didn't matter. He nodded. "I will talk to De Beaujeu."

De Villaret clasped his shoulder briefly and then drew himself back to his feet. He gazed down at the younger man with a curious expression approaching envy. "You are blessed, Jean. Did you know that?"

"What are you talking about? I just lost three-quarters of my company, Tripoli is burning and we have probably lost the Holy Land itself. What, in the name of Christ Almighty, is blessed in all that?"

De Villaret smiled at him. "That in spite of all that you exude nothing but concern and affection for all around you. Remember that Christ did not liberate Israel from the Romans – he was crucified."

Nazareth
March 1290

Mass was being sung and the voices of the monks blended and resonated, spilling into the circular ambulatory around the altar and down into the nave of the church. The smell of incense and candles hung thickly in the air and the light that filtered through the narrow windows in the thick walls was hardly enough to see by – especially for anyone coming from the blinding light of the Palestinian day outside.

Jean halted abruptly inside the door, less to adjust to the sudden darkness than to minimise the disturbance of his entrance. The harmonious calm of the Gregorian chant rebuked him for his loud, hurried and tardy entry. In remorse and shame he crossed himself with the holy water in the shell by the door and dropped his left knee to the floor, bowing his head until the leather thong holding his chainmail coif grazed his right knee.

Only when the chant was ended, succeeded by the slight rustling and creaking of monks readjusting themselves, did he rise. Taking care to keep his spurs from scraping distractingly upon the black and white chessboard of the marble floor, Jean advanced to stand at the foot of the nave. Behind him, scrupulously following his example, came the knights, sergeants and lay brothers of his company. All bore the marks of the long road from Acre on their faces, surcoats and chainmail leggings. The pilgrims they had escorted had been delivered to the hospice attached to the Cathedral of the Annunciation, but Jean always sought accommodation for himself and his company at the more modest Augustinian establishment of St Joseph.

Reputedly built on the site of St Joseph's carpentry shop, Jean was drawn to the church because it was almost entirely the work of artisans from the Languedoc. While the older and native churches bore the heavy mark of Byzantium and the newer churches were influenced by the more elegant and airy architecture of northern France, this church was like a transplant from Jean's homeland. No glittering mosaics glinted in the candlelight here, and the squat, heavy pillars supported rounded rather than peaked arches. The capitals were adorned with beasts and vines like the ones which had fascinated him as a child, and Jean looked up to them now, noting with sadness that the paint was fading and chipping.

St Joseph's, like all the churches allowed to operate in the Muslim world, suffered from severe poverty. The pilgrims who came in an ever-declining trickle rarely had the resources for a donation after paying the expenses of the long journey from the West. The churches themselves were allowed to own no land and furthermore were subject to a variety of special taxes. The churches and the monks who maintained them were utterly dependent upon their mother houses in Christian countries. This little community of Augustinians was all but forgotten by an order embroiled in local politics in Italy and Sicily. It was kept alive by subsidies from the Templars, and indeed the very bread and wine used in the Mass were brought in regularly by the Templars performing the escort service to Nazareth.

The mass was over. Two by two, still singing, the black-robed canons left their stalls, bowed to the host, and then filed out in pairs with their lighted candles. The chant grew thinner and fainter while the monks departed until only the echo of their last praise to God lingered like the scent of incense in the still air of the now nearly darkened church. Again Jean dropped down to his knee and bent his head, and, then rising, he crossed himself.

Around him the other Templars were also rising from their knees and crossing themselves to the inevitable clatter of scabbards and spurs and the chink of chainmail. They were weary and hungry. It had been a strenuous journey. Since the fall of Tripoli each journey into the Sultan's territory was a dance with death. To be sure, the Sultan claimed Tripoli was an 'exception' not covered by the general truce. The right of pilgrimage to Nazareth had been explicitly reaffirmed, but no Christian trusted the Sultan any more.

Many in the order questioned the wisdom of continuing the pilgrimages, and the first whispers suggesting a withdrawal to Cyprus had been heard. De Beaujeu turned deaf ears to any such talk. He insisted that it was the order's sacred duty to defend the Holy Land

and pilgrims thereto. As long as pilgrims were willing to risk the journey, the Templars were sworn to provide protection, at the cost of their own lives if necessary. The fact that many pilgrims arrived in blithe ignorance of how dangerous their journey really was could not exempt the Templars from their vow to provide all protection humanly possible.

Jean supported De Beaujeu in this policy generally, but each journey entailed risking the lives not only of himself and his company but the pilgrims themselves. The fact that they had a Tripolitan noblewoman among the pilgrims on this trip made the task all the more trying and nerve-wracking. He would not really sleep, he thought, until he had her safely back in Acre.

Leaving the church for the cloisters, Jean was abruptly confronted by a Franciscan. The friar towered a good six inches over him, although he hunched his shoulders and bent his hawkish face between his bony shoulders like a bird of prey.

"Did it never occur to you," the Franciscan opened without preliminaries in the accent of the Île de France, "that you offend our Merciful Lord by wearing swords in His house? And that in the middle of mass!"

"We wear them in His service." Jean replied sharply, instantly bad-tempered. He might be humbled by the presence of the host and the harmony of the Gregorian chant but not by any self-righteous friar. He started to push past the friar, but the man blocked his way, glowering in holy indignation.

"Christ abhorred the sword!"

"If you doubt the Christianity of the Knights Templar, take up your discussion with the Pope!" Jean retorted and behind him George had to stifle a laugh.

They started as a group down the cloister aisle, but the friar called after them, "I was warned about the arrogance of the Templars, but I had not wanted to believe it."

Jean spun back on the friar. "Arrogance? Which of us is presuming to preach to the superior of another holy order? You have no right to sit in judgement on me!"

"I do naught but deliver His holy message. He came among us to preach the word: love thy neighbour! He who would not take up the sword to free His own oppressed people and land from the yoke of Romans condemns with His whole life and His whole testament the use of violence to preserve the rule of degenerate, selfish, bickering Christians here in Palestine. He condemns the use of violence against any man – regardless of how misguided by false prophets he may be. You" – the friar flung out his arm and pointed accusingly at Jean and then the other Templars in a slow, sweeping gesture – "offend Him. And you will pay the price of offending Him by dying here in vain and burning hereafter in hell!"

The friar's impassioned eloquence was starting to have its effect on some of Jean's company. They were risking their lives in a cause that was patently hopeless, and now they were being insulted and scorned for their sacrifice by a representative of the Church they were defending.

Jean lifted his head and his voice as he would to give a command and his eyes glinted. "You, Brother Friar, will be the first to scream for our help when the Sultan's soldiers arrest you!"

"Never! I am here to convert the heathen with the power of Christ's word – not to pervert His message by delivering it at the point of a sword."

"Then you will soon have the pleasure of meeting your maker – unless, of course, you prefer to embrace Islam."

"I would rather the skin was torn from me living than even contemplate acceptance of a false religion. But I have nothing to fear. He who lives by the sword shall die by the sword, but as I come weaponless except for the truth, not even the Sultan will dare to lift his weapons against me."

"I would laugh if I weren't so damned tired." Jean did not often swear, but he was perversely compelled to provoke the friar even further. He turned his back on the friar once again, and determinedly led the way to the refectory.

The refectory was a vaulted chamber with a row of crudely decorated pillars running down the centre. There were no windows so the smell of stale grease, fish and wine clung to the walls persistently, not fully overpowered by the scent of fresh-baked bread and steaming artichokes. The canons were taking their places to the loud scraping of benches on the uneven, tiled floor. Half-breed lay brothers were thumping pottery jugs of wine, platters of artichokes and bowls of some watery soup on to the trestle tables. A cheery confusion and the babble of voices greeted the Templars as they entered and dispersed to find a place according to their rank. Jean proceeded with his two troop leaders to the high table, where the prior stood in discussion with one of his canons.

The prior was a small, delicate man with a fringe of grey hair framing his shiny scalp. He glanced over at the advancing Templars and smiled at once. "Commander! I was just seeing if we couldn't find some meat for you and your brothers." It was Lent and the Augustinians were duly observing it as they should, but the Templars were exempt from fasting while on active service.

"It would be much appreciated." Jean accepted at once, with a glance down the room where his weary serving brothers and sergeants had squeezed in beside the lay brothers and his knights were mixing with the canons.

"It will take a few minutes," the Augustinian cook told him, "but we can probably purchase baked lamb from the inn at the bottom of the street." Jean at once opened his purse and gave the cook two silver dinhars. The cook departed and the prior indicated that Jean should take the seat next to him, offering him a finger bowl in which to wash his hands as soon as they were seated.

As Jean untied the leather thong and shoved his chainmail coif from his head, the prior remarked, "It is a pleasure to see you again, Commander. You have escorted pilgrims for the Feast of the Annunciation?"

"Nearly two hundred," Jean confirmed.

The prior crossed himself. "Brave and blessed souls! That cheers me greatly. And is there news from the West? Is a new crusade being planned at last?" The anxiety and hope were impossible to disregard.

Jean considered the man beside him with sympathy. The prior was the child of Frankish parents born and raised in Christian Palestine or, as it was called in France, Outremer. The Christian kingdoms in the Holy Land were his homeland not only spiritually but physically – and he could not possibly imagine how far away and irrelevant these sacred places were to the bulk of Europe's population and rulers. Jean tried to be gentle with his answer, but the bitterness was plain nevertheless. "Perhaps. But Edward of England is preoccupied with Scotland, France and the pope are quarrelling with Aragon about Sicily. The Holy Roman Empire is embroiled in Prussia..."

In open desperation the prior looked up at the young knight and pleaded, "But surely, now that Tripoli has been so shamelessly sacked, the pope will..." His hopes died on his lips as he saw the Templar's expression harden. He looked down.

"The Mongols are a better hope, Prior Anselm. Their khan is well disposed to Christianity and many of his nobles have been converted. He has sent an ambassador to the courts of Europe proposing joint action, that much I know, and he has the ear of the king of Armenia."

The prior's face was clouded with worry. "I pray that you are right. It would be a great miracle indeed if such barbarians might, through the Grace of Our Loving God, renounce their past of butchery and bloodshed. Do you think it is possible?"

"The Mongols are great warriors, Prior Anselm; that is why they would be great allies. It is too much to expect them to become monks as well as allies."

The prior paused to consider this answer, looking up at Jean with surprise. He seemed to want to say something, but at that moment the Franciscan friar re-emerged. Although the prior was clearly superior in rank to the friar, Jean noticed that the prior at once sat straighter and nervously glanced along the table like a schoolboy afraid of a reprimand. "Commander, you have not yet met Brother Elion, I think. He only arrived two weeks ago." The prior hastened to introduce the friar, who presumptuously took his seat on the prior's other side.

Neither Jean nor the friar was inclined to refer to their encounter in the cloisters, and the prior continued like a conscientious host, explaining to the friar, "Commander de Preuthune frequently escorts pilgrims and provisions from Acre. He just brought two hundred pilgrims, he tells me." Then, turning to Jean, he explained, "Brother Elion is an intimate of Charles of Anjou."

This explained the prior's evident deference toward the friar, the deference of a provincial towards a man who has been near the seat of power. On the basis of accent and manner, Jean suspected, furthermore, that the friar came of a noble family – possibly illegitimate, but with powerful connections.

The prior was continuing, "He has come direct from Rome to re-establish a house of his order here in Nazareth."

Jean spluttered on the wine he had just swallowed and had to cough his windpipe free before he could look at the friar in utter disbelief. "Have you gone mad?" he asked bluntly. He had taken the friar's previous boasts for mere rhetoric. "There is no way the Sultan will condone the establishment of new Christian establishments. It's rather a question of *when* he will move against the ones already here! We can't protect you in Nazareth!"

"I don't want your protection, Commander," the friar responded with perfect disdain. "Christ and St Francis are all the protection I need."

"Where were Christ and St Francis when they sacked the Franciscan houses in Antioch and Tripoli and sold your brothers and sisters in the slave markets of Cairo?"

"My brothers and sisters in Antioch and Tripoli had forgotten their vows of poverty and chastity. They had collected vast wealth, dressed in silks and scented themselves like Muslims. They maintained hawks, hunting dogs and horses. They ate without regard to the rules of fasting, and even engaged in carnal pleasures with one another. In short, they lived like oriental lords and ladies, just like the selfish secular lords. As God smote Sodom and Gomorrah, so he let Antioch and Tripoli fall into the hands of a merciless foe."

Jean looked at the prior as if to ask if he had heard correctly, and the prior looked down in embarrassment. Even the Islamic world had been shocked at the brutality of the sack of Antioch. After capturing the city, the Sultan had ordered the gates locked so the population could not escape and then had hunted the citizens – not just the garrison – like vermin. Only as the troops themselves wearied of the bloodshed had the Sultan been content to collect the remaining Christians and then divide them, like the rest of the loot, among his emirs and his soldiers. In Tripoli they had set fire to the city and then levelled it entirely.

"Were you ever in Antioch or Tripoli?" Jean managed to ask at last.

"Of course not, but we had very reliable reports."

At this moment, one of the lay brothers arrived with a plate of sliced lamb and set it before Jean. The friar wrinkled his nose and drew back from the pungent scent of lamb spiced with rosemary as if it were repulsive.

"Have you forgotten this is Lent?" the friar demanded furiously of the prior.

The prior cringed visibly under the assault, and Jean answered for him. "Father Anselm has forgotten neither Lent nor the fact that Templars are exempt while on service. My men have not had a warm meal since leaving Acre and they have been in the saddle since prime."

"Such excuses must make the founder of your order blush with shame, Commander! You are no better than the others corrupted by the wealth of Outremer! Grown soft and self-indulgent, you offend God more than the ignorant Musselman! You – who dare to wear His cross and claim to serve Him – serve only the aggrandisement of the Temple. You have become the moneylenders in the temple against whom Christ raged! You are the real cause of the misfortune here in the Holy Land and you – not I – will feel the bite of retribution."

It was bad enough to condemn them for being knights, but to establish a causal relationship between the Temple's activities and the destruction of Christian Palestine was too much. Of course the Templars performed some banking functions, safeguarding the deposits of kings and khans and expediting the movement of goods with letters of credit, but they did not lend money, much less charge interest. It was simply that no other institution had such an extensive network of mighty castles stretching from Scotland to Palestine and a private army to guarantee the security of deposited funds. But the Temple had not sought this function; rather it had been imposed upon it by nobles and merchants seeking security and flexibility. It was unfair to compare a service offered to fellow Christians with the usury of Jewish moneylenders. "If Saint Louis did not disdain the services of the Temple who are you to criticise us? Or do you claim to be better than a saint?"

"If you are referring to King Louis of France, he has not been canonised by the pope."

"I know that – but do you doubt he will be?"

No one who had served the Count of Anjou would dare disparage the memory of the count's uncle. The friar recognised the trap and deftly went on the offensive. "Why, if not on account of your sins, has God let His kingdom of Jerusalem be reduced to this state?"

The question found its mark. Jean felt it go home in his breast, and it robbed him of words and breath. He could neither evade it nor answer it. He could not believe that the sins of the Temple or the citizens of Outremer were responsible for their present plight. He did not think that they had sinned any more than people throughout Christendom. But he had no alternative theory. He did not understand why they suffered defeat after defeat, and his heart and mind protested in outrage to a God who seemed to have turned his back upon the people who sought to honour Him by preserving the sanctity of His homeland.

Brother Elion smirked in triumph.

*

The following morning a messenger arrived from Lady Melisende requesting Jean's attendance. Lady Melisende was a daughter of the De Montfort family. She had married into the equally powerful Embriaco family and settled in Tripoli. A widow by the time of the siege, she had been evacuated by ship from Tripoli while the Mamelukes poured through the breach in the city walls. Thereafter she had taken up residence with her De Montfort kin in Acre. During the journey, she had been an uncomplaining, cooperative and reticent traveller, utterly unobtrusive in her widow's weeds and never demanding special treatment. Still, the responsibility for a lady of such high birth and with such important connections was a burden, and her summons could not be ignored.

Jean rode to the Hospice of the Annunciation accompanied by Sergeant Pirenne and Brother Paul. He did not allow Pierre to accompany him on these journeys into enemy territory because Pierre was not a Templar. Sergeant Pirenne, however, had assumed the post of bodyguard ever since Jean had been promoted to commander. As commander, Jean was also entitled to the full-time service of a serving brother and Paul had asked for the post. Since Lucien had been killed in the skirmish for Tripoli and none of the Templars in Tripoli had survived the fall of the city, Paul and Jean were the only Templars from Cahors left alive in the Holy Land.

Self-consciously, the three Templars clattered through the crowded city streets, attracting attention by the size of their mounts and the brazen red crosses they wore upon their breasts and shoulders. Some youths called out insults before darting for safety in an alley and several old men spat or mumbled prayers while the women turned away as if afraid they would besmirch their honour merely by making eye contact with the hated infidel.

At the hospice, Jean left the horses with Paul and entered the spacious but barren reception with Pirenne. Lady Melisende, who had been waiting patiently upon a stone bench with her maidservant, rose and advanced toward them, her silk veils and surcoat fluttering about her. On the trip from Acre, she had ridden with the veil forward, covering her face, and this was the first time Jean had seen her with the veil thrown back over her head.

Her round face matched her round, short body and her kindly eyes went perfectly with her gentle voice. "I did not realise you wouldn't be staying here or I would have sought to talk to you yesterday, Commander," Lady Melisende told him as he bowed over her hand. "I don't know if you realise why I have come to Nazareth." She indicated the bench and Jean obediently sat down with her, while Pirenne drifted discreetly to the other end of the chamber and the maidservant took up lace-making on the other bench.

"I presume for the Feast of the Annunciation, Madame."

"No." She paused. "Commander, you know I escaped from Tripoli as the city fell?"

"Yes, Madame, you were extremely fortunate," Jean replied politely, inwardly irritated because he felt he had more important things to do than sit here and chat with a middle-aged lady about her escape from Tripoli.

"Yes, I was, but many were not. My stepdaughter, the illegitimate daughter of my husband, who served me as devotedly as if she were my own child, did not get out." Again she paused and searched Jean's face for some response. He did not know what was expected of him and made a neutral sound. "She saw me safely aboard one of the Genoese galleys, but insisted on going back for her three children. Her husband, of course, was fighting with the garrison and we knew he was lost. But she had three children. She refused to leave them behind, and the Genoese refused to delay their departure to wait for a serving woman and her children." Again she paused, and still Jean could think of no appropriate response.

The Genoese had panicked and abandoned the city before it was really lost. He felt nothing but contempt for the Italians who enriched themselves by trading with the Muslims and were more concerned with preserving their own skins and their own wealth than the lives of Christians and the survival of Outremer.

"I have no children of my own, Commander. I am barren. My stepdaughter was like my own child; her children my grandchildren. And I left them behind in Tripoli."

Jean sighed inwardly, expecting that the lady would now declare she had made some extreme vow of penance that would place her in greater danger than she was already.

He was startled when she continued calmly. "I have made extensive enquiries, and learned that a certain slave trader, Ibrahim al-Athir, bought up the bulk of the Christians captured at Tripoli from their captors. He lives here in Nazareth and I intend to pay him a visit. My hope is that he can help me locate my stepdaughter and her children. I would be grateful if you would be so kind as to accompany me. I fear a woman alone would not be received." Her hands stroked nervously at her lap, and Jean suspected that she was, perhaps, a little afraid of her own courage now that she was actually here. "And... and, she added with an embarrassed smile, "I don't speak Arabic."

*

The address given to Lady Melisende proved to be the slave trader's residence, and his steward angrily sent the Christians around to the opposite side of the large, palatial complex where Ibrahim al-Athir had his business offices. They were greeted by the stench of crowded humanity emanating from a tract of buildings with high, barred windows, housing the 'merchandise'. From the windows of the smaller building came the high, garbled sound of female voices, and Jean saw Lady Melisende blanch, but she did not falter as they proceeded into the office.

There was a busy coming and going of merchants and tradesmen, all of whom cast curious glances at the unexpected figures of a Templar commander and a Christian woman. The young clerk in the outer office who asked their business was evidently flustered by their request for an interview with Ibrahim al-Athir himself. "The worthy and devout Lord Ibrahim - may Allah have mercy on him - is very, very busy. Do you have an appointment with him?" The implication was that without one there was no chance of an interview.

"No, but we have come from Acre, and I am certain he will find time for us." Jean's Arabic was far from perfect but it was entirely serviceable. He left no doubt about the fact that he expected to be received, an impression greatly strengthened by his generally commanding appearance. Arab and Turkish officers were concerned to show their wealth and status in the richness of their clothes and so covered their armour with embroidered shirts, billowing trousers, tasselled boots and brocade vests and turbans. In contrast, Jean was encased in chainmail from head to toe, which was only scantily covered by his sober surcoat.

The clerk looked sceptical about the prospects of an interview with his awesome master, but did not dare further contradict the Frankish knight and so hastened away to whisper with another, more senior employee of the wealthy slave trader. This older man came back and after only a moment's hesitation bowed to Jean – not too deeply but respectfully nevertheless. "You wish to see our worthy master Ibrahim al-Athir?" The man inspected first Jean and then Lady Melisende, and Jean was glad that he had taken the time to visit a public bath-house that morning and changed into a clean surcoat. Paul had even removed the worst of the mud and rust from his chainmail.

"Indeed we do."

"Is our worthy master expecting you, gracious sir?"

"Very unlikely."

"And what is your business?"

"Trade. We are here to buy four slaves." The man's astonishment did Jean good. "Four specific slaves, you understand. Christian slaves. Slaves taken captive at Tripoli."

"Ah." Understanding dawned. "May I tell our master the name of his honourable visitors?"

"Tell him that Commander de Preuthune of the Knights Templar at Acre is here with and on behalf of the noblewoman Lady Melisende de Montfort." That sounded impressive enough, and the clerk bowed more deeply and retreated through the hanging beads into the room beyond. The man soon returned and assured them that his master would receive them 'presently' – as soon as his delicate negotiations with a trader from Sudan had been concluded.

Jean and Lady Melisende waited in the outer office while Pirenne returned to Paul, who was holding the horses in the street outside. Jean seated himself where he could see out of the door to the comings and goings in the courtyard. Customers were led into the room across from the office, and slaves were then brought for inspection either one at a time or in groups of two or three. Some slaves were quite well-dressed and were allowed to proceed without any external restraint. Others had their wrists bound and some had their feet in irons.

At length they were summoned. Passing through another room, where clerks were evidently keeping the accounts and handling the money, they entered an inner chamber. The air was cool and scented with lotus blossoms. Blue tiles covered the walls and inscriptions from the Koran provided an elegant border. Through the filigree woodwork in the arched windows came the chirping of birds and the splattering sound of a fountain. In the relative darkness, they hardly noticed their host, seated cross-legged before a magnificently carved and mother-of-pearl inlaid table. He rose as they entered and bowed to Jean, before indicating a cushion opposite him. Of Melisende he took no apparent note, but there were two cushions ready for them.

Lean and meticulously dressed with manicured hands, the trader made the impression more of a scholar than a trader. His face was deeply lined, and his hair was greying. At the clap of his hands, a male slave entered with a tray of tea and nuts, which were offered to Jean. Jean indicated that Melisende should be served first and the slave glanced at his master for instructions.

Melisende shook her head. "I couldn't possibly drink or eat anything," she whispered to Jean.

"Take the tea and sip it, Madame," Jean advised as he took a cup and handed it to her before taking the second cup for himself.

The slave withdrew. Ibrahim al-Athir opened with the usual pleasantries about how joyful and honoured he was to receive them and asked how he could be of service.

"We are looking for four Christians, captured at Tripoli. We were told you could help us."

"I am flattered." The trader bowed his head. "But I should think you would be pleased to know that no Knights of your Temple allowed themselves to be taken alive. Your sergeants too fought to the last man. Only two score or so of your servants fell into our hands – craftsmen and the like. I sent all but one of them to my establishment in Cairo because it is well known that if they are in cities where there is even one church – much less the possibility of encountering a Templar Knight" – he bowed his head to Jean – "they constantly try to escape. It is safer to send them to cities so far from the reach of the Temple that they accept their fate sooner. Better for them as well as their masters. One of your servants was a trained mason, however, and I sent him to a customer in Aleppo who was desperately searching for such a slave and had commissioned me to find someone qualified."

Jean was for a moment taken aback by the thought of Templar brothers – even serving brothers – in slavery, but, reminding himself of his mission, he replied, "Thank you for the information, but I am here on behalf of the Lady Melisende and she is looking for four civilians. A lady and her three children."

"A lady? I was not aware that any noblewomen fell into our hands," Ibrahim retorted with a slightly sceptical note in his voice.

"The lady is the illegitimate daughter of the House of Embriaco."

"I see." He raised his eyebrows and gave Melisende an appraising look.

She remained hidden behind her black veils.

"And she had three children – a youth then fourteen, a daughter of eleven and a boy of eight," Jean continued.

"I see," the trader responded, and then when Jean said no more he prompted, "And can you describe these persons in detail?" He seemed almost mocking in that moment, and Jean turned to Lady Melisende, half afraid they were on a fool's errand.

"He wants more specific descriptions of the four people we are seeking."

To Jean's surprise and relief, Lady Melisende was well prepared for this question. She removed a parchment from her purse and handed it to Jean. "I used to try my hand at sketching. The children were my models," she explained. "These are the best sketches."

They were astonishingly good and Jean handed them on to Ibrahim, whose expression changed at once, and he glanced again at Lady Melisende. "Anna..." Lady Melisende sighed. "I have no sketch of Anna. I tried to do some from memory, but... they were no good. Anna is now thirty-two. She is a hand taller than I, with curly brown hair and golden eyes. She has an upturned nose and lips that pout somewhat. Her teeth are not very good – all crooked and yellowed. But she is definitely pretty when she keeps her mouth shut."

Jean translated as best he could.

Ibrahim shrugged with one shoulder. "Is she full-breasted or flat-chested? Is her ass firm or flabby? Are her thighs fleshy or shapeless?"

Jean stared at the trader, his expression a rebellious refusal to translate these questions to a noblewoman seeking her stepdaughter. The slave trader shrugged again. "A pretty face is good, but it is only one factor when selling a woman. At thirty-two she is not prime stock. I doubt that I bought her. I rarely buy women over twenty."

Jean translated only the fact that Ibrahim did not believe he had ever purchased Anna. "He specialises in younger women."

"But who... where... can't he give us any information?" Lady Melisende insisted desperately.

Jean asked the trader if he might suggest where they could look and he shrugged. "Some of the caravan dealers take older women and try to sell them as if they were younger. If she was plump and pretty of face she might still sell to the Bedouins... I will have one of my clerks give you the names of one or two dealers." Then, of his own accord, he returned his attention to the sketches and, pointing to the one of the girl, he announced, "This girl I purchased. She is fair and plump and very lucky. The soldier who took her captive recognised that with so many other women to be had for practically nothing she was worth more to him unviolated and sold her to me intact." He was talking about an eleven year old child. The picture showed a plump, round-faced little girl with big eyes playing with a kitten. Jean felt his stomach tighten. The trader continued professionally. "Although I had to pay a high price for her virginity, I found a buyer who was prepared to take her into his harem. I doubt he would consider selling her back to you for any price, but..." He shrugged. "That is his affair."

"And where do we find this man?" Jean asked as calmly as he could while Lady Melisende watched his lips, trying to understand the Arabic.

"He has a house here in Nazareth. His address too I will have my clerks give you."

Only now did Jean inform Melisende that they had located the girl and could seek out her new owner. Lady Melisende let out a little cry of joy and then crossed herself fervently. "God be thanked! God be praised!"

Meanwhile Ibrahim was considering the last two sketches. "This youth was a troublemaker." He indicated the elder boy. "I purchased him because he was well-built and strong for his age, but he was too angry and wild. Such troublemakers only spread restlessness and discontent. So I sold him again shortly afterwards to one of the traders who supply the galleys. He had the shoulders for it and, chained to the oars at sea, there is not so much opportunity for him to do any serious damage. Such youths soon settle down."

Jean gazed at the man with a fury he dared not express. He could remember being fourteen and could imagine how he might have reacted to slavery. Christ! He had sometimes bristled and baulked at even the well-meant discipline of the Captal de Buch during his five years as a squire. He knew too the life of galley slaves – confined in the bowels of a ship, seeing nothing but the sweating back in front of them, breathing in the stink of their own sweat, urine and the filthy bilge water. Their labour was the ultimate in monotony, offering no variation, no chance to think or even to ingratiate themselves with their owners. Devoted household slaves might attain responsibility, even authority over other slaves and might win the affection of their masters, receive gifts and women. A galley slave was like a part of the ship itself. It was kept in repair as long as possible, but if it broke down entirely it was dumped overboard. No one bought former galley slaves. Their legs were ruined from being chained to the benches and otherwise unused so that they could hardly walk, and furthermore they had a reputation for mindless brutality. Not even quarry slaves were more disdained than the galley slaves, who were treated and perceived more like animals than men.

"What is it?" Lady Melisende pleaded. "What did he say? Does he know where we can find Armand?"

"Armand is dead," Jean told her without turning his head or breaking eye contact with the trader.

Ibrahim al-Athir shrugged and smiled almost in embarrassment. "It was God's will that he should fall into our hands. God is great. If the boy is intelligent enough to recognise the Only God, then Allah will be merciful to him."

"'I am the resurrection and the life. He who liveth and believeth in me, though he be dead, yet shall he live.'" Jean spoke in French but he ended by crossing himself and the trader's face instantly darkened.

"Not in my house!" he warned sharply, as if he had been insulted or even threatened.

"Commander, what is it?" Lady Melisende begged nervously.

"Nothing," Jean assured her, still not taking his eyes from the trader. "What of the younger boy?" he asked, directing the trader's attention back to the sketches.

Ibrahim al-Athir considered the last sketch for a long time. "A boy of eight, you say?" Jean nodded. "That is a good age. Not so young that he must still be mothered, but young enough to accept his fate and to convert to Islam with his whole heart. Boys are cheap at that age too." He reflected more than informed while he studied the sketch. "But I do not remember this boy. Was he fair-haired like his sister?"

Jean conveyed the question to Lady Melisende, who nodded. "Fairer. The children were all born with light hair, which darkened as they grew older."

"Hmm." The trader considered.

"He... he had a club foot," Lady Melisende ventured in a whisper, tears welling in her eyes.

Jean looked at her in horror but her tears indicated that she knew already what the consequences might be. He turned to Ibrahim al-Athir. "The boy had... had..." He did not know the Arabic for club foot. "A big foot, misshapen."

"Ah! Of course! But I never deal with deformed or sick slaves," Ibrahim informed him shortly. "It would ruin my reputation. He was sold to one of the caravan dealers for sure. Though... you could look at the dye factory here in Nazareth. They employ many slaves of this age and it might make no difference there if the boy had a club foot or not." The business now evidently concluded, Ibrahim al-Athir handed the sketches back to the Lady Melisende.

"What did he say about little Jacques?" she asked Jean tremulously.

"That he may be in the dye factory here, but he isn't sure. He did not buy Jacques and does not know where he ended."

"But he might be in the dye factory?" She clung to the positive news.

"They employ many slaves his age and his handicap would make no difference. We can go and look."

Jean bowed to Ibrahim, returned his tea cup and Lady Melisende's to the table, and then got to his feet and helped Lady Melisende up. She turned to the trader and expressed her thanks profusely in French, to the evident displeasure of the trader.

Ibrahim al-Athir addressed Jean. "It is not right to bring a woman on business dealings. Women belong in the protection and seclusion of the house. Your Temple is wise to allow no women to enter."

Jean paused, torn between hatred for this cold-blooded merchant of humans, and caution. The trader evidently respected the Temple, but disapproved of Jean's behaviour toward Lady Melisende. The slave trader spoke with the utter confidence of a man convinced that his opinions and his culture were vastly superior to all others.

And why shouldn't he think that so long as God gave Islam victory after victory against His own Church, His own knights? Jean lifted his chin and smiled a faint, tired smile. "My orders are to assist the Lady Melisende in her search."

"You Christians are made weak by your women. They interfere in everything! You even let them rule you! Allah is great and we will destroy you in the long run. But you make it easy for us by setting women where they do not belong. Only the military orders ever really defied us."

Jean declined to answer. What was the point? He bowed and withdrew with Lady Melisende.

They were received more graciously than Jean expected by the merchant who had purchased Lady Melisende's step-granddaughter. Dried apricots, dates and almonds were offered with the tea while they sat in the cool of a decoratively tiled room looking out on to a courtyard through the scalloped, Islamic archway of the two doors. The courtyard was paved with freshly scrubbed marble and contained an elaborate fountain depicting fighting lions. Potted orange trees filled every second arch and an arcaded gallery ran around the upper storey of the courtyard. Not only did the noise, heat and dust of the city seem miles away, but the sordid business of selling human beings was equally distant.

Jean had first assumed that the merchant was roughly fifty years of age, judging by his bulk and his shortness of breath when he walked, but when they sat opposite him Jean reduced his estimate downward by a decade. The man was not really old, just unathletic and self-indulgent. He had inherited his trading empire, he gladly informed Jean in a flood of friendly chatter. His father and grandfather had built up the trade and he had nearly a thousand camels with which he could carry goods from Sudan to Constantinople and back. He had traded with all the Templar castles, he informed Jean proudly. And he liked doing business with the Templars. They struck a hard bargain, but they paid promptly and in full. He never had trouble with Templar customers. Very punctilious, he assured Jean with respect, and Jean was compelled to smile and bow his head and thank him for the compliment.

"Not flattery!" the man insisted with a sharp movement of his hand. "You and the Hospitallers were excellent customers. I was sorry to lose the trade at Krak de Chevaliers and at Safita." He shook his head sadly. "But I still trade in Acre. My nephew keeps my business there. Perhaps you know him? Ali ibn-Ahmad Talib?"

Jean shook his head and apologised. His host shrugged and helped himself to some dried fruit.

"You know," he reflected, "it would probably be cheaper if you let my caravans carry the grain and wine you deliver to the Church of St Joseph than bringing the things in yourself. You have to pay for the camels and the camel-boys and they aren't always the best. My caravans are first class," he told Jean definitively. "And they are safer. No robber dares attack the caravans of Mahmud ibn-Qaraga!"

"I have yet to meet a robber I have to fear," Jean answered boldly, bowing from the waist and smiling to reduce the impudence of his remark.

Mahmud laughed delightedly. "You Templars have the Mameluks' own arrogance! Allah have mercy on your infidel souls. So what do you want from me, Templar?"

"I have come on the behalf of the widow Melisende. She is looking for a certain girl – her granddaughter." It was better to make the bonds closer, if they were to appeal to the man's pity. "She was taken captive at Tripoli and Ibrahim al-Athir said he sold her to you. The widow is prepared to pay a very high price for the return of her granddaughter."

Mahmud's face betrayed first surprise, then hostility and finally a forced geniality. He bowed his head slightly toward Lady Melisende. "I am honoured to meet the noble grandmother of my dearest pet and dove, Lucie."

Lady Melisende turned her head rapidly to Jean for a translation. Her breathing had grown so heavy from sheer nervousness that it lifted the silk of her veil. Jean translated, and could sense more than see that Lady Melisende broke into a smile. "He will give her back? She can return with us today?"

"We have not got that far," Jean tried to check her euphoria.

"You must tell the honourable widow that I treasure her granddaughter above all my other concubines. She is like a little ray of sunshine among the others, who are all dark. And she is as sweet as sugared almonds." He kissed the tips of his fingers. "You can assure my Lucie's grandmother that her granddaughter will want for nothing – nothing that her heart desires could I deny my little pigeon."

'Except her freedom,' Jean added mentally, but he confined himself to turning to Lady Melisende and translating. "Mahmud assures you that your granddaughter is his favourite and will want for nothing."

"His favourite? She is a child! He cannot mean he would keep her? Why she is not even old enough to breed!" Lady Melisende protested, then, remembering that nearly a year had passed since the girl was captured, she added, "Or hardly old enough. He must return her to me. When can I see her and what price does he demand?"

Jean turned back to the merchant. "The good widow points out that her granddaughter is very young yet. She begs you to have pity on her, for she lost all her grandchildren in Tripoli and this is the only child she has been able to locate."

The merchant shook his head in a gesture of profound sympathy. "That is very sad. Very sad. But how much more joy the good widow must feel to know that this child is so well provided for! I am a wealthy man. I have dozens of houses. A thousand camels. You can see yourself the comfort I provide." He gestured vaguely to the room around them and the courtyard beyond. "What more can the good widow wish for her precious little dove? If you take her back with you to Acre, you cannot even be sure she will survive the journey. And what happens when Acre falls into our hands?" The confidence with which he assumed that this was just a matter of time sent a chill down Jean's spine. "The first soldiers to seize a girl are not always so temperate as Lucie's captor in Tripoli. Now that she is no longer virgin, her price would not be so tempting in any case." He gestured helplessly with his hands. "She is much safer here in my protection," Mahmud concluded smugly and bowed to Jean, indicating that he should translate this.

Jean's tongue was heavy in his mouth and he took a sip of tea, ignoring the way Lady Melisende leaned forward and gazed at him with alarmed, anxious eyes. "Madame, Mahmud refuses to return your granddaughter at any price. He has already... already..." Jean took a deep breath. "Lain with her."

"But she's immature!" Lady Melisende protested again. "He can't have... I don't care. No! Especially if he has violated her, I must take her home. How can any man use a child?"

Mahmud responded to the obvious outrage and anguish in Melisende's voice. "I will send for my turtledove and let the good widow assure herself of her welfare." He clapped his hands and gave an order to the slave. Shortly thereafter an older woman dressed in a chador, with the black veil pulled across her face so that only her eyes were exposed, entered and went on to her knees before Mahmud, touching her forehead to the floor in abject submission. Mahmud gestured for her to rise and come to him. He whispered to her at length, and she slipped out of the room again. Meanwhile, Jean explained to Lady Melisende that Lucie was to be brought so she could question her.

It seemed to take a long time and Jean saw the woman in the chador passing along the gallery above the courtyard. She entered a room opening off the gallery and for a moment the cackle of girlish giggles and the tinkling of windchimes escaped into the courtyard. Mahmud offered them both more tea. Lady Melisende's hands were trembling violently.

At last the chadored woman re-emerged escorting a short little girl by the hand. The girl was dressed in bright turquoise silk veils which spilled from a golden circlet on her blonde head. Beneath the turquoise veils she wore a pink silk blouse that encased her childishly plump torso but left her waistless belly bare. She wore baggy turquoise trousers and sandals with bells. Lady Melisende gasped, covered her mouth with her hands and physically forced herself to bite back her sobs before she lifted her head and called out, "Lucie!"

The chadored woman hissed in the girl's ear and, though the girl's head jerked as if she wanted to turn in the direction of the cry, she kept her eyes on the figure of Mahmud and dropped on her knees to crouch before him as the chadored woman had done. Mahmud benevolently called her to come to him. She scrambled clumsily to her feet and advanced obediently. Mahmud pulled her up on to his lap and sat fondling her as he gazed back at the two Christians. "You can see how fine I have made my little turtledove. Ask her anything you like."

"Lucie! I've come to take you home! I promise I'll spend the rest of my life making this up to you!" Lady Melisende fell on to her knees and reached out her arms to the girl.

Lucie turned her head away and buried her face in the fat neck of her master. She burned red with shame and dug her fingers into Mahmud's ample flesh, but she could not bring herself to answer or look at the woman who had known her in her childhood.

"You see?" Mahmud declared triumphant and proud. "My little pet is happy with me. She does not want to return to her old life – to the dangers and the filth. She is safe with me here and happy."

He bounced the knee on which she sat and pinched her cheek to make her smile, cooing endearments to her as if there was no one else in the room.

Lady Melisende dropped her face into her hands and broke into violent sobbing.

Jean rose to his feet. "You will excuse us," he told Mahmud, and, raising Lady Melisende by the elbow, he led her from the chamber and out into the courtyard.

"How could he! How could he! My poor Lucie!" she gasped through her tears, her whole body shaking with sobs, her hands trembling more violently than ever.

The chadored woman came up behind them and hissed at them in heavily accented French. "Hurry and leave! You have done enough harm already."

Stunned, both Jean and Lady Melisende spun around and stared at her.

"Get out, I tell you. You do no good here. The girl was just settling down and learning her duties, and now she will start wetting her bed again. If Mahmud were not so besotted with her, he would have lost patience long ago. She doesn't know the first thing about pleasing a man!"

"She's a child!" Lady Melisende protested yet again.

"A girl child! What else does she need to learn? You Franks are fools, filling a girl's head with letters and numbers. God did not make women to be scholars!" she scoffed contemptuously. "Women have only one purpose: to sweeten the sowing of their man's seed so that he will sire many children upon them! If Lucie learns that soon enough, she can live like a queen for two or three years, before he buys a new girl. If she gives Mahmud a son before too long, her position will be secured forever."

"And what if she doesn't?" Jean asked as Lady Melisende collapsed against him in incoherent wailing.

The woman shrugged. "Then she will be like me and will have to care for the new favourite or the children of the more fertile concubines. It is not a bad life. Much better than being made to work or service the lust of countless strangers like an ordinary slave."

"She is not a slave to us. She is a child and would live with her grandmother."

"For how long? You would marry her off some time. Who is to say her husband would treat her so well as my lord Mahmud? He is very gentle and indulgent to his harem. And what would happen to her when Acre falls?" There it was again, the absolute certainty that Acre would fall to the Sultan.

"Help me!" Lady Melisende moaned as she started to chant the rosary. Jean half-led and half-carried her out of the merchant's palace to the curious whispers of Mahmud's other slaves.

*

The dye factory was located in a shabby, run-down quarter of the town. Here it was the sight of well-trappinged, full-blooded horses and the glitter of expensive steel equipment which attracted attention. All three Templars dropped their right hands to their sword hilts automatically, and Jean ordered Pirenne up on Melisende's other side so that they flanked her completely while they rode through the streets.

When the street people crowded in too closely around them, Jean rode ahead, chasing the beggars and loiterers out of the way. The sight of his massive iron-shod stallion and the unsheathed four foot long broadsword was sufficient to elicit respect even from the most insolent thieves and they melted into the alleys.

The factory itself was backed up against the city wall. The gutters around the factory ran with dye and the walls had been splattered with so many various colours that they were a filthy purple colour at the base. The stench that emerged was unnatural and revolting.

Jean left Lady Melisende with Pirenne and Paul, both with drawn swords, and went alone into the factory. His plan was simple. He would show the owner or overseer the sketch and offer him a cool thirty dinhars for the boy. According to Ibrahim al-Athir's clerks, a boy cost between fifteen and twenty dinhars and a boy with a club foot would hardly command more than ten.

Inside the factory the stench was almost unbearable. Great vats of steaming liquid putrefied the air, and the clouds of steam hung beneath the ceiling while tainted condensation on the walls had fostered sheets of mould that contributed to the stench. On precarious catwalks built between the vats, bony boys dressed only in filthy loincloths perched and clambered. They stirred the vats with long wooden sticks. As his eyes adjusted to the gloom, Jean could make out other boys, their sallow skin glistening with sweat, crouching under the vats to feed the fires. Jean had the sensation of having entered hell, and he crossed himself.

"You! What do you want? Who are you?"

"Commander Sir Jean de Preuthune of the Knights Templar at Acre!" Jean replied in a voice that echoed and made the boys jump and stop in their labour. His eyes swept their faces looking for the one in the sketch, looking for blond hair. But they all had large eyes, unformed noses and narrow faces. The dye of days and months stained their faces, their hair, their hands and chests.

"What? An infidel? May Allah see that you rot in an unmarked grave with your whore of a mother! I tolerate no infidel under my roof! Get out!"

A turbaned man in robes hardly less filthy than the loincloths of his slaves was storming toward Jean from the other end of the chamber.

"You would throw away the chance to earn thirty dinhars?"

The turbaned apparition stood still. "How?"

"I am looking for a boy with a club foot."

"I might have seen him."

"Seen him? Does he work here?"

"No, would I employ a boy who can't climb?" He pointed to the catwalks. "But he begs down in the square."

"Describe him to me." Jean did not think a slave would be allowed to beg.

"Twelve, thirteen – tall and burly, except for the foot."

The man was bluffing, assuming that Jean would want a strong youth rather than a weakling.

"Pity. That isn't the boy I'm looking for. Do you know of no other with a club foot?"

"Of course," the turbaned man rejoined. "There's the whore's brat..." If the mother was known it could hardly be the boy he was looking for.

Jean felt something pawing at his ankle and he leapt back, his skin crawling with instant revulsion, thinking it was a rat or something similar. He looked down into the miscoloured face of one of the boys who had been feeding the fires. The boy had wriggled forward on his belly to avoid being seen. "*Monsieur*," he lisped in French, "*Monsieur le Templar*. Please take me with you. I'm Christian."

The boy was nothing but skin and bones and he had black eyes under a shock of black hair. Jean glanced at his feet. They were stained black but were narrow and well-formed. He was not the boy they were looking for.

"Our Father Which art in Heaven. Hallowed be Thy name. Thy kingdom come..." The boy began the Lord's Prayer in a rush of Latin, apparently afraid that Jean did not believe him.

"Where are you from? How did you get here?"

"Tripoli, *monsieur*. My father was a bo'sun in the Venetian fleet. My mother—"

The turbaned man was suddenly there, and he reached down and grasped the boy by his skeletal arm and flung him back toward the fire, landing a kick on his behind for good measure. The boy sprawled on to the dirt floor, his arm fell into the fire and he howled in genuine agony. Instantly, of course, he withdrew his arm, balled himself up and held the burnt arm against his belly, yelping like a wounded puppy. The overseer took his cane from his belt and started raining blows on the boy, cursing him furiously.

Jean reached out and pulled him off the boy with ease. The Arab felt the bite of his sword-hardened fingers and whimpered in surprise. He had not suspected so much strength could be in the hand of the elegant young man.

"Leave the boy alone."

"He is a worthless whiner!" The man spat at the boy, who still rolled back and forth, clutching his arm. Jean suspected he was consciously acting now, but it made no difference.

"Is he a slave?"

"What else?"

"Where did you buy him?"

"At the market, where else?"

"How long ago?"

The man shrugged. "That worthless brat? Six months ago at least."

"Was he taken at Tripoli?"

The man shrugged again. "Might have been? Did he say that?"

"Yes."

"Speaks nothing but your shitty Frankish gibberish! Too stupid to learn Arabic and the Koran! He'll rot in hell!"

"I'll give you seven dinhar for him."

"Seven? I paid fifteen and now he's a trained dyer and has learned his manners better."

"He's got a burned arm and his face and feet are stained. I'll give you eight dinhar."

"Fourteen."

"Eight and a half."

"Twelve."

"Ten."

The man held out his hand and rubbed his thumb and forefinger together.

Jean drew his dagger with his left hand and held it casually at the ready before reaching inside his surcoat and extracting his purse. The boy had gone abruptly still and the Arab watched Jean with unblinking eyes. He was carrying far too much coin on him, and Jean reproached himself. But he had to trust his skill with the dagger. He had practised using it with his right hand tied behind his back often enough.

He pried into his purse with his right hand, feeling the coins for size and weight. He brought out a five dinhar piece that instantly disappeared into the Arab's hand. The empty hand was held out again. Jean was aware that the Arab would not make change but disappear with whatever he removed from the purse. At last he found a smaller coin and withdrew it. Half a dinhar. It too disappeared and the empty hand was held out again. He withdrew another coin: five dinhar again. It was gone and the turbaned man was bending over the boy and hauling him to his feet. He indicated Jean. "Your new master, you little wretch!" He gave him a last kick almost affectionately.

The boy ran forward and grasped Jean's hand. He started kissing it wildly. "Have you bought me? Have you really?"

"Come on."

As they emerged once more into the daylight, Jean heard Lady Melisende cry out in joy, and then cut herself off. Jean was half blinded after the dim light in the factory and he made his way forward squinting.

"But Sir Jean, this boy... this boy..."

"Is Christian. Would you have me leave him there? Jacques was not there. The boys have to climb on catwalks. No one with a club foot would be suitable. Nor does the man know where he might be." Taking the boy under his arms, Jean lifted him up to Paul.

"*Monsieur le Templar?*" the boy called to him shrilly. "*Monsieur le Templar!*" He held out his arms and tried to clamber down from the horse, but was evidently afraid of the fall.

Jean returned and hushed him. "What is it?"

"You are my master now. Please don't sell me or give me away. You are my master."

"No, you are free. But Brother Paul will bring you to the Hospice of the Annunciation and there the good brothers will see that you are cleaned and given clothes."

Lady Melisende was suddenly beside him, tears running down her face again. "You shame me, Commander. I will care for the boy." Then she smiled at him through her tears and asked his name.

"Marco, Madame," the boy answered, but his eyes lingered on Jean's back as he went to mount his stallion.

*

In the heat of the noonday sun, the slave market was all but deserted. The dealer and his drivers had retired into the nearby tavern, leaving only one elderly eunuch who dozed against one of the buildings lining the square. The slaves waited listlessly in the shade of improvised awnings, finishing the mash of chickpeas and lamb fat that had been their midday meal. No customers came at this time of day, and only the stray dogs slunk about the edges of the square looking for rubbish.

Madeleine squatted near the edge of the awning. Her stomach revolted against the daily mash, and, after two dips of her fingers, she set the bowl aside. At once the fat woman beside her nudged her with her elbow and gestured toward the bowl. Madeleine nodded her head wearily. The fat woman at once seized the bowl and shovelled the contents into her own mouth, leaving smudges of the muck on the outside of her lips in her haste. Then, satisfied, she sank on to her ample buttocks with a satisfied burp.

Madeleine turned her head away and closed her eyes. She no longer even smelt the stench that perpetually surrounded her: the accumulated sweat; the fat and bits of food that had spilled on to her bodice over the months; the rubbish, urine and animal shit that had become ingrained in the toughened soles of her bare feet. But the flies that landed on her cracked and crusted lips and alighted on the putrefaction which oozed from her right eye irritated her. She waved them away angrily, and then tried to sleep.

Sleep was her only escape, but it would not come. Instead her thoughts circled idly to the food she had failed to eat. She was lucky that the trader had not been present for he often forced her to eat, standing over her with his cane and beating her if she tried to put the food aside. But she had her revenge, she thought with a faint smile, when she vomited it all up again. He then tried to tempt her with sweets and other delicacies like dates and almonds. But she had lost all appetite even for such things. So she grew thinner and weaker with each passing day, to the despair of the trader who watched her value shrink with her body. One of these days he would carry out his threat to cut her free of the rope that bound her to the other women and leave her to die in the wasteland between market towns.

Madeleine did not fear this. Her only fear was that someone would buy her before the trader was driven to this act of despair. The thought of being purchased made Madeleine stir uneasily despite the utter stillness of noon.

Though she could hope that things might be different now that she was skinny and ugly, she could not convince herself that her next owner would not use her like the last. And for all the filth and hardship of life in a slave caravan one thing was certain: it was in the slave trader's self-interest to ensure that no males – free or unfree – tampered with his female merchandise. Pregnant females were almost worthless.

Madeleine envied the women who enjoyed copulation. They flirted openly with prospective masters – some coyly and some brazenly. They encouraged the probing hands, expertly arousing the lust of the customers with their gestures and eyes. But the instant a man looked at her with the slightest hint of lust, her insides hardened and her stomach twisted in on itself while her heart beat in furious panic.

She no longer knew how many men had raped her – for each coupling had been a rape, even if she had been too weak and helpless to show her resistance. She had stopped counting after the night when her master had had a dinner party for eight friends and let each have a turn at her. That had been in the first month of her slavery when raping a Christian nun had still seemed a novelty to many Islamic men. Her master had had her bathed but ordered her dressed in her increasingly dirty and ragged habit when he sent her to service his friends because it was the habit as much as she herself that aroused their lust.

Later, when she wore only the usual garb of an Arab slave woman, she had learned that her best defence was utter passivity. No matter what they forced her to do, she allowed herself to show neither resistance nor anger, pain nor disgust. The men quickly lost interest in a zombie lover, and though her master cursed and beat her to try to make her respond she preferred any other abuse to the routine rape that was the alternative. Finally her master's first wife intervened because she was pregnant, and then she was left alone for four glorious months until, in a flood of blood and agony, she miscarried the baby.

She had never loved her baby, for all that she was thankful for the protection it had temporarily offered her. It was a product, a symbol and reminder of the brutal process by which it had been conceived. Sometimes she had wondered which of the faceless, nameless strangers who had helped themselves to her body had left behind the seed that took root. Had it been one of the virile, impatient young men who expected her to be impressed by their instrument of torture, eager for the degradation of penetration? Or one of the older men who had been unable to perform the act at all until they had made her arouse them in other ways?

Madeleine gagged on the memory, and shook her head to clear it. But there was nothing else to think about. The future was a blank that ended either in death on the side of the caravan road or back in that world of perpetual humiliation. The past started with the fall of Tripoli. What had gone before was too irrelevant and too unreal. It might as well have been a different world, a different life. Certainly it belonged to a different person.

That Madeleine, born and raised in a rose-covered castle in sunny Poitou, had flitted through life like a happy lark. She was pretty and loved and spoilt by her parents and her five elder brothers. She had ponies and pet dogs and pretty dresses and bright ribbons for her hair. She had sung and danced and learned her catechism with equal delight. But her father's Château du Lys-St-George lay only five miles from Neuvy-St-Sépulchre. Year after year, she stood in wonder in this church built by a pilgrim from the Holy Land in imitation of the Church of the Holy Sepulchre in Jerusalem.

Year by year the desire to travel to Jerusalem and see the original had grown and with it a sense of religious vocation. When she turned fifteen, that Madeleine had rejected the as yet anonymous knight her father would have found for her and taken the veil instead. Madeleine joined the Cistercians with a joyful heart – though her mother cried and all but one of her brothers said it was a 'waste'.

And, as with everything else in the life of that Madeleine, she soon had her own way about the Holy Land. She had talked her mother superior into letting her travel to Tripoli to join the Cistercian nuns there. Tripoli was, after all, closer to Jerusalem than France. The Cistercian nunnery in Tripoli was beautiful, peaceful and soaked with sun. Madeleine had felt Christ's nearness, had heard his sandalled footsteps on the tiles behind her, seen him disappear around the corner of the alley riding on a donkey, felt his hands bless her as she bowed her head at Mass. She had lived in a kind of joyous rapture, waiting unconsciously for a yet greater miracle, the step still closer to Him.

The siege came instead. It had not frightened her at first because Madeleine never dreamt that the Christians might be defeated. She waited in a kind of nervous exultation for the miracle that would rescue Tripoli. She had blithely expected Saint George or Saint Michael or the Archangel Gabriel to appear. The sight of the Templar and Hospitaller reinforcements clattering up from the port had moved her to a day of absolute fasting while she waited for the victory that must follow the arrival of the Soldiers of Christ.

Even when the panicked shouts of fleeing citizens told the nuns that the walls were breached, that Madeleine had expected the miracle would come – must come – very shortly. She had accompanied her panicked sisters in that crazy rush to the port, but always with a look over her shoulder, not wanting to miss the sign that He had come. And even when the last of the Genoese galleys cast off from the quay only half-full and Italian – Christian! – crossbowmen fired into the crowd on the quay to prevent them from storming the galley, she had not realised that all was lost. She had turned her back on the Italians with contempt and faced back toward the city thinking, 'We are the chosen ones, for we will see Him when He comes'

He did not come. The Mamelukes came. They killed all the men and old people and rounded up the women and children. Madeleine and most of her fellow nuns were herded together into a church and left there under guard. Despite or because of the horror of the slaughter she had seen in the streets, she was in too great a state of shock to clearly comprehend what had happened to her. The very fact that she was still with most of her sisters and they were in a church did much to deceive them. They spent their time in prayer, an island of apparent sanctuary while around them the city was sacked and its citizens slaughtered. Gradually the sounds of killing and destruction faded, the light faded from the day, the coolness of the evening gripped the church. And then the Mamelukes who had rounded them up returned.

They were in high spirits, laughing and chattering, wiping their bloody swords and putting them away. They went into the sacristy and started dividing up the valuables they found there after clearing the altar. This loot divided, they came back into the nave and started circling the cowering nuns. There were roughly a dozen Mamelukes and thirty-five nuns, three apiece. They took their time selecting, yanking off the veils to see the colour of their captive's hair and pulling up their habits for a look at their legs. Now it started to dawn on Madeleine – even on that Madeleine – that they were not going to be spared or treated with respect but dishonoured, humiliated, violated like common whores.

While some of the nuns were elderly, frail and ugly, Madeleine had a plump prettiness that attracted the attention of more than one of the Mamelukes. They kept coming back and lifting her skirts for another look and there followed some friendly arguing before at last one man took her by the wrist and pulled her away.

The instant his hand clasped her wrist like an iron band, she knew what he intended, but she couldn't - not even then - believe that God had abandoned her. She screamed and tried to hold back. But when she refused to follow him willingly, he simply dragged her. He hauled her to one of the side chapels. Her hip crashed against the shallow step and the bruise of that blow left her lame for almost a week, but at the time the pain was obscured by her panic. The Mameluke released her wrist at last but he was standing over her, astride her, while he unbuckled his sword belt.

Madeleine clasped her hands together in prayer and petition and tried to rise to her knees. Tears were streaming down her face - tears of pain, fear, self-pity. The Mameluke pushed her back on to the floor with the toe of his boot.

"Please!" she begged. "Please don't. Please! I'm a maid! A virgin! A nun! Don't you understand? A nun!"

The man had rid himself of those articles of clothing that might get in his way, and he lowered himself on top of her firmly and expertly. He was a man of roughly thirty years of age, she guessed. No longer young and fresh, but not yet old and weathered. He was sleek and powerful as a cat. His big hand wrapped around both her wrists as she held her hands together in fevered supplication, shoved her hands up over her head and held them there.

Madeleine rolled her head from side to side gasping, sobbing, begging for mercy. The Mameluke pulled up the skirts of her habit with his free hand and pulled down her drawers.

"No! Please! I'm a virgin!"

"You are a whore!" The man surprised her by speaking in very understandable French. "A whore!" he repeated as his hand started to work - expertly as she would soon learn - to make her moist enough to receive him. "Married to three men at once!" His chest rested heavily on her and he spoke directly into her ear in a hissing, harsh French.

"I am a maid!" Madeleine protested again in a desperate wail. "I am a bride of Christ - Jésu Christi!"

"And his father and his slave. Three men at once! You are a whore!" As Madeleine grasped that he meant the Trinity, the Mameluke decided she was ready and jammed himself into her. The pain alone made her scream, and then the realisation that no begging, no fighting, not even death could save her any more, made her scream turn into a high-pitched howl that echoed in the dome of the church and drifted down upon her more fortunate sisters huddled together in the nave.

The howl did not end. It went on and on as the Mameluke worked against the scandalised flesh which had never known an intrusion before. The Mameluke was deaf to the howling. Sweat beaded on his forehead and glistened on his neck. His breathing rasped in his throat and bathed her face with the smell of garlic. His hips worked faster and faster, and he began to chant into her ear, "Allah is great. Allah is great. Allah is great. Allaaaahh!" He pinned her to the floor and his whole body trembled in triumph. When he recovered his breath, he pulled himself out and off her and spat on her. "Whore! See what good your three husbands are! There is no God but Allah!"

She didn't remember what happened immediately after that exactly. They were kept in the church for a long time without food or water, and then the slave traders came and bargained with the Mamelukes who had captured them. With their right ankles tied together, the nuns were led outside for the first time since their capture. Around them lay the smoking ruins of the city and the rotting corpses of the inhabitants. Only the stone buildings, like the church, were still standing.

The prisoners were loaded on to camels, two or three apiece, and tied to the saddles. Then the caravan swayed out of the ruined city through the Aleppo Gate. Here the Mamelukes had lined the road with spikes, each crowned with the head of a Templar, Hospitaller or Teutonic Knight. Madeleine vomited, and the camel driver laughed. The nun beside her on the camel crossed herself and started to pray. Madeleine stared at the woman. She was a brittle nun already approaching forty and the Mamelukes had disdained to rape her when there were so many younger and prettier woman to be had.

"Have you forgotten how to pray?" the older nun scolded when she saw Madeleine staring at her, and it was in that instant that Madeleine realised that she had indeed 'forgotten' how to pray. For a tortured moment, she tried to join in the other nun's prayer, but the words stuck in her mouth. In her head she heard only the rasping breath of a Mameluke rhythmically repeating: "Allah is great!"

She had never again uttered a single word in prayer, and not once, regardless of how young or old, tall or short or fat the man was, had she failed to hear the hissing words as the thrusting between her legs reached its climax. "Allah is great." The words buzzed in her head now like the flies that tried to light on her lips and eyes. She shook her head irritably and tried to swallow.

The sun had continued its journey and now slanted in under the edge of the awning. Madeleine felt the heat and became aware of her thirst. That was the one thing she had not learned to master. The trader could always get her to eat in the end by denying her water until she had consumed the food he put before her. She licked at her lips and tasted the layer of dust upon them with revulsion.

A shadow fell across her, abruptly blocking out the sun. At once her body cramped as she registered that it could only be a customer. He had stopped directly before her and she could feel his eyes studying her, boring into her. She closed her eyes more tightly and tried not to move, to not even breathe. Surely any man would be repulsed by what he saw: the hair dyed the colour of straw a month ago and – she presumed – already growing out at the roots into its natural hazelnut colour, the sallow skin prematurely aged by the Syrian sun, the lips painted on larger than life with a fatty red cream.

The man – she could tell it was a man by the smell of horse sweat and leather – did not move, and nervously her eyes fluttered just enough to let her peep through her lashes. She saw two chainmailed feet and a shudder went through her. Only soldiers wore chainmail – though she could not remember seeing a Muslim in chainmail leggings. Her eyes cautiously ran up to the leather garters buckled just below the knee to keep the leggings in place. Her heart was thundering in her chest; no Muslim dressed like this.

Her eyes flew open and she gasped in terror. Looming over her was a militant angel – white surcoat over glittering mail and a head of golden hair framed by a halo. "Gabriel!" she gasped in wonder. She had died.

And then the man dropped down on to his heels and the sun remained high over his head and he was not an angel after all.

Madeleine swallowed and her eyes fixed upon the red cross on his breast. Though he was dressed like a Templar, she had seen with her own eyes the heads of all the garrison and relief on the stakes before

Tripoli. And since he could not be a Templar, he could only be an apparition sent to admonish her for her loss of faith.

"What did you say?" he asked her, and she was startled by the gentleness of his voice. Her eyes were released from the cross and sought his face. It was a handsome face: tanned and weathered with deep lines creasing his cheeks and crows' feet about his grey eyes but retaining a youthfulness and a kindness. The eyes searched her face, prying into every crevice, registering the cracks on her lips and the infection in her eye, seeing the dust and the sweat.

Madeleine started to tremble with shame. She felt as if she were naked before him. But this was a different nakedness from the matter-of-fact disrobing of a slave girl. It was as if the eyes could read her very soul. "What are you?" she asked the apparition.

"I am Commander Sir Jean de Preuthune of the Knights Templar at Acre," came the answer.

"Acre too is fallen?" she asked in alarm. "You are enslaved?" But then she realised how absurd the question was. A Templar commander did not allow himself to be taken alive – and if he did, the Muslims killed him because the Temple forbade ransom. "You are a spirit!" she concluded.

"No," he told her calmly, and she saw pity in his eyes, which made her want to cry. "I am very much alive and free." Seeing the disbelief and confusion, he explained. "We still have the right of pilgrimage to Nazareth."

"Nazareth?" she repeated, lifting her head and staring about her. "Are we in Nazareth?"

"Yes."

"Nazareth?" she repeated again, and suddenly it was too much for her and she dropped her face in her hands. Squatting in the dirt He had trodden, she had not even known she was in His city. She had not felt His presence here where He had lived, though she had imagined it in Tripoli where He had never been.

"Who are you?" he asked her gently. "Your accent sounds almost as if you were from the Languedoc…"

"Poitou. From Poitou." She lifted her face and looked at him again. "From Lys-St-George. My father is the lord of Lys-St-George. My name is Madeleine."

The village was obscure and Jean did not know Poitou, but he nodded and smiled. "And you came on pilgrimage?" he asked cautiously. "You were captured *en route*? Your father was killed?"

"No... I came... I was a sister at the Convent of St Helena in Tripoli—"

"You want this woman?" The trader had at last returned from his midday meal and, seeing Jean conversing with Madeleine, he hurried over. "You have an eye for a bargain! Skinny as she is now, I'll let you have her for a mere twelve dinhars! But she'll soon fatten up if you treat her right." He smiled lecherously.

Jean turned on the trader and would have made a sharp retort if Paul had not suddenly grasped him on the arm. "Commander! Come quick! It's my brother! I've found him!"

"A Templar?" Jean asked eagerly, as he let Paul pull him away from the female to the male slaves.

"No, my real brother!" Paul corrected. "You remember that he left for the Holy Land four years before I did and I was hoping to find him here." Now that Paul reminded him, Jean did remember.

Paul led Jean down the line of abruptly roused and curious slaves to a man who at once fell forward on his knees at the sight of Jean. His hands were bound together with leather bands but he lifted them up clasped together. "Noble sir! Have pity on a poor Christian who has spent years in the hands of the Muslims! Please, sir!"

The slave was a little man wearing nothing but baggy knee-breeches coated with dust. His torso was scrawny, his shoulders bony and sliced with two whip scars. He had very short, skeletal legs and feet so knobby and deformed that they hardly seemed human. His mouth contained only half its teeth and his breath while he pleaded was repulsively foul.

Behind Jean, Paul begged with equal fervour, "Please, Commander. I'll find some way to pay you back. Please don't leave him here!"

Jean turned on Paul. "What have I done to deserve such mistrust?"

He clapped his hands and the trader, hovering only a half-dozen steps away, ran over and bowed. "You want this slave too, master?"

"What does he cost?"

"He is a very expensive man – lean and tough! Twenty-five dinhars."

"His health has been ruined by abuse and bad diet," Jean answered automatically. "I'll give you twelve dinhars only because my brother wants him." He indicated Paul, who was beaming with relief.

"Not under twenty!"

"Twelve!" Jean insisted, aware of the anxious looks of Paul and his brother and becoming ashamed of the haggling even though it was expected.

"Nineteen and not one dinhar less!"

"Twelve." Jean insisted again, wishing that Paul and his brother did not look so desperate. He could not even pretend to walk away as long as they both looked to him as if he were Christ Himself.

"This is a strong young man! The girl you can have for eight dinhars!" he told Jean in exasperation. "For five even!" What did he have to lose? She would die soon anyway and no one but a crazy Christian would want her. "But for this man you must pay eighteen!"

"Done." Jean agreed instantly for the combined price was the same now. He reached for his purse and Paul's brother fell on his face and started kissing his feet.

"You'll never regret this! Never. I'll serve you for life—"

Jean backed away from him and signalled for Paul to lift him up. *Non nobis, Domine, sed nomini tuo da gloriam.*

The man stared up at him blankly as Paul caught him under his arms and helped him to his feet. "It is the Templar slogan, Jacques," he explained as he cut his brother's bonds with his knife. "'Not to us, but to You, God, goes all the honour and the fame.'"

As Jean handed over the coins and Paul released his brother from the bonds, a voice was lifted from among the other male slaves. "Commander! I too am Christian. Buy me too!"

"Me too!"

"And me!"

A whole chorus of voices erupted. Throughout the throng of humans who lay bound under the awning, one man after another rose up in hope and supplication. They scrambled to their knees, reached out their hands and cried out for pity and succour.

There were almost a dozen of them, Jean estimated, and they would cost a small fortune. A fortune that he - vowed to poverty - did not have. Every dinhar he spent was Templar money, money he had to account for. It had been one thing to purchase a child, a nun and a relative, but could he justify several hundred dinhars for another dozen slaves? Could he turn his back on Christians trapped in slavery?

"Are they Christians?" he addressed himself to Paul's brother, and the newly freed slave looked back at the others and, pointing with his finger, confirmed one after another. "Yes, that German was captured by robbers, and those two Venetians were taken by pirates off Cyprus and sold to Egypt, and those three men there are all Spanish friars who were on pilgrimage to Bethlehem. That man there is also from the Languedoc, sir, from Toulouse; those are native Christians from Antioch; and that is a Greek Christian – if that counts," he added somewhat sceptically with a sidelong look at the Templar.

Most of these men, like Paul's brother, were either physically inferior, sickly or past their prime. Good slaves did not end up in a slave caravan which travelled to weekly markets, but were either kept by their masters or traded by established and respectable slave merchants such as Ibrahim al-Athir.

Jean turned to the eager trader, who waited with squinting eyes. "I'll give you one hundred and fifty dinhars for all these Christians."

"One hundred and fifty!" he cried in horror. "You are trying to ruin me! You want my children to go begging in the streets! My wives to sell themselves! One hundred and fifty dinhars for so many magnificent slaves! You are a scoundrel!"

"Probably."

No Arab could shrug off an insult so this simple answer confused the trader more than any vehement protest would have done. "I do not deal with scoundrels! With pigs!" he retorted indignantly, jumping up and down in agitation.

Jean shrugged. "Then don't." He turned his back on the trader and the slaves. A roar of protest went up from the men who had thought themselves rescued and now saw their hopes dashed. Jean ignored them and strode toward his waiting horse.

"Sir! Commander!" It was Paul's brother, who came hobbling after him. "Save at least the man from Toulouse! Please, sir, I vouch for him."

"I don't intend to leave any of them behind," Jean told him in an undertone without looking back.

Having reached his stallion, he unbuckled his saddlebag and removed his mantle. With this in his hand, he returned to Madeleine, who still crouched under her awning unaware that she had been bought and paid for in the transaction regarding Paul's brother.

"Come. I'll deliver you to the Hospice of the Annunciation where you'll be fed, bathed and given clean clothes. You may have to wait until you reach Acre for a proper habit. From Acre you can return to a Cistercian convent on Cyprus or in France."

Madeleine gazed up at him in a kind of dazed uncertainty. It was less a matter of disbelief than a new fear: how could she return to a Christian world after what she had become? How could she enter a church again without remembering the Mameluke smashing her maidenhead to the words 'Allah is great'? How could she mix again with women who were as pure and self-contained as she had been before? How could she face a mother superior or a confessor, knowing that her heart was empty of faith? Could she go through the rituals, recite the prayers, sing the hymns and kiss the cross in a perpetual routine of deception?

Jean bent and severed the rope that tied her to her fat neighbour. Then he held out his hand to her, and she – ashamed to take it – tried to scramble to her feet without help. But she went dizzy from trying to stand too abruptly, and almost lost her balance. Jean had to reach out a hand to steady her. His hand was warm but gentle – not like a man's hand, for it sought neither to dominate nor humiliate her. It offered her support.

She seemed so fragile to Jean as she swayed on her stick-like legs that he was afraid to hold her firmly. Her very bones seemed to have shrunk until they felt as though they would break in two if he closed his fist upon them. He released her and swung his mantle over her shoulders. She staggered under the weight of the wool.

Madeleine gasped and looked up at him with huge, shocked eyes. "I can't wear this! The white is for purity, the cross..."

"Christ died for our sins, Sister. For yours as well as mine." He took her hand, but she tripped over the mantle which bunched on the ground around her feet. Jean bent and swept her up into his arms in a single, fluid motion that left her no time to protest.

Suddenly Madeleine was a little girl again, being carried into the warmth and safety of Lys-St-George by her father after a long, tiring journey. She turned her face into the powerful, warm chest of her protector and blocked out the rest of the world.

The slave trader came running after Jean. "Master! Don't be so hasty! You have me on a good day! Look, I gave you the girl for practically nothing! For two hundred and eighty dinhar, you can have all eleven men!"

"I can't afford them," Jean told the trader without deigning to look at him. "Keep them."

The trader glanced back toward the slaves and quickly calculated the chances of selling any one of them today – much less so many at once. The slaves he didn't sell he had to feed until he reached the next market and who was to say that he'd sell them there? A bird in the hand... "Two hundred dinhar – that's less than twenty apiece!"

"Some of them are old men you couldn't sell for fifteen separately. One hundred and seventy-five dinhar for the lot."

The trader hesitated to give in so soon, but Jean had lifted Madeleine up into his saddle and was collecting his reins while Paul had mounted and pulled his brother up behind him. They had deliberately left Lady Melisende behind today.

"All right!" the trader gave in angrily. "You Christian dogs! You ruin me, but I am a poor man, and must have offended against the Almighty! He punishes me by forcing me to deal with swine like you! But now I will rid myself of all you pigs, and then the All-Merciful will favour me again, God willing!"

Jean did not dismount. He ordered Paul to dismount instead, and told him to release all the men who had been identified. He was then to lead them to the Hospice of the Annunciation, and let them know that the return journey to Acre would commence the day after the Feast of the Annunciation.

Sergeant Pirenne stopped Paul with a gesture of his hand. "Commander."

Jean looked over questioningly.

"Please grant me this privilege – in atonement for what I did."

"Pirenne, only a priest can grant absolution, you know that. But if you wish to be the one, then by all means, release them."

Pirenne solemnly dismounted and handed his reins to Paul, while Jean emptied his purse into his hand and counted out the one hundred and seventy-five dinhars. He had not exaggerated previously. He would have to budget carefully for the journey back to Acre or buy on credit.

When the Christian slaves realised that they were to be released after all, a great cheer went up. Some of the men got to their feet and danced about. Others went down on their knees in gratitude or prayer. Others flung their arms around an embarrassed but grinning Sergeant Pirenne.

In the midst of all the jubilation, an old slave with a long white beard, dressed in dirty but once expensive robes, suddenly spoke up for the first time. "I too am a Christian, Brother Templar. Ask your commander if he will buy me as well." The man spoke educated French.

"No! Not him!" two of the other freed men shouted abruptly.

"He's no Christian," the German spat at the man. "I've seen how he prays five times a day just like the other Musselmen!"

"That's true!" Others joined in. "He is as much a Musselman as old Ali al-Masurh!" They indicated the slave trader contemptuously, tasting their freedom already.

"Not only was I baptised and did I take communion like the rest of you," the man continued calmly, "but I have taken holy vows and I am a priest."

"A heretic!" the Spanish Dominican friars spat out. "Heretic!" They cursed the man in a flood of vehement Spanish, but the old man ignored them.

"Buy him that he may burn at the stake as he deserves!" This merciful suggestion was put forth by the man from Toulouse.

Confused by the turmoil around him, Pirenne turned to Jean.

Jean nudged his horse to the edge of the crowd and gazed down at the old man. He held Madeleine supported in the crook of his left arm and the reins in his right hand.

"Are you literate, Commander?" the old man asked condescendingly from where he squatted in the dirt, his bare ankles tied together by leather thongs.

"In French and Latin," Jean replied, provoked.

"The Temple has improved since I knew it," the old man responded in Latin as if to test Jean. Then in the same tongue he continued, "Who are you to judge me, Centurion? Until you have known the indignities of slavery, you cannot know the baseness of your own soul. We are not all graced with the souls of martyrs." As the man spoke, his grey-blue eyes, one of which was filmed with a cataract, stared up at Jean accusingly.

"Who are you?"

"I am Father Bernard of the Dominican Order. I was with King Louis of France on the Seventh Crusade and fell into the hands of the Egyptians during the retreat from Mansourah."

The shock that went through Jean at the mention of Mansourah set his stallion prancing and Madeleine clung to him, frightened.

"King Louis ransomed all the Christian captives taken at or after Mansourah."

"King Louis thought he did. There were hundreds of prisoners who were never returned."

Jean had heard this from other sources as well, and it was probably true, but he argued nevertheless. "A Dominican priest is hardly a nameless prisoner. Your superiors – if not King Louis himself – would have made enquiries."

The man shrugged. "They may have been told I was dead, that I had died of the fever or the scurvy which took so many thousands of our soldiers' lives."

"Why should the Sultan lie? What did he have to gain?" Jean did not want to believe this man. It was partly the antipathy of the other slaves which had communicated itself to him and it was partly a deep-seated aversion to the Dominicans. They had burned his grandmother at the stake and tortured his mother for two years.

The man shrugged. "What did they have to lose? King Louis paid a lump sum and every captive they did not return made the deal more lucrative."

Though there was no arguing with this logic, still Jean did not want to believe him. There were ample examples of spies and assassins who had gained access to information and Christian leaders by claiming to have converted to Christianity or to be long-lost Christian knights. Shaking his head, Jean declared bluntly and in French, "I do not believe you." Then, addressing the curious crowd of freed slaves, he urged them to disperse before the slave trader changed his mind, suggesting they would be safest with the pilgrims at the Hospice of the Annunciation. "I am taking Sister Madeleine there, if you wish to accompany me."

He swung his stallion to ride past the alleged Dominican, and the old man called out after him in a voice that carried to the ends of the square. "Where did you get De Sonnac's sword, Commander?"

Jean spun about, his stallion scrambling and flinging his head in surprise. The old man stood with his arm outstretched, pointing at Jean's sword.

"What makes you think this is De Sonnac's sword?"

"Only the Master of the Temple ever carried the sword with John the Baptist's finger. It is one of the Temple's most treasured relics, and it was said that no man could be killed by unbelievers so long as he held St John's hand in his! De Sonnac survived the attack on Mansourah only to die three days later – after he had belted that sword around a novice's hips. What became of that novice, Commander?"

"He lived to sire me."

Around them the freed slaves and even Pirenne and Paul were staring in awe and excitement at Jean's sword.

Jean, meanwhile, was trying to work out how this old slave had learned of an otherwise obscure incident which not even the other Templars knew about. Paul knew only that the sword had been a gift from Geoffrey at their departure from Aigues-Mortes. Pirenne knew nothing of the sword – other than the fact that De Beaujeu let Jean retain it.

"I was in King Louis's tent when he knighted your father. The King gave him a pair of state spurs as well – blue enamel with diamond fleurs-de-lys."

Jean could no long pretend that the man was not what he claimed to be. He must have been with King Louis to have been a witness to his father's knighting. And even if the man had indeed converted to Islam and did not deserve his freedom, Jean could not ride away from a man who had been at Mansourah.

Jean looked around for the slave trader and found him hovering nearby. As soon as Jean's glance fell on him, he bowed and smiled. "You wish to buy this man as well, master? A great scholar, a man of many languages and capable of writing. A man worth fifty dinhars—"

"A man who has twice renounced his faith: first when he converted to Islam and just now when he claimed to be a Christian." Jean's voice was harsh and condemnatory and the slave trader responded with genuine shock.

"You claim now to be Christian? You pig!" The trader swung out his leg and kicked the old man on the shins with religious outrage. "Almighty Allah, show this stinking pig your wrath!"

The old man was felled by the trader's kicks. He cowered on the ground and lifted his arms to protect his head. The trader continued to kick and cuff him, raining curses in a flood of fluid Arabic.

After a few seconds, Jean intervened coolly. "Give him to me, and I will turn him over to his Christian masters who will deal with him as he deserves."

"Give? A scholar is a scholar even if he is a piece of Christian shit! Fifty dinhars!"

Jean shrugged and put his spurs to his stallion.

"Come back!" the trader called. "You can have him for thirty dinhars. The pig!" The trader swung his foot and landed an expert and violent kick in the old man's gut. The old Dominican crumpled up, clasping his hands over his belly, retching.

"With a ruined belly he isn't worth ten!" Jean retorted, his sympathy for the old man aroused despite himself.

"Please, Commander." It was Pirenne, suddenly sidling his stallion nearer. "I'll pay the thirty dinhars if I have to beg them on the streets of Acre. Don't leave the priest here."

Jean understood Pirenne. He had killed a Templar knight on request rather than freeing him, and now he wanted to free a man in atonement – not just cut the bonds of men Jean had already freed.

"Then take him to St Joseph's, Pirenne, and keep him under guard. His superiors will decide his fate."

Pirenne thanked him and jumped down, while Jean with a sigh took out his near empty purse and handed over the thirty dinhars.

*

"Commander! Commander! Come quick!" The voice was that of Pirenne, muffled by the heavy wooden door, and it was supported by insistent knocking. Jean dragged himself from his confusing dream and the straw cot of the guest chamber at St Joseph's and stumbled to the door. Pirenne stood in the light of a badly trimmed torch, his face drawn and his eyes wide. "Commander! They came for Father Bernard and tried to remove him!"

"Who came? Who is Father Bernard?"

"The old priest we bought at the slave market yesterday. The Spanish Dominicans we released at the same time came with the

Franciscan. They demanded that we release him to them. They say he belongs under their jurisdiction."

The sleep was gradually clearing from Jean's head, and without comment he turned and groped for his hose and chainmail leggings and then his hauberk. Pirenne propped the torch in the empty metal bracket on the corridor wall and ducked into the chamber. He buckled Jean's garters and spurs while Jean pulled his surcoat over his head. Then, grabbing his sword, Jean indicated they could go. Pirenne took the torch in his hand and led the way down the corridor. Jean followed, buckling on his sword as they went.

They descended a narrow, worn stairwell. The light of the torch cast dancing shadows and obscured as much as lit the uneven footing. The smell of dampness greeted them and the chill of the underworld enclosed them as they wound their way under the surface of the earth. Here, in a windowless chamber beside the catacombs was the prison cell of the Augustinian Order and it was here that Jean had ordered the old priest to be confined. Although he had also given orders for straw, blankets and a hearty meal with wine, he was already regretting his harshness. The damp would be unbearable for an old man.

Pirenne led him down the narrow passage from which the catacombs opened. As they passed, the torch briefly lit up the recesses crammed with bones. Rows of skulls leered in apparent outrage at the intrusion and then sank back into oblivion. At last they reached the only chamber with a door and a barred window.

The Templar sergeant at the door took two steps toward Jean as he appeared, his young face drawn and anxious. "Commander, your orders were not to let the prisoner out under any circumstances. I didn't know that the Dominicans might..."

Jean calmed him with a hand on his shoulder. "You did well, Bethlen." And he pushed past the sergeant to the door, Pirenne and Bethlen on his heels. The door was unlocked and it creaked as he shoved it inwards. He half fell into the room, which was a good six inches lower than the door.

The scene that greeted him made his hair stand on end. They had tied the old man's hands behind his back and then suspended him by them from a iron ring in the ceiling. The ceiling was rather low so the man swayed only a few inches from the ground, but the effect on his wrenched shoulders was no less than if he had been yards higher.

The man moaned and mumbled, sweat dripped from his brow, and around him four dark hooded figures clustered.

Jean overheard the question they put to the man in Latin: "How long did you resist renouncing Christ's divinity?"

"I never..." the old man blubbered.

"You never resisted?" It was the arrogant, piercing voice of the Franciscan. One of the Spanish Dominicans jerked on the rope suspending the prisoner, and the abrupt tightening of the rope provoked a wail of pain.

"Release the prisoner instantly!" Jean shouted in Latin to make sure he would be understood by the Spaniards as well as the Franciscan.

Startled, four heads turned to him, their faces shadowed into obscurity by their hoods. None of them made the slightest move to release their victim.

"This is not your affair, Commander," came the cool voice of the Franciscan. "We are here to investigate the heresy of this Dominican on the authority of the patriarch of Jerusalem!" The Franciscan removed an impressive looking document from the sleeve of his habit and held it in Jean's direction.

The only answer Jean gave was the rasping of his sword as he drew it and then came the cry of the old man as he fell to the floor, the rope suspending him severed cleanly by the honed sword. The squawk of protest from the Spaniards and the roar of outrage from the Franciscan echoed in the cavern, but Jean might as well have been alone for all the notice he took. He dropped his sword back in its scabbard and strode between the dark-robed monks. Kneeling beside the whimpering prisoner, he severed the bonds binding his swollen blue hands with his dagger and massaged the old man's shoulders gently.

"I repeat. You have no right to interfere here. I am authorised by the patriarch of Jerusalem and my father, Charles of Anjou, to investigate crimes against the faith here in Outremer."

"So you *are* a bastard," Jean remarked as he helped the trembling old man to sit up.

"You will regret that remark, Commander," came the furiously calm voice of the Franciscan.

At last Jean deigned to look over at the Franciscan, who was trembling no less than his victim – from fury rather than pain and fear. Again he held out a parchment to Jean, at which Jean glanced cursorily. There was no mistaking the seals of the patriarch of Jerusalem and the king of Naples and Sicily, erstwhile king of Jerusalem.

"The Templars, as you know, are subject to no authority outside the order except His Holiness the Pope."

"This man is not a Templar!" The Franciscan pointed at the prisoner.

"He is in Templar custody."

"By what right do you keep a monk of another religious order in custody?"

"He is in the protective custody of the Temple until he can be turned over to the proper authorities of his own order," Jean replied, increasingly conscious that he was on thin ice.

The Franciscan actually smiled. "But, Commander, these three Dominicans constitute the chapter of the Dominican Order in Nazareth and they have requested my assistance in questioning the prisoner and determining his guilt."

The Spaniards bowed slightly in Jean's direction in confirmation.

Jean felt a chill creep up his spine. Then he swallowed down his fear with the same determination he had strapped on his helm before Tripoli. Helping the old man to his feet, he faced the four inquisitors, apparently unimpressed. "These three men who claim to be Dominicans were also purchased in the slave market. What evidence do you have that these men did not also convert to Islam while enslaved?"

"Slander!" one of the Spaniards called out, while the other two burst into floods of protesting Spanish.

"How dare you question the faith of three devout men who have suffered cruelly for their religion?"

Jean looked at the three men with detachment. Compared to Madeleine, who had hardly been able to walk for weakness, these men looked robust. Nor had he noted whip marks or other indications of abuse upon their naked torsos in the market. He shrugged. "I merely said that we have no evidence but their own testimony to their faith while in captivity. I therefore question their right to sit in judgement of Father Bernard."

"Who better than men like he, who have known the trial of slavery? In any case, as the only representatives of their order, they are entirely justified in seeking the assistance of the Inquisition – which I am authorised to represent."

Jean was not versed in Church law, and was aware that he could not bluff for much longer. He could hardly use force to eject the Franciscan and the three Spaniards, so he opted for a less confrontational course. Starting toward the door where Pirenne and Bethlen stood alertly, he escorted the old man between the Inquisitors. "It is not my intention to interfere with an investigation, Brother Elion, but the Temple does not and will not allow the use of intensified interrogation methods. Tomorrow, in my presence, you may question Father Bernard." He had reached the door and gently shoved the old man forward to precede him. The old man stumbled over the step. The two sergeants had backed toward the door and now stood between Jean and the others. The three Templars slipped one after another through the door and then closed it behind them.

The Inquisitors rushed to the door, shouting in protest and terror. But Jean had not locked it. They spilled out into the hall and found it utterly dark and deserted.

Pirenne had brought a tray with wine, and the old man sat on the edge of the cot holding the goblet in both hands. When he lifted it to drink, his teeth clattered against the lip of the chalice audibly.

"You must regret speaking up in the market yesterday," Jean remarked, watching him with compassion. He leaned against the wall opposite, exhausted and tense. He felt guilty for what had happened and was uneasy about what the morrow would bring. He did not trust Brother Elion – indeed some part of him was afraid of the man. He evidently had powerful connections and Jean had given him every reason to hate him. But especially because the old man had voluntarily identified himself and asked to be restored into Christian hands, it shamed Jean that it was his Christian brothers who had thrown him into a dank dungeon and then tortured him.

The man lowered the silver chalice and gazed at Jean with his half-blind eyes. "You think I would have preferred to remain a slave?"

"Wouldn't you?"

"No." He said this decisively, and the chattering of his teeth stopped abruptly. He set down the chalice. "No. You think I have no pride and no character. To you I am a worm." His tone was accusing and self-righteous, and Jean lifted his head to protest, but the old man cut him off. "You look at me, Commander, and you either despise me or pity me." Jean clamped his mouth shut for this was true: his emotions toward the old man vacillated between exactly these extremes. "But you do not know me and you have not known slavery."

"Then educate me," Jean retorted, noting that he disliked this man no matter how much he pitied him and regretted what had been done to him. He slid down the wall to sit on the floor with his elbows on his knees, his hands hanging loose.

"I am a son of the Brienne family. My father saw that I received the best education. A Dominican friar was my tutor from the age of seven. I entered the Dominican order at the age of fourteen and was ordained at twenty-one. When King Louis asked for ten clerks to accompany him on the crusade, I was recommended by my superiors and joined the king at Aigues-Mortes. My duties for the king were initially trivial – copywork and translations – but I was frequently a witness to discussions between the leading noblemen of the court. De Sonnac was also frequently in attendance upon the king. An impressive man, De Sonnac, with an education quite exceptional for a Templar. Half of you can hardly read and write your own name." He waved his hand in a gesture of dismissive contempt.

Jean felt his dislike for the man harden, but confined himself to a dry retort. "If you count our serving brothers and sergeants certainly – but then I doubt if Dominican lay brothers can read or write either."

"I was speaking of your knights, who for the most part are singularly illiterate monks. You substitute fanaticism for understanding. Even De Sonnac himself, intelligent as he undoubtedly was, lacked the subtlety to distinguish between martyrdom and your damned Templar pride. At Mansourah Robert of Artois needed only to taunt him with cowardice, and the great De Sonnac threw away the lives of his bravest knights! He knew it was pointless to storm the city and he knew what it would cost him. He told the count, 'Templars are strangers to fear. We will accompany you into Mansourah, but none of us will come back.'"

Jean felt the sweat, sticky and stinking, as it broke out on his back. In the silence of the Nazarene night, his ears caught the distant ringing of combat and the fingers of his hands tingled.

Unaware of the effect his words had had upon his listener, Father Bernard continued his narrative. "De Sonnac received a head wound in Mansourah and a novice – it must have been your father – pulled him on to his own horse and carried him out of the city to the safety of our lines. Only one other Templar Knight from the van survived that day."

Jean forced his fingers to close and open, defying the sensation that they were severed.

"But you must know all that from your father. You must know too that what followed was nothing less than the wholesale, sordid collapse of the crusade. The army was seized with scurvy and then dysentery. Soldiers, knights and nobles lay in their own filth and died like flies. The king himself tended to the sick and dying, and we priests went with him or were sent out by him to hear the confessions of the dying and administer the last rites. Nothing was left of the glory or the might that had sailed with King Louis from Aigues-Mortes.

"When the withdrawal began, we were harassed by the Egyptians. The stragglers were picked off by the Bedouins, who received a coin for each Christian scalp they could deliver to the Mamelukes. Sometimes they did not bother to kill their victims before removing the precious scalp. When the surrender finally came, I had dysentery. I remember only vaguely that I was squatting over the latrine when suddenly I was surrounded by mounted Mamelukes with drawn but clean weapons. I tried to run, tripped on my robes and ended face down in the muck. The Mamelukes roared with laughter, and one of the French soldiers remarked listlessly that there was no point trying to flee because the king had been taken captive." The old man paused, apparently lost in thought.

Jean felt the tension easing from his back and, straightening his legs, readjusted his position.

"I was put with the prisoners who were deemed ransomable, but separated from the king and his nobles. They did not know I belonged to the king's household and I was too ill to tell them. Many of the men around me died. I sometimes wished for death, but mostly I was unaware of my surroundings.

"Then one day the guards came and asked if any of us could read and write. I was too ill to wonder why they were asking the question. I made it known that I could do both, and they dragged me out of the compound with expressions of contempt and disgust and delivered me to a very well-dressed man with fine, aquiline features. He raised his eyebrows at the sight of me, enquired via a translator who I was, how old, where I had learned to read and write and the like. I answered his questions to his satisfaction apparently, because I was ordered to go with him. In my weakened condition I could hardly walk, so a black slave was ordered to carry me on his shoulders. Later I was transferred to a camel and I remember nothing more of the journey that followed.

"When I came to myself several days later, I was in a cool, darkened room. My clothes had been removed and my body washed. I lay on a soft mattress with a clean sheet over me, and beside me an turbaned old man was squatting. He held a bowl in his hand and indicated I should drink the hot soup in it. This I did, and within days I was starting to recover. I did not know where I was, nor could I communicate with the old man or the boy who alternated caring for me. At first, I gave this no thought. I assumed I was in some kind of hospital. I imagined the king had intervened on my behalf, or that sheer veneration for an educated man had induced this special treatment." The old man smiled cynically. "It came as a shock to learn that I was a slave. The aquiline man who had put the questions to me on the first day had purchased me from the Mamelukes."

Father Bernard reached for the chalice and drank slowly and thoughtfully. Jean did not prompt him.

At length he continued. "Abu Abdullah al-Ma'arra was a physician and he had taken it into his head to study a number of books on medicine written in Latin. Because he did not think it right for a Muslim to learn Latin, his plan was that a literate Christian slave should be taught Arabic and then translate or expostulate on the texts to him. As soon as I was well enough, he explained his plan via his translator – another Christian slave, incidentally, but one of low birth who was not literate and furthermore a base, greedy, grovelling man whom I learned to detest utterly.

"When I had learned the elements of Arabic, Abu Abdullah put me in the care of one of his more educated Kurdish slaves and slowly we came more and more into contact."

At last Jean was provoked to comment. "And you accepted slavery just like that? No protest? No attempt to escape or establish contact with the king? No rebellious refusal to learn Arabic?"

"See? That is just what I mean about the fanaticism and false pride of the Templars. You think it would have done any good to protest? Where do you think rebellion would have led me? I can tell you: it would have caused Abu Abdullah to sadly sell me to a trader. The more I protested, rebelled or sought to escape the more brutal the treatment would have become and the cruder the master willing to purchase me would have been. An educated and refined man like Abu Abdullah does not believe in brutality against his slaves, so when his slaves became troublesome he simply dispenses with them – and lets someone else do the dirty work of disciplining them. And how should I have established contact with the captive French king? I did not even know where I was. It turned out that I was in Alexandria!

"No, rebellion would have served nothing. As it was, I was well fed, clothed, housed – even offered slave girls for my sexual satisfaction – and I learned Arabic."

"Did you make use of the slave girls?" Jean asked with a sneering edge to his voice. He was thinking of Sister Madeleine.

"Not at first, only after I had converted to Islam."

The calmness with which he said this made the blood rise in Jean's head.

"You condemn me, Centurion," the old man noted harshly. "You condemn me in ignorance! I took to wife a Christian woman, a slave like myself, and she was grateful to me the rest of her days! She was no beauty, and Abu Abdullah had put her in charge of his lame mother. His mother was bedridden and, until her marriage to me, my wife had to bathe her, feed her, change her bedpans, and otherwise be at her beck and call.

"Arab women are raised in golden cages for the purpose of sex and reproduction only. Daughters and wives are never allowed outside the home, never allowed contact or communication with any man outside the family; indeed their husbands only seek them out for a few moments of carnal pleasure – never for conversation or companionship.

"My wife had been married to a merchant before she was taken by pirates and sold into captivity. She had managed her husband's business whenever he travelled. She nearly went mad in the harem where the only topics of conversation were the various positions for copulation and the Koran."

Jean was duly confused by this speech. He could well imagine that marriage to a Christian was better than slavery to an Egyptian, and yet he hardly found it appropriate for a Dominican priest to marry anyone, much less sound proud of it.

"Where was I before you so rudely interrupted?" Father Bernard asked, but when Jean bristled, he smiled faintly and shook his head as if to say he was only joking. Jean allowed himself to be soothed – and then wondered if Bernard had survived his slavery with this tactic of impudence softened by disarming charm. "Yes, as I learned Arabic, I had more and more contact with Abu Abdullah. He was a brilliant man, an excellent physician. I came to admire him greatly. Of course, I translated the books he wanted, but this was not merely a matter of translating word for word. How was I to know Arabic medical terms? No, I had to try to explain what was meant by the texts using the vocabulary I had. In the course of trying to explain, Abu Abdullah would naturally voice his surprise, his approval or shock. Often he dismissed what I told him as nonsense, but just as often he agreed that this was correct, exactly what he too would do with one ailment or another. Occasionally, he would be intrigued with some remedy and resolve to try it himself. Is it any wonder that I became interested in medicine?"

Jean did not respond at first, thinking the question had been rhetorical, but when Bernard asked the question insistently a second time Jean admitted that it was not in the least surprising.

"Then it will not surprise you that I soon asked to be taken with Abu Abdullah, or that I started to function as his assistant. We developed an excellent relationship. Once he noticed that I was gifted" – humility was clearly not one of Bernard's traits – "he gave me ever more responsibility. Soon I was tasked with the follow-up visits to patients where the diagnosis was clear and the cures were already working. Within three years, we had become so good a team that Abu Abdullah took pleasure in asking me for my diagnosis and suggestions for cures. He was proud of me, as any teacher is proud of an apt pupil.

"After four or five years with Abu Abdullah – and I must stress he treated me better than many a prior treats his monks! – I asked to be taught how to read Arabic so I could read Arab medical texts. Suddenly Abu Abdullah grew cold and dismissed me from his presence angrily. I was perplexed and hurt. I did not know how this request could have offended him.

"Our relationship had grown so easy and familiar that I had forgotten I was a slave. Now he reminded me. I was not allowed in his presence, nor was I allowed out of the house. Abruptly I was not the physician's assistant, but a prisoner.

"When at last, some three days later, Abu Abdullah sent for me, he explained that he had been upset because he did not think it right for any man to read Arabic unless he used this knowledge first and foremost to read the Koran. It was an insult to God to read Arabic for the sake of some profane knowledge. If, however, I was prepared to read the Koran first, then he would consider teaching me to read and write in Arabic. What would you have done?"

"There is no harm in reading the Koran - only in accepting it as divine word."

"Ah! You are more clever than I expected."

"My father could read and write in three languages by the time he was twelve," Jean snapped back.

"Your father? That novice who saved De Sonnac at Mansourah? I never would have thought it. And you?"

"I am not his firstborn. He did not teach me Greek. Only French and Latin. And you may have noticed that I've taught myself Arabic."

"It is obvious that your Arabic is self-taught for you mispronounce as many words as you say correctly, but it is to your credit that you have bothered to learn the language at all," he conceded. "Have you read the Koran?"

"No, nor have I any desire to."

"That is a bigoted attitude to a great theology."

"Are you familiar with the works of the Cathars?" Jean countered sharply. He did not see why one should be any more familiar with Islam than with Catharism.

"That is heresy!" Father Bernard was clearly outraged by the comparison Jean was making.

Jean was not a Cathar - even if his mother's inchoate and inarticulate belief in reincarnation had taken a grip on his soul ever since his arrival in Acre. So now he merely shrugged. "So you read the Koran and were converted."

"No, not converted but I was impressed. Deeply impressed. And Abu Abdullah became passionately devoted to converting me. He had a dream this was his greatest mission: far more important than rescuing the bodies of the sick from death was the task of rescuing my soul from hell. How could I insult him by not complying?

"I put up some resistance, of course. I argued with him on theology. After all I had a good education. But I allowed him to convince me and then I humbly converted, to his great joy."

Jean just gazed at the old man, whose expression was one of conscious superiority.

"After that I was allowed access to Arab medical tracts and became a proficient physician. Abu Abdullah sent me in his place if he had no time or was not feeling well – which was increasingly the case. I had my own patients. I was a respected man." The old man was reminiscing, his eyes misty with pleasure at his faded and forgotten glories.

Jean was tired, stiff and increasingly irritable. "But you were still a slave," he reminded the great doctor cruelly.

"Yes." The old man lowered his eyes and squinted at Jean resentfully. "Yes. I was still a slave, but then I did not think it was important. Then it seemed an irrelevant detail, of no more significance than the colour of my hair or the shape of my nose. I married. We had no children for my wife was over forty and barren, but I can't say I missed children much. When my wife died fourteen years later, I considered remarrying a younger woman. As Abu Abdullah allowed me to retain most of the fees I earned, I could even afford the bride price for a slave girl, and I discussed the possibilities with Abu Abdullah, who was delighted at the prospect.

"And then suddenly and without warning Abu Abdullah died. He had suffered for years from periods of dizziness and shortness of breath, but nothing that a couple of days of rest could not cure. Then one day, while rushing to a patient who was said to have appendicitis, he crumpled up, clutching his heart and fell to the bottom of the steps dead." The stillness which followed this was heavy with Father Bernard's shock.

"Of course they sent for me. I did all I could to revive him, but only God – the One and Only God, whatever you wish to call him – could have raised Abu Abdullah from the dead.

"In my grief, I did not realise what this meant for me. I mourned Abu Abdullah sincerely, for he was an intelligent, honest and kind man. A great physician. I was still in shock when suddenly his son arrived.

"Abu Abdullah had four wives, but only one of them had blessed him with sons, and only one of these had survived. This worthless spendthrift had been the scourge of his father's existence for many years. Totally spoiled by the womenfolk and vain beyond all belief, this boy had grown up into a rake of the worst variety. He drank wine – to his father's mortification – and he gambled inveterately, running up huge debts. He was involved in one scandal after another, even breaking into the harem of another Alexandrine scholar and seducing the man's wife. She claimed it was rape, of course, but could not produce the necessary four witnesses to her struggle so was stoned to death, which created bad blood between her family and Abu Abdullah, much to his regret. His father tried to marry his son off, in the hope he would settle down, but the ungrateful pig sent the bride back as being 'not to his taste', which only alienated another important family – especially since it turned out that she was returned violated. It took a great deal of tact and money to mollify the offended relatives of the rejected bride, and after that Abu Abdullah banished his son from Alexandria.

"But, of course, he was still the heir and as soon as his father was dead he returned in triumph. I knew we were in for bad times, but still – because I had never known any master but Abu Abdullah – I could not imagine how bad. This man, now well over forty, fat from overindulgence and wearing the marks of dissipation on his sagging face, was not above insulting his own mother! When she tried to rebuke him for his undisguised crowing about his father's death, he slapped her roughly across the face and called her a slut – his own mother!

"And this" – rage made the old man's pulse flutter and his hands shake even now – "illiterate brute owned me! His first words to me were a threat. He said I was to remember my station or he'd have my eyes out! By my station he meant that I was to go on my knees and bow my head to the floor whenever I addressed him! He put his foot on the back of my head and smashed it to the floor if he felt I was too slow or too proud!

"One day I was in the courtyard, returning from seeing a patient, when he went to mount his horse. Because he was so heavy, the saddle shifted under his weight and the horse staggered. He went into a rage, and sent for the slave who had saddled the horse. When the unfortunate man cowered in terror at his feet, he hauled him up by his hair and stabbed him in the gut. I ran to the man, prepared to do what I could for him, and my master ordered me to leave him alone. He said if I so much as touched him, he would do the same to me. Nor would he let anyone else touch the groom. We had to watch him bleed to death in great agony – all for not having tightened a girth properly. That, Commander, is slavery!"

"Allah Akbar, Father Bernard?"

"Don't mock me, young man!" the Dominican raged. "Where was Christ at Mansourah? Where was he when King Louis surrendered? Would he have helped me against this selfish, arrogant bastard?"

"No, but nor did Allah, it would seem."

"God is great – we do not understand His ways."

"I could say the same for Christ. What happened next? How did you end in the slave market here?" Jean's patience had run out and he needed sleep.

"This man demanded that I turn over all that I earned as a doctor to him! The fruits of my labours, my knowledge, skill, and intelligence, were to go to feed his insatiable need for gambling and wine. I therefore refused to attend any patients."

Jean raised his eyebrows; this seemed a courageous act in the light of the scene he had just described – and courage was not a trait he would have attributed to Father Bernard.

"Abu Abdullah's son had me stripped naked and assigned me to the most demeaning and filthy household tasks – even cleaning the latrines! After several weeks of this he asked which I preferred, continuing in these tasks or performing my duties as a doctor and surrendering to him my earnings. Since the patients always paid my master directly, there was no way I could cheat him. Abu Abdullah had given me that portion of my wages he thought fair. In the beginning it had been only a fraction, because I was still his apprentice and owed all that I earned to him, but in the end it had been the entire fee. But I refused to enrich his son, and he again set me to performing the most menial tasks. But one day, without warning, he had me bound and taken to a slave trader. If I would not earn the physician's fees for him, then he could make more money from me by selling me and using some cheap fool for the menial tasks."

"And that is when I bought you?"

"Oh, no, that was five years ago. But, you see, once a slave is sold – and that means rejected – he is tainted. No one really believes that a sold slave is valuable.

"I was first purchased by a man suffering from stomach ulcers who thought I would cure him instantly. When my initial cures did not have the desired effect he beat me, and finally sold me – this time as a quack. I was not young and strong; buyers had to believe what the trader told them about my great skills – and who believes a slave trader praising his wares? Eventually I was bought by a shopkeeper who needed a scribe, and for three and a half years I lived free of abuse but in squalid conditions – for he was not himself a rich man – in Aqaba. Then one day he sold me to pay for a new mule – which was more important to him! That is how I ended up in the market here."

Dawn was breaking. The silence was pierced by the distant wailing from the nearest minaret. The faithful were being called to prayer. Thirty years of habit made Father Bernard start and almost fling himself upon the floor. Then he remembered where he was and forced himself to remain seated and still.

Jean considered him with a mixture of pity and hostility. How could he know how he would have responded in the priest/physician's shoes? Might he not have converted? Might he not have adapted? How does a proud man maintain his self-respect in slavery, other than with the sly combination of exterior submission and internal contempt?

Stiffly, he pulled himself to his feet, and took the empty goblet from Father Bernard's hand. "You probably know better than I what you can expect from the Inquisition."

The old man looked up at him with weak, watery eyes that blazed with scorn. "Yes – I know. If I deny my heresy, then I must be tortured until I confess. What I confess under torture can be used as evidence against me, and so to condemn me to death for heresy. But to retract any confession made is to be a relapsed heretic who must be burned at the stake. But why should I deny what I did? I will confess my heresy, repent and put myself at the mercy of the Church."

"The mercy of a man like Brother Elion is cold as ice and soft as marble."

"But not arbitrary," Father Bernard insisted. "If I cower and play the penitent abjectly enough, he will be flattered and pleased with his efficiency. Then he will be merciful in order to demonstrate his superiority and his power. But, you see, it is my decision. It is my free will. It is better than slavery."

Jean took a deep breath. It went against his grain to turn this man – or anyone – over to Brother Elion. "Those three Dominicans want only vengeance."

"More than that, they want to be rid of a witness who can testify to their crimes."

"What crimes? Did they convert to Islam?"

"You think that is the worst crime a man can commit?" Bernard countered scornfully. "Those three are true sons of the Church, which did not prevent them from making sketches of every Christian city and castle from Tripoli to Acre!"

The sense of alarm that this information awoke in Jean made his response more sharp than it otherwise would have been. "How do you know that?"

"From their own mouths! They assumed no one else could understand Latin so they used that tongue among themselves. They were incensed that their emir had sold them when the last sketch was complete and they could think of no further valuable information to impart to him. When they first found themselves in the slave caravan, they talked incessantly – each trying to outdo the other in stressing the value of the information he had offered the emir. They could not comprehend how the emir could have then 'betrayed' them. Indeed, he almost executed them because – being an honourable man himself – he hated men who would sell their co-religionists for the sake of life and bread. But then, in a gesture of greater contempt still, he sold them to the slave trader of ill-repute instead."

"Can you ride?" Jean asked abruptly.

"You mean a horse? No, there was no need for that, not even in Abu Abdullah's service."

"A camel?" Jean persisted.

"Oh, yes, I can manage a camel."

"I'll arrange then for your transport to Acre – I will send you with an Arab caravan doing business there. Once there, it is your decision whether you turn yourself over to the authorities of your order or disappear."

*

William de Beaujeu received his visitors in the audience chamber of the Temple at Acre. This cavernous, cross-vaulted room had been built to receive delegations from sultans, popes and emperors – and to impress them all with the wealth and power of the Temple. The ribs of the vaulting were gilt, as were the stars scattered across the azure of the ceiling. The wall frescoes were militant scenes in vivid colours depicting the biblical fall of Jericho, the historical fall of Jerusalem to the crusaders in 1099, and – the most recently completed – the Jewish defence of Masada against the Roman 10th Legion in AD 72-73.

De Beaujeu, entering from a side stair that opened directly on the dais, did not stand on ceremony but hastened down the steps to offer greetings to the solemn visitors. He was dressed not in armour but in the long white habit of the order, with a red cord at the waist and the red cross on his left breast. His once dark hair was now an iron grey, though his trimmed beard was only salted with silver.

"My dear Father Guichard," he addressed the prior of the Dominican Order in Acre and its senior officer in the Holy Land. "To what do I owe this honour?" The tone was friendly, almost jocular, but it was received with cold disapproval.

The hostility between the orders could not be bridged with light words, the prior felt, and in reply he bowed his head stiffly. Then, indicating the tall, gaunt Franciscan with fierce eyes who accompanied him, he announced, "May I introduce Brother Elion, a devout servant of the Church, who has been commissioned by his father, Charles II of Anjou, to investigate charges of heresy here in Outremer." The Franciscan held out a sealed parchment.

De Beaujeu raised his eyebrows in a gesture of restrained disbelief. "Does our beloved friend, King Charles, have reason to suspect that heresy is a significant problem here in his former kingdom of Jerusalem?" As he spoke he took the offered document and seemed to study the seals carefully before unfolding the parchment.

"Is not the fall of Tripoli itself reason to suspect treason, heresy and corruption, Master De Beaujeu?" the Franciscan asked sternly, reprovingly.

De Beaujeu appeared not to overhear the reproach and replied evenly, "No, the fall of Tripoli, like the fall of Antioch, Jerusalem and Edessa before it, needs no more complicated explanation than mathematics. So long as the Sultan's armies outnumber ours a hundred and more to one, we will not be able to defeat him at arms." Then, while scanning the letter, De Beaujeu remarked without lifting his eyes from the text, "You are an illegitimate son of Anjou, I presume. I have met all His Grace's legitimate sons." It was a double blow, not only reminding the friar of his origins but also reminding both visitors that the Temple had long maintained a particularly close relationship with the House of Anjou.

Brother Elion blushed but he answered doggedly. "It is because of the loyalty and friendship you showed my grandfather and father for so many years that I came here expecting support and assistance – not the reverse."

De Beaujeu lifted his eyes from the parchment and studied the angry young friar, whose face was livid with indignation. "I have not denied you assistance, young man. I merely asked if you had cause to suspect that heresy, treason and corruption are rampant in Outremer. You have not answered my question." His tone was mild, but the rebuke was sharp enough even so. Brother Elion burned a darker shade of red, and Father Guichard felt compelled to come to his aid.

"Master De Beaujeu, we have come here with a specific complaint. One of your knights, a commander no less, has interfered with the investigation of a former Dominican friar who converted to Islam. No fewer than three of my brethren testify to the man's heresy, but your commander not only interrupted the interrogation – he used force to physically remove the heretic from the justice of my order and – though he had given his word that the interrogation could be continued the following day – he refused to let either my brethren or Brother Elion see or question the heretic again. Apparently this known heretic is being protected and hidden within the Temple. You must agree that this is a highly irregular, suspicious and provocative act which must raise questions about the faith of the Temple itself."

"Indeed," De Beaujeu agreed readily, the crease of a concerned frown cutting his forehead in two. "I am scandalised. If your accusations are correct, I would have to share your conclusions. But, you must understand, this is the first I have heard of the incident. And I can assure you that no unauthorised person – much less a renegade Dominican – is being harboured here. You are welcome to search the entire compound." He opened his hands in a gesture of disarming openness.

"The incident occurred in Nazareth." Brother Elion took up his own case again. "The heretic might have been given refuge in any of the Templar strongholds throughout the Holy Land. But the commander responsible is here in Acre – that I have already determined. And, as he continues in his rank and duties, it must be assumed that the Temple supports his actions."

"I can hardly punish a man for an incident about which I knew nothing," De Beaujeu countered lightly.

"Is interference with the Inquisition so routine that it is not even reported to you?" Father Guichard enquired bitingly.

"It is, to my knowledge, completely unheard of, Father Guichard. The Inquisition has not been active in Outremer."

"A grave mistake which – with the help of Brother Elion – I mean to rectify!" Father Guichard announced fervently.

De Beaujeu considered the Dominican prior with an unreadable expression, and then remarked reflectively, "Let us hope that your investigations do not lead to dissension which can be exploited by the Turks."

"How can the Inquisition lead to dissension unless heresy is widespread?" Brother Elion countered with a sparkle of smugness in his eyes.

"Because, my dear Brother, the zeal to manifest one's own devotion to the true faith can cause harmful rivalry. Look at the two great militant orders: the Temple and the Hospital have in the past been so obsessed with proving the superiority of their devotion to Christ and a Christian Jerusalem that they have more often competed with one another than cooperated for their common cause. The fierceness of their competition for the honour of being the most Christian of Christ's soldiers led at times to outright clashes between the orders. Don't you think that the activities of the Inquisition here will have similar consequences? The Genoese will try to prove the Pisans are heretics, the Pisans will accuse the Venetians of godlessness and so on and so on. And while we are busy accusing one another of being less pious than ourselves, the Sultan will swallow what is left of Outremer."

"You paint an ominous picture. If you have so little faith in the future of a Christian Holy Land, why do you remain at all?" Brother Elion scoffed.

For the first time a remark seemed to pierce Beaujeu's armour. Hotly, the master retorted, "because I have sworn a vow to die rather than abandon the Holy Land to the Muslims!"

"Wouldn't it be better to convert the Mohammedans than to die in a fight you yourself acknowledge cannot be won?" Brother Elion enquired, with missionary zeal lighting up his entire face.

"That is another topic," Father Guichard intervened hastily, with an annoyed look at his young *protégé*. "We came here to ascertain if the Temple – or merely one of her commanders – is opposed to the Inquisition. Since you assure us you had no knowledge of the incident in Nazareth, I am prepared to accept this was the act of a single knight without the sanction of his superiors. But I expect that the knight will now be accordingly disciplined."

"Indeed. Of that you can rest assured," De Beaujeu agreed readily, even ardently. "If you would be so kind as to identify the offender, you can be certain that he will be disciplined in a most appropriate manner." De Beaujeu was scowling now and his voice was stern.

Brother Elion could not stifle a slight smile as he stated distinctly, "Sir Jean de Preuthune is the offender, Master."

"Sir Jean?" De Beaujeu displayed great astonishment. "A most courageous knight! He rescued the Count of Tripoli when the count was utterly surrounded and outnumbered in his attempt to relieve Tripoli during the siege. His father was knighted by King Louis for his courage at Mansourah."

"No one has questioned De Preuthune's courage, Master De Beaujeu, only his faith!" Brother Elion retorted.

"It is beyond my comprehension how a man who is willing to lay down his own life for the Cross and the Holy Land can be lacking in Christian faith." Beaujeu's voice had taken on a certain hardness which suggested he was less pliant than he had appeared only minutes before.

"You are quite right, my lord. Brother Elion did not mean that Sir Jean's faith itself was in question, merely his respect for the Inquisition and holy orders other than his own. Sir Jean is a haughty man, and as such he does serious damage to the reputation of your order, Master De Beaujeu. You would be well advised to curb his pride before it is no longer manageable."

"You can be assured, I will look into this matter rigorously and without delay," De Beaujeu replied, apparently mollified by Father Guichard's words.

Father Guichard appeared equally mollified and indicated to Brother Elion that they could now depart. The three clerics took a coolly polite leave of one another, and De Beaujeu remained where he was while the two friars turned and started for the door at the far end of the chamber. A breeze, already heated by the oppressive heat outside, swept from the door, and the brown habit of the one friar and the black robe of the other fluttered around them. Their sandalled feet scraped on the turquoise tiles and left behind a trail of sand. Then they passed out into the blazing Palestinian sun of the courtyard beyond, and De Beaujeu sighed.

*

De Beaujeu ordered Jean to report in the intimacy of his own study, a small octagonal room in a tower perched over the sea. The breeze through the open casements was relatively cool and scented by the sea, and the cry of gulls provided a counterpoint to the conversation. Though he at first listened to Jean's narrative with apparent calmness, De Beaujeu became increasingly caustic and sarcastic as the tale proceeded. "And you gave more credence to the excuses of this twofold traitor than the testimony of three Dominican friars?" he scoffed.

"The friars were themselves traitors, trading information about our defences and garrisons for the sake of their lives," Jean contended, sweating nervously under the increasingly hostile interrogation.

"How do you know that? It couldn't be that this Father Bernard told you as much, could it? Even you – God grant me patience – aren't so naive!"

Jean could only answer with embarrassed silence.

"Christ's nails!" De Beaujeu slapped the table top with the flat of his hand. "Were you born yesterday? And Brother Elion? Didn't you know who the Franciscan was? Didn't he identify himself?" he demanded in a harsh, disbelieving voice.

Jean had rarely seen De Beaujeu angry and he was as much disconcerted by this fact as uncomfortable about the confrontation with Brother Elion. "I had been told he had close connections with the House of Anjou, but it wasn't until he was torturing the old man that he informed me Anjou was his father."

"But it was after that when you spirited the heretic away! How could you be so bloody stupid?" De Beaujeu was nearly shouting.

"I don't see why a bastard blood relationship with the House of Anjou gives a man the right to employ torture." Jean mustered a touch of defensive indignation.

"You don't see why a blood relationship with the king of Naples is relevant," De Beaujeu mocked. "That's the kind of stupid, dogmatic answer I would have expected of an unimaginative, half-literate knight like Jacques de Molay. I thought you had more sense!"

Jean could only stand before his master and silently accept the abuse. It wasn't so much the absolute obedience he had vowed on entering the order, but a sense of sincere confusion that inhibited his self-defence. The fact was that he had been uneasy about his decision to free Father Bernard in Nazareth, and now regretted his spontaneous gesture. If he had it to do over again, he would never buy the old man!

Jean had been severely rebuked and criticised in chapter for having spent such huge sums of Templar money to secure the freedom of so many 'worthless' slaves. The Treasurer had suggested that he should not be allowed control of Templar funds until he learned 'more responsibility' – which amounted to depriving him of his command. And De Molay had equated his misuse of funds with the careless loss of Templar property – an offence that could be punished by a year and a day of degradation to sergeant. In the ensuing debate, Jean had enjoyed the support of many of the younger knights, but of the senior officers only Peter de Sevrey had spoken energetically in his defence. Yet Jean did not regret his decision to buy the other slaves and had defiantly proclaimed that he was proud to accept whatever disciplinary action the master decreed for the sake of Sister Madeleine, Marco, Paul's brother and the others. In the end De Beaujeu had left him in his command, but he had not been given escort duty since his return from Nazareth.

The incident with Father Bernard was another matter altogether, one he could not defend with equal self-assurance. Still, he had not expected De Beaujeu to react this violently. De Beaujeu, after all, came from a leading noble family. His paternal grandmother had been sister-in-law to King Philip Augustus. He was not a man Jean would have expected to be awed by a bastard of the count of Anjou – even if the count's father had made himself king of Naples and Sicily and bought the crown of Jerusalem from the rightful heir.

De Beaujeu ran a hand through his curly grey hair and sighed deeply. He shoved back his chair and went to stand by one of the windows. His anger was abating, and when he turned and looked at Jean he saw a young man of intelligence and courage who appeared both bewildered and contrite. He was neither a hothead nor a fool, he was neither irresponsible nor incapable. He was a bright and competent young man who had made a mistake.

'Oh God,' De Beaujeu thought with a silent moan, 'how many mistakes have I made in my life?' Cringing internally, he thought back on all the misjudgements and bad decisions he had made since he had become master of the Temple. He had been the master now for seventeen years, and each of those years had brought a lifetime of wisdom. But all that wisdom could not undo what he had done. The impetuous, overconfident mistakes of his early years had reaped a harvest of mistrust within the Temple and without.

And one of the most serious of his mistakes had been supporting the claims of Charles of Anjou against those of Hugh of Cyprus for the crown of Jerusalem. At the time he had perceived Charles of Anjou, the brother of King Louis, as the Christian monarch most likely to mobilise new enthusiasm for a crusade. By the time he recognised Anjou for the petty, grasping, short-sighted man he was, it was – in all probability – too late. After King Charles's death, De Beaujeu had ceased to support his son Charles II and given the support of the Temple to Hugh's heirs. This had at last given the Cypriot king the united backing of all the military orders, the nobility of Outremer and the citizens of Acre, but it had also earned De Beaujeu and the Temple the enduring enmity of the House of Anjou. It was a price worth paying if it saved the Holy Land. If not, De Beaujeu thought with a sigh, he would not be alive to bear the consequences.

Patiently he tried to explain the situation to Jean. "Whether he's a bastard son or not, a man with powerful connections is always dangerous. The Angevins are especially dangerous. King Charles has by no means forgiven me for supporting King Henry of Cyprus. He thinks I should have sacrificed unity of purpose here in Outremer for the sake of his claims to the throne of Jerusalem. And you have now given him new ammunition to use against us. Your actions have already been perceived as a calculated insult to the Inquisition and the House of Anjou. It is presumed that you were acting on orders or at least have received my sanction for your behaviour."

Jean went slightly pale, thinking that the gravity in the master's expression stemmed entirely from contemplating the consequences of his rash and senseless clash with Brother Elion. Too late he began to guess at the wider implications of what he had done so impulsively. "If I had known..." He left the lame excuse unfinished, and dropped instead on one knee, bowing his bared head to his superior. "Forgive me, my lord, and punish me as is fitting and in such manner as to banish any doubt that you supported my impudent behaviour."

Jean was armoured and armed. The coif of his chainmail hauberk hung down his broad back, obscuring the upper arm of the red cross. The skirts of his white surcoat brushed the tiled floor, and his scabbard scratched them harmlessly. Beaujeu's eyes strayed to the hilt of his sword and with a start he was reminded that it was De Sonnac's sword.

De Sonnac had begged his successors to take Geoffrey de Preuthune into their staff, their confidence, their hearts. He had had a dream, and 'for all that the visions of men with one foot in the grave are worth' he had perceived in Geoffrey de Preuthune a future master of the Temple. But Geoffrey had not returned to the Temple, he had sent his son instead. Didn't the son deserve what would have been given the father?

"Jean, I have half a mind to take you into my staff."

Jean looked up in alarm. The master was entitled to two knights as his personal companions and these 'companions' enjoyed a special status which often opened the way to other positions of power. But the companions served in the master's personal household and had no authority over other knights except in the master's name. In short, it meant that Jean would lose his command, and this seemed a punishment worse than months in a dungeon. But he had just begged for punishment. He could hardly protest for his own sake. "My lord, that is hardly a punishment designed to convince Brother Elion that you disapprove of what I did."

De Beaujeu laughed with abrupt and unexpected heartiness. He had seen the look of horror on Jean's face and he understood the real reason for the objection – which was why the clever argument caught him by surprise. Still grinning, he answered simply, "You're right, but I can hardly treat you like a criminal – lock you in the hermitage until your joints and eyes are ruined or degrade you and set you to mucking out the stables. You have not violated the rule. You are guilty of an error of judgement not a sin!" He paused, reflecting on what he had said and observing the knight on his knee before him. "I think I had best consult with Peter and Etienne on this. Go into the chapel and pray until I send for you."

Jean pulled himself to his feet and with a nod of his head started to withdraw obediently. At the door he abruptly halted. Angrily he tugged at the buckle of his sword belt and, removing it, he offered it to an astonished De Beaujeu. "I don't deserve to wear this, my lord!" Without meeting Beaujeu's eyes he dropped the sword with a clatter, and flung himself out of the room.

*

Jean's knees ached. The *Pater Noster*s ran together meaninglessly. The chapel had grown dim and almost gloomy. Jean stretched himself face down on the floor and reached out his arms, so that he lay in the form of a cross.

"Oh, Christ," he prayed formlessly. "Is there nothing about us which pleases You? Have we offended You so much that the torturers of the Inquisition are dearer to Your heart than the knights who have sworn to defend the sites of your Passion? Are our sins so unforgivable that it is worth the entire kingdom of Jerusalem to see us humbled, defeated, and exterminated? Would you sacrifice the Holy Land to Islam simply to punish us?"

"What sin have you committed, Brother Jean?" The voice came out of the darkness that had enveloped the chapel.

Jean's heart missed a beat and he held his breath, not sure whether the question was rhetorical. The voice, familiar and yet slightly distorted in the echoing of the chapel, was that of the senior Templar chaplain, Father Etienne.

"Well?" the priest prompted invisibly. "You lie like a penitent in the grip of deep remorse. What sin have you committed?"

Jean turned his head just enough so that his words would not be spoken into the floor. "I... I have interfered with the Inquisition," he admitted, assuming that De Beaujeu had consulted with the chaplain, who had come to pass judgement upon him for what he had done in Nazareth.

"You consider that a sin?" came the sceptical – even critical – answer.

Jean considered the question, the inflection and answered honestly. "No."

"Then what sin *have* you committed?" The question was put by a different voice, that of the commander of the kingdom of Jerusalem.

Jean felt the hair on the back of his neck stand on end. Around him and over him breezes danced. The skirts of habits brushed like whispers upon his chainmail and made his skin creep. Candlelight danced in the darkened chapel.

'Christ!' he prayed in inarticulate terror. His father had warned him that the punishments of the Temple could be brutal. De Beaujeu was not vindictive, but De Beaujeu had phases when he was astonishingly weak or indecisive. He let others attack him, sway him, usurp his powers or shame him into doing things he did not really want to do. The commander of the Kingdom of Jerusalem was the treasurer of the Temple; he had been outraged that Jean had spent hundreds of dinhars to buy slaves without the slightest authorisation. The funds issued to commanders on escort duty were very specifically designated for the needs of the escort and pilgrims during the journey. He had, along with De Molay, been the principal critic of Jean, heartily recommending the degradation of Jean. Jean could only too well imagine what he would think of his having spent Templar money to free a heretic! Jean broke out into a sweat.

"None of us is without sins, Brother. What are yours?" It was yet another voice, again familiar although Jean could not place it in his present state of mind.

"I have misused Templar funds." He forced himself to the confession, though his heart protested even as he spoke. How could he have left Sister Madeleine in captivity? It was perverse to think that Templar gold was more sacred than freeing fellow Christians from Muslim captivity! Hadn't the Temple used its money to ransom the poor citizens of Jerusalem from Saladin?

"You consider that a sin?" Again it was the disbelieving voice of Father Etienne.

"What do you want of me?" Jean cried in an eruption of anger, hating them for playing with him like cats with a captured mouse. Why couldn't they just condemn him? He was willing to mouth the words of penitence they expected. Did they expect him to betray his soul as well? "Do you want my submission to your damned authority or do you want the truth?"

"The truth." That – at last – was De Beaujeu himself, and he spoke in his characteristically relaxed manner, as if unaware that Jean felt crucified.

"Then, no!" Jean raised his head slightly so that his words were louder, more emphatic. If they insisted on this, then he would fight them. "No, I do not think it was a sin to buy the freedom of my Christian brothers! I would give all the gold of the Temple if it would free all the Christians held in Muslim hands. If you care more for your hoarded wealth than the fate of Christians, if you think it is more important to play the moneylender in the temple than to lead Christ's children out of Egyptian slavery, then strip my mantle from me. I am ashamed to wear it!" His words echoed in the arches of the chapel and drifted back down to him, making him go rigid with horror at what he had said.

"And what", De Beaujeu put the question calmly, "would you use to buy fodder for our horses and bread for our table? How would you maintain our equipment and our fortresses? How would you pay for the spies at the Sultan's court, who keep us informed of his mood and even his intentions? How would you save the very people you freed from a second captivity?"

The silence in the chapel was brittle. Jean recognised that – again – he had been too preoccupied with his little world to see the larger picture. He now understood that the treasurer might not have been jealously guarding his prerogatives, but sincerely concerned about a shortage of funds. Could the wealthy Temple really be short of money? Jean was reminded with embarrassment of the lecture he had once given a Templar sergeant at Peyroles so long ago in France. Could he judge what it cost to maintain these precious outposts in the Holy Land? Of course he couldn't; only the senior officers could know what the real income and expenses of the vast Templar apparatus were – which was precisely why ordinary knights, sergeants and brothers were expected to obey the instructions of their superiors.

"*Mea culpa*," Jean murmured humbly into the tiles.

"You have misunderstood us," De Beaujeu informed him. "That the policy of the Temple must be more judicious and more balanced than implied in the wholesale repurchase of Christian captives, does not make what you did in Nazareth wrong – much less a sin. How can it be a sin to save a Bride of Christ from a heathen brothel? Not even the purchase of the former Dominican, Bernard, is a sin – even if it was a foolish waste of coin. Would you insist that Sergeant Pirenne did penance for the gesture?"

Jean had not told De Beaujeu that it was Pirenne who had insisted on buying Bernard. He could only have this information from Pirenne himself or from Paul. "Pirenne wanted to save a life in atonement for the one he had taken."

"Is that a sin?" Father Etienne pressed him.

"Christ!" Jean exploded again. "You're the priest. You tell me!"

"We are here to consider your sins, Brother Jean" – this was another voice that he could not place – "not those of Sergeant Pirenne."

Father Etienne added, "Confess to us your sins – not the ones you think we want to hear, but those that weigh upon your conscience."

Jean rebuked himself for his outbursts of defiance. He had vowed obedience. He had chosen the discipline of this harsh order. He closed his eyes and forced himself to surrender to the mercy of the tribunal. He sought an honest answer, stuttering at length somewhat ashamed, "I – I have broken my vow of chastity dozens of times." This could cost him his rank, could mean degradation, a year of menial service, eating from the floor, excluded from the companionship of his fellows.

"With your squire?" came the sharp, shocked question from the commander of the city of Jerusalem. So they knew then about Pierre's inclinations, Jean registered.

"No, with women – mostly whores," Jean told them.

The answer seemed to astonish nevertheless; he could feel glances exchanged over his back.

"Your father never broke his vow of chastity, not even as a novice," De Beaujeu reminded him disapprovingly.

Jean had no reply. He knew De Beaujeu was right, but he was not his father. Then he remembered something else, what his father had told him about Mansourah. "But my father denied the divinity of Christ."

"Yes," De Beaujeu confirmed, though Jean felt the uneasy stirring of others around him, the ghostly habits brushing against his arms and legs.

"Have you doubted the divinity of Christ?" the commander of the kingdom of Jerusalem asked.

Jean clenched his fists in sudden terror. It was as if they had seen into his heart and seen the doubts that festered there. He swallowed, and his forehead ground the tiles as he tried to allow more air into his compressed nose. "Sometimes... I don't understand how Tripoli could have fallen. How He could have allowed Tripoli to be taken? It is, Brother Elion assured me, on account of our sins. But have we sinned more than others? Did Sister Madeleine sin more than her sisters in Poitou and Ireland and Portugal? Why should she pay such a price? Why should we? What sin is so great that it is worth sacrificing all of Outremer to Kalaoun?"

"Brother Elion", De Beaujeu told him with a note of acid irritation in his voice, "is like a child who thinks that every thunderstorm was caused by his misbehaviour!"

"But if it wasn't our sins, then why? Is Allah more powerful than Christ? Is Christ merely a prophet lacking divinity?" The words were out, and Jean held his breath, waiting for the reaction.

"So your father never found the answer to that question," De Beaujeu reflected.

"My father said the Devil won at Mansourah," Jean admitted.

"No." De Beaujeu was suddenly decisive. "The Devil didn't win – the Sultan did. The Sultan beat the armies of the king of France. God does not fight His own battles, He lets us fight them for Him.

"And if we are too foolish to recognise our own weaknesses and limitations then we will lose! It is that simple! It is time you too grew up, Brother Jean, and stopped expecting God to come to your... our assistance. In this world we have only the strength of our own hands, hearts and minds. Miracles happen only in the imagination – and in the heart." With his hand he gently but firmly lifted Jean from the floor.

Jean lifted his head, and found he was surrounded by the officers of the Temple in the east: the master, the seneschal, the marshal, the commanders of the city and the kingdom of Jerusalem, and the chaplain. Only the draper, turcopolier and commander of Acre were absent – because they were sergeants, not entitled to sit in judgement of a knight. Stiff and slightly disoriented, Jean pulled his knees under him and, with Beaujeu's hand under his arm, scrambled to his feet. He looked at the officers in their white robes, their faces only faintly decipherable in the dark of the chapel.

"Brother Jean," De Beaujeu still had him by the elbow. "We have decided that we must make a show of punishing your 'disrespect' toward the Inquisition." His tone was friendly and he sought to break the news gently. "In light of your mother's association with the Cathar heresy, the fact that your grandmother was burned at the stake, and – more suspicious still – your uncle's execution for murdering an Inquisition judge, it is relatively easy to claim that your actions were those of an individual. The order is spared the suspicion."

Jean understood, but he could hardly rejoice at the prospect. He was pale though calm as he let his eyes sweep the faces of the men who had condemned him out of expediency. He was afraid of their judgement and with his eyes he sought their mercy. Father Etienne smiled at him and Peter de Sevrey winked. Jean looked sharply at De Beaujeu.

"Jean, you must be seen to be confined and fasting, but at the end of your sentence you will be restored to all your former duties and honours – and your sword. But I hope you will find the three months valuable in their own right."

And then De Beaujeu gave him the kiss of peace.

Acre

August 1290

Some people later claimed that the massacre was triggered by a Christian shopkeeper who discovered his wife's infidelity with a Muslim neighbour. Others said it was a gambling brawl between newly arrived papal mercenaries and Arab caravan drivers. In the end, it didn't matter how it began.

It started near the marketplace and spread from there. The shouting and screaming, the smashing of crockery and furniture and the clash of weapons penetrated the massive walls of the Temple only faintly, the sounds reduced to harmlessness by their indistinctness. But a serving brother who had been at the market came breathlessly through the gate, announcing that some Italians were rampaging through the town, killing every Arab they could lay their hands on. Within minutes, other citizens were clamouring for protection, and the great alarm bell of the Temple started clanging, to be echoed by the church bells all the way to the Saint Jean d'Acre.

The Templars left whatever they were doing and scrambled to collect arms and armour. De Beaujeu assigned each company a sector of the town, and ordered them to restore order – at any price – and the companies rode out as soon as the bulk of their members were assembled and mounted. There was no time to wait for stragglers and latecomers.

By nightfall the disturbances were extinguished and a couple of hundred papal mercenaries were locked in the city gaol, though there was no telling how many had escaped and lay hidden. Across the city, the keening of the mourners and the wailing of the bereaved competed with the mullahs and the bells. The death-wagons creaked through the streets, and royal troops patrolled the city uneasily. Pickpockets darted from the shadows to rob the uncollected dead, while thieves combed the vandalised houses for valuables overlooked by the bloodthirsty mercenaries. The estimate of the casualties rose by the hour until it reached roughly a thousand.

Jean had just sat down to take his evening meal in silence with the other knights when Master De Beaujeu sent for him and Jacques de Molay. They left their unfinished meal and joined the master and marshal in the courtyard beyond. Here they found their horses were already being led from the stable fully tacked, along with the master's and marshal's stallions.

"Two representatives of the Sultan Kalaoun have just arrived on fully foundered horses. The city council has been convoked to discuss their embassy."

The masters of the Templars, Hospitallers and Teutonic Knights all had seats on the city council. In the past De Beaujeu had often taken De Sevrey with him when he expected the council to discuss military affairs, but the inclusion of Jacques de Molay and Jean was unprecedented. De Beaujeu, however, owed no one an explanation and he obviously did not intend to give one. He stepped down into the ward, collected the reins in his left hand and went to mount his favourite stallion.

"Kalaoun couldn't possibly know about the riots already," De Molay protested, as he too went to mount. "It must be pure coincidence."

"Kalaoun knows exactly what happened – even if he hasn't obtained the names and numbers of the victims yet. And he'll have those by tomorrow at the latest," De Beaujeu retorted as he swung himself into the saddle. De Beaujeu had taken the time to don his finest silk surcoat and cloak over his chainmail. He wore his mail coif over his head with the chin and throat flap closed. The red leather thong binding the coif to his forehead was like a bloody crown covered by neither cervellière or helm. His stallion was a massive white warhorse in black and white trappings that imitated the Baucent.

As Jean went to mount he managed to ask Peter de Sevrey in an undertone what De Beaujeu wanted with him.

"Your friend De Villaret will probably accompany De Villiers. De Beaujeu thought it would be helpful if you also attended." That was plausible. Although Jean and De Villaret had managed to arrange one secret meeting between the two masters, it had failed to bring any tangible results and had not been repeated.

"And De Molay?" Jean asked, lower still.

De Sevrey glanced at the master and De Molay, who were both mounted now and impatiently awaiting the others. "De Molay can be expected to oppose any decision the master takes. William hopes that he can win him over if he participates in the making of the decision."

Then De Sevrey flung himself into the saddle and Jean followed his example, sending his stallion forward even before he took up the off-stirrup.

The city council of Acre was composed of the governor of Acre, the papal legate, the patriarch of Jerusalem, the masters of the Templars, Hospitallers and Teutonic Knights and a representative of each of the city's twenty-seven districts. Correspondingly, the council chamber in the roomy royal palace had been built to accommodate a large number of councillors. But when members were accompanied by numerous advisors, as in Beaujeu's case, even the spacious chamber was soon filled to overflowing. Despite the setting of the sun, the temperature had hardly fallen and the air in the chamber was stifling. De Beaujeu took his place at the table, but the other three Templars stood against the wall. Jean nodded greetings to De Villaret, who had indeed accompanied De Villiers.

At length, the governor concluded that all – or sufficient – councillors were present and he opened the meeting by asking the papal legate to pray for wise counsel. He then informed the council that the Sultan Kalaoun had sent a message which he ordered read aloud by a secretary because he could not bring himself to 'mouth the words the Sultan used'.

The Sultan was – or employed – a skilled master of rhetoric. The message that was read aloud sang and vibrated with outrage, floods of abuse and threats of revenge all poetically phrased in the best Arab tradition. The use of metaphor was brilliantly employed so that, for all the flights of descriptive fancy, the hard vicious core of the message remained unobscured: the city of Acre would turn over all the individuals responsible for the massacre to the Sultan for 'justice' or they would drown in their own blood and the blood of their wives and children.

Jean felt a chill run down his spine as he listened, but more than one of the councillors mocked the message, saying that Kalaoun could threaten all he liked, he could never carry out his threat, while others considered the message an insult that deserved a brusque rebuff. How dare the Sultan interfere in the internal affairs of the free Christian city of Acre? they demanded in a tone of indignation.

"Among other things, because we have a treaty with the Sultan," the governor reminded the citizens uncomfortably. The governor was a practical man. He was a competent administrator and for the most part managed to juggle the diverse interests of such a heterogeneous city well, but this crisis seemed too much for him. He kept rubbing his bloodshot eyes and pulling at his heavy jowls. "A treaty in which the lives and property of all Islamic citizens are expressly guaranteed," he elaborated when he had the attention of the majority. It was clear to Jean that he feared the Sultan's anger not least because he knew it was justified.

"The treaty does not guarantee the lives of the Muslims in Acre – no treaty can do that. Life and death are in the hands of the Almighty. The treaty merely places the Muslims of Acre under the protection of the civil authorities." The papal legate, Monsignor di San Gimignano, was an ambitious Italian prelate who took a lawyer's pleasure in correcting the governor.

"It comes to the same thing," Patriarch Nicholas retorted – as much out of dislike for the papal legate as because this was the simple truth. "The city council is responsible for the lives of the Muslims living in Acre and now over eight hundred of them have been brutally murdered!"

The remaining two hundred casualties were Jews and unfortunate Christians mistaken for Muslims or Jews.

"You missed my point, Your Excellency," Di San Gimignano replied with a patronising smile. "Because no mortal can guarantee lives, our duty of protection is simply to offer the same civic services that we offer all our citizens. But when a crime cannot be prevented then it must be punished. That is our responsibility now: to punish those responsible for this incident."

"Kalaoun demands that we turn them over to him." The master of the Hospitallers, De Villiers, pointed out calmly. De Villiers was a man approaching seventy, with fine aristocratic features grown sharp and almost skull-like with age. His pale blue eyes watered almost constantly and his hands had a tremor. He had been elected, so it was rumoured, as a compromise candidate to the German and French factions within the Hospital, because he was a man all revered equally. But he was very jealous of his dignity – which was why he insisted that the younger De Beaujeu court him and not the reverse.

"Nonsense!" the papal legate retorted dismissively. "He would only kill them all!"

"Better them than the entire population of Acre," the governor suggested, wiping the sweat from his brow with his sleeve.

"That is nothing but Arab hyperbole," Monsignor di San Gimignano scoffed.

"Ah, the great Arab expert Di San Gimignano speaks!" the patriarch sneered. "Tell us, dear Brother, how many years did you study Arabic and the Koran while in Rome? We all know you haven't been in the Holy Land even a year yet!"

The legate flushed. "The study of Arabic and the Koran are activities closely related to heresy, Your Excellency. I would never endanger my soul by intimate or prolonged contact with such filth."

"Ah, but you presume to know the Arab mind and how a Sultan thinks? That, dear Brother, is presumptuous pride. God punishes the over-proud!"

"Your Excellencies. Please!" The governor, used to the perpetual bickering between the competing prelates, intervened in a tired but insistent voice. "The issue is whether we should turn over the prisoners to the Sultan Kalaoun or expose the entire city of Acre to his wrath. Let us not forget what happened at Tripoli."

"Tripoli did not have half the defences Acre has!" the master of the Teutonic Order pointed out with a contemptuous gesture. "Acre has nothing to fear."

"No fortress is invincible and cities even less so," De Beaujeu remarked in his casual way.

The Teutonic master cast De Beaujeu an irritated glance, but it was the papal legate who answered him in a tone of theatrical outrage. "Would you prefer to turn the pope's soldiers over to certain death – possibly torture and mutilation – at the hands of the Sultan than even risk a defence of Acre? Did you not beg for papal reinforcements in every letter you have written for twenty years?"

"Indeed. I have repeatedly pleaded with the Holy Father to send us reinforcements – but not common criminals who sate their bloodlust on peaceful citizens under our protection. Such reinforcements are – as we have learned all too pointedly – a liability. I say we are better without them, and if we can avert the Sultan's anger by sacrificing them, then in the name of God the Merciful, let us do it today rather than tomorrow."

Jean stood up straighter and tried to get a glimpse of De Beaujeu's face. He had rarely heard him speak with so much suppressed passion, and it made him uneasy. De Beaujeu, it seemed, was no less afraid of the Sultan's threat than the governor and the patriarch.

"You would seriously consider handing men in the service of the Holy Father over to the Sultan! Are you Christian?"

"You would risk the lives of all the Christian men, women and children in Acre, Monsignor? Are you human?" De Beaujeu retorted.

"To give in to the Sultan's demands is to show weakness!" the master of the Teutonic Order declared. "If we show weakness, they will only be encouraged to new affronts and new demands. We must show strength instead!"

"We must promise to punish the offenders in our own courts," one of the representatives of the city districts suggested.

"After all the treaty doesn't promise any more." Someone else took up the suggestion.

"You think the Sultan will be content with that?" De Beaujeu asked the room at large. "Not unless we are prepared to kill them all ourselves."

"We cannot afford to kill papal soldiers," came another voice, seconded by a rumble of assent.

"We cannot afford not to. Kalaoun will not be content with anything less. We must either execute those responsible in our own courts or turn them over to the Sultan," De Beaujeu insisted.

"How can you even contemplate killing the very men who came to help us, protect us?" Di San Gimignano protested in shocked outrage, and now a chorus of protest joined in.

Jean glanced at Peter de Sevrey in alarm, and then Jacques de Molay, who seemed to be actually enjoying the master's discomfort.

De Villaret stepped behind his master and spoke into his ear. The old man nodded, and De Villaret called for silence. The old Hospitaller lifted his head and his voice was thin but penetrating. "My dear Master De Beaujeu is right. The Sultan will be content with nothing less than blood – an eye for an eye..."

"Eight hundred Muslim dead," the patriarch took up the theme, "demand eight hundred Christian lives in return. Wouldn't you rather it was the men who committed the crime than your wives and daughters?"

"But there aren't eight hundred papal mercenaries," someone pointed out.

"Then empty the gaols of every criminal we have!" De Beaujeu suggested with a gesture of exasperation.

"This is outrageous!" De Molay protested, though he had no right to speak. "You would send innocent Christians to their deaths?"

Not only De Beaujeu but the other councillors as well gazed at De Molay in stunned silence, but in the next instant the papal legate hastened to exploit the weakness of his opponent and declared triumphantly, "You see! Your own order would not follow your traitorous suggestion!"

De Beaujeu flushed with shame, and De Villiers reached out a fragile old hand in apparent sympathy. He leaned and murmured something in De Beaujeu's ear, while De Villaret looked sharply at Jean, a frown hovering over his face. Jean burned with embarrassment, and seven years of uneasy animosity toward De Molay hardened into hatred. "You traitorous bastard," he whispered in Molay's ear. De Molay stirred uneasily although his face was a rigid mask of self-righteousness.

Around them the debate continued. Some took up De Beaujeu's suggestion that other criminals should be sacrificed to appease Kalaoun. Others pointed out that the Sultan would not be fooled by the trick – he had far too many spies who would report exactly what happened. The patriarch proposed that both the papal mercenaries and other criminals be sacrificed – the exact number of Christians as Muslim victims.

De Beaujeu was too humiliated to raise his voice again, and though De Villiers attempted to advocate the sensible course of action he was a weak speaker. When it came to the vote those in favour of sending an apology and promising quick Christian 'justice' in accordance with the treaty had the majority. Only ten of the thirty-three councillors voted with the patriarch, De Beaujeu, De Villiers and the governor for the surrender of eight hundred criminals to the Sultan.

Before the royal palace, the Templars waited for their horses to be brought. De Beaujeu had neither spoken nor looked his companions in the eye since De Molay's insubordinate outburst in the chamber so they stood together in uncomfortable silence.

It was De Sevrey who finally broke it. Turning to De Molay, he announced, "The lives of every Christian in Acre be on your conscience, Jacques de Molay. May God have mercy on your soul."

Acre
September 1290

The Falcon, a great ship purchased from the Genoese and now the pride of the Templar fleet, manoeuvred alongside the quay to the ribald orders of her captain, Sergeant Roger de Flor. The sergeant, seeing a contingent of Templar knights awaiting him on the quay, could not resist a bit of showmanship. Raised on the dockside of Brindisi, Roger had been more comfortable in the rigging of ships than at home from the time he was eight or nine. He had sailed in Templar ships from the age of fourteen onwards, and commanded his first galley at twenty-two, when he had joined the order as a sergeant. Now, proud of his command and feeling himself under the eye of the master of the Temple, he approached the quay at an acute angle and a risky pace, only to pivot at the last minute and glide into position. The oars of the port side were raised with a flourish, splattering those on the quay with a shower of harbour water.

Roger shouted profanely at his sailors to secure the springs and hawsers. Cursing in a cacophony of languages, the sailors wound the hawsers around the wooden pylons, straining until the veins bulged at their knees and temples, to try and break the momentum of the ship before she smashed into the Venetian galley ahead on the quayside. Ship and hawsers protested, but the Templar ship was brought to a standstill a yard short of the next stern, and then hauled steadily back to be made fast directly before the waiting knights.

Grinning, Roger de Flor sprang from the poop on to the quay and came to bow before his superiors. He was slightly disappointed that the master was not among those on the quay, but he recognised the subtle insignia of two commanders and bowed deeply. "Roger de Flor, captain of *The Falcon*, at your service, Commanders." Then standing upright, his eyes shifted hastily from one man to the other, trying to decide which of the two was the more important.

The elder commander wore a traditional but unfashionable untrimmed beard and his expression was grim and disapproving. The younger commander, who stood somewhat apart from the other knights, had a decidedly more pleasant face and he considered Roger with a touch of amusement. The red cord lacing his mantle at his throat was twisted with black and white threads, indicating that he was the personal companion of the master.

It was the elder of the commanders who spoke sharply. "As soon as you have offloaded your cargo, you are to deliver me and my companions to Clontarf," De Molay informed the captain, indicating his squire, Deacon de Fleury and two sergeants. "We will go aboard at once. Send slaves to collect our baggage." A half-dozen iron-reinforced, locked chests waited beside De Molay.

"It will take us at least a day and a half to offload, Commander," Roger de Flor countered, unimpressed by De Molay's tone. "I have a cargo of hay, grain and vegetables from Apulia as well as twenty-six horses and these recruits there." He gestured almost deprecatingly to the Templars clustered along the poop rail of the ship. "You will be much more comfortable in the Temple", he said as he gestured vaguely toward the towers of the Temple looming behind the warehouses, "than aboard ship."

"That is for me to decide," De Molay told him. "You have your orders." De Molay started toward the waist of the ship, where the gangway was being prepared. Besides De Fleury and the others who would be travelling with him, he was accompanied by Fulk van der Burg and several other knights who had come to see him off.

"The cabins must be cleaned and prepared, Commander," Roger de Flor pointed out, calling after his turned back.

"Then see to it, Sergeant," De Molay flung over his shoulder without stopping.

The sergeant-captain cast daggers with his eyes in De Molay's back and snarled curses under his breath.

"He is being sent to Ireland against his wishes." The other commander moved to stand beside the shipmaster and explained in a low voice.

"Whoever longs for Clontarf?" the Italian retorted. The main Templar house in Ireland was a primitive backwater compared to

Roger's own Brindisi. "Especially at this time of year? Do you know the kind of weather we can expect in Biscay and the Irish Sea?" The question was rhetorical.

"Master De Beaujeu thought that if any master would be willing to cross Biscay in October, that you were he, but if—"

"I didn't say I wouldn't brave Biscay!" The Italian took the bait angrily.

Jean nodded, satisfied, and his gaze shifted to the gangway, where De Molay was charging aboard ship, trailed by his well-wishers, without giving the arriving Templars a chance to disembark first.

Jean watched him depart for the West with distinct unease. He remembered too vividly how the novices, knights and servants trapped in the mundane life of the provincial houses idolised any knight from Outremer. De Molay, with his long beard and weathered face, would seem like a living legend. He had been in the Holy Land nearly twenty years now, and he had been a brave knight. He carried his share of wounds and glory with him so his opinions would be endowed with weight far in excess of their actual value in the eyes of the admiring provincials. In the absence of others with firsthand knowledge to contradict him, Molay's voice would he louder in the West than ever it could be in Acre.

If the Sultan's threats led to new defeats, De Molay would be in a position to attribute them to the imperfect – not to say weak – leadership of De Beaujeu. He could condemn Beaujeu's subtlety and leniency as the source of all failure, and in the eyes of the simple lay brothers and naive younger knights he would seem like a fiery reformer cast out by a corrupt or at least degenerate leadership. It would be easy to present himself as the incarnation of the ideal of the order – the devout, solemn, simple but brave knight. It would be equally easy to collect a following anxious to see De Molay raised to a position of power within the order. There would be pressure to offer him the first vacancy among the senior officers, and, with full-scale war now threatening, vacancies were all too likely.

Who in the West would recognise that the qualities De Molay had were not enough for the difficult task of retaining a Christian foothold in the Holy Land? The provincial masters would realise this certainly, for they were experienced men with service in the Holy Land, men who knew De Beaujeu well. But the younger men – even men like Bourgneuf, who had spent their lives administering Templar houses –

would easily be impressed by De Molay's self-assurance and conviction. Jean sighed, aware that there was nothing he or anyone else could do.

The disembarking knights had managed the perilous crossing of the gangway on their unsteady legs, and stood about looking somewhat bewildered. Jean hastened forward to welcome them, counting as he advanced: there were eighteen knights and roughly three score sergeants. By the fairness of their hair and skin, burned and peeling or littered with freckles, he guessed that they were English or Irish.

"Welcome to Acre, brothers," Jean addressed them collectively.

A tall, barrel-chested man with an abundant light brown beard at once turned to him and held out his hand. "William de la More," he introduced himself. "From the commandery at Sandford. We heard you needed some help out here." His tone was bluff and a gleam of amusement lit his green eyes. "So I've brought you the fifteen best English knights and forty-eight sergeants who can handle a longbow – a weapon I'll wager you've never even seen before!" He indicated the English sergeants with evident pride.

"Welcome to Acre," Jean repeated this time in English.

"We're no' all English!" a tall, red-haired knight snarled under a scowling brow. "Duncan Graham of the commandery at Balantrodoch." The Scotsman was in his early twenties, and he might have been attractive were it not for his intensity and his frown.

Jean felt an instant antipathy toward the man, which he consciously repressed as he forced himself to welcome the Scotsman graciously – in French. He added with a touch of rebuke, "Here in Outremer we are Christians – and Templars – not English, Scots or Provençal."

"Tell the bloody English that!" Sir Duncan snapped back. "I'll no' have them treating us like a poor relations or vassals!"

The Temple had only seven provinces: France, England, Poitou, Aragon, Portugal, Apulia and Hungary. The Templar houses in Scotland – as with those in Ireland – were subject to the authority of the provincial master of England. Of course, that did not imply that an English knight was automatically superior to a Scottish one.

Jean glanced at De la More, who raised one corner of his mouth and shrugged slightly as he remarked in a fluent Latin, "The dignity of youth is oversensitive because it is so fragile."

Jean laughed without thinking and then cast a guilty glance at the Scotsman. Duncan Graham was glowering at him furiously.

"Brother Duncan does not speak Latin," De la More informed Jean, "but I'm sure that fact in no way impedes his knightly skills – certainly he proved the best sailor of us all." It was a sincere effort to soothe tempers and was delivered in French, but Graham was not prepared to be appeased.

"I've no need of your patronising!" he retorted.

De la More shrugged, and the second Scottish knight murmured something to Graham in an apparent effort to calm him. De la More changed the subject, addressing Jean. "I carry a letter from King Edward of England—"

"May God curse his putrid soul!"

This provoked a growl of protest from more than one of the English knights and the English sergeants made threatening gestures toward the Scotsmen, who responded belligerently. For a moment, Jean thought the two contingents of arrivals were about to come to blows with one another. De la More, however, sharply called his men to order, and the second Scotsman was hissing in Graham's ear to hold his tongue.

"Brothers! If you would rather fight each other than the Turks, then I beg you to reboard at once!" Jean pointed toward *The Falcon*. In the embarrassed silence that followed, Jean let his glance sweep slowly across the pale faces – some eager, some sullen, some shamefaced, and some amused. He sighed inwardly, and then turned again to William de la More. "If you would accompany me, Brother William, I will escort you to Master De Beaujeu." Then, remembering himself, he added "Jean de Preuthune, companion to the master."

*

De Beaujeu had pressed the post of 'companion' upon Jean in the aftermath of the disastrous city council meeting following the massacre. Nothing could have induced Jean to disappoint De Beaujeu at that point in time, even though it cost him his command. It came as some consolation that immediately thereafter all pilgrimages had been halted and the opportunity to exercise command correspondingly curtailed. There was even a certain compensation in the duties of companion because for the first time Jean was given insight into the decisions taken by the senior officers and allowed access to information that was otherwise a closely guarded secret.

When he brought William de la More into the master's study to deliver the letter from Edward of England, Jean recognised the seal of the letter already opened upon the master's desk: that of Emir al-Fakhri, De Beaujeu's friend and spy at Sultan Kalaoun's court.

De Beaujeu looked older than he had a month earlier. There were dark smudges and puffy bags under his eyes and his skin seemed to sag at the jowls. Even his beard seemed greyer than before. Yet his eyes lit up at the sight of De la More and he smiled broadly at the Englishman. "Brother William de la More, isn't it? We met during my last trip to England."

"My lord!" De la More went down on one knee and bowed his head before the master in a gesture that was particularly moving from such a burly, self-confident man. "I'm amazed you can remember me!" he declared, pulling himself up again.

"I never forget a man who can unhorse me!" De Beaujeu retorted easily. "My ass ached for weeks after our little exercise in the tiltyard!" he laughed.

De la More smiled, but then hastened to change the subject. "I've brought a letter from King Edward."

"And when is he arriving with a crusading army?" De Beaujeu joked, holding out his hand for the letter.

De la More blushed. "My lord, King Edward hasn't forgotten his crusading vows – of that I can assure you. He is sincerely concerned about the fate of the Holy Land but you must understand that—"

"I know, I know. There are always more pressing problems at home – in Wales, in Ireland, in Gascony or Scotland." De Beaujeu ended the sentence for de la De la More. He had become resigned to this state of affairs. He was, after all, a realist. "With the Scottish throne so conveniently vacant and an actual invitation to intervene, what Plantagenet could resist interfering?" De Beaujeu continued with an attempt at levity which partly succeeded as he laid the letter, unopened, on his desk. "Have you come alone, Brother William?"

"No, we are fifteen knights and forty-eight sergeants – including the two Scots knights and ten sergeants who joined us at La Rochelle."

De Beaujeu nodded, satisfied. "And you have just disembarked. Jean," he turned to his companion, "escort Brother William to Thibald so that they can be assigned quarters and horses, then return to me here. Did De Molay embark, incidentally?" he added with poorly disguised tension as Jean went to leave.

"Yes, he went aboard at once."

"Who was with him?"

"Fulk van der Burg, Father Hubért, Fabian de l'Haye."

"And your friend Brother Elion?"

Jean started. "No. Not that I saw..."

"That's good," De Beaujeu remarked and then nodded to indicate that Jean could leave.

*

Alone together, De Beaujeu showed Jean Emir al-Fakhri's letter. Jean could not read Arabic, but De Beaujeu summarised: the Sultan had agreed to a desperate plea from De Beaujeu and was willing to spare the city of Acre from 'certain destruction' at the price of one Venetian gold sequin (the smallest Venetian coin) for each Christian in Acre.

"Do you believe him?" Jean asked, somewhat incredulous.

"Emir al-Fakhri? I would stake my life upon his word."

"And the Sultan's?" Jean persisted.

"Never. You are quite right: Emir al-Fakhri is reporting accurately the Sultan's stated response to my envoy – but only God knows if the Sultan means what he says. I think..." He paused and reflected, and then concluded with conviction, "I think that he would allow himself to be bought off until the end of the truce – that is, after all, only a little more than two years."

"It's a high price for two years," Jean remarked, calculating roughly in his head.

"But maybe Edward of England will have swallowed Scotland by then and be ready to bring his victorious army east." De Beaujeu shrugged as he spoke, to indicate that he didn't really believe this himself. "Or maybe the Mongols will be harassing Kalaoun's rear."

"I thought miracles only happened in our hearts."

"And imagination!" De Beaujeu rejoined, with a weary smile of self-ridicule.

*

Somehow the news had spread that the master of the Temple had received an envoy from the Sultan Kalaoun and crowds had collected before the royal palace, where the council had again been summoned. It was a mixed crowd of anxious citizens, idle sailors, beggars and thieves. Jean thought he caught sight of Rachel's father among a knot of Jews huddled together on the edge of the crowd. And there were a number of nuns clustered beside the enclosed litters of the wealthy Italian women whose husbands attended the council as district representatives.

A ripple of excitement went through the crowd when De Beaujeu arrived on his white stallion. As before, he had dressed in his best armour and wore his coif over his head and fastened shut at the throat. Jean and Peter de Sevrey, who flanked him, had had time to dress accordingly, and they had brought a small escort of six knights, including William de la More. The crowd parted for the Templars, who dismounted and tethered their horses beside those wearing the red trappings of the Hospital.

"Commander!" One of the nuns had left the little group and caught Jean by the arm.

"Sister?" He turned to her politely but impatiently as De Beaujeu and De Sevrey started up the steps to the palace, leaving the escort with the horses.

"You don't recognise me," the nun stated in the face of Jean's neutral response.

Jean tried to concentrate on the nun, but her pale, thin face dominated by wide-set blue eyes and framed by the pristine white wimple of her habit was unfamiliar to him.

"You purchased me in the slave market at Nazareth."

He started violently. "Sister Madeleine?" He could hardly believe it. "You're still here?" His astonishment and alarm were undisguised. He had assumed that she had sailed for home months ago.

She nodded. "Commander, please tell me the truth. Is there any chance that Acre will surrender to the Sultan?"

"Not without a fight. But if the council will agree to the Sultan's price, we might get an extension of the truce."

"But the Sultan doesn't respect truces," Sister Madeleine reminded him, a look of desperation sharpening the lines of her face; now Jean could see traces of the slave girl he had bought in the sunken, pleading eyes.

"The Sultan has never broken a treaty with the Temple," he tried to assure her, aware that the other nuns and citizens were pressing close to hear his words. He dared not say in public what he would have told her privately: to get out of Acre at the earliest opportunity. "Please forgive me, Sister. I must attend the master."

She released his arm with a nod, but as Jean hastened up the steps of the palace he could feel her eyes boring into his back.

As before, the council chamber was crowded and stiflingly hot. Here there was little willingness to make way for a tardy Templar, and Jean had to push and elbow his way to a place near De Beaujeu and De Sevrey. De Beaujeu was seated between De Villiers and the grand master of the Teutonic Knights. Jean greeted De Villaret, who stood behind De Villiers's chair, with a nod.

The governor called for order, and the murmur of voices died down.

De Beaujeu rose to his feet. Jean knew that he was nervous no matter how well he was able to disguise it from the others. "My lords, honoured citizens. I have received a message from Sultan Kalaoun. The Sultan is prepared to spare the city of Acre in exchange for one Venetian sequin per Christian in Acre. This offer deserves careful consideration. To reject it is to burn our last bridge. The Sultan refuses to negotiate further. This is a final offer – and one which does not even cost us Christian blood." De Beaujeu was at pains to point out the advantages of the proposal.

"A Venetian gold sequin *per capita* is a bloody fortune!" one of the Genoese councillors protested nevertheless.

"But payable," De Beaujeu countered firmly.

"Then let the Temple pay!" someone shouted from the back of the crowd. It was impossible to tell who had spoken. De Beaujeu did not deign to reply.

"It is a ridiculous sum to pay to prevent something that isn't going to happen anyway," the grand master of the Teutonic Knights declared gruffly. "Kalaoun can't take Acre!"

"What makes you think that?" De Beaujeu demanded irritably.

"It took two years to take Acre a hundred years ago, and since then the walls and towers have been greatly reinforced. We have control of the sea and Kalaoun doesn't even have siege engines."

"But he's building them," De Beaujeu countered.

"How do you know that?"

"I have spies."

"Well, even if he does," the German dismissed them with his tone and an impatient gesture of his hand, "I say Acre cannot be taken except by treachery or cowardice. It couldn't be that you, my dear Master De Beaujeu, have grown so fond of intrigue that you have lost the stomach to fight?"

De Beaujeu sprang to his feet. "How dare you!"

Jean broke out into a sweat. 'Christ,' he thought, 'it is Mansourah all over again.' Sense was being called cowardice and the Templars, who surely had no need to prove their courage, would prefer to die than let even a breath of stigma linger upon their reputation.

But before the German could reply, the papal legate enquired of De Beaujeu in a clinical tone, "Why did the Sultan put this offer to you and not to the Council of Acre?"

"Because I wrote to him," De Beaujeu replied equally coolly, as he reseated himself, torn between gratitude for the intercession, which had prevented an unnecessary confrontation with the master of the Teutonic Knights, and resentment at the question itself.

"Directly? Without consulting us?" The legate's question released a new flood of outrage.

"Yes." De Beaujeu was breathing heavily and his hands were sweating. Nothing angered him so much as petty wrangling over issues of competence, but he was at pains not to let himself be provoked again. "The Temple is subject to no secular power, not even that of kings and emperors. There was no reason why I should not correspond directly with the Sultan."

"What did you tell the Sultan?"

"That we want peace." Beaujeu's tone could have been called haughty. He was angry that they would discuss his actions and not the content of the message.

"Why buy what we already have?" one of the Pisan representatives asked sullenly.

"Are you mad? The Sultan has called up his army from Egypt – even now it is being mustered!"

"How do you know that?"

"I have spies," De Beaujeu replied for a second time.

"Spies or ties?" someone quipped.

"Whose interests do you serve? Ours or the Sultan's?"

It was one insult too many. De Beaujeu was trembling visibly. "If I served the Sultan's interests I wouldn't be here!" De Beaujeu shouted, his voice hoarse with emotion.

"The Temple always serves its own interests!" one of the Genoese representatives scoffed.

"As does Genoa!" a Pisan retorted angrily.

The patriarch was demanding the floor and the governor rapped the table with his gavel for order. The patriarch rose to his feet. "This, of all times, is not the moment for recrimination and suspicion. The noble William de Beaujeu has brought us an honest proposal, one which—"

They would not let the patriarch finish.

"Honest? How much will the Temple charge for the transaction? What percent of our gold will go into Templar coffers?"

"Treason!" someone called. "It is treason to conduct secret negotiations with the Sultan without our permission."

De Beaujeu shoved back his chair and started out of the chamber without another word, followed by shouts of, "Coward!"

"Wait!" De Villaret sprang after him, catching Jean by the arm as he followed the master. "Stop him! This is our only hope!"

"Then say so!" Jean snapped back furiously with an angry look at the master of the Hospital who sat hunched in his chair, a picture of misery, with tears running from his pale, weak eyes.

"Wait!" De Villaret shouted in his commanding voice. "This is madness! Master De Beaujeu has found a way to spare your lives and you can think of nothing better than to insult him!"

"It's not our lives he is concerned about but our gold!"

The mood of the chamber had communicated itself to the crowd outside. The shouts of traitor and coward had escaped through the open windows, and the ruder elements were quick to take up the cry. There were, among the crowd, papal mercenaries who had heard that De Beaujeu would have sacrificed them. Now they had their revenge. "Traitor! Traitor! Death to the traitor!" they urged.

Bewildered, William de la More met the three Templars emerging from the palace. "What is this?" he demanded.

De Beaujeu shook his head and reached for his stallion's reins.

"It is heresy to maintain secret correspondence with the Musselmen!" a voice called out, and Jean felt a chill run down his spine even as he sweated under gambeson and chainmail in the Palestinian sun. It was Brother Elion. He had apparently been in the council chamber for he called from the palace steps.

Marshal de Sevrey took quick measure of the crowd now pressing forward against the palace steps. The litters of the councillors' wives were already in flight, the nuns scurrying beside them. The Jews were nowhere to be seen and honest tradesmen were removing themselves discreetly. What remained was a bellicose crowd of resentful mercenaries, rowdy sailors and a collection of rabble – including not a few Muslim youths clearly enjoying the discomfort of the Templars.

"Mount!" De Sevrey ordered sharply, and the six knights of the escort sprang to obey, De la More leaving his question unspoken on his lips.

Jean too shoved his toe into his stirrup and swung himself into the saddle as the stallion turned to go after his fellows instinctively. As his seat touched the saddle he saw something flash in the sun, and beside him Beaujeu's stallion squealed and flung himself sideways into Jean's thigh. His eyes were rolling back and exposing the whites. Blood stained his chest in a gush. The handle of a dagger glittered in the sun.

De la More and De Sevrey drew their swords simultaneously and spurred their horses forward into the crowd. Jean and the other knights were only a fraction slower, closing around De Beaujeu with their swords glinting in the sun. De Beaujeu did not take his sword from the scabbard, but urged his wounded stallion forward grimly. The noble animal ignored the wound and responded to the commands of his rider, though the blood streamed from his chest with each stride and sweat soaked him from ears to hock. The crowd gave way before the compact body of armoured knights and their powerful, well-shod stallions. Only the shouted insults, ridicule and laughter followed them as they clattered out of the square before the palace.

They were greeted by shouts of alarm when they cantered through the main gate into the ward of the Temple. Beaujeu's stallion was stumbling, and no sooner had he gained the ward than he sank on to his knees with a whimper. De Beaujeu stepped free of the stallion as his haunches crumbled and the horse lay down, heaving and pawing in a confusion of pain and exhaustion. With his own hands, De Beaujeu removed the dagger which had been meant for him and with his best cloak he tried to staunch the haemorrhaging.

Around him his knights clustered. Those who had not been with him asked what had happened, and in whispered undertones they were briefly informed. The sergeant-veterinary surgeon shoved his way through the crowd. The word 'assassin' was passing through the ranks of the Templars.

"If it had been an assassin," De Beaujeu lifted his eyes from the stallion and swept the faces of his shocked knights, "this would be my blood." He held up his blood-soaked hands, the ring of office coated and obscured by the vivid red liquid.

Gaudin had made his way through the crowd and now took the dagger from De Beaujeu, studying it professionally. "It is a Damascene dagger – the kind you can buy at any bazaar from Cairo to Aleppo for two dihnar."

"A thief's dagger," De Sevrey agreed. "Easily concealed until it is useful."

"What common thief attempts to kill the master of the Templars?" the seneschal enquired sharply. "This was no thrust in a dark alley with a hand reaching for your purse! It was a public attempt to kill you at the very moment when you have found a means to appease the Sultan. The man who threw that dagger wants war!"

"Or wants another man to be master of the Temple," De Beaujeu suggested under his breath, so only Jean heard him.

From the stables, Ian MacDonald had brought the donkey who shared a stall with Beaujeu's stallion. At the scent of his friend, the stallion lifted his head from the pavement and let out a piercing and pain-filled whinny. The donkey brayed in response and stretched out his neck to lick his friend on the withers. The exchange between the two four-legged friends distracted the bulk of the Templars for a moment, and Jean exploited the situation to ask De Beaujeu intently, "What do you mean? Who wants another master of the Temple?"

De Beaujeu shook his head. "It was just an idle thought. You saw the crowd. It could well have been one of the Sultan's men, or merely a fanatical Muslim. More likely, however, it was one of the papal mercenaries taking revenge upon me for even suggesting that we turn them over to the Sultan."

"A worse collection of thieves, thugs and pickpockets I've never seen," De la More concurred in his booming voice.

"And the worst of it," De Beaujeu reflected sadly, "is knowing that we are going to give our lives for the likes of them."

Acre
April 1291

The Sultan's army enclosed Acre like a human sea that stretched unbroken from the foot of the walls to the foot of the bluffs beyond the plain. The colourful tents of the emirs were sprinkled amidst the masses of troops and horses that writhed with constant activity like ants around their nest. More ominous than the silk tents fluttering with gold-stitched banners were the mangonels and catapults that loomed above horse and human – the siege engines the Sultan wasn't supposed to have.

Now that they could no longer deny it, the citizens of Acre outdid themselves and one another in guessing at the numbers and power of the forces gathered against them. Sixty thousand horsemen and two hundred thousand foot, they said, with five hundred siege engines and thousands of engineers to undermine the mighty walls of Acre. Sultan Kalaoun had died during the winter and it was his son Khalil who led this formidable force, and when he rode through his army the troops shouted themselves hoarse as they flung themselves down before him in homage – as if the victory were already won.

No sooner had the first missiles from the siege engines begun to rain upon the roofs of the city – shattering tiles and splattering Greek fire – than the Genoese packed their ships with all they could carry and sailed away. The Pisans and Venetians, however, remained. The ships which they sent to Cyprus, loaded with women, children and the disabled, returned carrying Cypriot troops dispatched by King Henry under his experienced brother Amalric. Counting every able-bodied man willing to stay and fight, Acre had some twenty thousand defenders – nine hundred of them knights.

The walls of the city, with their twelve towers, were divided into sectors. The Venetians, Pisans and Commune of Acre with their citizen militia of untrained troops were given the strongest and shortest section of the double walls running north–south on the eastward side of the city and anchored in the south on the harbour. Prince Amalric, as commander and representative of the king, took for himself the vulnerable angle where the wall turned sharply west. Here, in a cluster of towers named for their builders – King Henry, King Hugh, King Edward of England, the Countess of Blois – the Cypriot knights and troops replaced the garrison. The Teutonic knights reinforced the royal forces. The Hospitallers took the next long stretch of wall, and the Templars the last northern salient ending on the Mediterranean shore. Volunteers from the West were scattered throughout the lines, wherever they could best communicate with the other defenders.

As in every other siege of their two hundred year history, the Templars implemented a duty roster for manning the walls. This ensured that both knights and sergeants were regularly relieved, had time to rest and eat, and that there was always a reserve ready to respond instantly to an assault. As long as the Muslims confined themselves to the tedious business of a siege, the strain was not excessive. Unlike most sieges, after all, there was no danger of running low on supplies. There was no sea blockade and Christian ships moved freely in and out of the harbour. The Venetians had even built a catapult that could be mounted on a barge, and bombarded the Sultan's army from the sea. The amount of damage it did was insignificant, but the catapult made a major contribution to morale.

The situation was not, therefore, entirely hopeless. True, the Sultan could wear down the garrison in a long war of attrition lasting years. Or, if he were inclined, he could force a decision earlier by undermining the towers, then setting fire to the wooden supports of the mines, causing the towers to collapse; after that the Sultan's hordes of troops would simply overwhelm the defenders. But as long as the sea was in Christian hands, it was possible that effective relief would arrive in time to prevent either end. Hadn't the legendary Richard the Lionheart arrived from the West to seize Acre from Saladin almost exactly one hundred years ago? Could not his great-nephew, the merciless but strategically gifted Edward of England, play the role of rescuer now? Edward had been in the Holy Land once already. He had sworn to return. Wales was subdued, and Scotland... What was that barbarous, icy wasteland compared to this strategic seaport at the threshold to Christ's homeland? The arrival of a contingent of English knights under the command of Otto de

Grandson, a knight high in Edward's favour, strongly reinforced this hope.

The bombardment began on April 6 and from that date it continued day and night without interruption. The crews of the ninety-two giant catapults could eat, rest and sleep at leisure, without causing an overall halt to operations. One or another of the siege engines was always in action – except at dawn and dusk when the cry to prayer wailed through the enemy camp and all attackers bowed to God.

More demoralising than the great engines, which concentrated their fire upon the walls and towers, trying to crack and weaken the masonry, was the Greek fire, flung over the walls by the mangonels. Many more buildings were lost to fire than to battering, and buildings that had been gutted by fire soon succumbed to the pounding of the solid missiles. But it was when Greek fire landed directly upon something living that it took the greatest toll. The tar-like substance stuck like glue to the victim and could be extinguished neither by water nor smothering. Any material, even leather, ignited when it came in contact with the burning substance. Most victims merely spread the flames from one part of their body to the next as they desperately attempted to put out the flames.

Just over a week after the start of the siege, a lucky Muslim battery captain delivered his load of Greek fire over the double walls and through the arched doorway into one of the public baths. The pottery container shattered in the small drying room, splattering dozens of men with the flaming substance and setting aflame their clothes, towels and even the wooden benches. In panic, the victims rolled about on the tiled floors or rushed back into the baths to fling themselves into the water. Both were to no avail. By the time help arrived in the form of citizens with the presence of mind to collect sand from the street and fling this at the victims, most of the men had received burns over too much of the body to recover. Nine Templars were among the wounded.

Up to now the bulk of the casualties had been minor – flesh wounds from arrows, the occasional broken bone from the other missiles. The loss of nine men at once was a serious blow at this relatively early stage of the siege.

None of the burnt men was in a condition to be moved any great distance, and so they were taken to a nearby house. Word was sent to the Temple, and within an hour De Beaujeu himself arrived.

Ducking to enter the humble residence, the stench of burnt flesh met the master and his companions like a wall, causing them to hesitate for a fraction of a second. There were only narrow windows, and the grilled shutters had been closed, keeping out the fresh air and the light. As Jean's eyes adjusted to the dimness, his gaze fell upon the torso of a man swathed in a charred and blistered matter that had once been skin and muscle. Jean broke into a sweat, the images of his father's wound – raw, pulsing, scarlet – flashed across his memory. He had held a bowl for his father to vomit into as they cleansed the wound and wiped the vomit from his lips and the sweat from his brow. He had held his father in his arms as he writhed with agony when they applied the salve. But his father had been in full armour when Greek fire coated his back and shoulder. And he had been able to dive into the sand and extinguish the flame in a relatively short period of time. Even so he had fainted and been close to death for nearly a week – and wore the hideous scars of the burns to this day. One look at the surgeon confirmed Jean's amateur opinion: the surgeon had imperceptibly shaken his head and signalled to Father Alphonso that the casualties were his concern.

The priest went down on his knees beside the nearest man. This victim's face was so badly burned that it was a mass of raw flesh lacking lips, brows and eyelids. The nostrils emitted a stream of liquid, the teeth were bared. The breath rasped out of the unrecognisable face. The priest did not attempt to take hold of the man's hands: they were curled into claws, the muscles totally consumed and a yellow slime coated the remains of ligament and bone. "In the name of the Father and the Son..."

De Beaujeu crouched beside the master mason. Although technically only a serving brother and illiterate, he was a man of great skill and commanded considerable respect. Altogether four of the victims were masons, and their loss would be severely felt in the days ahead when the damage to the walls and towers demanded skilled repairs. "Brother Baldwin," De Beaujeu addressed him by name.

"Master De Beaujeu?" The mason's eyes opened and he tried to turn his head.

"Yes, Brother. I came at once—"

"Master, you must appoint Brother David in my place. I know he is only a half-breed and the others will mutter – they may even call him traitor for his mother's Egyptian blood – but he is the best mason. You will need his services—"

"I know! I need your services! You must fight a little longer!"

"Master, I cannot." His head shook almost imperceptibly, and he closed his eyes to signify his resignation. "Brother David is skilled. Listen to his advice. The mines are the greatest danger."

De Beaujeu nodded. He knew that without the mason telling him.

"They are concentrating on the angle."

Again De Beaujeu nodded, then, realising that Brother Baldwin could not see the gesture, he said, "I know."

"Fill the cellars with rubble from the shattered buildings," the mason advised. "It could delay them – if they have not dug deep enough."

"Yes. I'll give the orders."

"Pray for my soul. I am a miserable sinner. So much on my conscience. Before I joined the order, Master, I... I..."

"It is not for me to hear your confession, Brother. Father Alphonso is here. We will read masses for your soul – yours and the others. All of us together."

A faint smile seemed to lighten his face. "Then God will be merciful – so many good men praying for me..."

Father Alphonso, a relatively young Portuguese priest, had joined De Beaujeu, and the master pulled himself to his feet, crossed himself, and then led Jean back out into the street. They were startled to find the street thronged with Templars. The word of the tragedy had spread, and not only the masons and other serving brothers had collected, but many off-duty knights and sergeants.

"Will they live, Master?" one of the masons enquired, while others asked the names of the victims.

"Is there nothing we can do?" one of the younger knights demanded with obvious frustration at the inactivity.

"We will say masses for their souls," De Beaujeu answered.

"And their murderers? Is there no way to revenge them? Can't we build a catapult as the Venetians did?" one of the elder masons cried out in anguished reproach.

"Not without wood, and the Sultan's siege engines are out of range of our bowmen," De Beaujeu informed him wearily.

Wood was always a scarcity in the desert, and catapults called for large solid timber, which had to be imported. The Venetians had their own supplies but the Temple was not so well stocked. For two whole days, De Beaujeu had allowed the crossbowmen and even the English with their longbows to attempt reaching the nearest of the mangonels, but in the end he had ordered them to desist. They were wasting ammunition they would need later. Still, he understood the frustration. The besieged is condemned to receiving but never inflicting injury, and the desire to strike back is natural to man, the helplessness particularly galling to fighting men.

It was not surprising that it was a knight who now demanded, "How long are we going to just sit here?"

But seeing that the spokesmen was one of De Molay's *protégés*, De Beaujeu responded with excessive sharpness. "If you have not the courage to withstand this siege, Van der Burg, then you have no right to the mantle you wear!"

"I'm not talking about leaving!" Van der Burg shouted back, insulted to the quick. "I'm talking about a sortie, an attack! We're nearly three hundred knights and twice that many sergeants. We can mount a sortie that will teach the godless Muslims that we are not frightened women and children!"

"Oh, we can mount it – and the rest of the city can watch as we are swallowed and consumed by the enemy. It will do wonders to boost morale when the Mamelukes hold our heads on their lance tips and dance around the walls to show them to the remaining garrison. Not to mention that the city will be far better off withstanding the Sultan's assault with all of us already dead!" The sarcasm was acid, and De Beaujeu started forward toward his waiting stallion to indicate that he did not intend to discuss the suggestion any further.

"We dinna all have take part in the sortie," another knight pointed out stubbornly, and Jean recognised the Scotsman Sir Duncan. He was, as always, scowling.

"No, of course not," De Beaujeu stopped in his tracks. "A select few can damn themselves with suicide!"

His words were hardly out before, with a howl, a huge boulder swept in over their heads and smashed into the house where the wounded lay. The earth shook and several of the men lost their footing or flung themselves down. Dust, shattered tiles, mortar and plaster rained upon them, turning Beaujeu's hair solid white. From the house came a long drawn-out wailing scream.

De Beaujeu spun around and started to scramble over and through the rubble toward the scream. One of the masons grasped him by the shoulder, and when De Beaujeu shook himself free the man clasped him around the waist and dragged him back with brute force.

"Let me go!" De Beaujeu ordered the mason furiously.

"No, Master, you can do no good like that! You will only cause the rubble to shift and endanger yourself and the men in there! We have to do this carefully."

The scream faded into a whimpering. De Beaujeu stood immobile gazing toward the sound.

"We will recover them, Master." It was another of the masons coming forward, the half-breed Brother David.

De Beaujeu seemed to stare as if he did not recognise the man, but, dark as an Arab, there was no mistaking or forgetting him.

"Brother Baldwin named you his successor," De Beaujeu informed him at last, and then, without awaiting a response, he moved away from what had been the house.

"That was from the catapult they call the 'al Mansour' – the victorious," someone in the crowd informed them all.

"Mansourah," Jean murmured to himself, and for the first time since the siege began he was afraid.

"If we could just put that and a half-dozen other catapults out of commission!" Fulk van der Burg pressed again.

"No!" De Beaujeu spun around to face the speaker. Jean could sense the intensity of his emotions, as if he were on the brink of exploding. His hands shook from the strain of trying to control himself. "I said 'no!'" he repeated and mounted his stallion.

*

"But there is a lot to be said for the idea," Peter de Sevrey insisted privately when De Beaujeu told his marshal of the incident. "The last thing the Sultan expects is for the garrison to take any offensive action. Remember the panic the Venetians' lone catapult produced?"

"Only initially," De Beaujeu countered.

"It still unnerves them. And at night they don't even maintain any serious kind of watch. If we were to mount a sortie after darkness, ride straight for the 'Victorious' and set it ablaze, we could probably knock it out of commission with hardly any losses at all."

"Do you seriously believe that?"

Peter looked a little embarrassed in face of the master's evident conviction that this was nonsense, but he was a straightforward Englishman and admitted, "Well, yes, I do – at least I'd be willing to give it a try."

"You?"

"I am the marshal." De Sevrey replied simply and De Beaujeu made a grimace as if to suggest he doubted the wisdom of the decision he had taken when making the appointment. He refrained from comment, however. "All I need is, say, fifty knights and two hundred sergeants," De Sevrey continued. "Enough men to seem like a formidable force in the darkness, well mounted so that we can flee when the work is done with little risk that close pursuit will endanger Acre itself."

"And if you burn one catapult there are over ninety others left! The loss of one won't make the slightest impact on the balance of forces. And they'll be waiting for you the next time."

"The enemy troops and slaves are superstitious, Will. The moral impact of seeing the greatest of their engines, the one called 'Victorious', burning among the corpses of her crew will undermine their faith in victory."

"The Sultan and emirs are hardly likely to be equally intimidated by a symbolic defeat."

"True, but the audacity of it will teach the Sultan to respect us. We need his respect."

"Do we?"

"Only respect for us will ever induce him to abandon the siege and accept some form of treaty."

De Beaujeu looked at his friend sidelong. Though in general he was correct, Beaujeu's informant in the sultan's court reported that the new Sultan had staked his prestige upon the capture of Acre. Anything less would endanger his own position, make him vulnerable to the kind of plots that always threaten the person of a new, untried sultan. "For all your experience, Peter, you are at heart no different from the other hotheads who chafe at the inactivity."

"Maybe. But if I speak for them, then I can only beg that you let us have our chance. The worst that can happen is that you are proved right."

"And I will have lost fifty knights and two hundred sergeants when I cannot afford to lose a single one of you."

"William." De Sevrey lowered his voice and an urgency was audible. "Can you afford to lose the respect of those young hotheads who already mumble 'Jacques de Molay would not be afraid to fight'?"

De Beaujeu caught his breath. "Are they saying that? Who? When?"

Peter shook his head. "Does it matter? You need them all. And you need them behind you. It is better to let the hotheads have their way and learn their lesson if necessary than have them feeding the rumours of your cowardice here in Acre."

"My cowardice?" De Beaujeu repeated as if he was unsure of the meaning of the word and was puzzled by it.

"The word fell at that last council meeting."

"They called me traitor!" De Beaujeu corrected, flushing with remembered anger.

"And coward."

They stared at one another.

"And to wipe away the stain of that word I must send others to their death?"

"There is no certainty that even one of us would die – much less all of us."

"Two hundred and fifty men amidst an army two hundred and fifty thousand strong?"

"In darkness and on the periphery. The Victorious does not stand in the middle of the host."

"Is there nothing I can say to dissuade you?"

"You can command me, Will, I am bound by my oath to obey you."

"So are they all." De Beaujeu reflected "But I cannot command respect – or love."

"No." De Sevrey mouthed the word silently, but then he lifted his head, adding, "But there are many of us – greater in number than the others – who do love and respect you. We know you are no coward, Will. Your problem is not lack of courage but an excess of vision. You are a man cursed with too much intelligence. You can anticipate, understand and analyse events and relationships which more common men do not even perceive. No matter what we discuss, you are always three or four steps ahead of me – and I am not the slowest or least educated of our knights. But what good did it do you to know nine months ago that the Sultan intended to destroy Acre? No one wanted to listen to your words of warning. No one wanted to believe. It will do you no good to say that the lives we could lose on a sortie are more valuable as defenders against the assault which the Sultan must sooner or later launch. You are undoubtedly correct. But that is not what young men want to hear, not what they are prepared to believe. They want action, the opportunity to demonstrate their courage, the opportunity to take revenge upon the enemy for the deaths of their brothers, the opportunity to live up to their dreams. What young man has ever joined the Templars without seeing himself in the shoes of the legendary heroes of the Second, Third, and Seventh Crusades?"

De Beaujeu sighed, and, not daring to look at his friend, he murmured, "Make your sortie, and let us hope the footsteps you follow are not those of Riddeford and De Sonnac."

*

The selected knights and sergeants mounted by the light of torches in the great inner ward of the Temple. Except for the men on duty on the walls, there was not a Templar, knight, sergeant or servant who was not there to watch them. What was sleep at a moment like this?

It was rare for so many horses to be tacked up at once, and the horses jostled one another, whinnied, bit and kicked out while girths were tightened and stirrups adjusted. After all, it was over a week since any of them had been properly exercised, and the suppressed nervousness of their riders could not be disguised from their mounts.

The knights wore chainmail leggings and hauberks but De Beaujeu had ordered them to leave their distinctive surcoats behind. Their success was largely dependent upon surprise and not being easy targets once they were in the midst of the enemy. The sergeants in black were well camouflaged, but the white surcoats of the knights would only have endangered them. Neither knights nor sergeants wore their great-helms over their cervellières. The heavy helms, which saved lives in open battle, would only impede vision and mobility in this kind of raid. Besides, it was hoped that the enemy would not have time to arm and fight.

They had taken the darkest horses from the stables. Not a grey nor hardly a horse with a white blaze or sock were among the two hundred and fifty mounts that now stamped and snorted in the ward. Even in the torchlight, the shapes of horses and riders seemed only partially distinguishable. In the shadows they lost all form and melted into the walls.

Peter de Sevrey had the command, of course, but many others had vied for the right to accompany him. Reluctant to risk commanders they might desperately need later, Peter had consciously taken many of the younger, less experienced knights and sergeants. He had also been careful to include the most vocal opponents of Beaujeu's policy of caution: Fulk van der Berg, Ludolf of Köln and Duncan Graham.

The portcullis creaked up and the gate of the Temple was flung open to permit the taskforce to spill out into the sleeping city. The horses, so long confined, stretched out their necks and their stride. Their shod hooves clattered on the cobblestones. Sheathed swords clanked. Even Templar discipline could not prevent a certain low murmuring among the men as they set forth in improvised troops, four abreast.

The exceptional commotion roused those citizens who slept lightly or were, for whatever reason, still awake. The shutters were flung open. People came to their doorways. "The Templars! The Templars ride!" The word ran like the balmy sea breeze off the Mediterranean sea from the Temple at the south-west corner of the town to the walls north and east.

Soon the citizens, rich and poor, waited for them already awake, alert, and excited. Women hung from the balconies clothed only in sheets wound like shrouds, and the boys scampered along beside them, tripping in the uneven gutters but not noticing their falls. "The Templars advance!"

There were shouts of encouragement, shouts of blessing. If any one noticed that they were just a pitiable two hundred and fifty men, or thought of the disproportion of two hundred and fifty pitted against two hundred and fifty thousand it left them speechless with pity or awe.

Reaching the northern sector of the wall, Peter drew up and waited for William de la More, who had the watch, to report that all was ready. There had been no unusual activity noted in the enemy camp. All lamps had been extinguished more than an hour earlier – except up near the Sultan's own tent where, it seemed, some festivity was in progress.

"All the better," De Sevrey concluded. "If the emirs are celebrating together their men will be leaderless."

De la More confirmed that he had prepared quarrels with flammable tips. He would fire these if he noted any movement in the camp. At the sight of such a signal, De Sevrey would abandon caution and ride full tilt for the objective. An arrow with a blood-red flame was a signal that there was a trap of some sort, and the sortie should be called off.

De la More stepped back, and gestured to the men at the gate to open it for the taskforce. "God be with you, Brother!"

"And you, Brother!" De Sevrey gently nudged his stallion with his spurs.

Some of the citizens started to raise a cheer, and De la More roared at them for silence. "Do you want to betray them before they can do any good?" he demanded rhetorically. The cheer faded into rebuked silence so that only the clatter of hooves and the snorting of the horses filled the night. The noise rose in volume in the confines of the gate and then lost itself in the vast open space beyond.

When the last rider of the taskforce was through the gate, De Beaujeu and Jean, who had both followed unobtrusively behind, dismounted and climbed to the roof of the gate with De la More. From here they could follow the progress of the band of riders across the plain spread out before them.

The enemy camp started just beyond crossbow-range, roughly a thousand yards away. When the taskforce had crossed just half of the distance, De Sevrey increased the pace to a trot. At two hundred yards, they broke into a steady canter and at just fifty yards, they could be seen to spurt forward. The cry of, "Vive Dieu St Amour!" carried back to the walls of Acre and sent a tingle down Jean's spine. He grasped the rough surface of the rampart and hung forward into the night, straining his eyes and ears.

For three or four heartbeats there was no response to the Templar battle cry. Then a muffled shout reached them, a scream cut short, a wail like a mullah and a woman's shriek. Jean looked hastily at De Beaujeu.

"The emirs have their harems with them – and there are always ample slave girls for the troops." De Beaujeu's gaze was fixed on the darkness where the enemy began – a clear line of black against the lighter colour of the desert floor.

The screams and shouts were becoming entangled now and the clash of weapons rang through the air.

"Something has gone wrong!" De Beaujeu announced and the tightness of his voice made it seem almost alien.

"But what—"

"They're going down!"

It was hard to see at that distance, but there was no denying that the progress of the mounted men seemed to have come to an abrupt halt. The first light appeared, a torch or a lamp. First it was a point of light, then it erupted into a sheet of flame as, apparently, an entire tent caught fire. By the light of the burning tent, they could briefly make out the chaos of hand-to-hand combat. The Templars were laying about with their swords to good effect. The enemy – evidently unarmoured – were falling in droves. But there were always more, and the Templars were making no forward progress. The great catapult which was their objective lay fully five hundred yards away, engulfed in darkness and apparent calm.

"The horses are going down," De la More announced. "Whenever they try to advance toward the catapult, the horses collapse. They must have set up stakes or some other kind of lethal barrier."

"There! At the Sultan's tent!" One of the English sergeants drew the attention of his superiors. They could now see torches being lit near the Sultan's tent. Horses were being brought and the Sultan and/or his guests were mounting, spurring toward the conflict.

"Signal!" De la More ordered.

The waiting crossbowman fitted the quarrel carefully and lit it with a flint. As it flared up, it blinded all of them for a moment. Jean tried to shield his eyes with his arm. The crossbowman was a professional. He steadied his weapon and with great calm and precision released it through the night. The yellow flare arched like a slow falling star and landed short of the chaos. Whether anyone involved in the tumultuous combat could have seen it was unclear.

"Again," De la More ordered.

De Beaujeu banged his head against the nearest rampart. "Jésu! Why I am so weak? Could You not grant me strength?"

Jean grabbed him and pulled him away from the wall. "My lord!"

De Beaujeu looked at him as if he were a stranger.

"We are not alone," Jean murmured.

"My lord! The marshal is disengaging and withdrawing," De la More reported. His eyes flickered to Jean as De Beaujeu turned his attention back to the conflict on the edges of the night.

Whether it was De Sevrey himself or someone else it was impossible to tell, but it was clear that the Templars were no longer even trying to advance toward the catapult. Instead they were clearly moving – slowly – in the direction from which they'd come. It was not isolated men in flight. It was still a coherent body of warriors in a fighting withdrawal. But the enemy leaders had also reached the scene of the engagement. Even from this distance, the sound of their orders carried. Jean thought he heard the Arabic word for 'pigs' and the order to 'stop' – which was surely not the order to stop killing but rather to stop the escape that was gaining momentum.

De la More called for his archers. They came pounding up the spiral stairs from the room below. Their longbows already leaned against the ramparts, and now they strung them, flexed them and took up positions along the wall.

A small rearguard from the taskforce was holding the mounted enemy at bay while the bulk of the riders broke free and galloped full tilt toward Acre. As the men reached the safety of the walls a shout went up, which was joined by the men along the walls. Only now did Jean register that he and De Beaujeu were not the only men who had come to watch the outcome of the raid.

Whether it was coincidence, timing or this cheer, the rearguard now also broke off their fight and made their dash for safety. They were pursued by the Arabs in ever-increasing numbers on fresher, fleeter horses. The scene was like the end of a hunt when the dogs surround a stag and, snarling and snapping even as he flees, start to drag him down.

"Ready!" De la More ordered.

"You'll kill our own men!" De Beaujeu seemed to wake from a trance. "Let them in! We are enough to finish them inside the walls!"

"My lord," De la More answered steadily, "the English longbow makes up for its short range with accuracy and rate of fire. If one single Templar is so much as wounded by one of our arrows, you may cut out my tongue. Archers! Fire at will!"

Jean yanked his head around sharply but even so he missed the actual volley, seeing only the impact. As if an invisible hand had struck them, the Arabs pressing closest and hardest upon the heels of the Templars were now rolling in the dirt or turned into a heap of dying flesh upon the desert floor. And before he could hardly register what had happened a second and a third volley of arrows had taken their toll of the pursuers.

"Jésu!"

The rate of fire was indeed at least three times that of crossbowmen.

The rearguard of the taskforce was nearly at the gate, and the Arab pursuers of the second rank made a last attempt to close the gap left by their dead comrades and catch the Templars. With a cry, they spurred forward, raising their scimitars over their heads. The moon, which at the outset of the sortie had been below the horizon, had come up. Unexpectedly it caught upon the steel of the weapons. They flashed briefly and then the darkness closed over them again as they sank down – victims of the lethal longbow.

From below Jean's feet came the rattle of the portcullis as it was cut free. Shouting and clatter made its way from the gatehouse to the roof.

De Beaujeu yanked himself away from the ramparts, started for the stairs and then stopped. "Well done, Brother William. Thank you, Brother Archers!" Then he disappeared down the stairway.

In the gateway, men were falling or being hauled down from their horses. Sir Duncan's face had been sliced in half by a sword and his lips were hanging from his chin. At least two surgeons were already giving orders, and the wounded horses were being led away. De Sevrey was still mounted. In the light of the torches something glistened dark along his shoulder and down his right arm, but with his left he was still gesturing, giving orders. His eyes fell on De Beaujeu as the master emerged from the stairwell.

"You were right, William – as usual."

"I was..." De Beaujeu cut himself short. "How many men did we lose?"

"I'm not sure yet. At least ten – probably more."

"And what happened?"

"You'll laugh." De Sevrey had never looked so grim or so defeated.

"Peter?"

"The tent ropes. The horses couldn't see them in the dark so they kept tripping over them. We could make no progress."

De Beaujeu nodded. "How badly are you hurt?"

"Not bad. Van der Berg is back there. So are Brothers Georges, Olivier, Malcolm, Stephanus..."

De Beaujeu went and took hold of Sevrey's stirrup. "Come, let me see to your wound," he urged his friend gently.

"You were right," De Sevrey repeated, as he leaned forward against his horse's mane and slowly swung his mailed leg over the rump of the stallion.

"What good does that do?" De Beaujeu asked, his arm around his marshal to help support him as his feet touched the uneven cobbles beneath the gate.

"Can you ever forgive me, Will?"

"Can you forgive me? I was too weak to stop you."

"The Temple deserves better than this. Name another marshal!"

"Elect another master, Peter. Shall we call Jacques de Molay back?" De Beaujeu managed an accompanying smile.

"De Molay has to answer for the whole bloody siege!" De Sevrey burst out furiously. "If he hadn't defied you—"

"Never mind, Peter. It is too late to change things. Come, let me dress your wound. You will need all the blood you have left."

Acre
May 4, 1291

On the 4th of May, King Henry of Jerusalem and Cyprus arrived with no fewer than forty ships carrying two thousand fighting men, weapons and supplies. The citizens went wild. The bells clanged. Flowers were thrown on to the streets to pave the king's progress to the royal palace and the houses were decked with silk banners. A thanksgiving mass was sung at Saint Jean d'Acre as if the Sultan's army had already withdrawn, and the great church was thronged with so many that even the galleries were crammed. That night the taverns by the port came to life again after a month of slumber. The sailors sang and drank in unbridled merriment, the barrier of language washed away in shared drink and shared danger. Across the town the royal palace was lit by a thousand torches while all the leading citizens of the kingdom of Jerusalem collected at a banquet to honour their king.

The King himself was overly thin and excessively pale. His movements were slow, his speech reticent, his face carved with an inner sorrow. Jean knew, because De Beaujeu had told him, what most of the citizens collected here in their most extravagant finery did not know: the King was epileptic. It was not surprising that he preferred to send his more charismatic younger brother to represent him in military crises. Amalric, tanned and robust of build, exuded a certain competence which was reassuring to the masses – even though Jean had heard De Beaujeu refer to him as a blustering amateur. Yet the arrival of the King at this moment in time was a gesture of solidarity with his besieged citizens worthy of Saint Louis himself. Furthermore, though he was not a military man, his authority was so unassailable that he gave the defenders of Acre what they had formerly lacked: central command.

Before the banquet, the King had invited the masters of the military orders, his brother and the commanders of the Commune of Acre to report to him. He had heard them with great attention, asking intelligent and pointed questions, and at the end of the sessions he had bluntly told them all that Master De Beaujeu was his deputy and all his orders were to be obeyed without question or hesitation. It was a late victory, but Jean was encouraged by it.

Because no one had been expecting the arrival of the King, the entire banquet was improvised. While it had been possible to decide upon protocol for the prominent guests, those of lesser rank were left to seat themselves at the lower tables. In the resulting good-humoured chaos, Jean sought out De Villaret to congratulate him on his promotion to grand hospitaller, one of the senior officers of the Hospital, subordinate only to the grand master, grand commander and marshal.

Sadly, De Villaret owed his promotion to the death of his predecessor. The Hospitallers, shamed and inspired by the Templars' sortie of April 15th, had made a sortie of their own only a week later. It had ended even more disastrously because the Sultan had in the meantime instituted a watch and torches were at hand around the perimeter of the camp. These had been lighted at the first sound of approaching riders and the Hospitallers had been met with arrows and armed men. Their losses were proportionally higher and the casualties they inflicted insignificant. As with the Templar dead, the heads of the Christian soldiers were strung together and hung like a necklace upon a captured stallion which was then paraded under the walls of Acre.

"Such actions do not bode well for the diplomatic mission the King wishes to attempt," De Villaret reflected. "I would not want to be the ambassador. Does De Beaujeu still have a means of communicating with al-Fakhri?"

"Yes." Jean did not elaborate on how. "Al-Fakhri is convinced that al-Ashraf Khalil needs to take Acre or risk being deposed. He cannot afford to be bought off – and what can we offer him anyway?"

"But I heard a delegation of three knights, including one of yours, was to be sent to Khalil tomorrow."

"Brother Guillaume de Cafran has volunteered. De Beaujeu would never have ordered him to go. He is fluent in Arabic and can read and write as well as speak it." In fact, he could quote large portions of the Koran by heart and had frequently impressed, baffled and outwitted Arab negotiating opponents by employing their own scripture to support his positions. If anyone could talk the Sultan into giving Acre a reprieve then it was Guillaume de Cafran, who had been born in Antioch and raised on the banks of the Jordan, the descendent of one of the original crusaders of 1099. But neither Jean nor De Beaujeu himself seriously believed that Brother Guillaume had a chance.

De Villaret nodded, there being little to add in the face of their shared scepticism about the outcome of De Cafran's mission.

"I can't believe how many ladies are still in Acre." Jean nodded now to the women gracing the upper tables. These were without exception women of noble blood and they glittered in vivid silks and jewels as they flirted openly with the Cypriot knights newly come to their defence. "Don't they recognise how perilous the situation is?"

"Yes and no. They know what happened in Antioch and Tripoli, and you'll note there is not an Italian among them. They are all noblewomen from Outremer. Where can they go? Neither Tyre nor Sidon is as well fortified and garrisoned as Acre. If Acre cannot hold, the other cities are lost as well."

"They could retire to Cyprus, or return to France."

"To be exiles? Refugees? Impoverished distant cousins living at the charity of relatives they hardly know? They will stay to the very last possible moment, relying upon our ships to take them to safety when the walls start to crumble."

"And what happens if the Egyptian fleet arrives?"

Jules de Villaret took a deep breath. "Then I hope they will have the means and sense to kill themselves." He added thoughtfully, "I think if the Sultan could deploy his fleet against us, he would have done so already – before King Henry arrived with reinforcements."

"Unless he wanted to be sure he captured the King too."

De Villaret considered this and answered slowly. "Yes, you could be right, but we have no reports suggesting the Sultan has even attempted to collect his fleet. My suspicion is that he does not trust his admirals and prefers not to have them in a position to challenge his authority."

Jean meanwhile had found Lady Melisende among the more subdued of the women, and he thought of Marco and all the others he had freed in Nazareth. The Arabs of Nazareth had been convinced even then that Acre was doomed.

He started when he recognised Sergeant-Captain Roger de Flor among the crowd of bourgeoise women refilling their glasses from a fountain bubbling wine in the adjoining chamber. The Templar sergeant had his arm around the waist of a young matron who was leaning against his chest provocatively.

"Some women are very adept at ensuring their passage," Jules de Villaret commented dryly, following Jean's gaze.

Jean frowned at the Hospitaller, who burst out laughing. "Don't look at me like that. I don't believe your chastity is intact."

Though he had not once violated his vow since he had left France, Jean did not make a pretence of virtue, which would have won him no particular points with De Villaret who was tolerant of the weaknesses of others. Instead he pointed out, "I've never been so indiscreet. De Beaujeu is sitting right over there."

"Do you see De Beaujeu scowling?"

"When it comes to the evacuation, Jules, we can't let men like Roger de Flor decide who is taken aboard and who is abandoned."

"There are more than fifty ships in the harbour at present. Most of them are small, to be sure, but even so they are enough to evacuate virtually all the civilians. If De Beaujeu commandeers them all and keeps control of the evacuation, it might be possible to save everyone."

"That would mean commandeering your master's flagship, " Jean pointed out with a smile.

"I know – but De Villiers would welcome it if someone else would just start making the decisions for him."

"And it assumes that none of the fighting men flee."

"It assumes that all of us are dead, Jean."

"And the King and his knights."

"No, King Henry and his household will put to sea in the royal flagship as soon as the walls are breached. That is his duty."

"Sweet Mother Marie!" Jean swore, his gaze far across the room.

"What is it?"

"Forgive me, Jules, I must go and speak with someone." He was already swinging his legs over the bench, his spurs catching and almost tripping him in his haste.

He made his way through the milling throngs, his objective eluding him several times as people came between them. And then at last he reached the cluster of nuns sipping daintily from silver chalices and giggling with unaccustomed tipsiness. Right to the last, he hoped he had been mistaken, but as he came closer Sister Madeleine turned toward him and looked him directly in the eye. At the sight of him her eyes lit up and she took a step forward.

Jean lifted her hand to his lips with the casual gallantry he had learned as a youth, but he had no time for empty chatter. "Sister! I thought you had sailed for France long ago!"

"And who would have paid the passage, sir?" Madeleine replied evenly.

"Your father, your brothers, your order. Why didn't you come to me?"

One of the younger nuns behind Madeleine giggled behind her hand, and Jean realised that the whole cluster of nuns was watching him avidly. It was more than mere curiosity that enlivened their faces, it was a combination of wine and voyeurism.

One of them now made bold to ask, "May I come to you too, *monsieur*?"

An older nun at once slapped the questioner on her ear with the back of her hand and hissed that she should have more pride. "Sister Madeleine is a whore already, but you still have your honour."

Sister Madeleine was used to such remarks and stoically ignored it. Jean, however, spun on the vituperative nun. "You insult me and my order, Sister. Either have the courage to accuse me of violating my oath to Master De Beaujeu – here and now – or apologise." Jean was pointing with his right arm to De Beaujeu at the high table and with the other he was gesturing for the nun to accompany him.

The nun flushed and stuttered. "I don't know what this fuss is about. I didn't mean... Why should I insult... You are one of our gallant defenders. Everyone knows Templars—"

"What is the matter?" It was the cool voice of the abbess as she swept into the midst of her charges.

"I honestly don't know, Reverend Mother, this knight seems to—"

"This sister referred to Sister Madeleine as a whore – and implied that I had known her carnally. I insist on an apology, Reverend Mother."

The Abbess looked at him with detachment. He was a handsome man – dark blond and tanned. His spotless surcoat with its red cross emphasised his broad chest, and the chainmail of his hauberk encased his well-formed, muscular arms and legs like the scales of a snake. But she was an elderly woman no longer swayed by outward appearance. She looked Jean straight in the eye and saw the flint in his. He did not strike her like the kind of man who would be the debaucher of nuns, but she did not like the intensity of his emotions either. There was some kind of bond between this knight and Sister Madeleine – and any bond between monk and nun was illicit.

"I'm sure this is a misunderstanding, *monsieur*. Why should one of my nuns insult a Knight Templar? We are, every one of us, aware how great our debt is to you and your brothers. We are dependent upon your courage and your skill for our freedom and survival. As to Sister Madeleine, surely she is no concern of yours."

Jean recognised that he had been outmanoeuvred. He was not about to point out that he had purchased Madeleine, and what other, legitimate interest did he have in her fate? "None, Reverend Mother, but one..." He stopped though he had already turned away and looked back, his eyes holding Madeleine's though ostensibly he spoke to the Abbess. "*The Falcon* is the fleetest and best manned of our ships. When you hear the Muslim kettledrums heralding the assault, get thee to *The Falcon* – all of you."

He left them exchanging recriminations, explanations and excuses in flustered whispers, and went in search of Roger de Flor. If the sergeant-captain had orders to await the nuns from the Convent of the Sacred Heart, he might actually be prepared to hold space on *The Falcon* for them – and not cast off until they were aboard.

Moving away from the high tables to the lower end of the great hall, the noise level rose noticeably. Here the free wine had gone to many heads less inhibited than the nuns of the Sacred Heart. The scarcity of women also tended to make the tone rawer and more raucous than it might otherwise have been. Men were banging their goblets, fists or knives on the table and stomping their feet to accompany their hearty singing. Some of the Cypriot squires were dancing in a circle with their arms linked, as Jean had seen Greek soldiers dance. The occasional scuffles over wine or jests were quickly and amiably suppressed by companions intent on enjoying themselves.

Not seeing Roger anywhere, Jean followed his instinct and went out of a side entrance and into the royal gardens. Here more than one pair of lovers strolled in the balmy night air. The Holy Land, Jean reflected, was never more beautiful than in the spring. This year, the rains had lasted longer than usual, impeding the progress of the Sultan with his heavy siege engines, and allowing the desert to flourish more profusely than usual. In gardens such as these, with careful irrigation and cultivation, the flowers seemed to compete with one another. The fragrances mingled imperfectly so that now one and now another scent dominated the air that gently rustled the leaves of the lemon and almond trees and set the palms to waving.

Jean strolled slowly as if lost in thought, his eyes only surreptitiously focusing on the pairs of lovers embracing in the shadows of the trees or holding hands on the marble benches. The natural perfumes of the garden, the balmy temperatures of the luminous night, and the Commandaria wine in his veins combined to produce a melancholy that was only intensified by the sight of women surrendering to the caresses of other men. Jean felt a rush of desire followed by the familiar bitterness toward his brother for being the first born. He thought of De Villaret's assumption that he had not kept his vows scrupulously, and Sister Madeleine's face took form in his imagination. He shook his head in self-revulsion, seized by self-loathing at such a base thought.

Then he saw Pierre under one of the fig trees, his eyes shut and his face enraptured in an expression of sexual ecstasy. In the next second Jean registered that there was another figure under the tree with him, a youth with long blond hair. The shock of what he saw took his breath, then he gagged. Finally, collecting himself, he started to stride forward, his squire's name on his lips.

A hand on his shoulder stopped him. He turned. It was De Beaujeu. "Let them be, Jean."

"My lord! They're committing a mortal sin."

"I know. But it is their souls they endanger, not ours. You know Brother David's estimates: it will take the Sultan's engineers at very most ten days and probably less to undermine the towers of the outer wall. In two weeks we will all stand before the Judgement Seat. It is not our place to anticipate His justice."

"But the King has just named you his deputy."

"Only in military matters."

"That's what I meant. Now that you have overall command surely..."

"I can save Acre? Oh, Jean, you can't really think that that makes a difference?"

"Of course it does. You could have prevented the Hospitallers from their costly sortie – or now that you command the combined forces here assembled maybe we could mount a sally in sufficient numbers to rout – or at least maul – the Sultan's army."

"I need roughly five thousand knights to launch an attack on the Sultan's army and the total number of knights in Acre today – including those just arrived from Cyprus – is exactly eight hundred and sixty-seven. Either Edward of England – or someone else, though I don't know who it might be – brings me the missing four thousand knights in the next week, or we are doomed. It is that simple."

"Then why did the King appoint you his deputy?"

"So someone else will bear the blame for the defeat."

Jean looked shocked. "I can't believe King Henry—"

"No, not the King himself perhaps – but Prince Amalric will have been anxious to avoid responsibility for a second Tripoli."

"Is there nothing we can do?"

"To save Acre? No. But few men are granted such a splendid opportunity to save their souls. Come." He clasped Jean on the shoulder and steered him out of the garden and back into the palace.

Acre
May 16, 1291

By the 6th of May, the defenders of the tower of King Hugh, forming the pinnacle of the angle in the city wall, could hear the chink and tap of Muslim sappers boring in under the exposed barbican. Templar masons managed to dig a counter-mine which intersected the incoming mine, and in fierce hand-to-hand combat the Muslims were driven from the underground passage. But almost at once it became apparent that the Muslims had other mines already well advanced and they were able to switch their efforts to these. Since the tower was placed outside the line of the outer wall, the enemy could attack it above or below ground from three sides, and the defenders of the underground passageway could hear the progress and even the muffled voices of the enemy approaching from either side.

On May 8th, it was apparent that the tower was untenable so preparations were made to fire it as soon as the sappers had gained the cellar. The tower was soaked with kerosene and, when ignited, the flames shot up in a roaring column. The wooden floors and ceiling beams ignited, burned and collapsed. Flames licked out of the windows and danced along the ramparts like victorious devils. Small cracks emerged in the masonry, then visibly lengthened and widened until with the rumble of nearing thunder the tower started to crumble. Throughout the night flames continued to leap up, fed by God-knew-what, and by dawn the once great tower was a smouldering heap of ruin.

The Sultan's sappers turned their attentions toward the segment of the outer wall between the tower of King Henry, holding the angle of the wall behind the rubble of the tower of King Hugh and the largest and most important of Acre's gates, Saint Anthony's Gate, directly before the royal palace. The masons identified no fewer than five different mines being bored under the outer walls in this sector and the digging of counter-mines carried the risk of actually speeding the collapse of the wall.

The towers of Edward of England and the Countess of Blois were undermined and the shafts set alight by the enemy on the night of May 14. The defenders heard the muffled explosion of the kerosene being ignited and most managed to flee from the towers before the foundations collapsed and the towers sank in upon themselves. The tower of King Henry, the newest and mightiest of Acre's towers, held out a day longer, but on the 15th the outer wall of the tower abruptly collapsed, carrying dozens of the garrison to their deaths in a landslide of masonry that crushed them long before the triumphant Turks could strike. The remaining defenders, now fully exposed to the Turkish archers, panicked. Many were killed as they crowded into the narrow, spiral stairs and, losing their footing, were crushed and trampled by the men behind. If the Teutonic knights, who held the walls flanking the tower, had not rushed on to the rubble and put up a fierce and desperate struggle, the Sultan's forces would have occupied the tower immediately. But the loss of the tower built so recently by the King clearly broke the fighting morale of the Cypriot lords and troops. They demanded the immediate evacuation of the city and made every effort to persuade the King to give the necessary orders. King Henry refused. The inner wall, he pointed out was intact. He would not abandon Acre until this too was breached.

Throughout the night, the watch upon the wall observed and reported unusual activity in the Sultan's camp. Messengers came and went in a near constant stream. The clang of hammer and anvil betrayed the labour of the armourers and the snorts and whinnies of the horses registered the unease of the enemy mounts. Lamps burned in many tents undimmed until the dawn, when the wailing of the mullahs shattered the stillness of the breathless air.

As always, the churches of Acre responded to the mullah's challenge and within the walls of the city the prayers of Allah's children were drowned by the din of bells. Stiff and groggy from a near sleepless night, Jean rode with De Beaujeu through the still deserted streets of the city to the Gate of Maupas in the Templars' sector, and mounted the tower behind him.

Sir Duncan, his lower face held in place by a line of stitches that sliced across his face, came toward them at once. "What the bloody hell are they waiting for?" he demanded.

"For our nerves to become strained," De Beaujeu replied breezily as he stepped to the ramparts and focused his attention on the enemy.

Their prayers ended, the enemy could be seen collecting. It seemed an excruciatingly slow process accompanied by no apparent concern for haste. They knew perfectly well they were being observed, but they had no need for surprise; they had numbers on their side. The enemy battalions were drawn up with painstaking precision, inspected, then their emirs appeared to address their troops and then shouts of "Allah Ahkbar!" and other slogans were shouted in disjointed unison.

At last the enemy started to advance under their glittering banners bearing sayings from the Koran. De Beaujeu noted that the Sultan's elite guard, identifiable by their gold-plated helmets, was positioned quite far back. The entire body of troops, the foot leading, advanced on the three shattered towers.

The Teutonic knights had taken up positions in the shattered King Henry tower while the ruins of the towers of Edward of England and the Countess of Blois were held by the Hospitallers. Because the upper stories of these towers were no longer safe, the Italians and the Temple had concentrated their crossbowmen along the segments of the wall flanking the threatened towers. The Hospitallers had positioned all their crossbowmen on St Anthony's Gate. Although the combined fire of the crossbows felled not insignificant numbers of individual Muslims, the impact upon the advance of the Sultan's forces was negligible.

As the enemy front line came within fifteen yards of the city, they burst into a run and with shouts and yells flung themselves at the defenders. The battle cries of Christian and Muslim competed and mingled, punctuated by shrieks of pain and the astonished wail of the dying. The Templars clustered on the eastern side of the gate and strained to see what was happening along the line of the wall. Beaujeu's attention remained focused on the enemy. Though the front lines had already reached the city, the bulk of the Sultan's army was still advancing at a slow but steady pace. The lines of horsemen were checking their mounts. The Sultan's guard actually drew to a halt.

Beaujeu's fingers drummed on the stone of the ramparts and he squinted into the morning sun. The Templar knights and sergeants, clustered together where they could hear but not see the combat, cast ever more frequent glances over their shoulders toward the master, but De Beaujeu ignored them with sovereign nonchalance.

Below and behind them came the clatter of hooves and then the stamping of a man hurrying up the steps to the ramparts. Peter de Sevrey emerged from the stairwell breathless from the climb, his helmet under his arm and his chainmail glittering in the morning sun.

"My lord! The Teutonic knights have been forced out of Henry's tower and are holding the Accursed Tower against the Sultan's assault."

The Accursed Tower was the tower in the angle of the inner wall, the equivalent of King Henry's tower in the outer wall.

De Beaujeu nodded. "And our brother Knights of St John?"

"Having taken King Henry's tower, the Turks have penetrated the space between the walls and have surrounded the Hospitallers in the English and Blois towers. The Knights of St John can only retreat along the wall now."

"And are they?"

"They are—"

"Turks!" The cry came from one of the sergeants manning the Maupas Gate. Some of the enemy had rushed headlong between the walls, ignoring the Hospitallers still in the outer wall and now in their rear. They were obviously hoping that the entire garrison was concentrated at the three shattered gates to repel the assault.

"Clear the ramparts for the English!" the commander on duty ordered, at the same time hauling upon a rope that rang a bell in the guardroom below.

De la More and his archers came clattering up the stairs and deployed along the eastern wall in less than thirty seconds. De Beaujeu's confidence in them was such that he did not bother watching as they slaughtered the Muslims trapped between the mighty walls of the city. "Like shooting fish in a barrel," one of the English sergeants later remarked. The enemy responded to the unexpected deluge of cloth-yard arrows with hysterical confusion, running first right and then left and colliding with one another, tripping over their dead and wounded, screaming and praying and finally withdrawing. But De Beaujeu's attention remained fixed upon the Sultan.

The golden helmets of the Sultan's guard were in motion again. At first they advanced slowly, at a walk, and then with the distinctive staccato motion of men sitting a trot. They were escorting something on wheels. De Beaujeu frowned in concentration, trying to pierce with his eyes the tall, proud ranks of the Sultan's guard. A slight unevenness in the terrain at last gave him a clear view. They were escorting a battering ram.

"Saint Anthony's Gate!" De Beaujeu exclaimed aloud. Then he spun around. "De la More! You and your English remain here. Peter! Return to the Temple and collect all knights there and take them to Saint Anthony's Gate – mounted. Commander," he addressed the commander of the watch, "I want all the knights of the watch to report here at once." The commander gave the order to the sergeant-trumpeter, who blew the rally which called all the knights distributed along the length of the Templars' sector to the gate. The sergeants remained at their posts.

De Beaujeu did not waste time on pretty speeches; the ethos of the Templars left little room for them in any case. As his knights collected around him, he pulled his heavy, leather-padded helm over his head, drew his gauntlets over his hands and tightened the buckle of his swordbelt one notch before removing his shield from his back and taking it on to his left arm. Nearly a hundred knights who were collected around him followed his example without comment. As before Tripoli, Jean felt a nervousness seize his body and cause his hands to shake violently as he fitted his helmet over his head. He clapped his hand around the hilt of De Sonnac's sword so that none could see it shaking under his shield.

"Brothers," was all De Beaujeu said as he turned and started down the narrow flight of stairs leading from the ramparts of the gate to the wall walk ten feet below.

On the wall walk itself, they could walk three to four abreast, and Jean, Sir Duncan and another knight pressed in around De Beaujeu. He accepted their protection without protest.

The sound of battle was becoming louder and more distinct. Jean, now in the forefront, could see that the ramparts of St Anthony's Gate resembled a snake pit – a writhing bowl of bodies so tightly pressed together that it was impossible to tell where one man ended and the next began. Beyond, the wall walk leading from the tower of the Countess of Blois was carpeted with red and black – the surcoats and mantles of the Hospitallers who had given their lives for each foot of ground backwards. A glance downward confirmed that nearly as many dead lay heaped at the foot of the wall, where they had fallen or been flung as they fought. Here and there something moved feebly at the base of the wall, wounded men with broken backs, hips and legs who could neither stand nor crawl.

Suddenly a dull thud pierced the high-pitched crush of sound of hand-to-hand combat. For an instant, the fighting on the gate seemed to be suspended before it was resumed with new ferocity. The dull thud came again.

De Beaujeu threw back his head and roared, "Vive Dieu St Amour!"

Though his face was encased in iron, the shout still rang out with sufficient vigour to be heard and taken up by the others around and behind him. As he gave the cry, he drew his sword and plunged into the *mêlée*.

Like a river joining the sea, the Templars' momentum brought them deep to the centre of the tower roof before they started to dissolve among the more numerous enemy. The fear Jean had felt only moments earlier disappeared instantly. With clinical detachment, he wielded the four foot sword as he had been trained. At first it was easy. The cut and thrust eliminated one opponent after the other. It was not even necessary to lunge and manoeuvre, because the enemy pressed in so closely that he needed only stand his ground. The Muslims tripped over their comrades as they tried to reach him, slipped on the spilled blood and entrails and went down under the blade of his honed broadsword.

Yet gradually he became aware that the air was filled with wisps of smoke, and an acrid smell of burning tar, timber and heated metal made breathing more difficult than ever. He noted too that his back was more exposed than it had been. Out of the corner of his eye slit he registered that several of the bodies at his feet wore the white and red of the Temple. He glanced quickly to his left, but De Beaujeu was still fighting vigorously and Sir Duncan was swinging his sword with little finesse and all the more effectiveness.

Abruptly, the earth shook beneath his feet and a dull crash made him jump. From below came the hysterical screams of men. "They've breached the gate! The gate!"

"Back!" It was De Beaujeu pulling him as he himself withdrew. Beaujeu's hand on his white surcoat left a smear of blood. Jean stumbled as he tried to back up and someone else caught him under the arm. The body at his feet was that of Sir George, his neck nearly severed.

"Back! To the stairs!"

Jean understood. If the Mamelukes had breached the gate, the outer wall was lost and the danger was that the enemy, with their battering ram, would now force the inner gate and so gain access to the city itself. And there had been no order for the evacuation of civilians! Everyone had assumed that only the outer wall would be contested today. Everyone had assumed that they still had time – days, maybe even a week – until the inner wall was mined and the fight for the city itself began.

"Brother Diego! Take the news to Commander De la More! He is to pull back to the inner wall – immediately!"

The young Spanish knight who was farthest back did not bother to acknowledge the order, simply starting to run. He stumbled more than once as he ran along the wall walk, clutching his bleeding side.

Some of the Muslims realised that the Templars were withdrawing and came after them. Jean, Sir Duncan and a couple of other knights stopped their retreat to hold the enemy while the majority of the Templars gained the next tower and the stairs leading back to the ground. Jean and one of the other Templars were driven back toward the inner edge of the wall walk. Jean felt his heel land upon the edge and in panic he flung himself inward again, conscious of the drop of forty feet to the earth below. Beside him, his companion had stepped less luckily; with a wrenching scream he lost his balance and fell backwards into the abyss between the walls. "Christ God!" Jean screamed, whether in prayer or anger he did not know himself. He was sweating profusely, and sweat made the palm of his hand sticky; his wrists were numb from the relentless work with sword and shield.

Sir Duncan spun his sword over his head, decapitated one enemy and sliced open the chest of a second as he shouted, "Run for it!" Jean did not have to be urged a second time. He and the other remaining knight broke off fighting and ran for the tower behind them. As he turned his back something cut his calf, but the blow was not serious enough to stop him. The knight beside him, however, gasped and crumpled on to his knees. Jean grabbed him roughly under the arm and started to drag him along the wall walk.

"Leave me, Brother! I'm finished," the knight gasped.

Jean hesitated for a second, but he could not abandon his brother still alive. He bent to take a better hold around his comrade's chest and found that an arrow had pierced him from the back and was emerging from his belly.

"Get back!" Duncan shouted again. "I can't hold them much longer!"

"God have mercy!" Jean dropped the dying man back on to the parapet and ran toward the tower.

At the tower, two knights awaited with shields and swords at the ready. Jean was conscious of Sir Duncan hard on his heels, and as he glanced back he saw the two knights who had waited for them spring past Duncan and fell his pursuers. Then he ducked down into the stairwell.

At the first landing, Jean fell against the wall, so breathless he could not take another step. Sir Duncan and the other two knights clattered down the stairs after him and sank on to the stairs. Sir Duncan hung his head between his knees as if he were faint. One of the other knights leaned back against the stairs, his hand pressed to his thigh. The only sound was that of their rasping breath and from below the sounds which were battle.

Then the knight who had lain back sat up. "Do any of you have water?"

"There must be water in the barrel there," the other knight answered, pointing with his bloody sword. As if he were surprised to see the weapon naked in his hand, he gazed at it and then resheathed it.

The first knight pushed himself to his feet and went to the barrel kept in all of the towers to fight fire and provide the garrison with water. Removing his helm, he dipped both his mailed hands into the water and cupped them to his lips. Jean pushed himself away from the wall and joined him, as did the others. Jean set his helm on the floor and dropped his gauntlets beside it. Then he thrust his sweaty, swollen hands into the cool water. At once he felt calmer. He threw the water into his face to cool his head before slurping up the water from his cupped hands. He became conscious of the throbbing of his right shoulder and a stinging pain in his calf. He glanced down and saw that his chainmail had been sliced open and hung down, revealing a bloody gash in his leg. He nodded acknowledgement of the wound absently. They could not dally much longer.

The others were refitting their helms. Jean too pulled the heavy iron helmet back over his coif and cervellière. Then as one they continued down the stairs again, ever closer to the tumult of the battle still in progress.

They emerged into the space between the inner and outer walls and made their way back in the direction of St Anthony's Gate. The inner gate was closed of course, but already the battering ram had been deployed and was pounding the ironwork of the portcullis. From the opposite direction, apparently having sortied out of St Nicholas's Gate, came a body of mounted Hospitallers led by their marshal, Matthew of Clermont. Peter de Sevrey, with a body of Templars, was riding with them.

The Sultan's guard gave a shout and spurred their horses to meet the Hospitallers.

Jean had no time to watch the collision of chivalry. He joined the other Templars, still led by De Beaujeu, who were fighting on foot against the Muslim archers aiming Greek fire through the portcullis at the inner gate. Although reinforced with iron braces, the gate itself was wooden and thus vulnerable to fire. If the portcullis was wrenched from its housing by the battering ram, the gate, weakened by fire, would also give way before the battering ram. This was apparently what had happened to the outer gate. What Jean did not fully understand was why or how the inner portcullis of the outer gate had given way so rapidly – unless it hadn't been shut at all. If the defenders in their haste to reinforce the men fighting on the walls had failed to lower it...

Jean found himself on foot among mounted enemy, an uncomfortable and unaccustomed position for a knight. He was grateful that the enemy rode the light-boned, smaller horses native to Arabia and not European destriers. These horses were short enough for him to see over their backs, and they were unarmed and thus piteously vulnerable. It seemed unfair to expose these noble and spirited animals to the brutality of battle unprotected, and Jean initially concentrated his blows upon the riders attacking him. But the strain of raising his mailed arms and the broadsword a foot higher than normal soon became too great and he was rapidly reduced to slashing at the chests and bellies of the Arab horses to bring down their riders, where he could finish them off.

Matthew of Clermont had gained the battering ram and was hacking at the hawsers which formed the sling suspending the pointed beam. Despite the sharpness of the sword, the fact that the hawsers bent with each blow made progress slow. Furthermore, several of the Sultan's guard were trying to stop him. One man was trying to pull him from his horse while another attacked him with a scimitar and a third was raining blows to his helmet with a mace. He would not be able to hold out for long.

Jean was only yards away from the dangerous siege weapon himself. He fought his way forward and hauled himself over the wheels on to the platform. Taking his dagger in his left hand, he started to saw through the hawsers where they were held taut around the beam of the weapon. A man lunged at him and flung him down on to the platform. Through his eye-slit he saw the hate-filled face of a Nubian and felt the man clasp at his gullet. The mail of his coif completely covered his neck and throat, but the Nubian held a dagger with a triangular blade in his hand – a weapon that could easily puncture the mail if the blow was delivered with sufficient strength. Jean's response was both instinctive and drilled. He brought his knees up into the man's balls and thrust his own dagger into his opponent's kidneys at the same time. Then he rolled the dead man off him, and sat up.

He was amazed to see that Matthew of Clermont was still sawing at the slings of the battering ram, despite the blood now pouring from his left shoulder. Several other Hospitallers had, however, joined him and were either fighting off those of the Sultan's men who would have attacked their marshal or themselves trying to sever the hawsers.

Jean himself was attacked by another Muslim, who sprang at him from a horse and sent them both flying against the beam of the battering ram. This sudden jerking of the weakened ropes in a direction counter to the intended swing caused them to give way abruptly. All at once, the hawsers snapped and the beam of the battering ram came crashing down, shattering the axle of one of the wheels of the platform. It bounced once and then rolled along the ground. The platform itself lurched and crumpled over the broken axle, spilling Jean on to the ground.

When he came to again, Jean had no way of knowing if he had lost consciousness for seconds, minutes or hours. His helm had shifted so that the eye-slit was skewed. All that he could see was a negro's bloody hand: the palm was white where it was not smeared with blood, the fingernails were manicured. But the sound of battle jarred at his head, aggravating a tearing headache.

He tried to lift his arms to readjust the helm, and realised, still dizzy and disoriented, that one arm was pinned under him. He lifted himself slightly and freed it. Though stiff and bruised, it did not appear broken. He rolled over and tried to sit up. Nausea overcome him, and he sank back on to the ground. When the nausea had passed, he slowly sat up again and refitted his helm.

Now he could see the broken bodies littered about him. The crushed legs of a man on whom the battering ram beam had landed stuck out toward him and a whimpering from the other side of the beam suggested that he still lived. A Hospitaller also lay under the corner of the platform, his chest collapsed and the white cross obliterated with blood. But the fighting itself had evidently shifted away from the immediate area.

Carefully now, Jean pulled himself to his feet, using his sword to help him. He was amazed that his fingers were grasping the hilt; men often lost their swords when they were knocked out. What was it the old Dominican had said? That none could die at the hands of non-believers so long as he grasped the Baptist's hand in his? He could almost believe it after this day. Unfolding his fingers, he took heart from the sight of the finger bone encased in crystal, and then turned his attention toward the sound of fighting.

To his amazement he found that Acre's defenders had managed to push the Muslims back against the outer gate. They were also holding those of the enemy who were clambering over the rubble of the ruined towers of Blois and Edward of England. A solid line of Christian knights and sergeants, the white of the Temple and the red of the Hospital dominating but intermingled arbitrarily, stretched from the outer wall to the north of St Anthony's Gate to the inner wall south of the gate.

As he watched, Matthew of Clermont charged forward with two score of mounted knights including De Sevrey. They swept the astonished enemy closest to the outer gate back into it. From overhead came a shout, and then the sound of the portcullis chain rattling down its shafts. Jean looked up just in time to see two of his brothers dart out of the tower on the first floor and dash along the lower wall walk to the north. Below, the Hospitallers were flailing their horses forward while hanging off to the side to escape before the portcullis trapped them. Clearly the manoeuvre had been planned – otherwise it was unthinkable that they could have reacted so perfectly. Only three were trapped and one was pinned to the ground and killed by the portcullis itself when he fell from his terrified stallion.

The bulk of the Sultan's elite troops were suddenly caught beyond the portcullis, this time without a battering ram, and the troops who had come over the ruined towers were apparently confused by the sudden absence of the Sultan's guard. They hesitated. It would take several minutes for the Sultan to regroup and send his troops over the shattered walls by the towers – or bring up another battering ram. The order was given to withdraw, and the entire line of defenders started to give way, pulling back toward the Maupas Gate. Some of the knights of Acre who had rushed to save the St Anthony's Gate broke and ran for safety, but the Templars and Hospitallers made an orderly fighting withdrawal, Jean joining them as they went.

The Maupas Gate was open and the outer portcullis cranked upwards to admit the first of the men fleeing back into the city.

By the time the military orders had reached the gate, the Muslims were no longer pursuing the defenders. They had broken off and withdrawn beyond the rubble of the outer wall. With his brothers of both orders, Jean turned and passed through the gate into the city unmolested. The portcullis and gate closed behind them. Jean sank down into the gutter and leaned his back against the wall beside the gate in utter exhaustion, his eyes closed. Slowly his mind registered the fact that he was facing the sun. It was afternoon.

"Jean?"

He opened his eyes, startled.

"Are you badly hurt?"

"No, not at all, my lord."

De Beaujeu was standing over him, blocking out the sun. The master's once pristine surcoat was smeared and splattered with blood, much of it already dried and brown, some still bright red. It was tattered and half cut-away exposing the fact that the chainmail hauberk had also been badly hacked. One section of mail over his left hip had been cut through and hung down, revealing the padded arming doublet. De Beaujeu had removed helm and coif so that his sweat-soaked, grey hair stood on end, drying in the hot air. Smoke had left streaks of soot upon his face and the shape of his eyes stood out white.

Jean started to pull himself to his feet and De Beaujeu gave him a hand.

"The Sultan has pulled his troops back to regroup. I don't expect he'll attack again before tomorrow. We inflicted heavy casualties and he has no need to press the attack with weary men." De Beaujeu spoke with calm professionalism. "I must speak to the King about starting the civilian evacuation at once. I want you to get back to Thibald and have him arrange for the collection and burial of our dead. If there is time, the Muslim dead should be cleared out from the space between the walls so they won't putrefy the air too close to the city."

William de la More came up beside them, and De Beaujeu looked over expectantly. "My lord, my archers need to eat and rest. We also need to replenish our supplies of arrows. We should try to recover some of what we shot today."

De Beaujeu nodded. "Jean, see that the lay brothers detailed to collect the dead also recover any arrows that can be reused." Then, turning back to De la More, he added, "I will see that your men are relieved as soon as possible." Because of the intensity of the defence at St Anthony's Gate the routine watch system had broken down. "Jean, if Peter is able, have him make up a new duty roster. The walls must be manned by sergeants alone from now on. I need all knights for the reserve to counter the main assault wherever it occurs. We'll need exact information on our casualties."

The grand master of the Knights of St John rode up and, recognising De Beaujeu, jumped down from his white stallion before he brought his stallion to a halt. His head was bare and his white hair and beard framed his red face. Flinging open his arms, he embraced a somewhat abashed De Beaujeu. "William! Thank God you are alive!"

"It is to your marshal that the honours of the day belong," De Beaujeu replied. "He took the battering ram out of action and drove the enemy back beyond the outer wall."

"I have come seeking him," De Villiers admitted, his gaze shifting over Beaujeu's shoulder to the press of knights of both orders who, like Jean, had collapsed inside the gate as soon as they had gained its safety. "We have many casualties." De Villiers's eyes shimmered with tears, but he held his chin up and there was no excessive pathos as he turned back to De Beaujeu. "My own flagship and our next largest galley have been designated for the wounded. The serving brothers from our hospital and the surgeons have already gone aboard. You must see that those of your brothers who can no longer fight are taken aboard at once. We will keep them at the quay until the last possible moment."

De Beaujeu gazed at De Villiers with a sense of wonder and a touch of ironic humour. Only a year ago this same man had maintained a cool distance at every meeting – and indeed he had insisted upon lengthy and tedious marks of courtesy before he would even condescend to meet with the Templar master. True, he had backed De Beaujeu in council and there had been a distinct increase of warmth to him throughout the preparations for the siege. Yet there was still something touching in this gesture of fraternity. At last, after two hundred years of bitter rivalry, the two military orders were fighting and dying without distinction between the colour of their tunic. Now, when it was too late to save the Holy Land, they were finally acting like brothers. Then the thought struck De Beaujeu that they had always acted like brothers: jealous of the other's possessions and achievements, competitive to the point of vindictiveness, but in moments of crisis always banding together and fighting together against outsiders, whether it was the pope, the emperor or the Muslims.

His thoughts and feelings too many to express, De Beaujeu replied simply, "Thank you. I will see that our wounded are sent down to your ships as soon as possible."

The two marshals, seeing their masters in conversation, came over together. Both had dismounted and removed their head gear. Matthew of Clermont had a bandage wound about his shoulder which was already soaked through. Peter de Sevrey was limping. De Villiers flung his arms around his own marshal and then, for good measure, around De Sevrey too.

"We must get the King to order the evacuation of all women, children and disabled men." De Beaujeu brought the Hospitaller back to the pressing business still ahead of them.

De Villiers took a breath and nodded. "Yes, we should seek out the King. Take my stallion." Grasping the bridle, he handed it to De Beaujeu.

The Templar hesitated for a moment, but already one of the knights who had accompanied the Hospitaller was jumping down to offer De Villiers his horse. So De Beaujeu collected the offered reins and heaved himself upon the prize stallion of the Hospital.

Acre
May 18, 1291

Throughout the 17th of May, the Sultan kept his kettledrums pounding the ominous threat of assault. Mounted on three hundred camels, these gigantic drums beat out the seconds like a slow rhythmic heart: *thum-dum, thum-dum, thum-dum.* Neither the wailing of the mullahs nor the chiming of the church bells could halt or overpower the steady pulse of the drums beating like the heart of the city on the brink of death.

At the port the evacuation began. The King refused to order it, but civilians wishing to depart were given leave. De Beaujeu detailed Otto de Grandson to oversee the embarking of the ships, while Templars manned the harbour fortifications and controlled the chain across the entrance to ensure that no ship departed without authorisation – which meant without a full load of refugees. The small, slow boats were loaded first. Fishing smacks and Arab coastal dhows, big-bellied galleons, everything but the fleet and manoeuvrable galleys, were loaded with passengers and allowed to pass the harbour entrance. The two hospital galleys of the Hospitallers were moored directly at the quayside, and the most severely wounded of both orders were already aboard. They were few in number; the knights and sergeants of both orders insisted that they were still fit to fight if they could in any way stand and lift either arm – and many men had bled to death before they could be collected on the evening of the 16th.

Jean sent the faithful Pirenne to the Convent of the Sacred Heart and urged the sisters to depart at once. *The Falcon*, like all galleys, would remain in the harbour until the inner walls were breached and the Sultan's troops within the city itself. At that point, the remainder of the knights, sergeants and militiamen would have a last chance to flee – if they could gain the ships in time.

Jean was in the order's secretariat sorting through documents to be burned and/or loaded into chests for evacuation when Pirenne returned.

Jean looked up. "Are they all safely aboard one of the galleons?"

"Yes, sir – except for one."

"What do you mean?"

"One of the nuns refused to go, sir. I could hardly force her. She asked instead to be taken to *The Falcon*."

Jean's stomach knew even before his mind was willing to accept what Pirenne was telling him. "But *The Falcon* won't sail until the city is already lost."

Pirenne shrugged helplessly. "What was I supposed to do, sir?"

"Did Sergeant de Flor take her aboard?"

"Yes, sir. He welcomed her gallantly and gave her one of his best cabins – or so he said."

"Was it Sister Madeleine – the nun we..." – purchased was such an ugly word – "rescued in Nazareth?"

"Yes, sir."

"Christ be damned!"

"I beg you to watch your language, Brother. You are a monk in holy orders." This rebuke came from Father Etienne, who was helping sort through the documents.

"My apologies," Jean mumbled automatically, cursing himself for his overzealousness the night of the King's arrival. If only he had kept out of it, Madeleine would be safely on her way to Cyprus. Instead, he had her on his conscience if anything went wrong.

"This is a letter concerning your father, Brother Jean. You should be the one to decide if it is to be saved or destroyed." Father Etienne handed a parchment to Jean. The letter was addressed to the seneschal of the Temple and the broken seal on the back was that of Master De Sonnac. Jean's throat went dry as he realised that this had to be the letter dispatched by De Sonnac shortly before his death in Egypt some forty years ago. He held it in his hand afraid to open it: the night after the massacre in Mansourah his father had raged at De Sonnac, refusing admittance into the Knights Templar and denying the divinity of Christ. This was the letter the master had written to his deputy following that event.

Curiosity overcame foreboding and Jean lifted the folded leaves and scanned the elegant script. De Sonnac had evidently had no clerk available, for the entire letter was in his own hand. He wrote to his deputy and to all 'future masters of the Poor Knights of the Temple of Solomon." He told of his wounds at Mansourah, the situation of King Louis's army and spoke of his impending death as a certainty. He had lost sight in one eye as a result of a blow to his head in the fighting in Mansourah. 'But it is said that the blind are given second sight, and without knowing its worth let me pass on the dream of a man with one foot in the grave.'

De Sonnac had had a nightmare – surely induced by the horrors of the crusade – in which he had seen his brothers led into dungeons, tortured and burned like heretics. That was the worst of it, he commented, that they were not decapitated by the Muslims as infidels but burned at the stake like the Cathars. The dream was confused because he saw the master of the Temple being consumed by the flames of the *auto-da-fé*, but then he saw the novice/squire Geoffrey, aged and venerable, also in the mantle of the master. Geoffrey, mounted on a tall chestnut stallion, struck one of the men feeding the flames of the *auto-da-fé* with a sword and split him in two. From the two halves of the dead man – a Dominican – sprang two devils and Geoffrey fought them like St George against two dragons – a sword in each hand.

And while he fought, the brothers of the Temple who had been tied to a row of stakes broke their bonds and fled to the sea, where they jumped in and the flames which had clung to them were extinguished. But the devils kept multiplying. Though small and unarmed, they attacked Geoffrey like locusts or hornets until, exhausted, Geoffrey fell from his horse. By then all the fires were out, and a beautiful noble widow came and spread her cloak over him where he lay in the cold ashes at the foot of a row of empty stakes.

De Sonnac had refrained from trying to interpret his dream. He had merely urged his deputy and successors to accept Geoffrey into the order if he applied for admittance. 'If,' De Sonnac wrote, 'it is God's will that he be our master one day, then take him into your household and your heart, preparing him – as a man does his son – to assume the burden of that office that you yourself bear.'

Jean felt the blood in his head and the tightness of his throat. He knew now why De Beaujeu had always favoured him, forgiven his faults and indulged his waywardness. But he also felt an intense guilt. No one was more aware than Jean himself that he was not his father.

De Beaujeu had favoured the wrong man, placing hopes in him which he could never fulfil.

But what was the value of a dead man's dream anyway? All the images came from his own immediate experience. No man spent a lifetime fighting in the Holy Land without seeing men split in two. The civilians of Mansourah had seemed like locusts and hornets attacking the Frankish knights from all sides with their improvised weapons. And even after an adulthood spent fighting the Muslim enemy, the horror of the *auto-da-fé* witnessed as a child would never be wiped from the subconscious. There could be no doubt that De Sonnac had witnessed the *auto-da-fé* because he came from the Languedoc and his family had been tainted by Catharism even if he himself did not come from the heretical branch. It was therefore hardly surprising that he had mixed the horror of the battle he had just survived with the most horrid of his childhood memories. And in his dream he had transformed the youth who had rescued him from certain death at the hands of the Muslim fanatics into the rescuer of all those threatened by religious fanaticism.

Jean handed the letter back to Father Etienne. "It is not an important document, Father. We can burn it."

Father Etienne considered the monk-knight with an unreadable expression, and then, nodding, he put De Sonnac's letter on the pile to be burned.

*

All hope that dusk would silence the kettledrums proved vain. Through the night the drums kept up their ominous *thum-dum*, robbing the defenders of their sleep or harrying them in their dreams. There was no change in their pace or rhythm to mark the actual assault. In the eerie mist of early morning on the 18th of May, 1291, the final assault began.

The battle cries of the enemy pouring in over the rubble of the shattered towers at the angle of the outer wall roused the garrison from their sleepless daze. The Sultan offered extraordinary monetary rewards for each Christian head and the mullahs promised immediate entry to Paradise to those 'fortunate' enough to give their lives in the holy war. The Sultan's soldiers flung themselves at Acre with that explosive mixture of greed and piety that had characterised the conflict between Christian and Muslim throughout the Crusades.

The Sultan had sufficient troops to scorn a concentration of troops on any one point, and, after pouring through the ruins of the outer wall, the Sultan's troops spread themselves along the inner wall, pinning the garrison down for its entire length. At the Accursed Tower, in the angle of the wall, the enemy attacked from three sides. With the help of ladders, grappling hooks and even mobile platforms, swarms of turbaned and lightly dressed Muslim soldiers scaled the walls while mounted archers set up a barrage of arrows that darkened the dawn.

The Italian crossbowmen and the English archers sent to the Accursed Tower to counter the assault were overwhelmed within an hour. Because of the sheer numbers swarming up at them, they could not fire fast enough to prevent some men from reaching the ramparts. In hand-to-hand combat they were utterly at the mercy of the scimitar-wielding enemy. Whether it was Prince Amalric or his knights who were the weaker link, the Cypriot defenders of the Accursed Tower proved unequal to the task they had claimed for themselves. They fought until the last archer was slaughtered and then they broke and fled for their lives.

Both the Templars and Hospitallers had held back the bulk of their knights back, fearing that the concentrated attack on the Accursed Tower was a diversion and the major attack would be launched against the weakened St Anthony's Gate. Seeing the Cypriot defence collapse, however, De Beaujeu and Matthew of Clermont spurred forward with their mounted reserves and met the enemy as they burst out of the tower into the streets of Acre in a fever of triumph. The lightly clad enemy went down like wheat beneath the hooves of the European horses and the weapons of their riders. More than two hundred Muslims found their way to Paradise at the base of the Accursed Tower before the remainder took refuge in the tower itself, forcing the knights to dismount to pursue them.

Now it was the Sultan's troops who enjoyed the advantage of defending themselves within the walls of the massive tower. The Christians could only drive them back out of the tower by first forcing an entry through the narrow door and fighting their way up the spiral stairs – twisting clockwise to give the defender the advantage.

The enemy was being constantly reinforced by comrades scaling the now undefended ramparts of the tower, while each Christian lost was irreplaceable. The blood of the dead and dying mingled together, indifferent to the religion that had driven men to spill it. In the dark and the confusion, the Knights of Christ were driven back more by the sheer weight of the Muslims pouring down the stairwell than by their weapons. The Muslim soldiers joining the fight from above were fresh and driven by the thirst for glory, plunder or heavenly reward. While those who had been driven back into the tower had lost some of their *élan* in the sheer reality of the fighting, the new arrivals ran down their weary comrades in their eagerness to get at the hated infidel.

Forced again into the streets of Acre, Jean was amazed to see that old De Villiers himself was there beside them. De Beaujeu seemed to notice him at the same time as Jean, and, pulling back abruptly, he grabbed the master of the Hospital by the arm. "My lord! No one expects this of you!"

"I am not so old that I cannot die for my faith!" De Villiers protested, shaking himself free of De Beaujeu's arm and plunging back into the fight.

De Villaret sprang after him, and it was his sword more than that of the seventy year old which kept the Muslim scimitars away from the grand master of the Knights of St John.

Even as Jean fought with one Egyptian soldier he dropped dead at Jean's feet with an arrow through his neck. In horror, Jean glanced upwards toward the ramparts of the tower hanging over them. Muslim archers had gained the ramparts of the Accursed Tower and were now firing down into the street. The Europeans, encased in armour and wearing their iron helmets, were considerably less vulnerable than the Saracen fighters, but, with apparent indifference to the casualties they would inflict on their own comrades, the Sultan's archers pumped volley after volley from the tower into the *mêlée* below.

Jean became aware that Templar serving brothers, Augustinian canons, boys and even some women had joined the knights, fighting with clubs, paving stones or weapons taken from the dead.

Pierre came up beside him. "Sir! We..."

He sank down at Jean's feet, the smile of greeting still upon his face, his intestines spilling from his fatal wound.

'Christ have mercy on his soul. Forgive him his sins.' Jean was aware of tears running down his face, unseen behind the iron mask of his helmet. His broadsword fought on, indifferent to the identity of the victims.

De Beaujeu was shouting, "Get him out of here! Back to the galleys!"

"I can still..." De Villiers protested with the shrill petulance of an old man. His sword was gone and his entire shoulder seemed to have caved in; his collarbone had apparently collapsed under a blow.

"For Christ's sake, one of us should be a witness to what happened here!" De Beaujeu insisted, adding to De Villaret, who was supporting the master, "Get him down to the ships!"

De Villaret hesitated, looked about for someone else who could fulfil this task for him, but De Beaujeu shouted at him in mounting rage. "Don't you understand, you idiot! If you don't get down to the ships and take command, there'll be chaos in the harbour! Your duty is to the sick and wounded, *Monsieur le Grand Hôpitaller*." He used De Villaret's new title to remind him of the duties it implied and carried.

De Villaret started, then nodded. The hesitation was gone and a determination took its place. He spoke to De Villiers and the resistance of the old man dissolved. Meekly, the master of the Hospital let himself be led back from the line of fighting.

The enemy still pouring down from the Accursed Tower had pushed the defenders far enough away from the base of the tower to be able to start spreading along the back of the inner wall. They poured along the passageway attacking the garrison – still manning the wall against the assault from outside – from behind. They set to slaughtering the men defending the gates, preparing to open them from the inside.

Jean heard a cry beside him and, despite all the tumult and the shouting and screaming of men around him, it sent a chill down his spine. He spun around and saw De Beaujeu with his sword arm still lifted over his head – and an arrow sticking out of his armpit. De Beaujeu staggered backwards, his sword falling to the cobbles. Jean sprang to catch him and found himself shoulder to shoulder with Father Etienne. The priest had pulled a chainmail hauberk over his cassock and was fighting bareheaded with a mace. Together they held De Beaujeu.

De Beaujeu fought to right himself. With his left hand he reached under his right arm and felt the wound and the arrow.

"The ships," Father Etienne suggested, and Jean nodded.

"The Temple," De Beaujeu corrected. "No need to waste a berth that might save another."

They took a step backwards.

"How dare you desert us!" a furious civilian knight shouted directly in Beaujeu's face. "If you pull back we are lost!" He grabbed at Jean with his mailed fist as Jean tried to get the master away from him. Jean could not recognise his coat of arms, as his surcoat was too tattered and filthy.

"I am not withdrawing." De Beaujeu struggled for breath as he replied with dignity. "I am dying." And with these words he lost consciousness.

"Can't you see the wound?" Jean furiously demanded of the astonished knight, while Father Etienne demanded Jean's shield. Jean slipped it off his left arm and dropped it, inner side up, on to the ground behind De Beaujeu. He sheathed his sword and, together with Father Etienne, laid the master on the shield. One on either side of the shield they carried De Beaujeu away from the *mêlée*.

They stumbled through the shuttered and deserted streets, the sound of the conflict ever further away but never entirely silenced. Jean could hear Father Etienne's breathing becoming increasingly laboured. He suggested they pause to rest, but then he realised that Father Etienne was sobbing, his eyes and nose running with tears.

Jean wondered why he couldn't cry. He wanted to. There was even a tension at the base of his throat like the start of tears, but he could not cry. The tears he had so briefly shed for Pierre were long since dry – or rather mingled with the sweat that soaked his face under the iron of his helmet in the heat of the Palestinian sun. At the junction where the roads leading to the harbour and the Temple separated they stopped in indecision. It was only a short two hundred yards to the harbour and from there they could clearly hear shouts and crashing sounds competing with the noise of battle behind them. By mutual consent, they started down toward the water in defiance of Beaujeu's wishes, but they had underestimated his will power.

At some point during the journey De Beaujeu had regained consciousness and now he recognised the route they were taking. He grasped Father Etienne's wrist. "Etienne, as you love me, do as I say. Take me to the Temple."

"What is the point?"

"Do you think I don't know when I'm finished? Take me to the Temple and let me die here in the Holy Land – not on the promiscuous sea."

Father Etienne was crying too hard to answer. They changed course and followed the narrower alley along the back of the Pisan quarter and then into a wider street again that led to the gate of the Temple. The Temple was manned by lay brothers and elder sergeants, those not thought fit enough to take part in the actual fighting. They rushed to relieve Father Etienne and Jean, aware instinctively that these men would not have left the fighting to carry anyone of less consequence than the master himself.

There were no surgeons left in the Temple for they had all gone aboard the two hospital ships. Ian MacDonald at once said he would run down and fetch one, but De Beaujeu forestalled him. "There isn't any point, MacDonald. Just take me to my chamber."

MacDonald and two other serving brothers shouldered the shield between them and did as they were bidden. Father Etienne and Jean followed behind. Jean was torn between a sense of urgency to return to the fighting and a love for De Beaujeu that did not permit him to turn his back on the dying man.

The brothers transferred De Beaujeu from the shield on to the bed, and then stepped back. Father Etienne had collected himself. The tears and sobbing had stopped. He knelt beside the bed and prepared to administer the last rites.

Jean leaned over De Beaujeu and removed first his helmet, then his cervellière and coif. "Would it help if I removed the arrow?"

De Beaujeu shook his head. "Just hold my hand for a moment. I know you are anxious to return to the fight."

It embarrassed Jean that De Beaujeu could read him so easily – even with his eyes closed and on the brink of his own grave. He removed Beaujeu's gauntlet and his own so that they held hands skin to skin. The sweat which had soaked them inside their gauntlets and helms was gradually cooling in the chill of the room facing the sea. It was still before noon and the chamber was in shadow.

There was so much to say that Jean's mind was blank.

Father Etienne broke the silence. "William, are you ready to confess?"

De Beaujeu nodded, squeezed Jean's hand one last time and then removed it. "Go back to the fight, Jean. Peter needs you. Help him and obey him as you would me. He is the best of us."

Jean grasped Beaujeu's hand and kissed it. "You will be remembered for your courage, my lord."

"I will be remembered for losing Outremer," De Beaujeu countered cynically.

Thibald Gaudin burst into the room. He was in full armour except for his helm, which he held under his arm. He stank of sweat and blood, as they all did. Thibald had command of the Temple itself, but apparently he had joined in the fighting. "My Lord?"

"Ah, Thibald! Come, kneel beside me – no on the left. Jean, give me your sword – De Sonnac's sword."

Jean was too confused and distressed to question or wonder. He drew the dulled and bloodied sword from its sheath and handed it hilt first to De Beaujeu. De Beaujeu lay with his right arm over his head so that the arrow would not thrust any deeper into the wound, so he took the proffered sword with his left hand. "You are my witnesses – all of you," De Beaujeu addressed the serving brothers still clustered against the back of the wall. "I, William de Beaujeu, master of the Poor Knights of the Temple of Solomon in Jerusalem, do hereby knight you, Thibald Gaudin."

Lying flat on his back and losing pints of blood by the minute, De Beaujeu could not control the four foot long broadsword. It swung and swayed dangerously through the air, its edge still lethal though dulled and nicked from the violent encounters with steel and bone. Sergeant Gaudin drew his head between his shoulders and Jean reached forward to take the blade between his thumb and finger. He guided it from one shoulder to the other.

"Rise, Sir Thibald, Brother Knight of the Temple of Solomon."

The white-haired sergeant was so moved that he had difficulty clambering to his feet. "My lord..." he stuttered. "My lord..." He was not of noble birth. The honour was more than he could have ever hoped for. It was one he did not feel he deserved.

"What is it, sir?" De Beaujeu smiled at calling him sir, and sank back into unconsciousness.

*

When Jean left the Temple he was aware that the sound of conflict was not only nearer but that a certain diffuseness had replaced what had once seemed coherent. Smoke marked the fires set within the city, panicked horses clattered riderless through the alleys. People – soldiers and civilians, some bloodied, some laden with sacks of belongings – rushed across his path making for the harbour. He caught a glimpse of Paul's brother, the man whose freedom he'd purchased in Nazareth, shoving his way past a woman with two children; overburdened with her valuables and a baby in her arm, she stumbled and nearly fell.

The sound of hoarse shouting mingling with the rumble of a crowd reached him from the right. Abruptly, he turned toward the water and stopped at the head of the street where he could see down to the port. The King of Cyprus's flagship was already beyond the harbour entrance, its flag fluttering above an unfurling sail. To his surprise, Jean could make out *The Falcon*, still under oar at this time, but on the brink of passing the harbour entrance. Roger de Flor had apparently taken things into his own hands for his orders had been to wait until the enemy could be seen on the quay. He had a dozen crossbowmen aboard to ensure that he could still cut his hawsers and put to sea before the enemy could seize the galley. But if Roger de Flor was being insubordinate and even cowardly, Jean was nevertheless relieved for Sister Madeleine's sake. It was one less burden to carry this day.

The Hospitallers' two galleys, in contrast, were still at the quay, and De Villaret, with several knights and sergeants, was defending the gangway against a crowd of desperate civilians. 'Where have they all come from and why hadn't they left yesterday?' Jean wondered. Then he realised that they were beggars, Jews, half-breed Franks and even Arabs, apparently afraid they would be tainted with collaboration and slaughtered or enslaved, just like their Christian and Jewish neighbours. They were those elements of society with no money for bribes and no one to turn to for help and support in a strange country.

Even as Jean watched, the crowd suddenly left the end of the gangway and fled like a flock of frightened fowl toward another point on the quay. At first puzzled, he realised that a ship which had been anchored just offshore appeared to be approaching the quay. Jean saw that this ship was flying the banner of the patriarch of Jerusalem. Realising that the crowd on the quay would try to storm the ship, however, the captain kept his ship hovering a good hundred yards off shore. At last Jean noticed the patriarch himself, escorted by dozens of priests, lesser clerks and servants, who had just reached the quay. The old man went down the steps of the quay and a skiff was launched from his ship to take him aboard.

As soon as the people on the quay saw what was happening, the braver or younger of them started leaping into the water. The weaker called for help. The patriarch was confused. He stopped, turned back, was evidently urged forward by his household. He was helped into the skiff and it set off. The swimmers splashed forward with obvious desperation. The men in the boat tried to fight them off as they laid their hands on the gunnel. The patriarch reproached them and offered the swimmers help. The swimmers increased their efforts. More and more risked the leap into the filthy harbour and swam for the little skiff. Now it had come to a halt in the middle of the distance between the shore and the waiting ship. More and more people were climbing aboard. The skiff settled deeper and deeper into the water. Jean wanted to scream at the idiots to stop letting people into the boat. He looked hastily at the Hospitallers, but they were too busy attending to a cluster of men who came half crawling and half limping out of the street from the east. Jean thought he recognised Otto de Grandson among the men helping the wounded to the quay.

A cry from the harbour drew his attention back to the drama on the water. The inevitable had happened. The little skiff had capsized. Now sailors were diving from the ship into the water and in the midst of it all several non-swimmers, including the patriarch, were flailing in the water in panic.

Jean snapped himself out of his fascinated daze. What was he doing standing about watching people drown? He was tired, his muscles ached, the wound in his calf was bleeding again, bruises of a hundred blows throbbed, but he was fitter than most fighting men left in the city. His place was with those holding the enemy back so that the others could reach the ships.

Making his way by ear back to the battle, Jean realised that St Nicholas's rather than St Anthony's Gate must have fallen first. It was from the east rather than the north that the enemy was pressing deepest and most vigorously into the city. From the north the citizens were fleeing, apparently still protected by a line of Templar sergeants withdrawing in an orderly fashion and holding back an enemy that was numerous but not overwhelming. Beyond the line of withdrawing Templars, the frustrated enemy was plundering goods and setting fire to the buildings. From the east, fighting men as well as citizens were fleeing, and the enemy, sensing success, had no time for plunder and arson but sought feverishly to achieve the final breakthrough. If they succeeded, they would break through to the port, cut off the remaining Christians from the ships and possibly even capture some of the ships still tied up at the quay. It all depended upon whether they could break through suddenly and strongly enough to take the port entirely by surprise.

Just beyond the Patriarch's palace, Jean met the battle line as it was driven by the Muslims past the headquarters of the Teutonic knights. Both the Germans' fortress and the royal palace had fallen into Muslim hands already and were flying the green and gold of the Sultan. Though the Hospitallers' castle was still in Christian hands, it sat inland and north of the Italian quarter and could offer no halt to the enemy driving for the port. Nor did the patriarch's palace lend itself to military purposes. The only advantage the Christians now had was the narrowness of the streets, which prevented the enemy from bringing their numbers to bear directly. The enemy had to be content with wearing down and wounding the defenders, confident that their own losses could be replaced while the Christians' numbers shrank with each backward step.

Jean made his way to the foremost edge of the defenders, conscious that he was relatively rested and had quenched his thirst before leaving the Temple. He located Peter de Sevrey and took his place beside him immediately. De Sevrey staggered slightly when he saw a knight arrive so unexpectedly from behind and drive his sword against the enemy with an energy he had lost hours ago. "Jean?"

Jean nodded.

"He's dead."

Jean nodded again as the great blade of De Sonnac's sword cut through the neck of an opponent and shattered his collarbone. Behind the protection of Jean's rested arm, De Sevrey leaned upon his own sword and struggled for breath and clarity of thought. He glanced over his shoulder and was horrified to register how close they were to the harbour. He had known they were being driven back, but had not realised how far. After all, each step had been hard fought; the enemy trod upon a carpet of dead. Yet now the water could be seen shimmering and glittering at the foot of the street. He made a rough count of the men he had left: maybe two dozen Hospitaller knights and twice that many sergeants. Half again as many Templar knights but hardly any sergeants – they were still holding the line on the northern sector. There were a handful of Teutonic knights and crusaders, but the Cypriots and Otto de Grandson with his Englishmen were no longer fighting, having either been killed or made for the harbour. There were another hundred native militiamen with a few Frankish knights stiffening them. Altogether some two hundred to two hundred and fifty fighting men left, and then an odd assortment of priests, monks, women and Jews fighting from sheer hatred and with awe-inspiring self-respect. These were truly people who had decided to die fighting rather than face the humility of slaughter or captivity, though no oath and no professional pride dictated this destiny. De Sevrey felt humbled by their courage and took up his sword again.

From behind them came a sudden uproar, hysterical screaming different from the shouts of battle. Jean threw up his shield so that he could turn and look back over his right shoulder. The enemy had somehow managed to find their way through the houses into a back alley, thereby outflanking the small force of Christians holding the street. While some of the enemy were now slaughtering the defenders from the rear, the bulk were pouring down toward the harbour to seize the ships.

"The Temple!" De Sevrey ordered, and already he was moving back along their lines giving the order to change the direction of their withdrawal. They could no longer save the port, but by pulling back abruptly into an alley cutting between the Genoese and the Venetian quarters they could evade the enemy's pincer and gain again the safety of a yet narrower street.

From the harbour came the confused babbling roar of fighting. 'Let De Villaret get away with his galleys!' Jean prayed, and for a second time he was grateful that Roger de Flor had not waited till the last minute to take *The Falcon* out.

While the remnants of the defenders of the Accursed Tower and the eastern sector withdrew westwards, De Sevrey sent a knight to the north to order the immediate withdrawal of the Templar sergeants. Neither body of troops was hard pressed at the moment for the enemy was concentrating on the harbour, and it was not long before they could hear the hooting and chorus of shouts that indicated triumph: "Allah Akbar! Allah Akbar!"

Jean's throat went dry thinking of De Villaret in his blood at the foot of the gangway and the enemy pouring aboard the hospital galleys to slaughter the wounded while they lay helpless in the straw.

'Yes, Allah is great indeed,' he thought bitterly, but then he heard De Beaujeu's cynical voice in his ear remarking dryly, "Allah's greatness can be measured by the fact that it took two hundred and fifty thousand of his soldiers to defeat one thousand Knights of Christ."

They could tell by the shouting that the Sultan, who had not once bloodied his hands or his silken robes with actual fighting, had now ridden into the city to receive the tribute of his troops for his great victory. But behind them loomed the great gate of the Temple. It stood with yawning portcullis casting the entire street in shadow against the afternoon sun. The black and white banner of Templars was flying out straight on a stiff breeze.

Fortunately, a line of black-clad sergeants was flanking the street on the north. Otherwise, the enemy, which had entered by the northern gates and had been held back by the Templar sergeants all day, would have cut them off from their last refuge. Jean could make out Pirenne, half a head taller than the men around him, fighting with astonishing vigour still. It was a comfort to think he had survived so long.

From the gate itself came the first volley of quarrels, driving those few tenacious pursuers in the street behind the knights to dive for cover. De Sevrey gave the order to run for it. Knights accompanied the rag-tag collection of civilians and clerks broke off the struggle that had lasted three-quarters of the day and fled with utter abandon for the safety of the castle. The sergeants waited just long enough for the others to get behind them, and then they joined in the desperate sprint to gain the safety of the masonry. Out of the corner of his eye, Jean saw Pirenne fall, a flung lance sticking up out of his torso. The sergeant tried to lift himself and Jean broke stride to go to his aid. De Sevrey roughly grabbed him and shoved him forward. They clattered through the barbican still at a run, and as Jean twisted to look back at Pirenne the first of the portcullises dropped before his face. De Sevrey was dragging him still. He stumbled into the courtyard as the gates were banged shut and barred. The second portcullis crashed down with a shudder that made the entire courtyard tremble.

Doubled over, his hands on his thighs, Jean struggled for air. His temples were pulsing and he felt faint. Dropping his sword on to the cobbles, he reached up and shoved his helmet from his head so he could suck more oxygen into his heaving lungs. Slowly the faintness passed. With a last deep breath, he righted himself and his heart stopped. Spread out before him like a tapestry were literally hundreds of people. The fighting men who had just gained the safety of the castle lay gasping for breath and clutching their wounds upon the cobbles of the inner ward. Beside them lay all those civilians who had been fighting with them, no less exhausted and equally bloodied. But in addition to these were scores upon scores of others who had been in the northern sectors of the city and therefore cut off from the harbour. Some still clung to sacks full of their most precious belongings while others mourned their dead openly, keening and crying.

The refugees crouched in the arcades, squatted along the walls, spilled up the steps to the chapel and had flooded into the audience chamber. Among a party of Jews, Jean noticed little Rachel clutching a woven basket in her scrawny arms. There was no sign of either her father or her sister. She, like all the others, had found here a last refuge – but one no less vulnerable to the Sultan's sappers than the city itself had proved.

Acre
May 19, 1291

At dawn on the 19th of May an eerie calm reigned in the Temple at Acre. Food and water were plentiful. The baths were so extensive that they enabled even the most humble of the refugees to wash away the dirt of years. Though the surgeons had withdrawn to the galleys before the fall of the city, the wounded nevertheless found adequate linen for bandages, salves and the means to cauterise those injuries which would otherwise fester. The Temple at Acre, built at the height of the Templars' power, could easily accommodate the roughly eight hundred people now besieged within without undue squalor. There were three great dormitories designed to house serving brothers, sergeants, squires and novices respectively. Owing to Templar casualties, all the Templar sergeants and serving brothers could sleep together in the sergeants' dormitory and the remaining two dormitories were large enough to offer all the refugees a pallet. The surviving knights and squires, whether Templar, Hospitaller or civilian, could pick and choose among the vacant cells of the Templar knights. The kitchens, ovens and refectory were not in the least strained by the burden of providing for so many – once a number of the refugees had been moved to volunteer their services.

As the sun climbed up the eastern sky, the occupants of the Temple had to shake themselves out of two kinds of shock: the knowledge that Acre was irretrievably lost and the shock of their own survival. All had witnessed the slaughter that had decimated the garrison in the gruelling, day-long battle that climaxed a six-week siege. All were mourning friends, relatives and brothers. In short, the survivors in the Temple were in no state to rejoice over their own survival. Almost all had some kind of injury. Many of the fighting men were nursing serious wounds.

Though water, food and the cleansing of body and clothing did much to reinvigorate the flesh, the mental and spiritual daze was only increased as the survivors watched from the ramparts the plundering and arson of their homes, bazaars, warehouses and churches. They watched too the disrespectful treatment meted out to their dead; the bodies of the Christians were heaped upon dung-wagons and tipped into burning houses and warehouses – unless of course they happened to be members of the military orders. The Sultan ordered the bodies of the dead Templars, Hospitallers and Teutonics carved in pieces, the heads skewered upon lances and the lances propped up within view of the Temple. Particularly painful for Jean was seeing Pirenne's head at the top of one of the lances.

When, at dusk on the 19th, the Templars read the requiem for De Beaujeu, they prayed for all their dead. Of the roughly three hundred knights and eight hundred sergeants with whom they had commenced the siege, there were now only thirty-two knights, one hundred and twenty-seven sergeants left alive, and even the serving brothers – rushing lightly armed into the streets in the final phase of the fighting – had lost more than half their number. All the Temple's senior officers except for Peter de Sevrey and Thibald Gaudin had died in the fighting.

As the requiem bells rang out from the Romanesque chapel, the refugees – except of course the Jews – crowded in to hear the service, remembering in their hearts their own dead. And when at the end of the service the Templars lifted De Beaujeu's austere coffin from its place before the altar, the refugees – including the Jews – joined the brethren in escorting his body to the graveyard. De Sevrey and Gaudin, as the only officers of the Temple still alive, Jean and Father Etienne, one sergeant and one serving brother, as members of De Beaujeu's household, carried the coffin. They were followed by a somewhat piteous train of knights, sergeants and serving brothers – bandaged, limping, with improvised crutches and canes and slings.

On the morning of the 20th, Marshal De Sevrey began organising the refugees. By evening all had been assigned duties in the kitchens, the stables, the baths, the laundry, the bakery or brewery. Those men willing and able to bear arms had been detailed to the watch and took their turn manning the walls. Among the monks and canons of other religious orders who had managed to gain the sanctuary of the

Temple, there were several with medical experience and these took over the infirmary under the direction of a Jewish doctor.

In recognition of Gaudin's knighting, De Sevrey named Gaudin commander of the kingdom of Jerusalem and appointed another senior sergeant to be commander of Acre. His right as marshal to make these appointments was, of course, dubious, but both the master and the seneschal were dead, making De Sevrey the senior officer, and no one in Acre that day even thought to question his authority unless it was Gaudin, who felt himself excessively honoured.

It was clear to all of them, however, that the initiative lay entirely with the enemy. They had neither the resources to buy their freedom nor the means to escape. The Templar Rule prohibited the payment of ransom for a captured knight, much less purchasing one's freedom in advance, and De Beaujeu had evacuated the Treasury on the 17th in any case. There was, to be sure, a sea gate in the cellars of the Temple with direct access to the Mediterranean, but there was only one small, light skiff at the quay and an old, open longboat – of dubious seaworthiness – lying keel-up in the boathouse. These boats together might carry one hundred to one hundred and twenty people, but De Sevrey showed no desire to make a selection among his charges – at least not yet. With the consent of all the Templars, including the sergeants and serving brothers, the decision was made to defy the Sultan.

On the 21st of May, having apparently celebrated his victory in sufficient splendour, counted his plunder, overseen the initial dismantling of the walls and buildings of military value and observed with satisfaction the burning of the rest, the Sultan at last took note of the Temple, still defiantly flying the Baucent. Troops were sent against the last remaining Christian stronghold, but they showed little real enthusiasm for dying in a cause already won. Furthermore, in his haste to destroy Acre, the Sultan had allowed even the houses directly before the Temple to be burnt, thus denying his own troops any cover during their assaults. The attack was quite easily repulsed with boiling water, some projectiles containing Greek fire and crossbow volleys.

The repulse of the enemy did much for morale inside the Temple, and De Sevrey ordered some casks of the master's best wine breached and distributed to all who had taken part in the defence. They slaughtered two calves as well and roasted them for the entire garrison.

On the 22nd of May, the Sultan repeated his offensive against the Temple with more determination. He sent some of his elite troops, and when they also withdrew after an intense but nevertheless unsuccessful attack the dervishes were sent to inspire religious fervour. The Christian defenders had the rare pleasure of shouting ridicule at these usually invincible opponents with absolute impunity; the fanaticism of the dervishes neither frightened nor impressed the masonry of the Temple and they all died at the foot of the brooding walls.

At this point the Sultan lost his temper and sent in his own guard. They rode to the attack in their golden breastplates with their banners streaming behind them, but it was hard to see what they hoped to gain. William de la More had only a dozen of his archers left, but there were nearly eighty other sergeants and as many civilians who could manage a crossbow with moderate efficiency. The armoury of the Temple in the undercroft of the sergeants' dormitory provided them with more ammunition than they could expend in a year. From inside the wall and from the ramparts they were able to put up a barrage that – while not comparable to what the Sultan himself could have launched – effectively broke the charge of the horsemen.

Those Mamelukes who reached the portcullis were at once subjected to boiling oil tipped through the murder-holes in the floor of the barbican directly over the space before the portcullis. The screams of the horses wrenched many of the defenders' hearts and caused the Templars' own horses to whinny in sympathetic distress from their stables.

"The beasts have a better love of their fellows than man does," Ian MacDonald remarked as he helped carry another barrel of pig's fat up to the barbican where it would be heated over a fire.

"Hm," Sir Duncan grunted in agreement. The stitches of his face wound had been partially torn out during the fighting on the 18th and his whole face was now a swollen, misshapen mass, despite the best efforts of the Jewish doctor. He spoke only with difficulty and barely intelligibly. Even so, he could not leave the fighting to others.

The choice of pig's fat for the boiling oil was, of course, a means of adding insult to injury for the Muslim enemy. Even now, as they prepared to empty a second vat of the liquid lard down the murder hole, Jean could hear the bitter curses of the men below who recognised the smell of the weapon being employed against them. It was a petty kind of revenge for all that the enemy had inflicted on them, but Jean savoured it with uncharitable pleasure. The second vat was as good as wasted. No sooner had they started to tip it down the holes than the enemy fled the barbican with wild furious threats of revenge – and seemed to keep riding all the way to the Sultan.

The best wine was shared out again and pigs were slaughtered for the evening meal. Invaded as they were by civilians outnumbering them nearly two-to-one, the Templars made no effort to maintain the rule of silence. Nor did anyone attempt to mount the pulpit and read holy texts. When far down the table one of the civilians stood and started singing, De Sevrey actually smiled – for the first time since his sortie more than a month earlier.

"A pity the Sultan cannot see the candelabra burning here tonight," Jean remarked wistfully to William de la More sitting on his left. Not one of the great iron chandeliers nor one of the standing candelabra was without burning candles. No one really believed they could hold out for long so they were not even trying to husband their supplies. Better to burn the candles themselves than let them fall into the Sultan's greedy hands.

"I was wondering about that," De la More replied with the professional enthusiasm that characterised him. "From the sea it must be possible to see the light burning in the hall here."

"Yes, but our lookouts have not sighted any of the Sultan's fleet yet."

"The fishing boats will have his spies aboard," De la More responded. "He must be anxious to know how many of us are here. Is there any weakness in this fortress which a prisoner might be forced to reveal?"

"Not that I know of."

"Then you think we are impregnable?"

"From the sappers that brought down the King Henry tower? Hardly."

Jean felt something tugging at his sleeve and looked over his shoulder in surprise. Rachel stood at his elbow, her surcoat dirty at the knees and torn at the shoulder. Her feet were bare, but she had wrapped a threadbare, faded shawl around her head, covering her dark, listless hair as if she were a grown woman. "*Monsieur?*" she asked him, her eyes big as saucers in her pale face.

"Rachel!" He tried to sound pleased, but his heart sank to be reminded that she had not made it to the boats on the 17th.

She reached for his hand, and he let her take it, but he looked somewhat nervously down the hall to the other Jews. "Where is your father, Rachel?"

She nodded with her head toward the outside wall.

"In the city?"

"He refused to leave my mother. She is crippled. He and my sister refused to leave... but... but I was so frightened – I ran away. I came here." The tears were quivering in her eyes and her fingers wound themselves in his with desperate intensity.

"Ah, Rachel!" Jean freed his hand so he could fling his arms around her and draw her against his breast. She burst into tears, and buried her face in the white surcoat with the red cross and wept her heart out.

William de la More was watching him with a bemused expression, and Jean smiled somewhat apologetically across Rachel's heaving back. Her shoulder blades stuck out sharply and he was reminded of how fragile Sister Madeleine had been when he carried her from the slave market in Nazareth. He was reminded too of the jeers of Sir Ludolf and Sir Fulk who had called him Jew-lover, and he looked again more defensively to Sir William. But De la More's expression remained more amused than disapproving.

Gradually Rachel's sobbing ebbed and Jean took his goblet and offered her his wine. She looked up at him first, her eyes rimmed with red but shimmering with tears. They were the eyes of a doe, pretty even if her hare lip made her face ugly. With one hand, she helped guide the silver goblet to her lips and tasted his wine with a daintiness and a sidelong glance that was almost coquettish.

De la More burst out laughing, slapped the table with his palm and then reached for the pitcher to pour them all some more wine. "You've made a conquest of that little one, Brother, whether you intended to or not!" He spoke in English, a language he knew Jean understood but the others at the high table did not.

"Don't be ridiculous! She's a child. A Jew. The daughter of a shopkeeper who – incidentally – treated her harshly. I don't think she ever learned the meaning of the word 'play' and you can see how poor she is!"

"And she's head over heels in love with you." De la More found this immensely amusing precisely because he could see that Jean neither returned her affections nor knowingly invited them.

De la More's loud laughter both discomfited Jean and attracted attention, so that he now firmly set Rachel aside and told her to return to the other women.

Rachel did not seem offended. Collecting her skirts in her right fist, she started to sprint away, the child overpowering the woman. Then just as she was about to disappear behind the dinners at the side board, she stopped and flashed a smile at Jean before bounding away. De la More laughed even louder, and Jean scowled in embarrassment and confusion.

*

On the morning of the 23rd the Sultan sent an ambassador in full diplomatic splendour, escorted by two emirs and a squad of Nubian slaves. He bore the white flag of truce. De Sevrey mounted to the ramparts of the barbican and let the master's translator, a half-breed turcopole, enquire the ambassador's mission.

"My lord and master, the all-powerful and from merciful Allah best-beloved Sultan of Egypt and Syria, al Ashraf Khalil, son of the illustrious and devout Kalaoun..." He went on at some length about his master's ancestors and achievements before finally getting to the point: "...sends his greetings." In light of the awesome victory Allah had granted him in purging the stinking, pig-eating infidels from the sacred soil of Palestine, his master was prepared to show great mercy to the remnants of a once arrogant legion on the condition that they removed their stinking bodies from his lord's territory and swore never to putrefy it again with their presence.

"Tell the Sultan to bury the heads of my brothers! Then we can discuss how to clean the air further!" De Sevrey pointed demonstratively at the lances still bearing the rotten, fly-coated heads of the Templars and Hospitallers. Then he turned his back and started to descend into the barbican without even waiting for the translation, much less the response.

At the base of the stairs, in the shadow of the guardroom, he stopped as if to catch his breath and leaned against the wall, closing his eyes. "Almighty and Ever-Loving God! Father, Son and Holy Ghost in one! Mother Mary! Saint George! Let it be true! Let the Sultan want a rapid end to this siege more than he wants our blood. Grant us this reprieve in the name of all our Brothers who have died in Your name. Grant me the wisdom to negotiate this truce and this withdrawal. God Almighty, maker of heaven and earth, save our miserable lives that we may praise Your name in all the years to come. Mother Mary, have mercy on your children for your son's sake, who died for our sins." He pulled himself together as he heard the translator coming down the stairs.

"Well, what did he say?"

"He withdrew to consult the Sultan. Now we must wait."

"You think I made a mistake?"

The turcopole shook his head slowly. "You were wise. Very wise. He knows now that we are not desperate for a truce. He has seen our defiance not only in the face of his anger but in the face of his mercy. That is good. Too much eagerness would have made him either lose interest in any agreement or make his terms very harsh. But... we will have to wait and see."

De Sevrey was in the infirmary when a messenger from the walls found him to inform him that the Sultan's slaves had removed the lances with the Christians' grisly heads. Shortly afterwards the ambassador reappeared with the same worthy escort and the ritual began again. This time De Sevrey ordered the outer portcullis raised to admit the ambassador. The inner portcullis was not lifted, however, until the outer portcullis had been lowered behind him and after he had passed it this too was relowered.

By the time the ambassador dismounted in the inner ward, his face was noticeably paler than it had been in the street. De Sevrey accorded the ambassador all courtesy due to his rank and mission. He was received in the audience chamber, offered a stool, iced water from the cisterns in the deepest cellars of the fortress and fresh bread lightly sprinkled with salt. Dates, apricots and almonds were placed in a bowl at his elbow.

De Sevrey had a working mastery of Arabic much like Jean's, but he still made use of his turcopole translator to avoid the embarrassment of grammatical error or misplaced nuance. He had

Jean and De la More flanking him during the audience, both as witnesses and to increase his own dignity. As these were the only surviving commanders and both were in relatively robust health, he hoped to give the impression of having more resources in manpower than in fact he had. Bluff was a major part of any negotiation.

The discussion started with a round of compliments. The Sultan expressed his great admiration for this little band of men who defied him in spite of the hopelessness of their situation. De Sevrey marvelled at the Sultan's military skill in taking a city as powerful and well defended as Acre. If the ambassador noted the irony in the flowery speech as De Sevrey stressed the vastness of the Sultan's army and the sheer awesomeness of his ordnance, he did not let it show. Ambassadors were trained to keep their expressions pleasantly neutral.

Instead, the ambassador stressed that, since Tyre had also surrendered, Sidon was the last infidel city still besmirching the land so dear to Allah.

The Sultan was anxious to expunge this insult to the true faith and did not have the patience to teach the miserable wretches here a lesson. He was therefore prepared in his infinite mercy and for the love of pity that Allah also preached (appropriate passages of the Koran were cited) to allow the remaining garrison of Acre in the Temple (he referred to it as the fortress of the Knights of Solomon) to withdraw.

"Withdraw where? And how?" De Sevrey demanded succinctly.

"To withdraw from Palestine, of course – to Cyprus or France or Ireland for all the Sultan cares. He does not care where you go so long as you are gone and swear never to return."

"How? Will he provide us with ships?"

"The Sultan is prepared to guarantee you safe conduct as far as the harbour where you will be free to hire ships – at your own expense."

"No." Jean was surprised by the sharpness of Sevrey's answer. Sensing the surprise of his companions, De Sevrey glanced up and murmured in French, "That is a trick. We get to the harbour and there are no ships or the masters have all been instructed not to give us passage at any price, and then the Sultan either kills us or takes us all into slavery for having failed to keep our word about departing at once."

Turning back to the ambassador who was sitting with an impassive face as if he had not understood, De Sevrey elaborated his answer for the interpreter. "We will not accept any terms other than a safe conduct guaranteed by the Sultan himself on the honour of his mother's virtue all the way to Cyprus. The Sultan must provide us with ships or allow Greek ships to enter for the purpose of our evacuation. The shipmasters will be reimbursed the expense after all of us have landed safely at Limassol, and the Sultan will receive an extra gift as well for keeping his word!"

"I cannot possibly make this offer to my lord and master as it would insult him and make him determined to destroy you. The word of such an illustrious and devout son of the true faith is sacrosanct and cannot be purchased." The ambassador's tone was sharp for the first time.

De Sevrey registered his mistake and, cursing himself inwardly, bowed his head slightly. "Then only the shipmasters will be reimbursed, but the Sultan must guarantee us safe passage to Limassol."

The ambassador said he would carry this message to his master. His expression and demeanour gave no indication whether he thought the offer might be accepted or not, but the turcopole interpreter was encouraged that he had not dismissed the idea out of hand.

The Sultan was apparently in a hurry to leave the smoking rubble that had once been the most prosperous trading port on the coast of Palestine. Before nightfall, the message reached De Sevrey that the Sultan had agreed to his terms. In the following negotiations it was agreed that the Sultan would send an emir and one hundred men to accept the Templar surrender. After they had taken possession of the Temple and raised the Sultan's banner over the ramparts, the survivors would be escorted to the harbour where ships would be waiting to transport them to Limassol. De Sevrey insisted and the Sultan ultimately agreed 'in his infinite mercy' that all the knights, sergeants and squires would be allowed to retain possession of their arms and armour. All the horses, ordnance and supplies stored in the Temple were, of course, claimed by the Sultan as his rightful spoils. The final issue was how many ships the Templars would need.

De Sevrey replied that he needed transport for one thousand men. He hoped the exaggeration was sufficient to keep the Sultan from changing his mind and deciding he could destroy them after all.

*

The news that they were all to be allowed free passage to Cyprus produced an almost hysterical joy among the refugees. Some fell on their knees and thanked God fervently while others cheered and flung their arms around each other, dancing and frolicking like children. There were not a few, however, who refused to believe the good news, thinking it was no more than a trick to get armed men inside the citadel.

When these doubts were reported to De Sevrey he nodded solemnly. No one was more aware than he that the Sultan's predecessors had often guaranteed free passage only to break their word and murder or enslave the garrisons with whom they had negotiated. "It is a chance we have to take. Since all the fighting men are allowed to retain their weapons, I can only assure you that we will go down fighting if need be."

*

On the morning of the 24th a nervous excitement dominated the mighty fortress. Father Etienne, assisted by the three other surviving Templar priests, read mass in the chapel before virtually every living Christian still in Acre. When the service was over and the refugees and fighting men went to the refectory to break their fast, Father Etienne and all the surviving clergy – the Templar chaplains, an Austin canon, a Franciscan friar, two Benedictine monks and a Cistercian novice – together extinguished the candles and packed away the host in reverent silence. They were conscious that this was the last time a mass would be read in Acre for unforeseeable years ahead. Nor was there any point in trying to save the treasures of the chapel – the jewel studded cross, the silver candlesticks, the gold and silk altar cloths, the vestments and sacred vessels – many of which were irreplaceable works of art. The Sultan would destroy them, melt them down or turn them to profane uses, but any attempt to rescue them might provoke the Sultan into cancelling the agreement. Instead, the remaining clergy tidied the church and even polished some of the vessels with the love of a wife laying out her husband's corpse. Then, when they could find nothing more to do, they left the chapel in a sad, proud little group.

Among the civilians there was less reticence about trying to rescue something other than their naked lives. The clergy, after all, could find food and shelter with their orders wherever they landed in the weeks to come. But only tradable goods or gold would enable the civilians to avoid beggary and destitution. Some of the refugees broke into the cellars searching for anything of value they could carry on their persons. When several serving brothers tried to stop them, they were roughly handled – the first serious incident of tension between the Templars and their 'guests' since the start of the siege. Several sergeants came to the assistance of their brothers and the refugees were arrested and confined. Their violent protests as they were locked in a cellar lent an ominous undertone to the morning. Meanwhile, more adept thieves had slunk back into the chapel after the clergy had departed and helped themselves to the very things the clergy had consciously sacrificed to the Sultan.

In the kitchen, the Templars were handing out salted and dried meat along with flasks of water and loaves of bread, extra batches of which had been baked during the night. De Sevrey had ordered that all the refugees should be provided with provisions to last a week because, even if the Sultan kept his word, there was no guarantee that he would provide food on the ships he put at their disposal.

When all had received their share, the kitchens too were closed and swept out for a last time. The fires were screened off and allowed to go out. In the stables and barns the livestock was fed and watered. De la More and more men and women collected in the great inner ward, their bundles of belongings strewn about them. By noon everyone was waiting with increasing tension for the promised release.

*

By the time the Sultan's troops approached, many had started to despair. After verifying the fact that only the specified one hundred Mamelukes under one emir were approaching, De Sevrey had his knights, sergeants and brothers draw up in the inner ward facing the entrance, with the Hospitaller and civilian knights behind them. The women, children and other non-combatants clustered on either side of the ward, like two scruffy wings reaching forward from the relatively neat line of the Templars in their black and white surcoats. De Sevrey positioned himself ahead of his brothers, flanked by Sirs William and

Jean a half stride behind him, and with the turcopole translator at his side. All the Templars wore hauberks and swords, their chainmail coifs pulled over their heads and held fast with a red leather band so that they made an appropriately martial impression. Their shields, lances, cervellières and helmets, however, were carefully stowed away to avoid the impression of combat-readiness.

At a signal from De Sevrey, the outer portcullis was cranked up and the gate opened. The emir, a young man on a prancing grey Arab mare, rode through the inner portcullis before it was fully open. The emir had made himself fine for the occasion. His baggy white trousers were spotless and tucked into boots of supple camel-hide. He wore a calf-length, green silk robe, slit up the front and back to enable him to ride, and over this a shorter surcoat of pale blue and silver silk brocade. Only the initiated could have distinguished this surcoat, lined with chainmail and cotton padding, from a civilian coat without protection. A turban of the same brocade, sporting a tuft of peacock feathers held in place by a thumbnail-sized sapphire, completed his apparel.

Behind him came the Mamelukes of his unit. All were notably light-skinned, marking them as Circassians from the Sultan's own guard. They were accompanied by a number of black slaves. None of these men, in their spotless silk trousers and turbans, made the slightest attempt to disguise the sense of triumph they felt. On the contrary, rather than showing their defeated enemy the respect of solemnity, many of the Mamelukes were openly grinning and exchanging comments among themselves. For troops who were usually so well disciplined, they seemed remarkably casual – as if the entire task was more a pleasure outing than a military surrender.

De Sevrey felt the sting of the insult and pressed his lips together, swallowing his desire to challenge the arrogant Mamelukes. Hauteur would be fatal, but dignity was vital – and the line between them very fine indeed.

The emir drew up before De Sevrey, and, leaning on his pommel, smirked down at him. He waited for De Sevrey to speak, but De Sevrey turned instead to the turcopole translator.

"Who is this man? I do not recognise him."

The turcopole enquired the emir's name.

The emir signalled for one of the slaves to answer. In flowery language, and at length, the African eulogised his master. The

Templar translator summarised: "He is the Sultan's nephew. He was promoted to emir for his exceptional courage during the assault on the 18th. He was granted the honour of accepting the surrender of the Temple by the Sultan as a further sign of his favour."

De Sevrey felt a profound unease at this news. Given the Arab custom of maintaining four wives and countless concubines, the term 'nephew' could refer to hundreds of youths and did not imply any particularly close bond to the Sultan. On the contrary, De Sevrey had the feeling that this youth was rich and proud as any prince, but not important enough to have been trained in the use of power. The fact that the Sultan had sent this spoilt puppy to accept the surrender of the Temple suggested that he was contemptuous of the survivors and more impatient than merciful in offering safe passage. Sevrey's experience with spoilt royalty suggested that spineless submission would invite ridicule and insult, but defiance often provoked outrage and boundless fury. He took a calculated risk. "Tell him that since this is the first time he has been employed on such a mission, I will assume that he is simply ignorant of the fact that it is improper to accept the surrender of a castle while still mounted."

The turcopole translator hesitated just a fraction of a second before he carried out his orders meticulously.

The emir flushed slightly though he made an effort to keep his smirk in place, and then ordered his men to dismount. Only when all the other men stood on the ground did he swing his leg over the pommel of the saddle and slip on to the ground in a gesture of exaggerated casualness.

"So," he spoke at last with a nod of his head in the direction of the men behind De Sevrey, "these are your disabled. Where are the other nine hundred men?"

"On and in the walls aiming longbows at you," De Sevrey answered, and had the satisfaction of seeing the emir spin about in alarm scanning the wall walks and windows.

Too late, he realised it was a bluff and turned back to De Sevrey with narrowed eyes. "You take me for a fool, but you will soon learn that I am not. Do you surrender this castle and your men to the mercy of the Sultan?"

"No. I surrender this castle and insist upon the terms of the agreement with the Sultan regarding the inhabitants – or is your sultan a man whose word is worthless? No better than a thief?"

"My Sultan is a man of the true faith – not like you Christian dogs!" He spat to one side, and behind him his men murmured their approval, tinged, so De Sevrey thought, with an undertone of impatience.

"Then send a man with the Sultan's banner to the ramparts." De Sevrey gestured toward the tallest of the towers where, in answer to his signal, a sergeant started to lower the Baucent.

The emir snapped out the order with a sharp gesture of his hand, and two of the Mamelukes started sprinting toward the tower. Then he gave a series of other orders and started to stroll along the line of Templars, inspecting them contemptuously.

De Sevrey glanced at the translator with a look of enquiry.

"He has ordered his men to search the buildings for other Templars."

And indeed a half-dozen Mamelukes were spreading out to enter the buildings through the various entrances. De Sevrey could not stop them, nor was there any point in it. The complex was being turned over to the enemy intact. They had the right to search it, plunder it, destroy it. The question was whether they would respect the other half of the bargain.

More and more of the Mamelukes were turning their horses over to the slaves and starting to disperse. A group of four set off up the steps of the chapel, another band made for the audience hall, some others followed their nose toward the kitchens and a large party set off for the stables, already chattering excitedly about the advantages and disadvantages of Frankish stallions. Other Mamelukes started to mingle among the civilians.

With increasing unease, De Sevrey watched them toe the bundles of belongings resting on the cobbles or grab them from wary refugees and search through them looking for valuables. De Sevrey exchanged a glance with Jean and William de la More. The refugees did not dare defend themselves, even protest. So the Templars moved into the ward to keep a better eye on what was happening.

With a shout of, "Allah Ahkbar!" the Sultan's banner fluttered up the flagpole overhead. The Mamelukes gave an enthusiastic cheer, and what had been casual – even leisurely – activities instantly became more aggressive. Now they started to slice open sacks of belongings and seize the rings from victims' hands. Jean saw a Mameluke thrust his hand down the bodice of a woman cowering by her ruptured sack, apparently looking for valuables. He caught his breath, held himself back from protest. Let the Mamelukes take all the plunder – so long as the Christians were allowed to keep their freedom.

But another Mameluke had pulled a boy to his feet and was inspecting him with an intensity Jean had only seen at slave markets. His stomach tightened, and his right hand slipped of its own accord to grasp the hilt of De Sonnac's sword. There were so many Mamelukes spread out among the refugees that it was impossible to watch them all, but Jean was aware of more and more laying hands not on the belongings but the refugees themselves. A woman's gasp drew his attention to the right and he saw that a Mameluke had ripped open her bodice. Beside him another Mameluke yanked a woman into his arms and started to lift her skirts while a third was shoving his hand into the drawers of a pretty boy. And then he saw a Mameluke grab Rachel and close his fist over her little breast – breasts he had never even noticed she had.

Jean didn't think, and he never knew if he led or followed. Suddenly he had his sword out if its scabbard and he was falling upon the man who was molesting Rachel – and he was not alone. Beside him and behind him he saw the cold glitter of drawn swords, felt men lunging forward, heard cries of outrage or inarticulate curses. Every Templar took a vow to defend all Christians, especially women. They could not stand by and watch the casual abuse of women clustered in their own Temple and under their protection. The reaction was spontaneous. No one gave an order and no one tried to stop them. When the first Mameluke was cut down by a Templar sword the truce was over and all hope of survival dead. De Sevrey, fortunately, was still in control of his faculties; while his knights hacked at a still startled enemy, the order rang out to drop the portcullises. Jean cleaved the turban and buried his sword inches deep into the brains of the Mameluke who had laid his hands on Rachel. The blade was well honed. He had had a week to see that the nicks and dullness were ground away.

Rachel stood, paralysed with horror, staring at the mangled corpse, and then her eyes met Jean's – wounded, confused eyes. The women and children around them were fleeing for the arcades or scrambling up the steps to the chapel.

The Mamelukes had recovered from their initial shock. With shouts and screams they drew their scimitars. Jean saw the blade gleam out of the corner of his left eye and he flung up his left arm to ward off the blow, forgetting that his shield was carefully stacked in the armoury.

The scimitar sliced through his arm as if it were butter. His eye recorded the fall of his severed arm on to the cobbles, but he felt nothing. With his right arm he brought De Sonnac's sword through the air in a sweeping arch and decapitated the man who had amputated his arm. He saw Rachel holding her skirts up so that her bare calves were clearly visible as she scampered for the arcades, and then he turned to face the next opponent.

Acre
May 25, 1291

It was the pain in his wrist and running up the length of his left arm that woke him. Then his consciousness registered that he had lost his left arm, had seen it fall to the ground, and he opened his eyes, shaking his head to clear it. He was lying in a darkened hall, lit only by candles. They highlighted the ribbed vaulting crossing over his head, but the shadows they cast wavered with each breath of air. A draft kept the shadows dancing.

Staring at the ceiling, Jean strained his memory for some clue of where he was. He felt the lumpy straw and his nose registered a mixture of urine and medicine. He must be in the infirmary. Venturing to turn his head slightly, he found that a serving brother was lying beside him with a white and waxy complexion. On his other side lay a sergeant with his head so heavily bandaged he could not identify him.

Jean was thirsty, desperately thirsty. Having noticed this fact, he could think of nothing else. He had to get a drink of water or he would die. He sat up and looked left and right the length of the infirmary. Since the fall of the city itself on the 18th, the infirmary had gradually emptied as the wounded either died or managed to get up and move around. Now it was full again – from one end to the other on both sides of the aisle there were pallets filled with wounded.

He saw the white face and beard of the doctor moving toward him, his dark robes hardly visible in the darkened chamber. The doctor leaned over him and spoke in a low, almost inaudible tone. "How do you feel, sir?"

"Thirsty."

"That is from the loss of blood. I'll have water brought to you at once. Otherwise?"

"I feel dreadful pains in the missing arm – am I mad?" He stared at the bandaged stump as he spoke, unable to understand how he could feel pain in a wrist and elbow that were no longer there.

"Such phantom pains are quite normal. Are you dizzy? Do you feel nauseous?"

"No."

"That is good. Lie down again. I'll see that water is brought to you."

Jean did as he was bidden, aware now of the faint murmuring of the mass coming through the slits in the wall slanting down to the chapel. The infirmary had been built backing up against the chapel so that the ill, infirm and dying could hear holy service even if they could not leave their pallets. The 'clerestory' windows of the chapel along the north wall were in fact ducts leading to the infirmary.

After a few minutes, which seemed eternal, Ian MacDonald leaned over him. "I've brought ye a mite to drink, Commander."

Jean sat up and let the serving brother support his shoulders as he took the proffered cup. It was cool water from the well, and MacDonald held a sweating pitcher in his hand, ready to refill the cup as Jean finished. When he had quenched his thirst, he looked up at the serving brother. "What day and what time is it?"

"It is matins on the Feast of Mary Magdalene, sir."

So he had only been unconscious some eight to ten hours.

"What happened? The last thing I remember is sinking on to the cobbles of the inner ward in the middle of a *mêlée*."

"The emir and every single one of his bastards are dead – we threw their bodies over the wall. The Baucent is flying again from the ramparts." MacDonald was proud of this.

"What did it cost us?"

"I don't expect any of us will survive now, sir – but what choice did we have? They clearly meant to sell us all into slavery. I for one would rather die – an' I haven't met a Brother who thinks otherwise. As for the others..." He shrugged.

Jean nodded wearily. It meant that Rachel and all the other women and children would fall into Mameluke hands sooner or later. All that had happened today was a postponement of their inevitable enslavement. Sooner or later, when there was no one left to defend them, they would be subjected to the same abuse – and worse – which they had suffered today. He should have known. Thibald had always been sceptical about the Sultan's offer. But De Sevrey had been right: they had to take a chance and as long as they were armed they would make any breach of faith costly for the enemy. But he was so tired of fighting. He wished that he could just go to sleep and never wake up. He did not want to witness any more bloodshed. He wished the pain would go away. He was infinitely weary...

"Here, sir." MacDonald was holding out the cup to him again. "I've laced the water with just a touch of wine. It will do you good."

Jean felt no desire for wine, but MacDonald was so anxious to do him a favour that he could not refuse. He took the cup again and sipped from it. The mass was over in the chapel and for a moment the stillness in the infirmary was absolute. Then someone moaned in his sleep and another patient shifted uneasily, rustling the straw of his pallet.

"Thank you, MacDonald."

"Jean?"

They both started. De Sevrey, apparently out of nowhere, went down on his heels beside Jean. He had removed his armour for the lighter and less confining white robes of a Templar monk.

"My lord."

De Sevrey brushed away the formality of the title. "How are you feeling?"

"As well as can be expected. I never knew something you didn't have could hurt so damned much."

De Sevrey put a finger to his lips and glanced up. Father Etienne came up behind him. But the priest was too weary to reproach Jean for his unnecessary swearing. He sank down beside De Sevrey.

"Jean, we've decided to send Sir Thibald in the skiff to Sidon with the remaining valuables and relics. He will take a handful of men to man the skiff and dispatches from me relating what happened here since the fall of the city. There will be room for a few others."

"Then send some of the women or—"

De Sevrey held up his hand for silence. "How am I supposed to make a selection? It is worse to favour a few among so many than to save none. There are only a handful of clerics here, however, and they will certainly be executed by the Sultan. I think they should be allowed to accompany the holy relics to Sidon."

Jean did not like the decision. The priests would indeed be slaughtered if they did not convert – and it was insulting to suggest they might – but was death for a true Christian really worse than slavery? Shouldn't the priests more than all others welcome martyrdom for their faith? His gaze shifted to Father Etienne, but the priest avoided his eyes. Jean did not understand. He had been prepared to risk his life helmless in a tattered hauberk in the streets of Acre, but now he was willing to slink away while women and children were left behind to bear the Sultan's rage?

"And who will minister to the dying? Hear our confessions and administer the last rites?"

"Two priests have agreed to stay," De Sevrey assured Jean. "Fathers Baudoin and Henri. As for the rest of us," De Sevrey was continuing, "there is no hope left. What happened today was... a tragedy. The emir was too young and inexperienced. He did not have a grip on his troops because they did not really respect him – any more than I did. But it was a mistake – I know, I drew my sword as well as any of you. But it was still a mistake. The emir – dying – asked why we were destroying our chances of survival, and I said because he had broken his word – or his Sultan had.

"He did not understand me. Jean, he honestly did not understand me. He said again and again, 'But the ships are waiting. You could have withdrawn to Cyprus. Why have you thrown your lives away?' And when I replied that you don't tear the bodices from women you intend to release, he said the agreement had always been for the Templars and the garrison – not for the civilians. They, he said, were 'naturally' spoils of war. It was only the fighting men the Sultan had honoured with freedom, out of respect for our courage – and to save himself the trouble of subduing us."

They stared at one another. "You're saying it was a misunderstanding. The Sultan didn't break the agreement as he understood it: we did."

De Sevrey nodded.

"Christ."

De Sevrey took a deep breath. "The Sultan will never treat with us again. We killed his nephew and one hundred of his own guard. He will kill us one way or another, sooner or later. We are dead men – including all the unfortunate civilians who put their fate in our hands." The burden of responsibility weighed upon De Sevrey, bending him and dragging at his once handsome face. Now it sagged with worry and exhaustion and despair. On top of that, he was mourning his best friend, neither glad nor proud to stand in his shoes.

Jean couldn't bear it. "There is the longboat," he ventured. "Surely we could send at least the women and children out in that."

"We don't even know if it's seaworthy, and we don't have a man between us who can rig and pilot a longboat – even if we could scrape together enough able-bodied men to man her oars."

"Oh, there's no' so much skill ta handling a longboat, my lord. I used ta do it as a wee lad – smaller longboat ta be sure, but the principle is the same, if you see what I mean? And Sir Duncan will ha' had his experience as well – no' ta mention that bloody Englishman – pardon, Father – Sir William. Tha's a man who has seawater in his veins. You can tell that just ta look at him." This helpful monologue was delivered by MacDonald, and though the marshal and Father Etienne looked at him with a certain astonishment there was more admiration than disapproval at his forthrightness. Only at the end did the serving brother seem to remember that he was speaking to the senior officer of the Temple and cast his eyes down with a certain humility.

"MacDonald's right." Jean hastened to support him. "De la More and Graham between them will be able to navigate, and you'll have no shortage of volunteers among the civilians for manning the oars. The longboat can certainly take a hundred adults – and all the children still here."

"And who is going to caulk it, get it in the water, step the mast and rig it?"

"Give me a chance, my lord." Jean felt energy pulsing through his veins. It was as if this was the only reason he had survived. "If we can launch and rig the longboat before the Sultan has breached the walls, let her sail with all the women and children aboard."

"We can't send the women and children out into the Mediterranean without oarsmen, pilot and at least a handful of fighting men to discourage pirates," De Sevrey pointed out.

"Surely we can spare so many men?" Jean could not comprehend Sevrey's resistance.

De Sevrey sighed and capitulated. "All right. See what you can do." Then he held out his hand to help Jean off the pallet.

For a moment, faint from loss of blood, Jean felt dizzy, and De Sevrey had to steady him, holding him firmly by his good arm. When the dizziness had passed, Jean nodded to De Sevrey. Together they started for the door to the infirmary and, reaching it, De Sevrey stopped. "Jean, do you know why we Templars are not allowed to marry, sire, adopt or sponsor children?"

Surprised by the question, Jean started, then answered readily. "So that we will be completely committed to the order."

De Sevrey shook his head. "No – so that we are willing to die. Only men without ties to this world can turn their backs upon it without regret."

*

To reach the sea gate to the Temple one had to descend by windowless stairs into the very bowels of the fortress. One emerged into a wide, cavernous chamber where the floor abruptly ended and the sea began. At low tide, a half dozen slimy steps led down to the water. At high tide the water lapped just inches below floor level. In a storm the waves roared and frothed through the iron portcullis and shattered against the very walls, carving away the stone and leaving great puddles behind. Even now, though the sea had been relatively calm for over a fortnight, puddles of water left from the last storm glittered in the light of Jean's torch.

The skiff rode happily upon the little waves, the mast lowered into place at the stern, the oars shipped and a canvas covering lashed over the cockpit. Jean turned his attention, however, to the ageing longboat, drawn keel-up, in the chamber beyond. Holding his torch above his head so it would not blind him, he bent over the boat and inspected the scraped and peeling bottom. To his layman's eyes it seemed in poor condition, and he felt his heart sink.

The sound of voices echoing in the stairwell drew his attention. Together with MacDonald, he had combed the Temple for men – civilian or monk – who knew something about ships. In addition to MacDonald himself, Sir Duncan and Sir William, they had discovered that two of the English archers and three Italian crossbowmen had spent various stages of their life at sea. There were a half-dozen civilians who had earned extra money helping with ship repairs, and no fewer than eight sergeants who had routinely served on Templar or Hospitaller galleys. They carried a half-dozen torches and the chamber was at once brightened.

Sir William, although nursing a leg wound, was in the lead – of course. He limped over to Jean at a brisk pace. "So we're to get this old wreck shipshape, are we?" He ran his hand along the planking and taking a torch, inspected the keel. "Hmm. Well, beggars can't be choosers. We'll need to caulk the keel line and there'll be no time for it to set properly, but what the hell," he shrugged.

Sir Duncan, scowling despite his face wound, made his own inspection of the hull, as did the civilians. These pointed to various damaged planks, and places where the caulking was crumbling.

"We need to get her in the water as soon as possible," one of the men said, "so the wood will swell. She'll leak badly at first and if we have to put to sea before the seams are closed it will be hard to keep her afloat."

But no one seemed to think – or wanted to admit – that the task was hopeless. From the storerooms opening off the 'harbour' they found reels of hemp twine, rope, barrels of tar and caulking tools. While the civilians and Sir Duncan set to work on the hull, the English and Italian archers inspected the mast, boom and rigging, all of which were neatly stowed on hooks on the wall. Much of the rope was rotted so they set to replacing yard after yard of rigging, splicing and tarring as they worked. Finally the canvas sail was dragged down from a shelf and spread upon the floor of the chamber. It was mouldy and stank, but appeared to be in remarkably good condition otherwise. MacDonald and four of the sergeants were given sailmakers' palms and set to patching and reinforcing the obvious weak points under De la More's direction.

All of this was work calling for a degree of skill and two hands. Jean, lacking both, was of little use. Taking two of the sergeants with him, he left the others to their tasks and set about organising barrels of water, bread, dried meat and dried fruits for the voyage. It was also essential that there be some means of providing shade or the merciless Mediterranean sun would bake the occupants of the open longboat. While the sergeants dragged the stores down to the sea gate, Jean went in search of one of the precious compasses. Although he himself had no idea how they worked, he knew that these navigational instruments were one of the most carefully guarded secrets of the Temple. De Beaujeu had claimed that the low incidence of shipwreck and relative good sailing times of Templar ships was largely a function of the use of these devices. *The Falcon* was fitted with the newest of them, but

Jean thought there might still be one in one of the master's locked chests. It had been impossible to remove everything of value.

As he ascended the stairs, Jean encountered Thibald Gaudin accompanied by a half-dozen Templar sergeants and the clerics.

"They have started digging mines," Gaudin informed him without preamble. "We can clearly see the sappers at work – even at night and, of course, just out of range of our archers. They must have a hundred men digging and removing the dirt, and timbers are stacked man-high, ready to be used for supports. At the pace they are working now, it will only take a day or two until they have reached the Temple."

Jean swore. How could they possibly get the longboat ready in so little time?

"My orders are to leave for Sidon," Gaudin told Jean, and the younger man could sense more than see that the old man was close to tears. "I begged De Sevrey to let me stay, but he insisted. He said I was not much use to him as a combatant. He says as a witness and chronicler of what had happened here I was invaluable."

"He's right, Sir Thibald. I'm sure Master De Beaujeu would have said the same," Jean tried to comfort him.

"But the good fathers here can write far better than I," Gaudin protested, indicating the priests and monks behind him. "I am a simple man, a man of humble birth, a sergeant. I am unworthy to speak for Master De Beaujeu and the good Marshal De Sevrey and the Templars of Acre."

"Let Marshal De Sevrey be the judge of that."

"It would be better if you went in my place," Gaudin persisted.

"No. I will see that the longboat is made seaworthy and that the women and children do not fall into the Sultan's hands."

It was so piteously little compared to all that they had lost, but Jean found that this mission alone filled him with energy and passion. De Sevrey might blame him for caring too much for the Rachels and Madeleines of the world, but for their sake and not for the Temple itself he was prepared to die.

"You do not have much time," Gaudin warned, and then he embraced Jean briefly but heartily before he continued down the stairs, followed by the clerics.

Jean did not blame the others for taking this rare opportunity to escape, but the sight of Father Etienne filled him with contempt. De

Beaujeu had raised him above all the other chaplains of the Temple; because the order had no bishops, Father Etienne was the senior cleric. And he was prepared to abandon his Brothers at a moment when they were all facing certain death. Jean promised himself never to forgive him.

Father Etienne paused before Jean, but, sensing his hostility, he scurried down the darkened stairs.

The dawn was breaking and from the besiegers' camp – now located around the basin of the harbour – came the wailing of the mullahs calling the faithful to prayer. By the light of day, the activities of the sappers were even more evident – the mounds of earth that had already been extracted grew minute by minute, and the stacks of wooden beams diminished. The sappers seemed like so many ants, busily carrying wood in and soil out with merciless efficiency. The mood of the garrison was correspondingly low.

Then, at noon, with great fanfare and glittering escort, the Sultan sent another emissary to the Temple. This ambassador suggested that the Templars send a delegation to negotiate an 'honourable' surrender.

"It is only a matter of time until you are forced to surrender." The emissary pointed to the sappers at work. "If you surrender now the Sultan will be merciful. If you wait, his fury will know no bounds."

"You are welcome to enter and discuss terms." De Sevrey let the translator reply, but the emissary shook his head.

"The Sultan is not willing to risk another misunderstanding. He wishes to negotiate himself – directly with your marshal, Monsieur Peter de Sevrey."

"And who will guarantee our marshal's safety while he is in the Sultan's camp?" the translator asked without prompting.

"The Sultan himself guarantees his safety and the safety of all those who accompany him. Diplomatic immunity is an ancient custom which the Great al-Ashraf Kalil would never violate. He values his own reputation far too much!"

De Sevrey stepped up to the ramparts and answered in Arabic for himself. "I will attend upon the Sultan at dusk." Then he left the ramparts and descended without pause to the sea gate below the inner ward.

Despite the daylight which filtered through the portcullis and illuminated the water, turning it an inviting aquamarine, the men working on the longboat still kept the torches burning in the interior chamber. De Sevrey found Jean painting tar into the seams filled with hemp twine with his one hand.

"Jean!" De Sevrey gestured to him and moved to the far side of the room, directly on the water's edge. "The Sultan has invited me to negotiate a 'honourable' surrender."

Jean laughed. "And he expects us to believe that? I am insulted!"

De Sevrey considered him from sunken eyes utterly in shadow in the dim light of the cavern. Then De Sevrey moved back toward the boat. "How are you coming along?"

Jean and Sir William showed the marshal what they had achieved. Since Gaudin had warned Jean that their time was shorter than anticipated, they had made much progress. The sail was patched and reinforced and lashed to the boom. The caulking was very nearly finished. The biggest problem was the rigging. This took the most skill and the sailors had warned that inexperienced help could do more damage than good.

De Sevrey nodded. "You'd best launch the boat at once so the planking can start to swell."

"What's the rush? The sappers can't possibly reach the Temple for another day or two."

"I have agreed to meet the Sultan at dusk."

"Are you mad? He'll kill you!"

"I am confessed."

They stared at one another. Then De Sevrey pulled Jean away from the others again. "You are right, Jean, our mission is the protection of Christians – pilgrims and crusaders and residents. Do you know what the rebel leader, Simon de Montfort, said to his followers on the eve of the Battle of Lewisham?"

Jean shook his head; he was from the Languedoc and knew only of the brutality of the Englishman De Montfort's father.

"He said: 'Commend your souls to God for our bodies belong to the enemy.' This is our situation, and I have made my peace with God, but I will die better knowing that I have left no chance – no matter how small – untried to save the others. Surely you understand that? Do you think William would have acted otherwise?"

Jean had the unpleasant feeling that De Beaujeu would indeed have acted differently. De Sevrey was a straightforward man. Jean knew no better tactician and no one who kept his head so well in the heat of battle. De Sevrey could fight brilliantly and he could lead men even better. De Beaujeu had valued him for these traits and raised him to marshal – a post he had certainly earned and honoured. But he was not a man who could read the unspoken motives of others nor one who could exploit such knowledge to his own ends as De Beaujeu had done. De Beaujeu had been a master of intrigue, and Jean suspected that he would have managed to spin some net to mislead, outmanoeuvre or at least confuse the Sultan. De Beaujeu would have played for time somehow. But without knowing how De Beaujeu would have done this, Jean could hardly offer De Sevrey other advice.

"I don't know and it doesn't matter. You are in command and we will all follow you to the grave. If you like, I will accompany you to the Sultan's pavilion."

"No. You were right about the longboat. If I cannot convince the Sultan to let all the civilians go free then you, at least, must see that the women and children escape. That is why I beg you – while all eyes are riveted upon the Sultan's tent to see how he receives me – get this longboat launched."

"But..."

Dusk was just five hours away. They couldn't possibly have the ship seaworthy by then.

"I'll see that all the women and children are collected and waiting," De Sevrey continued. "When I go out of the gate, I will send them down to you. You must load them as rapidly as possible and cast off. With luck, no one – not even a fisherman – will see the longboat put to sea. You must then close the portcullis so that the sea gate looks as sleepy as ever to the fishermen who will be casting their nets at dawn."

"I'll do my best," Jean promised, far from confident of success.

"Neither God nor I can ask for more."

*

The light of the setting sun cast glittering golden coins upon the breeze-ruffled sea beyond the sea gate. The longboat now lay alongside the gate, rising and falling with the gentle swell, creaking and leaking, but floating nevertheless. Six men had gone aboard her and sat with their naked legs ankle-deep in water, bailing. It was the second shift of bailers, but they seemed to be making slow progress against the water at last.

With some trepidation, Jean and William de la More agreed to load the supplies. The extra weight would cause the longboat to sit deeper in the water and in all probability the leaking would increase as new seams sank under the waterline. But they had to get these seams swelling, or no one would stand a chance. Three gangplanks were fitted and they started rolling the barrels of water, meat and fruit aboard both fore and aft.

Behind them, the riggers had finished the repairs and had started the more intricate business of actually sorting out buntlines, clewlines, halyards and sheets in preparation for rigging. Others were checking the condition of the oars and replacing them where necessary from the stores deep under the inner ward.

A sergeant descended from the ward. "Commander de Preuthune, Commander De la More?"

Jean and Sir William, who had both been watching the water level in the longboat with bated breath, turned and went over to the sergeant. "Marshal De Sevrey sends his greetings. He is preparing to go to the Sultan with Sirs Guillaume de Cafran and Sir Imbert d'Ibelin."

"Not yet!" De la More protested vigorously. "We have to at least step the mast and get it rigged. Then – if she's still watertight – we can think about taking the passengers aboard."

"Sir, the sun is setting."

"I'll talk to Peter," Jean told De la More and left with the sergeant.

Jean was feeling weak as they ascended the stairs and dizzy by the time they reached the top. He had to stop and lean against the wall, noting that his stump had started bleeding again some time during the day; the bandage was bloody and stiff.

"You should have the doctor see to that, sir." The sergeant gestured to the wound.

Jean nodded. "If the marshal will give us just one more hour…"

On the far side of the inner ward, women and children were clearly collecting with bundles of belongings. Here and there women clung to their husbands and children to their fathers, but most of the women clustered nervously in the shadow of the arcade, irritably reproving the irrepressible children running about and shouting while they played some game. Jean scanned the crowd for Rachel but in the dying light and confusion he did not catch sight of her. The sergeant was already starting up the stairway to the master's chambers.

De Sevrey had dressed himself with care. His chainmail gleamed free of rust and his silk surcoat had been bleached white; the red cross had been removed and resewn upon it – vivid, blood red. As Jean entered, he was tightening the buckle of his swordbelt, and Jean noted that he was wearing the ruby-studded belt De Beaujeu had kept for state occasions. The pommel of his sword was inlaid with rubies in the shape of a cross flanked by diamonds.

"Peter, I beg you, give us an hour more." Jean opened without preliminaries.

De Sevrey raised his head and at the sight of Jean he smiled faintly. "Can you sail in an hour?"

"Yes." He sounded more certain than he was. "The boat is in the water and loaded, but the mast has to be stepped and rigged."

De Sevrey glanced out of the double-arched window past the carved central pillar. A lizard darted up the spiralling vines of stone and disappeared on the back side. Only a glowing bump of sun remained above the horizon. "I told the Sultan I would come at dusk."

"Dusk is an indefinite term."

"It will be dark in an hour," he countered. "I'll have to make a great show of preparing to depart: trumpets and banners and we could put on some kind of open-air mass – anything to convince the Sultan that I am coming, which will buy you time. I'll keep it up as long as I can. When the women arrive, you will know I have passed the gate."

"Thank you."

"No, I have to thank you... You should see to your arm, Jean."

Jean glanced down at the bleeding stump with loathing. He hated the thing already – it hurt him and drained the strength from him though it was useless and hideous. But he had no time for it now. "There'll be time for that later," he told De Sevrey irritably, the pressure of time making him nervous and sending him toward the door. Only as he started out of the chamber did he realise in horror that he had not taken leave of De Sevrey. He turned back into the room and stared at the marshal, uncertain if he should bend his knee or offer a lame embrace with one arm. De Sevrey solved his dilemma by flinging his arms around him and muttering, "*Benedicite.*"

"*Benedicite*, Peter." Then, to take the edge off their parting, Jean added, "Till later." After all, he told himself, there was theoretically still the ghost of a chance that the Sultan was serious about negotiations.

"Later?" De Sevrey asked with apparent bafflement.

There was no point in pretending any longer. "Purgatory, I expect." Jean managed a crooked smile. "Unless you go straight to Paradise – then it could take a long time before we meet again."

De Sevrey forced a smile to his lips, but his eyes betrayed his despair.

There was no more to say. Jean departed, hurrying back to the sea gate despite the throbbing in his stump and the increasing pain in his missing limb. When he arrived, the men were in the midst of setting the mast. This was an extremely difficult business in the confines of the barrel-vaulted chamber with the longboat riding the gentle swells. Jean wisely sank on to the stairs to keep out of the way until they were finished. He dropped his head on his remaining arm and tried to collect his strength. What he would have given for a bath!

With an explosion of oaths and a loud bang the mast slipped on to the deck of the longboat, missing the mast well by a foot. De la More reverted to English in the heat of the moment, and both he and Graham began simultaneously giving orders which hardly anyone could understand. Several of the men who had been handling the mast had the skin torn off their hands and were cursing in their native languages. But, even as Jean dragged himself to his feet, De la More reverted to French and started giving comprehensible orders that were quickly followed.

They managed to lift the mast up a yard and guide it into the mast well. While four men held it in place, the braces were screwed more tightly around it and the stays were laced through the blocks fore, aft and on either side. The mast was roughly half the length of the longboat itself and approximately the same length as its boom, which now followed it aboard. Between the ceiling of the chamber and the top of the mast there were ten to twelve feet to spare, but navigating the exit under the portcullis would be a far more delicate manoeuvre. They had to take the longboat through the very centre of the arched exit, and, if a large wave lifted the long boat at the wrong minute, the mast would not clear the portcullis.

While the sailors set to rigging the boom and getting the sheets, halyards, clew and buntlines laced through their respective blocks and made fast along the pin-rail, Jean enquired after the state of the water from the bailers. They proudly reported they were making steady if slow progress. The planks were clearly swelling and – assuming they didn't run into a storm – they thought she would hold all the way to Cyprus.

The words were hardly out of their mouths when the high-pitched chatter of children and the flickering light of torches coming down the stairway announced the arrival of the passengers. Several of the boys ran forward when they saw the ship, shouting with excitement. They had to be chased back so that the rigging could continue unimpeded. Several infants were squalling, while the sight of the open boat induced two women to change their minds entirely. Rachel waved shyly at Jean from the crowd and he spared her a nod.

As soon as the sailors announced they were finished, Jean got the women to form into three files and enter the longboat by the three gangplanks. He himself and two of the sergeants helped the timid or handed the small children directly into the boat. Once aboard, the women were told to take their places as near the centre as possible. There was some dismay and protest at the fact that there were still some six inches of water in the bottom of the boat and belongings had to be held or they got wet. But Jean was considerably more concerned about how he was going to man the ship.

All the men who understood enough about boats to have helped get the longboat seaworthy were obviously predestined to take her out, and he met with no resistance when he ordered them aboard. In a short discussion among the sergeants, one was selected to take the steering rudder, and Sir Duncan and MacDonald between them prepared the springs for casting off.

Only William de la More hesitated briefly on the quay. "I expect Sir Duncan and MacDonald can handle the boat alone."

"She's undermanned, Sir William – we need another dozen men. There has to be some relief for the oarsmen and we may need men bailing while under sail. Go up and select some good men."

"You know our brothers better than I do," De la More pointed out. But Jean shook his head to indicate that he did not want to be the one to make the choice, and De la More was not a man who had to be urged twice.

In the boat the initial confusion and excitement had died away. Even the children had become quieter, and they all stared up at the quay waiting for the order to release them. Jean glanced at the portcullis which was now silhouetted against a luminous sapphire sky. It was time to get that raised, he concluded, and started in the direction of the great ratcheted drum around which the portcullis chain wrapped as it was hauled up. In fact, there were two such drums, one on either side of the sea gate, but it was possible to raise the portcullis by turning the handle of only one.

Halfway to his destination a shout went up from overhead – it was a dull shout but it spread like a roar and then cascaded down the stairs growing nearer, louder, sharper with each step. A sergeant plunged into the chamber, staggering as he reached the bottom of the stairs and screaming like a madman. "They killed him! They killed him! Seized him, bound him and decapitated him before our eyes! Didn't even let him enter the pavilion!"

Several other men had followed the first man down the stairs, and they too were shouting in rage. "Get the longboat out of here! They have betrayed us again!"

Jean used his good arm to gesture to the men to get aboard.

Two of the men were more than willing, scrambling with indecent haste to leap aboard without bothering with the gangways. The first of the sergeants, however, shook his head disdainfully and declared, "Nay, I'll stay and avenge the good marshal—"

"Don't question orders! Get aboard the bloody longboat!" That was roared by William de la More as he too came plunging out of the stairs with three other Templars and two Hospitallers. "Cast off fore!" He leapt into the boat, forgetting his leg wound, and landed with a loud cry which turned into an agonised moan as his wounded leg gave way under him and he crumpled up in the bottom of the boat.

Jean had no time to worry. While De la More lay in the bilge water, rocking with pain and cursing under his breath, Sir Duncan took over the command. Jean, meanwhile, hurried to the chain drum controlling the portcullis. Taking the iron handle in his right hand, he started to turn it. After the first half-turn, the slack was gone and with an audible crunch, the chain started to bite. The resistance on the drum handle increased dramatically. Jean bent his entire strength to turning the handle. Creaking and grating, the portcullis inched upwards. Sir Duncan cast off aft, and the oarsmen gently nudged the longboat away from the quay, pointing her bow to the centre of the gateway.

Jean had broken into a sweat and his breathing was becoming heavier as he strained at the drum handle. The portcullis had cleared the wave tops and the waves splashed against the pointed iron teeth. The longboat waited with its bow pointed straight at the centre of the opening, the oarsmen sculling gently to keep her in place.

Rasping for breath, his face beet red, the blood nearly bursting from the veins that stood out at his temples, Jean struggled not to faint. But the resistance of the portcullis seemed to be increasing. Abruptly, at three-quarters open, a metallic scraping sound echoed in the chamber and the drum jammed.

Only the depth of his despair gave him the strength to scream. "Nooooo! Christ, nooooo!" And Jean collapsed beside the worthless drum, the portcullis still ten feet too low to permit the longboat to depart.

Najac
June 1291

Eleanor woke weary from a restless night, and stared at the ceiling of her bed, reluctant to rise. The familiar carvings of vines and wild animals seemed strangely ominous today, like the confused remnants of an evil dream she could no longer remember. But she never slept well when Geoffrey was away, she reminded herself.

Dismissing her own foreboding, she forced herself to shove aside the curtains and swing her legs over the edge of the bed. Eleni sat dozing in the armchair by the fire, and Eleanor smiled indulgently. Eleni was a good six years younger than she herself, but uprooted from her Mediterranean home – and with no husband to quicken her blood – she had aged more rapidly. Her feet were gouty and her body shapeless, but she was still an attentive servant. She woke at once at the sound of Eleanor rising. "Madame!" she exclaimed, pulling her excessive bulk on to her painful feet and waddling toward the bed with Eleanor's dressing gown.

Eleanor let her maid wrap the quilted velvet around her and enquired after Eleni's health. The maid described her various ailments at great length, and Eleanor listened with only half an ear, her thoughts calculating that it was surely two or three more days before she could expect Geoffrey's return. He had escorted a transport of grain and timber to Marseilles where he intended to see it aboard ship for Acre.

The siege of the city preyed on his mind and he chaffed and brooded at his helplessness. He raged at the king of France who could indifferently stand by and watch the Holy Land for which his father had died succumb to Muslim forces. He bemoaned Edward of England's greed to master Scotland which was greater than his adherence to his crusading vow. He cursed a pope who was interested only in his own intrigues and power struggles while the Holy Land bled to death. Geoffrey would have sailed for Acre himself, if he had not been sixty-one and conscious of his own failing strength. He had offered to pay support for any volunteers – and had found a half-dozen youths eager for the adventure. But his own son Louis had angrily refused his call to arms and ridiculed him for being an old man no longer in touch with reality. The clash between father and son, the first open breach between them, had wounded Geoffrey to the quick. He had packed seven wagons full of timber and two with grain and headed for Marseilles with his volunteers, his sergeant and his squire.

Eleanor sighed and a wave of melancholy swept over her. She almost turned and crawled back under her covers. What was the point of rising? Marie ran the household now. She was sharp-tongued and insistent and no doubt there was less waste, less idling, and more order. But there were also fewer smiles and less laughter in the kitchens and stables, and sometimes Eleanor caught the echoes of dissatisfied mumbling with an undertone of resentment. Hatred and rebellion were built upon such mumbling, and Eleanor had heard of serfs rising against their masters, slaughtering, raping and plundering. Eleanor had no fear for herself, but sometimes she wondered what would become of her grandchildren, raised to an arrogance alien to herself and Geoffrey.

They were already spoilt, and Eleanor could see all too clearly how they would grow haughty on account of their Albret blood and arrogant because of their wealth. Geoffrey had rescued her run-down heritage and built a prosperous estate. For forty years they had laboured and saved, avoiding every extravagance and carefully calculating the cost of even the most necessary item built or bought. On himself, Geoffrey had spent almost nothing; his only indulgence were the clothes and jewels he presented to Eleanor and his daughters. He had laboured for her lands until he was bent and weathered and his bones grown gnarled, and all the thanks he had from his heir was contempt because he was not of noble birth. It was predominantly Marie's influence, of course, but the damage was done.

"Shall I brush your hair, Madame?" Eleni brought her out of her thoughts, and she dutifully sat at her dressing table and let her maid unbraid her grey hair. Holding a hand mirror, Eleanor considered her face with regret. If Eleni had developed a round, pasty face in which the eyes and nose seemed to merge, Eleanor's face was grown overly sharp. Her prominent cheekbones, square brow and long nose dominated a face where the brightness of the eyes had faded and the skin sagged below her chin.

Fortunately, during the day, her crown-like cap held in place with veils which wound under her chin hid her jowls. And there were many women her age and younger who envied her firm, slender but not yet fragile figure. Eleni dressed her now in a fine muslin delaine gown of pale blue trimmed with sapphire-coloured buttons and over this a loose sleeveless surcoat of royal-blue silk embroidered with silver Catherine wheels.

Thus armed in finery, Eleanor braved the day beyond her bedchamber. In the great chamber she found her youngest daughter Eloise curled in the southern window seat, her Chinese dog in her lap and a romance held before her short-sighted eyes while she absently ate strawberries from a bowl. Eloise wore the habit of a Benedictine nun, for she had entered the Benedictines some five years earlier. But it was a lax house with an abbess far too interested in accumulating wealth to care much about religious fervour. Whenever Eloise got bored with the routine and the squabbling of her sisters, she obtained leave to visit her perpetually 'ailing' parents. She did this with increasing frequency, to her mother's – not to mention Marie's – displeasure. She had arrived just two days ago, and bored them all with her tirades against the 'scandalous effrontery' of some new novice and endless bitching about the way the abbess's table groaned with delicacies while the sisters were fed stale, absolutely stale, cakes.

"You're late this morning, Mamá," Eloise observed with her mouth full. "Marie was here looking for you. Some old hag in the village was asking for you."

"What? Who?"

Eloise shrugged. "How should I know? Marie was in a bitchy mood, as usual."

Eleanor sighed. While Eloise was undoubtedly correct, she still disapproved of her daughter using such language. "I will have to find her and see what this is about. Have you seen Alice this morning?" Alice was also at Najac. She had been delivered of her tenth child, a sickly son, just over a month earlier. Ostensibly, she had come to show her son to her mother.

Eleanor was at once glad and unsettled by her elder daughter's visit. It was the first time since her marriage thirteen years earlier that she had come not for some festival or family event but simply for a visit – and come without her husband. Glad as Eleanor was to receive her, she sensed that Alice could no longer bear her unhappiness alone and had come in search of comfort.

Eloise shrugged again. "Alice rushed up to the nursery in a tizzy because Norbert supposedly has a runny nose."

Norbert was the youngest of Marie's children, a toddler of almost a year. Eloise could afford to be indifferent. She had never lost a child. But Alice had lost six. She would of course be terrified that her baby, Hugh, might be infected. An illness that a healthy toddler like Norbert could shake off easily could well kill the younger and sickly Hugh.

Eleanor did not hesitate but at once made her way through the hall and up the stairs of the small corner tower housing the nursery. There she was greeted by Marie's elder children, six year old Petitlouis and Natalie, who was four and a half. The children were in a tussle over a doll of Natalie's that Petitlouis had seized and was holding out of Natalie's reach. While Petitlouis was enjoying the game he could easily win, Natalie was becoming increasingly hysterical in her concern for her doll. Petitlouis threw the doll higher and higher, and just as Eleanor mounted the last step and was about to grab the unruly boy, he flung the doll with all his might back into the nursery. Both children belted into the room after the doll, leaving Eleanor breathless and limping on the landing.

As she entered the nursery, she found that Petitlouis had reached the doll first, and, holding it by the head, he was beating the walls with the body. "Your doll is a whore, Nata, and she has to be stoned!"

Natalie's reply was a wail of inarticulate, high-pitched outrage that seemed to shake the very walls.

"Louis Armand Philippe! Give your sister her doll this instant!" Eleanor ordered in her most authoritative voice.

Petitlouis looked over in sheer astonishment. His mother never addressed him by his full name and she was rarely angry with him either. More from surprise than obedience, he tossed his sister the doll. Clutching the doll to her breast and wailing, Natalie fled into the room beyond the partition.

Eleanor followed her granddaughter through the door in the partition. Here, in the sleeping chamber, the nanny was suckling

Norbert while Alice hung over the cradle where Hugh whimpered and whined.

The sight of Alice distressed Eleanor instantly. Dressed as she was now, in only her dressing gown, her hair loose about her shoulders, it was more evident than otherwise that Alice's health was poor. Her hair was lustreless, her skin sallow and her back was bent in a perpetual hunch. Mentally, Eleanor compared Eloise's glowing round cheeks and pert figure to Alice's worn frame and face. It was easy to conclude that Eloise had made the better choice by preferring the ease, luxury and independence of a convent to the prestigious bondage of marriage.

"How is he doing, Alice?" Eleanor asked, advancing to stand behind her daughter and look down at the baby. Hugh kicked with his tiny feet and held his hands in tight angry fists. His red face was puckered into a frown. Hugh was a pathetic little runt, small and thin with long black hair and splotchy red skin. Alice reached into the cradle and took him into her arms, opening the front of her gown to give him her nipple. Eleanor was shocked. "Are you nursing him yourself? No wonder you look weary and run-down! And no wonder Hugh isn't getting enough to fatten him up," Eleanor scolded out of affection and concern.

She had underestimated how broken her daughter was. Alice burst into tears. "Must you criticise me too? Antoine said Hugh wasn't worth the cost of a nurse! He said we should expose him to the elements and let him die!"

"Christ in Heaven!" Eleanor dropped on to her heels and pulled her daughter into her arms, nursing child and all. Alice collapsed into retching sobs and Hugh started whimpering. "Nurse!" Eleanor called over her shoulder. "Put Norbert down and take Hugh."

The girl was as simple and placid as she was healthy. Though unwed, she had had a baby every spring for three years in a row, each time disclaiming any knowledge of who the father was. "He was nice to me," she'd say. Or, "he was big and blond." Like a good heifer she dropped her babies in a barn and then fed them until the priest took them away to give to deserving childless couples. Just after the birth of her third child, Norbert had been born to Marie and the priest had suggested she come to the castle. She had given up her own babe and taken Norbert to breast without the faintest protest or indication of distress. Now, she just as readily put Norbert back in his cradle, ignoring his angry protests, and took Hugh into her arms. The moment Hugh's lips closed around her swollen red nipple, a look of bliss flushed his otherwise ugly face and he at once went still except for audible slurping and sucking noises that seemed out of all proportion to his tiny body.

But Eleanor had no time for her youngest grandchild; she was rocking the sobbing Alice in her arms. With her cheek on Alice's head, she tried to hush her with the endearments of her youth. It was a good thing Geoffrey wasn't home, she reflected. He had always had a special soft spot in his heart for Alice, and his relations with his son-in-law were already strained. Geoffrey considered Antoine an illiterate boor, a man whose conversation was confined to hunting, hawking and wenching. It had only been out of deference to Alice, who had maintained an unconvincing but insistent front of contentment up to now, that he had refrained from an open break with the Montfrancs. The sight of Alice sobbing here on the floor would have filled him with such anger that Eleanor feared what he might have done.

"Sweet child, listen to me. We'll find a good wet-nurse for Hugh, and then, you'll see. You'll get strong and pretty again and Hugh will grow so big and strong that Antoine will favour him best of all. There's no need for tears at all." But though she said this, she made no real attempt to dry Alice's tears, letting her make up for thirteen years of withheld or hidden tears.

Gradually Alice calmed herself. The sobbing died down, but Alice remained cuddled in her mother's warming arms, her head on her mother's soft breast. "Oh, Mamá, how can any man say such a thing about his own son? I know he has three others, but Hugh is still his flesh and blood! And the others are young. There is no guarantee that they will survive to adulthood – at least that is what he says to me when he insists on his rights."

Eleanor glanced at the nurse, uncomfortable with the thought of any serving woman hearing the details of Alice's humiliation, but the girl seemed blissfully unaware of anything other than the greedy baby suckling nourishment from her. She was in any case a girl of few words, not the type to carry the gossip of Alice's marriage to others.

Eleanor stroked Alice's hair and tears came to her eyes as she felt how coarse and unkempt it was. "My poor Alice. Do you not want Antoine to come to you?"

"Do you think I like being pregnant year after year? I'm so tired, Mamá! I'm so tired sometimes I just want to die – to lie down and sleep and sleep and wake up in heaven. But you see, I'm afraid to wake up in hell."

"Don't be silly, child." Eleanor kissed the top of her head. "Why should you go to hell?" If there is a hell, Eleanor added mentally.

"There were nights when I locked Antoine out," Alice confessed, starting to sob again. "I... I... caused him to seek his pleasures elsewhere. I forced him to sin and once he took a kitchen maid against her will. Everyone heard her pleading with him to let her alone, but he forced himself on her. After that she ran away and we never saw her again. It was my fault because I... I had told him it would damage the baby. I was carrying Annette at the time. I should be glad that Antoine still wants me," Alice admitted, the tears welling up anew. "And he never hits me. Not once, though his father still beats his mother so roughly you can see the bruises. Once he knocked her teeth loose."

"And they call themselves noblemen!" Eleanor spat out contemptuously. "It is the Norman blood – mercenary blood!" The Montfrancs had 'won' their lands by joining the Albigensian 'crusade' under Simon de Montfort. Though of noble birth, they had been impoverished before they had slaughtered and looted their way across the Languedoc in a 'religious' fervour to root out the Cathar heresy. They had been rewarded by the French crown with the lands of the families they had annihilated.

"Don't start that again, Mamá," Alice pleaded wearily, lifting her head at last and brushing away her own tears. The moment was past and her pride was reasserting itself. She had chosen Antoine. She had been head over heels in love with him. Some stubborn part of herself still refused to admit she could have been so wrong about him. She was just sick and weary after Hugh's birth. It had been a difficult pregnancy and, for such a small child, an unusually difficult birth. It was as if Hugh had not wanted to be born at all, and she had had to push and push and push. Just the thought of it made her weary again. She sighed. "Let me dress and then we can go to the village and look for a nurse." She glanced at the serene girl, who had transferred Hugh to her other breast and watched him as if he was the first baby who had ever taken her milk. "I don't suppose Marie would be willing to part with this girl here?"

"Not in principle – unless we could convince her the girl is inferior to someone else in some way," Eleanor added with a cynical smile.

"Give me half an hour, Mamá."

"I'll wait in the great chamber."

Returning to the sunny chamber behind the great hall, Eleanor was aware of her hunger. As on every morning, a loaf of fresh bread waited upon a sideboard along with cheese and butter. She cut herself a slice and spread it with butter. When Geoffrey returned, she resolved mentally, she would serve him breakfast in bed and they would laze there together till dinner – to the scandal of their children. The thought pleased her, and she smiled unconsciously.

She was startled from her reverie by Marie's sharp voice. "If you intend to eat us out of house and home, you might at least do some needlework!" Outraged at such impudence, Eleanor spun around, and saw Marie as she stormed into the solar, her veil and surcoat aflutter about her. In fact, Marie had not seen her mother-in-law and was addressing Eloise, who had finished off the strawberries and was now eating dates.

Marie had grown plump in the last six years. Four pregnancies had transformed her once pointed, upturned breasts into round orbs and thickened her waist. Her face, which had been vapidly pretty, was already marred by the frown lines that pulled the brows together and the dissatisfied downturn of the lips. Eleanor could not remember when she had last seen Marie smile.

Eloise looked up from her book and stared at her sister-in-law sullenly. "You have no business telling me what to do," she answered. "I'm in my own house."

"You are in *my* house!" Marie countered.

"No!" Eleanor corrected angrily, drawing Marie's attention to her presence. "Not until I die do you own this house. My daughters have as much right to be here as you do."

Marie's lips tightened and her eyes smouldered with resentment, but she dipped her head dutifully before at once launching into a new topic. "The laundress Raymonde was at the gate this morning, asking you to come and see her grandmother. She says the old hag is dying, but she hasn't sent for the priest. She isn't a heretic, is she?" The pointedness of Marie's question brought the blood to Eleanor's face.

"No one in Najac is a heretic!" Eleanor snapped back.

Marie avoided her eye and shrugged. Louis had told her that his mother had been held by the Inquisition for two years. She knew too that Eleanor's mother had been burned at the stake. "Well, now you know you were sought, it is up to you whether you go or not," she told her mother-in-law, and then collecting the wax tablet she had evidently come for, she departed again.

"I hope you never die, Mamá, and Marie never inherits!" Eloise declared, defiantly popping another date into her mouth.

"Your reasons for wishing me long life are less than flattering, my dear."

Alice emerged, neatly dressed in an amber gown of worsted linen and a lemon surcoat that matched her veils. Her starched white, linen wimple framed her face with matronly respectability and seemed to hold her head up for her. Gone was the confused, hurt girl who had cried in her mother's arms minutes before.

"We are going down to the village, Eloise. Would you like to join us?"

Eloise seemed tempted. "What are you going to do?"

"Look in on old Sybille and enquire about a nurse for little Hugh."

"No," Eloise decided, wrinkling up her nose. "Sybille always stinks. I'm sure she's never had a bath in her life."

Eleanor nodded. She had not really expected any other answer from this 'nun'. So she and Alice set off together.

It was a warm day with broken clouds chasing across the sky. Leaving the castle behind, the two ladies followed the narrow, paved path down from the castle and through the gate of the town into the bastide itself. The single street that followed the spine of the ridge was steep and poorly cobbled. Rubbish and dung collected between the stones in many places while rainwater had cut deep gullies that criss-crossed the path in others. At this time of year, grass and even blooming wild flowers adorned many of the tiled roofs, competing with the crude window boxes that housed the cultivated flowers of the more ambitious housewives. In the kitchen gardens, squeezed between the cottages and enclosed in low stone walls, peas, onions and carrots grew in neat rows, ending in the fenced-off pens where the chickens scratched and cackled in brainless discontent.

Looking from their unglazed and unshuttered windows, the women saw Eleanor and Alice and they came out of their crooked, low doorways, wiping their hands on their aprons to bob their heads and call: "*Bonjour, mesdames*! *Bonjour!*" Eleanor saw the smiles and heard the joy in their voices as they called out, and she reproached herself for coming so seldom into the village.

They had not gone far when one of the women came out into the street and, in guttural Languedoc grown unfamiliar to Alice's ears, excitedly explained that old Sybille was certainly dying. Madame must hurry.

"That's why I am here," Eleanor assured the woman.

"You are a true daughter of your mother, Madame!" the woman insisted, grasping her hand and kissing it fervently.

Sybille lived almost at the far gate, in a one room cottage built against the wall of the little bastide. Eleanor and Alice had to duck to pass into the darkened room. Despite the open windows the air was foul with the smell of decay and the wind blew the stench of the latrine hole at the rear of the cottage back into the room. Alice at once pulled her veil over her nose and tried not to breathe in as she hovered close to the exit. She admired her mother as she advanced without hesitation to the straw pallet on the floor against the back wall. Gathering up her skirts so they would not be fouled by the dirt floor littered with undefinable waste, Eleanor sank down on to her heels and greeted the toothless creature on the pallet.

Sybille was older than anyone knew. She said she was a hundred but it was as much a figurative as a literal description of her age. Certainly she was over eighty and there was no one alive who could remember the year of her wedding, much less her birth. She lay now, a skeleton sheathed in splotchy skin with tufts of white hair streaming from her head down on to the folds of skin that had once been breasts. The air that came from her mouth was foul in the extreme and even Eleanor had to swallow her revulsion, and lift her nose slightly, preferring the more familiar stench of the latrine.

"Madame!" Sybille croaked out, her head shifting and her hand reaching out. "The consolamentum. Give me the consolamentum."

"Christ have mercy!" Alice gasped, crossing herself hastily.

"Sybille, I can't," Eleanor answered her steadily. "You confuse me with my mother."

"No. I know what they did to your mother. They burned her at the stake. But there is no one else. All the Good Men are gone from here. You must give me the consolamentum."

Eleanor looked helplessly at Raymonde, who hovered near her grandmother. Raymonde whispered, "Please, Madame, she is afraid to die without it."

"Sybille, my mother never taught me her secrets. I... I don't know how to give the consolamentum."

Sybille, like most old women, did not like being contradicted. "You know! Why won't you help me? Can't you see I am dying? Help me quick!"

Once, just once, Eleanor had been witness to the rite. While travelling with her mother from Albi a man had stopped them on the road and begged her mother to come to his wife, who was dying in childbed. Eleanor had thought he wanted the help of a woman, a midwife. Maybe her mother had thought the same at that moment for she made no effort to send Eleanor away. They went together into the cottage. The woman lay surrounded by female relatives and the midwife was already there. It was the midwife who told Eleanor's mother in a lowered voice that she was helpless. Only a doctor who could cut open the woman could have saved her, she said.

The woman knew her condition. It had been in recognition of her approaching death that she had sent for her husband and asked him to fetch one of the Good Men. Realising that Madame de Najac was present, the woman had gasped out for the consolamentum, as Sybille did now.

At that point, Eleanor's mother had ordered her to leave the room. Though she dutifully did as she was bidden, her curiosity had been too great to resist peering around the edge of the door from outside. Her mother and the others were too intent on ministering to the dying woman to take any notice of Eleanor. Eleanor had seen her mother kneel and take the dying woman's hands in hers.

Now she did the same.

Alice could not believe what she was seeing. Her mother, after protesting so little, knelt beside the dying woman and took her hands in her own. When her mother spoke, Alice was afraid to hear the heresy that would issue forth. Clapping her hands over her ears, she rushed out of the cottage and into the street – directly into the path of a party of horsemen pounding down the slope from the road.

The riders drew up sharply, and Alice stood, terrified, with her hands on her ears and her eyes closed, convinced that she was about to be trampled to death for stepping into the house of a heretic.

"Alice! What are you doing..." Her father did not finish his question but flung himself from his lathered stallion to take his daughter in his arms.

Alice was her father's little girl. Without hesitation she flung her arms around his neck and started crying. "Papá, Sybille is dying and mother is there with her..."

Geoffrey's eyes went instantly to the run-down cottage and Alice felt the stab of jealousy she always felt when her mother so effortlessly claimed first place in her father's heart. In blind jealousy, she cried out, "She is a heretic!"

"Does it matter now?" Geoffrey answered, thinking she was referring to Sybille. "It is for God to judge her. But I must speak to your mother." Gently but firmly, he released himself from his daughter's arms. Only when he drew away from her did Alice register that he was coated in mud and his face was ashen, his eyes bloodshot.

"I will see to the dying woman." This was said by a young nun wearing an equally muddy habit. Alice did not recognise the young woman, though she spoke a cultivated, aristocratic French with the inflection of Poitiers, not unlike her mother-in-law's. Stiffly, the nun dismounted from her hired mare and started toward the cottage with Geoffrey.

"Sister Nun!" Alice called after her. "For your soul's sake do not enter there! The dying woman is a heretic! A Cathar! She has asked to be hereticated at death!" The shock in Alice's voice was genuine.

The strange nun looked at her with an unreadable expression for a moment and then turned and ducked into the cottage. Baffled, Alice looked up at the other horsemen. Her father's squire had also dismounted and stood holding the horses. All three horses stood with sunken heads, mud caking their cannonbones and splattered on bellies and haunches. Behind the squire, the sergeant of the watch, an ageing man who had come with her father from Cyprus forty years ago, sat on his exhausted gelding. It was this man, his French still betraying an English accent, who broke the news to her. "Your brother Jean is dead. Acre has fallen."

In the cottage, Madeleine fell to her knees beside the pallet. Raymonde's eyes opened wide and she seemed on the brink of protest, but Eleanor was already scrambling to her feet, dusting off her knees. Sybille seemed to have lost consciousness although her guttural breathing filled the room like snores. At the sight of Geoffrey in the doorway, Eleanor broke into a smile but the look in his eyes made it freeze upon her face.

She saw him with abrupt clarity. He was old, grey, haggard and bent. Her handsome knight had become an old man with ill-kept hair and a muddy brigandine, hose and boots. "Geoffrey." She whispered the name like a prayer, and already her mind had leapt ahead. He had been in Marseilles. She reached out her hand, and he took it, leading her out of the stinking cottage.

She was leaning on him by then, though he was hardly stronger than she at that moment. Tears were in his eyes. "Jean?" she asked in a whisper.

"*The Falcon* put into Marseilles while we were still loading. The Saracen breached the inner walls of Acre on the 18th of May. The Templars and Hospitallers together held the Turks long enough for the ships in harbour to put to sea – including *The Falcon*, loaded with civilians. All through the night the flames of the burning city lit up the eastern sky, allowing them to navigate without the stars. By the time *The Falcon* left Limassol for Marseilles even the fires had gone out."

The tears were running down his face. For thirteen years, Eleanor had pretended Jean was dead, but Geoffrey hadn't lost his son till now.

And now, when he was really dead, Eleanor did not believe it. "I don't believe it," she admitted, even as she wiped Geoffrey's tears with her hands.

"Sister Madeleine was on *The Falcon* – was in Acre."

"Your son sent a sergeant to see that I was safely aboard the ship, Madame." Sybille was dead and Madeleine had re-emerged from the cottage.

Eleanor turned and took note of her for the first time. She was an attractive young woman, despite the marks of exhaustion and the dirt of the road. But there was much more on her face than exhaustion and dirt, there was pain and depth.

"You knew my son?" Eleanor asked from a great distance. Jean, Jean, her heart was banging. I loved you more than the rest! Didn't you understand? Jean!

"I had the privilege, Madame, the very great privilege to have known your son."

She loves him, Eleanor registered. She loved him, she corrected herself. "Jean!" The word was torn from her, a cry and a shriek and a shout that, as if in a dream, emerged only as a little stifled croak as a chasm opened under her feet and swallowed her.

*

She woke in her own bed. Around her all was dark except for a sliver of light betraying the crack in the bed curtains. She shifted and felt Geoffrey's warmth and weight beside her and even after all these years she could not reach across him to open the crack in the curtains without dropping a kiss upon his naked chest. She rested her cheek upon the white hairs on his chest and listened to the rhythmic thudding of his heart. Then, kissing that faithful heart through its cage of rib and skin, she reached over and opened the bed curtains. It was night and the light came only from a candle by the bed. Apparently Geoffrey had returned to his Templar habit of lighting a candle in the chamber before retiring. It was nearly forty years since she had broken him of the habit, arguing that they could ill afford the candle and preferring the darkness for a lovemaking she found somewhat embarrassing by light.

Had Jean slept his last night with a candle? she wondered as she let the curtains fall closed and lay back beside her husband. In a city under siege, abandoned by all of Christendom, with ten hundred thousand Turks outside the gates, did the Templars still keep to their rule? Did they sleep in chaste pairs by candlelight and refuse to look a woman in the eye? Had this nun Madeleine fallen in love with her son without looking him in the eye? No. Eleanor decided. He had found her in a slave market and lifted her literally and figuratively out of the filth. He had wrapped her in his own white mantle and carried her in his arms. He had restored her dignity and her very humanity. He had not done that with averted eyes.

Jean! Jean! Listen to me! I loved you more than any of them! Jean! Answer me! Tell me you can hear me! Jean! Damn you, Jean! Answer me!

Eleanor sat bolt upright in the bed and held her breath. She listened. Her mother was there. Her mother had been in the cottage with Sybille, had given her the words for a rite she did not even understand. Her mother cast a shadow in the light of the Templar candle. "Mother?" Eleanor gasped for breath, unable to hold it any longer. The answer was there in the silence.

"Geoffrey!" Eleanor turned to her husband and shook him – far more harshly than he deserved. "Geoffrey!"

Groggy with exhaustion, Geoffrey roused himself. "What is it Eleanor?" His voice was gravelly with lack of sleep.

"We must go to Cyprus."

"Cyprus?"

"That's where the survivors will turn up."

"Eleanor." He was awake now and his eyes glittered in the light of his single candle. "There are no survivors. I know my brothers. They would not surrender, and even if they did the Sultan would kill them."

He did not say torture and mutilate them because he meant to spare Eleanor those details, but she read the unspoken thoughts in the strain on his face. He was tortured by the thought that Jean had fallen into Mameluke hands. Madeleine's information that he had been alive on the eve of the 18th was no comfort to Geoffrey. Geoffrey knew how Raoul had died.

"There are always survivors. Think of Mansourah."

She could see in his eyes that she had hurt him without meaning to. And she could see that he thought she was half-mad. But she also saw the look of indulgence that followed the spasm of agony, and she knew he was going to indulge her.

"All right. We can go to Cyprus."

Eleanor lay back down beside him with a sense of calm and relief that made her sleepy. She snuggled her head in the crook of his shoulder and with her eyes closed she murmured contentedly, "We can go to Kolossi."

"And ride along the road to Paphos."

"And then to Neophytos – do you suppose Brother Hilarion is still alive?"

"Of course," Geoffrey answered with a curious smile as he too closed his eyes. Brother Hilarion would have to be well over a hundred to be alive, and yet in that moment between consciousness and subconsciousness it was as if Brother Hilarion could never die.

"I will go and talk to him again." Geoffrey slipped from reality to dream, aware of slipping and yet unable to stop himself. "Eve..."

And the body beside him was smooth and firm and young again – like his own.

Marseilles
July 1291

The harbour at Marseilles was crammed with ships. Not a single berth was vacant along the two quays and at least a dozen ships waited at anchor or attempted to offload their cargoes on barges. The quay was correspondingly cluttered with wares, chandlery, the luggage of passengers embarking and disembarking, and the wagons of merchants delivering or collecting goods. Sailors, longshoremen, passengers and whores bargained, cursed and argued in all the languages of the Mediterranean. Customs officials in royal livery arrived with a squad of royal archers to make a raid upon a ship suspected of smuggling, and a band of pickpockets, the eldest of whom was no more than twelve, scattered into the nearest alley with yelps of delight to see 'a big fish' snared in a net. From the nearest tavern came a wail of drunken laughter and then a whore burst into the street, half naked, spitting and snarling in rage at the man who tripped over the leg of a fellow sailor as he tried to follow her out into the street.

Geoffrey drew up his stallion and glanced back at Eleanor with a degree of alarm. But Eleanor met his eyes and with an almost imperceptible nod of her head indicated that she was not in the least intimidated. Her mind was on the galley flying the Baucent at the foot the quay. If Eleanor was not distressed, Eleni, miserably perched upon a broad-backed plough horse, looked considerably more frightened, while Geoffrey's squire's eyes were popping out of his head as he twisted in his saddle to stare at the lightly clad whore throwing rubbish at the drunk in the doorway, to the raucous approval of his comrades.

The little party from Najac – Geoffrey, Eleanor, Eleni, Madeleine, Geoffrey's squire, six servants and seven pack horses – continued along the quay carefully. The horses pricked their ears and their nostrils quivered at so many unusual sights and sounds. Eleanor's highly strung mare nervously pranced and repeatedly balked as they made their way to *The Falcon*, still made fast where Geoffrey had left her two weeks earlier.

The Falcon, although she occupied a precious berth, lay quietly at the quay, neither loading nor offloading. A curious peace seemed to hang over the fleet fighting ship, and Geoffrey frowned instantly.

Geoffrey dismounted and went across the gangplank on to the deck of the Templar ship. He was not stopped until he was halfway to the aft deck. Then a Templar serving brother emerged from under an awning and shouted at him angrily, demanding his business.

"If I were captain of this ship, I'd have you flogged for letting me get this far!" Geoffrey retorted. "Where is Captain Sergeant de Flor?"

"He's—"

"Here." The answer came now from the poop, where de Flor emerged from his cabin, pulling a shirt over his tanned and muscular chest. Geoffrey had the unpleasant feeling that he had just dragged the man from lovemaking.

"Sergeant, my wife and I are seeking passage to Limassol. When do you expect to sail?"

Roger de Flor stood at the poop rail and considered the grey-haired man on the quarterdeck below him. He had made a fortune with the bribes extracted from the civilians desperate to flee Acre. It was money he had not the least intention of surrendering to the Temple – as the rule demanded – and he was acutely aware that he must soon 'disappear' or face severe punishment and possibly lifelong imprisonment. But he was extremely reluctant to abandon a ship as beautiful and seaworthy as *The Falcon*.

He shrugged in answer and, to emphasise his insubordination, he flung one leg over the rail and leaned his hand upon his knee, the foot swinging. "*The Falcon* will sail when the preceptors of France, Normandy and the Auvergne have arrived."

Geoffrey registered the insolence of the sergeant, but it was not his affair. Important was only the information that the Templars had apparently called a general chapter – as indeed they must to elect a new master to replace De Beaujeu. Without the preceptors of all the Provinces the chapter could not be held, and it could well take another week or two before the preceptors arrived overland from Paris and Rouen. That explained the incongruous peacefulness of the galley.

Roger de Flor was mollified somewhat by the fact that the old knight did not attempt to reprimand him, so he volunteered the information that a Hospitaller ship was on the eastern quay and was – if his information was correct – due to sail with the next tide.

"And when is the next tide?" Geoffrey enquired.

"Oh, the tide must be about to turn now," De Flor remarked with a listless arrogance, indicating the water lapping directly at the high water mark on the quay. Geoffrey turned at once to scan the opposite quay and located the black-hulled, red-trimmed galley of the Hospital. The bustle of activity at the quay and on deck indeed suggested that she was making ready to sail. He did not bother to thank the sergeant, but turned at once, ran back to his stallion and swung himself into the saddle. Pointing to the Hospitaller, he told the others to follow him. He then put his spurs to his stallion and turned him at the same time.

The stallion was tired but far too well trained to protest. Geoffrey cantered the length of the west quay, along the head of the harbour and down the east quay, scattering beggars, drunks and honest workers indiscriminately.

At the Hospitaller ship, he jumped down, even as they started to pull the gangplank onboard. "I must speak to your captain!" he shouted.

The sailors were startled but they called to the poop, even as a knight in the red surcoat and mantle of the Hospital emerged from the far side of the wheel house.

"Sir! Are you sailing for Limassol?" Geoffrey asked anxiously.

"Yes."

"I beg you to give me – and my party – passage."

"My lord." The Hospitaller had quickly assessed the value of Geoffrey's stallion, tack and armour for he wore his best long-sleeved hauberk and his legs were clad in the finest leather hose and over-the-knee boots. "This is a fighting ship of the Knights of St John of Jerusalem. We are travelling with dispatches for the master of our order – and desperately needed supplies and recruits. I beg you to understand that we are not a passenger ship – no matter what you wish to pay."

Geoffrey liked the answer and he actually smiled. "Sir, I do understand, but let me ask you this: were you at Acre?"

The Hospitaller's face went absolutely rigid and the jaw clamped. "I was – it was Master De Beaujeu of the Knights Templar who ordered me to take our wounded Master De Villiers to the ships and to defend them against the rabble."

"Then you may have known my son."

"Your son was at Acre?"

"My son was a Templar commander at Acre."

De Villaret suddenly knew, even though there was no real physical resemblance between his friend and his friend's father. But Jean had often spoken with deep respect and affection of his father and something about Geoffrey suggested that he had himself been on crusade, in Acre, a Templar. "Monsieur de Preuthune?" De Villaret asked.

"Yes, how—"

"You are welcome." Turning, De Villaret ordered the sailors to put the gangplank back in place. "How many are in your party, my lord?"

"Only my wife, a nun, my squire and five servants."

For a nobleman, that was indeed an extremely humble following and De Villaret nodded agreement.

Limassol
August 1291

The Hospitaller galley limped into Limassol harbour with an improvised foremast and a smashed port rail. In a violent storm, she had lost part of her deck cargo and four of the horses had had to be put down after breaking their legs in a frenzy of fear in the hold. But they had lost only one sailor and the galley was seaworthy. It swung in toward the dock smartly under oar, and made straight for the berth reserved for the master's flagship. Along the quay, there were no fewer than three ships flying the Baucent of the Temple, and Geoffrey quickly concluded that several of the preceptors – perhaps those from Aragon, Apulia and Aquitaine – had already arrived for the grand chapter.

Taking a cordial leave of De Villaret, Geoffrey and Eleanor disembarked with their little party. Eleni and Geoffrey's squire were sent with the other servants to find lodgings for them at one of the reputable hostels while Geoffrey, Eleanor and Madeleine made their way on hired horses to the squat white fortress that housed the Temple. It was almost forty years since they had seen it last, and it seemed subtly changed – or maybe it was the square around that had crowded in or the trees of the olive orchard that had grown. It was literally a lifetime ago that a barefoot sixteen year old had begged admittance to the Temple in a French that made even the serving brothers smile.

At the outer gate, two very young sergeants kept the watch and they promptly crossed their lances to prevent Geoffrey and Eleanor from entering.

Geoffrey was at a disadvantage on a gelding hack that gave him none of the dignity due a nobleman of France. His leather boots, streaked with salt and discoloured, made a sorry impression that even his diamond studded spurs could not overpower. His chainmail hauberk betrayed the beginnings of rust despite the best efforts of his squire, and his grey hair was untrimmed and somewhat unruly after the sea voyage.

But Geoffrey had never been someone to rely on outward appearance for his authority, and he drew up and considered the youthful sergeants pensively. They were much too young – beardless boys – and that said more about the toll of Acre than anything else.

"Boys, Geoffrey de Preuthune and his lady wish to speak with the senior officer here at Limassol," he told them, adding laconically, "Who is the senior officer?"

The sergeants exchanged a baffled look and then in a flurry of Italian seemed to discuss Geoffrey's question at length. At last, one of the youths looked up and in broken French said, "Monsieur, whom do you wish to see?"

"Who is commander here at Limassol?" Geoffrey tried.

"I heard that the commander took men to Acre with King Hugh. He didn't come back."

"Who is in command then?"

The Italian sergeants looked at one another, and then the spokesman shrugged in an eloquent gesture. "Master Gaudin arrived from Sidon and the preceptors of Aquitaine, Apulia, England and Aragon are here and the visitor-general."

"There is a new master? But the preceptors of France, Normandy and the Auvergne haven't arrived, have they?" Geoffrey found it hard to believe that *The Falcon* could have overtaken them even if it had escaped the storm.

"No, but—"

"Sergeant! What goes on there?" The voice was that of an older man, and after a moment Geoffrey could make out the figure of a knight striding forward toward the gate. "What can we do for you, Monsieur?" the knight enquired in a brusque, efficient tone that betrayed only the slightest Spanish accent.

"Geoffrey de Preuthune de Najac, sir. My lady and I have arrived this morning from France. We wish to speak with someone who can... tell us about the fate of our son, Commander Jean de Preuthune." The name obviously meant nothing to the Spaniard, so Geoffrey added, "He was Master De Beaujeu's companion."

The knight gave Geoffrey a look which flitted between respect and pity and then glanced past him to Eleanor, who sat her hired mare with apparent patience. In fact, Eleanor was so rigid with tension that a better horse would have been skitting about in nervous confusion. She had not really followed any of the dialogue between Geoffrey and the guards. Her mind had been too preoccupied with incoherent thoughts. She remembered arriving here forty years ago and watching Geoffrey being swallowed into the fraternity, hearing mass among his white-robed brothers rather than with the king. In the end, however, he had chosen her. But this cold, faceless fortress was not somewhere which could house her Jean. And if he were not here, he must be dead...

"Madame." The Templar knight had come to stand beside her stirrup and he offered her his assistance in dismounting. "I will take you to Monsieur Gaudin. He will have known your son."

She accepted his assistance automatically, and let Geoffrey lead her through the gate into the cramped courtyard. Auxiliary stabling had been created by spreading straw along the edge of the wall and rigging an awning to protect the horses from the sun. Native boys tended to the horses and from the kitchen complex came a cacophony of Greek, indicating that here too the Temple had resorted to native servants. Forty years ago they had had no such need.

Entering the keep itself by the external stair, Eleanor felt her chest constrict in the exact way it had forty years before. Here, inside the Temple, the rigid masculinity of the fighting monks was as predominant as ever. During her last visit, she had been in the entourage of the French king, and his courtiers had leavened the strict austerity of the Temple with their silks and jewels and laughter. Now the overcrowding and bustle was the product of so many high officials of the Temple itself being collected at this otherwise obscure commandery.

No fewer than three Templar chaplains were officiously descending the steps leading down to the chapel on the right, and from the left came the deep-pitched rumble and conversation of serving brothers dragging the heavy trestle-tables into place for the midday meal in the refectory. On the stair before them, knights, sergeants and serving brothers squeezed past one another on their way to and from their duties and the languages that cascaded down the steps included Spanish, Italian, and – or so Eleanor thought – a fragment of *langue d'oc*. Instinctively, she looked for the speaker from her homeland, but they were all dressed in the same white monastic robes with red cords, all bearded and tonsured. She shuddered inwardly and rebelliously cursed her son for having joined this damned fraternity.

The monks cast Eleanor discreetly curious glances. Madeleine, in her shabby and ill-fitting Cistercian garb, aroused less interest. But Eleanor was every inch a lady and she had chosen a green silk gown embroidered with vines and birds in gold thread that glittered in the candlelight of the windowless interior. As she limped up the stairs, the monks respectfully drew back to make way for her as she passed on Geoffrey's arm.

The Spanish knight led them to the relatively spacious chamber that served as the anteroom to the treasury. Here tenants of the Temple delivered their rent and pilgrims deposited or collected the money they entrusted to the Temple for safe keeping. A Templar clerk behind a table was counting out a sum for a traveller while another clerk was preparing a letter of credit for an impatient merchant pacing the whitewashed room. The Spaniard bade Geoffrey, Eleanor and Madeleine to wait, and continued into the chamber beyond.

Eventually he returned and bade them follow him. Passing through the treasury itself, they ascended a narrow stair into a darkened chamber. Geoffrey knew they had entered the commander's quarters by the indirect route. The chamber stank heavily of some herbal mixture and, propped up in a chair, was a white-haired man with a beard reaching to his chest. This man wore the robes and clutched the rod of the master of the Temple. Even before the man raised his left hand and tried to greet them, it was evident that he had been the victim of a stroke. The right side of his face was lifeless, his right arm and leg immobile.

Geoffrey went down on one knee and kissed the master's hand, and Madeleine followed his example. Eleanor confined herself to a polite but far from reverent curtsy. The Spanish knight excused himself, but from the corner a clerk came forward to stand behind the master's chair.

"I am Master Gaudin's secretary," he announced. "You have come to enquire about your son, I was told. A Templar?"

"Jean de Preuthune."

Thibald Gaudin at once started, his left hand jerked and from his contorted mouth came a garbled word. The secretary leaned forward, and Gaudin strained to get control of his tongue. "Jean! Jean was with De Beaujeu... when he died. He... was present... when De Beaujeu knighted me. De Sevrey..." He struggled but the words wouldn't come.

Embarrassed, Eleanor and Geoffrey exchanged a glance. The secretary urged Gaudin to relax, to take a deep breath, and he wiped Gaudin's high, gleaming, brow. They could hear his rasping breathing and his hand twitched spasmodically, but then after a bit he spoke again. "De Sevrey named... me... me... commander of the Kingdom. Jean was there. Jean..." Again the words failed to come and Gaudin's eyes bulged in his head as he struggled with himself. His face turned bright red and in alarm Geoffrey looked at the secretary. The secretary wiped Gaudin's brow and urged him to relax. He took a goblet from a sideboard and handed it to Gaudin, but the patient refused the tonic and angrily lashed out with his left hand. The Secretary managed to rescue the goblet just in time, but he cast Geoffrey a look of apology.

Geoffrey rose to his feet and stepped back beside Eleanor. "I think it is best we leave Master Gaudin in peace. Surely someone else can give us information about what happened to our son at Acre?"

The secretary sighed. "In the chapel perhaps. Several of the chaplains made it out with Master Gaudin."

To enter the chapel, they had to descend to the ground floor, below the level of entry. From the smell of incense it was clear that Mass had just been read and around the altar a novice was still dimming the candles. Most of the brothers would be at dinner in the refectory. Eleanor sank into a pew and waited while Geoffrey went forward into the choir to look for a priest.

A Templar chaplain knelt beside the altar. He prayed with his eyes closed and his lips moving in apparent passion. Geoffrey stopped abruptly and waited respectfully for him to finish. The sound of his spurs scraping the tiled floor, however, startled the chaplain and he looked over almost nervously – as if he had been caught in some illicit activity. His eyes widened at the sight of a secular knight.

"Forgive me for intruding, Father. My lady and I are seeking news of our son. He was at Acre. We were told that you – or one of the priests – might be able to help us."

The chaplain looked farther around until he could see Eleanor and Madeleine in the church. He looked up at Geoffrey more strangely than ever, but crossed himself and got to his feet. He came down into the choir to Geoffrey and kept his voice very low while he spoke, low enough so Eleanor could not hear. "I was in Acre when the city fell. If your son was among those who made it to the Temple, I may be able to help you."

"The Temple didn't surrender with the city?"

"Oh, no. The city fell on the 18th when the Mamelukes breached the inner walls and took the port. The Hospitallers took out a number of our wounded. Have you—"

"We have come from France with Sir Jules de Villaret. My son was not among the wounded. But if the Temple hasn't surrendered—"

The priest held up his hand and shook his head sharply to prevent false hopes from rising. "The Temple itself held out until the 28th, when it was undermined and collapsed upon the Sultan's troops when they tried to storm it. According to the fishermen and our information from a spy in the Sultan's court, every living soul in the Temple at the time – Christian and Muslim – was crushed under the mighty walls."

"But you survived," Geoffrey pointed out.

The priest flushed. "I was ordered out by Marshal De Sevrey – as was Gaudin – on the night of the 24th. We travelled by skiff to Sidon. We were twenty men: Gaudin, myself and the other clerics, and the oarsmen – all sergeants. I presume your son was a knight." It was unthinkable that the son of a knight might be a sergeant or serving brother but it was, of course, possible that he had been a cleric.

"My son was a commander." Geoffrey spoke with intense pride. Even though he had not allowed himself to believe that Jean might have survived, there was something about standing here in the chapel where he had spent his novitiate and speaking of his son's rise to commander which tore his heart anew. Jean had been the better Templar, he had risen further – and he had died for the Holy Land.

The priest started. "Only two commanders survived the fall of the city and made it to the Temple. William de la More and Jean de Preuthune."

The sound of his son's name on the other's lips was like a blow and Geoffrey blanched. The priest was staring at Geoffrey so intently that he saw the effect of his words and abruptly he grabbed Geoffrey's arm. "You... you aren't Geoffrey de Preuthune, are you?"

"Yes... How... Did Jean speak of me?"

The priest crossed himself and muttered a prayer. His eyes flashed and his entire face seemed to be enlivened. Gone was the sombre look of shared mourning. He nodded as he devoured Geoffrey with eager eyes. This was the man De Sonnac had dreamed would be master of the Temple one day.

"Jean is at Kolossi. He and De la More brought out a longboat filled with women and children the night after Gaudin and I sailed in the skiff."

Jean's survival was the one thing Geoffrey had no longer expected. He opened his mouth in astonishment or to express his thanks and joy, but no words came. Eleanor! He turned around and saw her clutching Madeleine's hand in her lap, and he could only shake his head in wonder. How had she known?

Her eyes widened as they met Geoffrey's. She could read his face and she was on her feet abruptly, Madeleine brusquely forgotten. She started forward, stumbling over her skirts, her lame leg betraying her, and Geoffrey went to meet her. "He's at Kolossi!" In boyish defiance of the memories of a harsh, chaste novitiate, he took his wife in his arms and covered her face with kisses. She was his greatest treasure, his life and heart's desire. And if she hadn't insisted on coming to Cyprus, they would have mourned unnecessarily for many months to come!

Father Etienne had come down the steps from the choir and stood at a respectful distance, smiling with indulgence and satisfaction at the joy he had ignited. He briefly considered the nun, who had fallen on her knees, crossed herself and appeared to be praying with sincerity. He presumed she was Jean's sister, and returned his attention to the grey-haired couple whose son had returned from the dead. He cleared his throat as husband and wife kissed blissfully. "Madame."

Eleanor ended the kiss but held Geoffrey defiantly close to her breast and looked at the Templar chaplain with triumphant eyes. It was not just the fact that she held her husband brazenly in her arms in the sacred heart of the Temple, it was also the fact that her heretical mother had told her Jean was alive.

"Madame." Father Etienne continued. "There is something I should warn you about." He was serious, so serious that Eleanor felt a touch of fear creep into her heart. "Your son lost his arm at Acre – just below the shoulder."

Eleanor felt Geoffrey suck in his breath, and she held him closer, comforting him. She could bear the thought of Jean one-armed better than Geoffrey. He had always had an intense aversion to any mention of amputation. He had seen Raoul with his arms hacked off.

Holding Geoffrey gently, Eleanor answered for them both. "Thank you for warning us, Father, but the loss of an arm is little compared to the loss of the son himself. We will make for Kolossi at once." She held out her hand to the priest, who bowed over it gallantly, but seemed reluctant to let them depart.

Father Etienne kept looking at Geoffrey. "Sir, were you not once a Templar novice?"

"Yes," Geoffrey answered somewhat stiffly, drawing back from Eleanor's embrace and taking her hand instead.

"You understand then something of the procedure for the election of the master?" the chaplain persisted.

Geoffrey nodded. He had been a novice for a little over a year when Armand de Périgord died. The election of his successor had been the most exciting event since he joined the order. They had talked of almost nothing else for the five months leading up to De Sonnac's election and for another two or three months afterwards.

"The slaughter of all our senior officers at Acre left the Temple here in the east virtually leaderless. The knights at Sidon, under siege already, elected Thibald Gaudin master when he arrived – almost like a miracle – by sea from Acre. They insisted it could only be God's will that he lead us, if he alone of all the officers of the Temple had survived. Thibald, however " – Father Etienne lowered his voice and, taking Geoffrey by the arm, drew him aside from Eleanor and Madeleine – "was a sergeant, the commander of the City of Acre."

Eleanor let Geoffrey go, but the blood rose in her head and her throat constricted, her fists clenched. A speechless rage momentarily overpowered all the joy of Jean's survival as she watched her husband conspire with the Templar chaplain.

Father Etienne was explaining to Geoffrey the circumstances under which Gaudin had been knighted and then named commander of the kingdom of Jerusalem. He explained that among the 'treasures' smuggled out of Acre on the skiff were the robes, rod and ring of the master, which he had personally removed from De Beaujeu's hand after his death. In Sidon, Father Etienne continued, De Beaujeu and De Sevrey were so revered that their promotion of Gaudin, combined with the fact that he had been entrusted with these symbols of the master, was interpreted as a virtual command to entrust the order into his hands. They had elected him master – much to his own initial embarrassment.

"But only a grand chapter can initiate the election of a new master," Geoffrey protested. Geoffrey remembered the procedure for the election of the master vividly because he had been young, impressionable and filled with the burning ambition of youth at the time of De Sonnac's election. The rule set out that a general chapter of all the leading men of the order from the West as well as Outremer must select two brothers. These two brothers – after a night of prayer – chose two further brothers. The four chose another two, and the six another two until they were twelve, eight knights and four sergeants. Together they selected a chaplain, making an electoral college of thirteen men representing the twelve disciplines and Christ. These thirteen Templars, ideally drawn from all the provinces of the Temple, then elected the master. They announced their candidate and the new master was then acclaimed by the entire chapter. In the first century of the Temple's existence, the brothers of the electoral college had then carried their new master into the Church of the Holy Sepulchre and placed him before the altar.

"Yes. Precisely. But once Gaudin had been carried to the altar and donned the master's mantle at Sidon, he considered himself duly elected. He took over the command, and he was tireless in his defence of Sidon – literally. I do not believe he lay down to sleep for more than an hour at a time for weeks on end. Inevitably the city fell, of course, on June 18, and the knights withdrew into the Castle Pilgrim. Gaudin resolved to sail for Cyprus and bring reinforcements. I sailed with him.

"Here in Limassol, however, we discovered that William de la More, unaware of the events at Sidon and Gaudin's election, had sent ships to all the provinces, calling a general chapter. By the time Gaudin and I arrived, not only were the preceptors of Apulia and Aragon already here, but the visitor-general had arrived as well. These senior officers, regarded Gaudin as a... joke – not to say imposter. They insisted that he could at very most call himself 'grand commander," – a title used for the officer elected to head the Temple in the interim between masters – "and vehemently refused to send any of the few knights they had managed to assemble to the Castle Pilgrim.

"Gaudin is over seventy. The siege of Acre and then Sidon had drained him of his remaining strength. Confronted with the arrogant attitude of the visitor-general and the refusal of all the other preceptors to recognise his authority at a time when the brothers left behind at the Castle Pilgrim were so desperate for relief, he become enraged, almost rabid. He shouted, screamed and threatened the others with eternal damnation – and they had the satisfaction of seeing him struck down. Now he is a bitter cripple, clinging to his own reality with remarkable tenacity, while the others calmly prepare for a general chapter and the election of another master. Meanwhile, the Castle Pilgrim was abandoned in despair on July 14, and the knights there feel a disappointment bordering on resentment toward poor Gaudin because he did not keep his word to bring reinforcements."

At last Father Etienne fell silent. Geoffrey considered the priest intently. The priest, with his weathered, kindly face and intelligent hazel eyes, had at first struck a sympathetic chord in Geoffrey, and Geoffrey was extremely interested in the detailed information he had provided – even if he could feel Eleanor's hostility turning the air of the chapel to ice.

But he could not understand why a Templar chaplain would tell an outsider so many intimate – and ultimately unflattering – details about internal Templar affairs. The election of the master of the Temple was a highly secretive affair even in the best of times. In the present catastrophic circumstances, the Temple could not afford any more damage to its reputation. Geoffrey disapproved of the priest's indiscretion. "Why do you tell me this?" he asked, his disapproval undisguised in voice and face.

Father Etienne winced and then looked at him sidelong with intensity. "Because your son must be persuaded to return to Limassol. As Beaujeu's companion and a survivor of Acre, he commands the awe of many younger knights and the respect of most of the senior sergeants. If he is here when the general chapter convenes – and that could be any day, as we are awaiting only the preceptors of France, Normandy, the Auvergne, and Portugal – he stands a very good chance of being selected for the electoral college."

Geoffrey did not like this answer. It suggested that the priest's interest in Jean was political – not to say manipulative. "Jean will hardly be at Kolossi voluntarily. If he was sent to the Hospitallers to recover from his wounds, then he should not return until he has recovered."

Father Etienne looked at Geoffrey completely baffled. "Kolossi hasn't belonged to the Hospital for a quarter of a century. It is a Templar house and Jean was sent there to train recruits. You can imagine, aside from the knights and sergeants the preceptors have brought with them, that men have flooded from the West on their own, offering their services on a temporary or permanent basis. They have all been sent to Kolossi to keep them away from the proceedings here, and Jean was entrusted with their training and the selection of those worthy of the mantle."

Geoffrey nodded. He could understand that. Commander de Bourgneuf had always spoken with enthusiasm of Jean's talent for training youths. "But if he was sent, then he can be recalled. It is not my business to interfere," Geoffrey insisted strictly.

"I am not suggesting that your son resign his command or abandon his duties – only that he come to Limassol for the critical period of the election. He can, I'm sure, find a deputy for a month or even two."

Geoffrey sighed and glanced back at Eleanor. She was glaring at him so furiously that he had to smile. He held out his hand, and – as he had expected – she refused to take it. He almost laughed. After all these years she was still afraid that he might abandon her for the Temple. He went and enclosed her resisting body in his arms. She was stiff with anger and brittle with resentment.

"What were you two monks discussing so intently?" she enquired acidly, refusing to return his embrace.

He kissed the top of her head and stroked her arms gently. "Eleanor, my love, you of all people should know that I am no monk. And if you doubt it," – he bent to whisper in her ear – "I'll prove it to you this very night."

She started to melt almost against her will. "Then what were you discussing?"

"Jean. I'll tell you everything on the way to Kolossi. And now it's time we set off." He turned then to Madeleine. "Sister, do you feel up to a further journey, or do you wish to follow us in a day or two with the servants?"

Geoffrey had rescued Madeleine from Sergeant de Flor by paying her passage with the same unquestioning generosity with which Jean had bought her freedom. He had offered her his protection, an escort home, paid for her hack and included her at his table. In short, he had treated her like a niece or cousin. So long as he expected to hear the news of Jean's death, he had not objected to her presence. But if he was to see his son for the first time in eight years, then he was less pleased at the prospect of a virtual stranger being present.

Madeleine, her self-regard so fragile, understood the rejection instantly. She seemed to shrink more deeply into her habit and, if she had been wearing a cloak with cowl, she would have pulled it forward to hide her face. "As you wish, my lord. I will await your instructions," came the wounded reply.

Eleanor went and kissed her on both cheeks. "Lift up thy heart, Mary Magdalene, for thou hast been to the tomb and found it empty."

Madeleine gasped and looked up with widened eyes.

"If He did not scorn to show Himself to the Magdalene before all others, then who are we to scorn you? Come with us."

But now Madeleine squared her shoulders and lifted her chin. "No, Madame, you are his mother. Go thee first to Kolossi."

Eleanor kissed her again, smiling. "Thank thee, child. But come tomorrow. Geoffrey will see that Charles escorts you. We know our way." She smiled over her shoulder at Geoffrey, who was watching her in puzzlement.

Kolossi
August 1291

A fleet of fishing boats bobbed upon the aquamarine waters of the wide bay at the foot of the cliffs. Beyond the distant headland to the west a spot of white betrayed an approaching sailing ship. Jean squinted toward the sail, but it was too far away to identify as galley or galleon. He let his gaze sweep inland to the rubble sloping up from the edge of the cliff. The collapsed masonry was meaningless now, though here and there the round surface of a pillar or fragments of carvings – a headless horse, a bearded face, a ship – bespoke once rich façades.

The sun had baked the countryside as far as the eye could see, and the parched earth gave up only dust. Dust coated the leaves of the olive and almond trees and blew with every breath of wind. It turned the coats of the horses to matted mud, now stiff as the sea breeze dried the sweat, and clung to the black surcoats of the riders, turning them grey. It worked its way through the rings of the chainmail to mix with sweat and streak the coif-framed faces with grime.

Jean considered the riders in file behind him one by one. With the exception of Ian MacDonald, whom he had promoted to sergeant, they were all new recruits. The white-haired Mario de Caril, a renowned Castilian knight, no less than the beardless Esteban Lopes from Navarre had offered their sword to the Templars. The fiery Stefan Hollosy came from Budapest and the shy Umberto from Siena. Imbert de Montfort was a son of the local branch of the family and his distant cousin Amaury came from Gascony. There were two Englishmen and a Bavarian, and the remaining eleven recruits all came from France or Aquitaine. Fully half the men were already knighted, but of these only four sought to join the order permanently. The rest had offered their services on a temporary basis in this 'moment of crisis' as Sir Lionel of Lincoln described it. Sir Lionel had been in Limassol, about to take ship for Acre, when *The Falcon* put in with the news that Acre had already fallen.

Jean could not know what motives drove them to join the Temple at this point in time, but he could guess that they ranged from genuine piety to bloodthirsty adventurism, while Umberto, for example, probably hoped to be admitted to an elite which would normally have been closed to him. Jean considered the young Italian more closely; he was squinting up his eyes and rubbing at his face with the back of his gloved hand, sand apparently in his eyes.

With the exception of Mario and Imbert, none of them was used to fighting in a desert climate. Jean could see the thirst on their dust-caked lips, and the exhaustion in their reddened, sweat-streaked faces. They were as finished as their horses, most of which stood with hanging heads and heaving flanks, having arrived some time in the last month and so being as unacclimatised as their riders.

Jean glanced at the sun hanging well above the horizon and just starting to turn a more mellow colour. He should turn them around and chase them back along the coast, make them descend the perilous trail to the shore and back – leading their reluctant mounts. He should keep them out all night, camped beside the cliffs with only the provisions they had on their saddles. He would wager that more than one of them had hastily tacked up this morning without bothering about food. They were used to relying upon squires, used to being able to go home when hunger called, used to being able to stop at a tavern to quench their thirst. Jean knew he could make their lives miserable, but what was the point?

They had lost the Holy Land. After Acre and Sidon, Tortosa and even the invincible Castle Pilgrim had been abandoned by their garrisons. There was nothing left of Outremer. Pilgrims seeking the Holy Places would have to put themselves at the mercy of the Muslims. No armed Christian knights could give them escort and no garrisoned Christian castles offer them protection and refuge. The poor Knights of the Temple of Solomon had lost the very reason for their existence.

Jean's missing arm was throbbing and hurting sharply. His remaining arm, doing the work of two, ached dully. His thighs and back were sore from riding, and the sand collected in every crevice of his body uncomfortably. In his memory flashed the image of the baths at Acre – cool and clean – and he felt the stab of loss again. The entire Temple was said to have collapsed in on itself and then fallen into the sea in a landslide, sweeping men and horses and all that it had symbolised with it.

Jean collected his reins in his remaining hand and put his spurs to his weary stallion, using his weight and legs to turn the horse around. Behind him, the others followed, but MacDonald's ageing gelding stumbled on the rubble and the Highlander, who had never been taught to ride properly, lost his seat and crashed on to the ground with a jingle of chainmail.

The high-pitched giggle of Esteban Lopez and guffaw of Norbert de Clères transformed Jean's initial exasperation with the clumsiness of the Scotsman to fury at the others. MacDonald had earned the promotion to sergeant by his invaluable service in repairing and manning the longboat. It was MacDonald, more than any other, who had proved he could handle the awkward steering oar even in heavy seas and had thereby saved the leaking and inadequately rigged longboat from foundering on its perilous journey. While Sir William and Jean himself had lain in the bilge water, only half-conscious for much of the voyage, Sir Duncan and MacDonald – in a curious mixture of comradeship and rivalry – had sought to outdo one another in the quality of their seamanship. But MacDonald was the worst horseman Jean had ever seen.

Esteban, by contrast, was the spoilt son of a wealthy cork merchant who had enjoyed the best riding masters and could perform on horseback almost any trick known to man. Norbert de Clères was simply the kind of brutish man who thought the misfortune of others was always cause for a good laugh.

Jean turned on Norbert de Clères first. "Dismount!"

The laughter died on his face and he looked at Jean, puzzled and resentful. "Why?"

Jean spurred forward, drew his sword and punched Norbert in the belly with the hilt as he rode past. The unexpectedness as much as the violence of the blow took Norbert totally by surprise, and he doubled up in the saddle and, falling forward, vomited past his horse's neck. The animal leapt sideways instinctively and Norbert tumbled into his own mess. It was better than what Jean had intended for him – except that none of the others laughed. Jean rode over to look down on him. "Templars do not question orders, Sir Norbert. I hope I've made that clear."

Then he rode over to Esteban. "Dismount," he ordered softly.

Esteban was in such a hurry to obey that he almost lost his footing as he hit the rocky ground. Then he looked up expectantly with wide, frightened eyes in his long acne-marred face.

"You and Sir Norbert can walk back to Kolossi," Jean told them. "MacDonald." Jean turned to the Scotsman, who was still struggling to remount his tall bay.

"Sir?"

"Take Sir Norbert's horse. Sir Friedrich, Sir Gautier, lead the extra horses." Without waiting to see his orders carried out or observe the exchanged looks of sympathy or outrage, Jean exacted a trot from his mount and set off for Kolossi.

By the time the little oasis of cultivated cane fields and citrus orchards marking the demesne of the Templars at Kolossi came into view, Jean was regretting his brutality. What had become of him? He had always hated commanders who dealt harshly with their men, and contended that it was an indication of weakness. Only leaders who could not inspire obedience had to resort to force. And that was the truth, he reflected. He lacked the energy to inspire men. How could he inspire anyone when he hardly had the will to keep going himself?

He drew up abruptly and glanced back. Two of the men drew back from one another guiltily and he could guess that they had been talking about him. The other faces betrayed disapproval, anger or fear. Only Mario and MacDonald met his eyes; Mario looking sad and concerned, MacDonald uneasy and guilty. Jean signalled for Mario to ride beside him. "You disapprove, sir."

"No, Commander. You are right to remind us all that the rule of the Templars is as unbending as the word of God."

"Then what disturbs you?"

"That you were angry, Commander."

Jean flushed in embarrassment for the Castilian was right. He wished he could resign his command and turn it over to Sir Mario. The Castilian was a widower who had put vanity, greed, ambition and passion behind him. He had turned his estates over to his heir and come to die in the Holy Land – or as close to it as he could get. But he was far from feeble, and though his strength was not that of a young man he had sufficient reputation at arms to command respect.

Jean resolved to recommend this to the next master, and then sighed at the thought of poor Gaudin.

They had reached the edge of the demesne and the complex of cream-coloured buildings rose among a cluster of Cyprus trees. Horses could be seen milling in the paddock before the stables and lay brothers in their brown robes were loading wagons beside the sugar factory. They rode through a low gate into the outer ward. Unlike Acre, there was no enemy on Cyprus against whom they needed to defend themselves and so the walls were low and thin, more a convention than a defence. Inside the outer wall the stables lay to the right and Jean dismounted stiffly.

MacDonald came up beside him and took hold of the bridle. "I'll see to him, Commander."

Jean looked at the Scotsman. "What's bothering you, MacDonald?"

"I'm not fit to be a sergeant, am I?"

"Because you fell off your horse?"

MacDonald looked down but didn't answer.

Jean sighed. Had he really made a mistake – as De Beaujeu had in knighting Gaudin – or was he just too tired to dispel MacDonald's doubts? Had he promoted MacDonald because he had demonstrated intelligence and responsibility in getting the longboat from Acre to Limassol or merely because he had saved his life? It was MacDonald who had dragged him aboard the galley before he and several others managed to unjam the portcullis and sail the longboat into the sea.

"Let's talk about this tomorrow – in private," he suggested, and started up the stairs that led towards the entryway into the keep. The steps ended upon a free-standing landing. A dry gap some twelve feet broad separated the stairs from the keep. The gap was bridged by a pedestrian drawbridge which could be raised to provide an extra shield for the door. Through the door, Jean found himself in the barrel-vaulted hall of the keep used as the refectory. The kitchens, wells and storerooms were on the level below. Turning into the spiral stairs on his right, he ascended to the floor above, heading for his own spacious quarters – quarters that had once housed the king of France himself.

As he emerged from the stairway he halted in irritation to find two civilians sitting in the window seat, and then his heart stopped as he recognised them. Unable to move, he looked from one to the other and his lips worked but brought forth no sound.

His mother hobbled to him and grasped his remaining hand, covering it with kisses. "Forgive me, Jean! Forgive me for all the wasted years. How can any woman be so foolish! So stupid!" She held his dusty hand against her warm soft face.

Jean wanted to laugh. She called herself foolish but she had been right – his entire life had been wasted upon a mission that was doomed before he ever joined the order. But he could not laugh, his throat was shut. She stepped forward and laid her head upon his breast and held him to her. He looked across her shoulders and met his father's eyes.

"It doesn't hurt," Jean lied, but he couldn't bear the pain in his father's face. "I swear – not like Mansourah."

His father's eyes widened in horror to hear his son confirm something he thought was only confused imagination, and Jean smiled faintly at him.

Eleanor slipped to Jean's left, holding him firmly in her right arm but turning back to invite Geoffrey to join her, freeing Jean's arm so he could offer his hand to his father. Geoffrey's embrace was more fierce than Eleanor's, and Jean could tell he was struggling to fight back tears.

"It's all right," Jean told his father. He had never seen him so moved, and it embarrassed him. "Don't you know you saved my life?" He tried to joke because his emotions were threatening to unman him. "De Sonnac's sword – they say no man can die so long as he holds St John's hand in his." Jean pulled back and unbuckled the swordbelt, ashamed that he had used the saint's hand to strike one of his own men. Holding the sword in its sheath to his father, he urged, "Take it back, Father. I had no right to accept it in the first place. It was against the rule – only De Beaujeu's respect for you induced him to let me keep it."

Geoffrey was staring at his sword held in his son's hand, but he made no move to take it.

"Please, Father, take it back. De Sonnac gave it to you."

Jean could feel how rigid his mother had become and realised too late that his father was hesitating on her account. "Don't worry, Mamá. The sword alone does not make him a Templar. But God alone knows who will be the next master. It would be wrong if he commanded me to give it up – if it were to pass into hands that had never known De Sonnac, never been to Mansourah."

Geoffrey looked at him sharply and his hand clearly itched to regain the proffered sword, but he stopped himself and turned to Eleanor.

De Sonnac had always been her rival – not the Temple itself but the master from the Languedoc who had Cathar kin. De Sonnac's ghost had fought hard for her husband's loyalty. But Eleanor was weary too. Her fight against the Temple had cost her thirteen precious years of her son's life, years in which she might have seen him, spoken with him, written to him, known his sorrows and hopes. With a deep sigh, she nodded. Geoffrey took De Sonnac's sword.

Limassol
August 1291

The Hospital of the Knights of St John at Limassol was located near but not contiguous to the commandery. It was built on a pattern repeated throughout the Holy Land with a large rectangular courtyard around which stables, cellars and storerooms opened under an arcade. An external stone stairway led up from the courtyard to the similarly arcaded gallery on the upper level where the actual hospital ward and sickrooms were located.

Sister Madeleine clutched her habit in her right hand as she navigated her way around the dung and rubbish in the street and followed a cartload of wheat into the hospital by the wide, arched gateway. The vaulted entrance was dim after the Mediterranean sun outside and the voices of the teamsters ahead of her boomed and echoed. Beyond, in the light of the courtyard, a wagon load of wine was being offloaded by rolling the barrels down planks. One barrel had apparently rolled off the plank prematurely because there was a puddle of ruby red wine spreading across the tiles while shouts of unwanted advice from a half-dozen bystanders rained upon the sweating wine merchant. The wagon and planks blocked the path of the wheat wagon, producing a further explosion of oaths from the teamsters, answered in kind by the already short-tempered wine merchant and his driver.

Madeleine attempted to slip behind the back of the wagon and gain the foot of the stairs leading up to the gallery beyond, but collided with a covered litter which was being carried out. The lead porter in the brown habit of a serving brother irritably told her to go around to the side entrance, and Madeleine at once retreated with profuse apologies.

Outside the hospital she drew a deep breath and tried to collect her courage. Part of her knew that she shouldn't be so lightly intimidated by the sharp tongues of low-born men. She couldn't imagine Eleanor running for cover, much less apologising. And she could picture more vividly still how the abbess of the Sacred Heart would have responded! But then they wouldn't have been alone, afoot, in a shabby, ill-fitting habit. And they had never been slaves in a strange land.

She sighed and drew another breath, repeating what Eleanor had said to her: she was a French noblewoman, not a slave or a whore. But it was hard to feel like a noblewoman in a frayed and travel-stained habit. She did not even possess a gold ring to identify her as a Bride of Christ; her first ring had been taken from her in Tripoli – she no longer remembered whether by the Mameluke who captured her or the first man who raped her – and the second, given her in Acre, had gone to Roger de Flor to pay her passage from Acre to Limassol. It was not surprising that she was mistaken for a lay sister, a menial.

Still, there was no point repeating her futile attempt at entry through this gate and so she resolved to look for the side entrance. Following the broad front of the hospital and turning into the next alleyway, she found a tall, arched doorway with a marble relief set above it bearing the arms of the king of Cyprus, the arms of the Hospital of St John and the arms of Portugal. The door itself stood twelve feet at the peak and was reinforced with iron, but a smaller door cut in the wood was ajar. At her timid push, it opened for her.

She stepped through the narrow door and found herself in a cool, darkened entry way. To her immediate left was a wooden stand, like a stall in a market, only instead of goods for sale there were ledgers, pieces of chalk and a bell. Beyond the stand she could see the bright light in the courtyard framed in an archway. The jumble of shouts, curses and banging still emanated from that direction. To her right a stone stairway led directly to the upper gallery. Since no one was in sight, she gathered her skirts again and ascended the stairs.

She emerged on the upper gallery at the apex of two sides. Doorways opened off the gallery every ten to twelve feet and two men in long, loose hospital robes leaned upon the stone railing of the gallery watching the activities in the courtyard below.

The billowing white robes of the two patients reminded Madeleine of Arab men and she at once opted to follow the other gallery, which led back toward the front of the hospital.

She had just passed the first doorway when an angry voice called after her. "Hey! You! Sister! Where do you think you're going?"

Her heart started pounding in fear, but she reminded herself that she had nothing to be afraid or ashamed of. A man in a black habit with the eight-pointed cross of the Knights of St John on his left breast was standing in the doorway she had just passed. Under the short-sleeved black habit, the red sleeves of his shirt emerged, shoved above his elbows. He scowled at her reproachfully while he absently wiped his hands upon a linen cloth – leaving great smears of blood upon the white.

"I am looking for the orphanage." Sister Madeleine tried to speak clearly and distinctly, to hold her head high and keep her shoulders straight as Eleanor had urged her. Yet her voice was frail and she unconsciously wrang her hands, trying to hide the naked ring finger. "I was told it was here," she added, more to give herself courage than to impress her interrogator.

"The orphanage? Whoever told you such nonsense? We can't have children disturbing the patients or exposing them—" The sergeant monk cut himself off with a sigh of exasperation; what was the point of explaining it all? "It's in the east tract..." He gestured vaguely beyond the courtyard.

"Thank you, Monsieur," Madeleine said politely like a well-bred little girl and turned away. She would have to pass along behind the two men after all.

"Wait!" The monk called. "You can't just wander around here. Didn't the concierge tell you that?"

"I didn't see any concierge, Monsieur. The door was open—"

The man started cursing under his breath and strode to the head of the stairs to shout down, "Brother Carlos! Carlos!"

A cracked and breathless voice of an old man called up. "Monsieur?"

"Where the hell have you been?"

"There's a wine wagon in the courtyard that—"

"Never mind! There's a nun here who wants to go to the orphanage." He turned to Madeleine. "Sister, would you be so kind as to return to the concierge and explain to him—"

"Brother Bertram!" The voice was familiar, a voice she had often heard raised in command over the last months, that of Jules de Villaret. Madeleine spun around sharply, ashamed that she should be caught obviously breaking the rules by someone as important as the grand hospitaller. She dipped into an apologetic curtsey. "Forgive me, Monsieur, I..."

Jules de Villaret was dressed in a scarlet habit with the white cross blazoned across his chest and a red cap covering his head snugly. Madeleine had never seen him out of armour before and the billowing clerical robes seemed incongruous to her, even though she knew he had been appointed grand hospitaller shortly before the fall of Acre. "Sister Madeleine!" He had just recognised her, and now he held out his hand to lift her up. "Can I be of service to you? Were you looking for me?" He tucked her hand into his elbow and guided her away from the infirmary. The sergeant brother shook his head and returned to the sickroom.

"I heard that Jean survived!" De Villaret was exclaiming enthusiastically. "They say he brought out a longboat full of refugees a week after the city fell! How like him! I long to see him again. Have you seen him?"

"Yes." Madeleine managed a smile, but she was not adept at disguising the pain in her eyes. Her encounter with Jean had been a nightmare. She had truly not expected anything very dramatic, but Jean's cold reception had embarrassed even his parents. Not only had he shown not the slightest pleasure to see her again, but he had brusquely rejected her stammered attempts to thank him.

"There is nothing to thank me for," he had cut her off.

"But you sent Sergeant Pirenne—"

"They decapitated Pirenne and set his head upon a stake propped up before the main gate of the Temple."

"You gave your arm—"

"For a Jewish shopkeeper's daughter – and God knows what has become of her. No one in Limassol can remember her. She was in the boat, I remember clearly, but now she's disappeared. She is an orphan. Penniless. And still a child, but the Mamelukes started to molest her. I cut one down before her eyes. It terrified her – and then I forgot I didn't have the shield on my left arm. She saw that too – the amputation. Poor Rachel."

"What's the matter, Sister?" It was the gentle voice of Jules de Villaret, not the acrid voice Jean had used to her.

"He... he lost his arm defending a... an orphan who had taken refuge in the Temple." Madeleine was ashamed to admit that it had been a Jewish orphan, that a Jewish shopkeeper's daughter meant more to him than she did.

De Villaret was nodding. "I was told the Templars had negotiated a safe conduct and that the Sultan had even put ships at their disposal. They preferred to defend the freedom and honour of the Christians in their care." His eyes were shining in admiration, bordering on envy. "Jean is privileged to have been allowed such a sacrifice."

"But he doesn't know what became of the orphan he defended." Madeleine tried to explain something she did not understand herself.

"But there were hundreds of women and children in the Temple at the time. The Templars defended them all – slaughtered the Mamelukes and rehoisted the Baucent."

"He spoke of a girl, an orphan, that the Mamelukes molested. He said he lost his arm defending her and that she was on the long boat, but disappeared after reaching Limassol."

Jean looked at Sister Madeleine sidelong, a touch of suspicion on his face. He had jestingly accused Jean of not being chaste, but he found it extremely hard to believe Jean had a mistress. And then he remembered. "Maybe it was Rachel! The fruiterer's daughter! Poor thing. Jean always had a soft spot for the girl. He gave her a white puppy on her tenth birthday." De Villaret laughed at the memory. The puppy had belonged to De Villaret's own squire and the youth had been about to drown the runt when Jean intervened and insisted on giving it to Rachel. There had been a hilarious scene with the squire suddenly demanding a high price for a puppy he had been about to drown and Jean cursing him with the profane vocabulary of a caravan driver. "And now she's disappeared?" De Villaret, like the professional soldier he was, redirected his attention to the problem.

"I thought she might be at the orphanage here," Madeleine answered hesitantly.

"Good idea. Let's go and enquire." At once he was striding along the gallery behind the two patients still gawking at the scene below and Madeleine had to half-run to keep up.

The orphanage was housed in an older, somewhat run-down building that backed on to the hospital from the east. The shrill clamour of children reached them as they descended by a narrow stair into the courtyard between the two buildings. Dozens of children of both sexes, ranging in age from toddlers to eleven and twelve year olds were playing in the barren courtyard. They were dressed in an odd assortment of clothing – evidently gifts – often far too large or too small for the wearers.

At the foot of the stairs, Sister Madeleine and Jules de Villaret were confronted with a child of five or six wearing a woman's surcoat as if it were a short toga. The flower pattern of the embroidery and the quality of the silk made a strange contrast to the dusty, bare feet protruding beneath the hem. With huge black-brown eyes and immense dignity, the child stared at Madeleine and De Villaret, blocking their way.

Then a nun started clapping her hands and calling. The child ran away like a frightened deer, and indeed all the children ceased their activities – more or less reluctantly – to form three lines facing the interior of the orphanage. There were the inevitable scuffles about places in line and the clamour of the children died only gradually.

Standing under the arcade were two sisters in black habits, one of whom hastened forward to greet De Villaret. "My Lord! We were not told to expect you today." It sounded almost like a reproach and the look she cast Madeleine was far from friendly – as if she could see through the shabby habit to the dishonoured body underneath.

Madeleine looked down in shame and shrank inside her robes. If De Villaret had not been holding her by the elbow, she felt as if she would have melted away entirely.

De Villaret either did not note or did not care about the nun's hostility to Madeleine. With the supreme confidence of a man used to authority, he announced that he had come to assist Madeleine in her search for a certain child. "The girl must be fourteen and she was in Acre – one of the children the Templars brought out after the fall of the city."

The nun raised her eyebrows and looked at Madeleine more closely. "And is the child related to you, Sister?"

"No," De Villaret answered for Madeleine. "We are looking on behalf of a friend." Twisting at the waist, he surveyed the lines of children, scanning their faces for a familiar one. He had, to be sure, only rarely had anything to do with Rachel and yet he thought he would recognise her; she had an ugly hare lip, he remembered. "The girl had a hare lip," he informed the nun.

"Ah! That girl!" the nun exclaimed with evident distaste. "But she was sick! And Jewish! We sent her away."

"Away?" It was De Villaret's turn to raise his eyebrows in disapproval. "The statutes of this Hospital state that any child – regardless of parentage – is to be taken in, fed and clothed. What gave you the right to send a child away – much less one that the Templars thought worthy of transporting from Acre?"

"She had some kind of skin disease – red, inflamed splotches all over her arms and legs and even on her face," the nun replied defensively. Madeleine noted that she would not meet De Villaret in the eye and that she was nervously toying with her rosary.

"Then she belonged in the hospital," De Villaret pointed out sharply. "This is not the first time you have acted uncharitably, Sister Clotilda – nor is it the last time I will concern myself with the issue."

"Should I have taken in a child so evidently sick?" the nun demanded in indignation. "I should have been neglecting my duty to the other children if I had been so foolish—"

"You have indeed been foolish, Sister Clotilda, but we will discuss it another time. For the moment, Sister Madeleine and I have to find the poor girl you rejected. When you turned her out, where did she go, do you know?"

"How should I? But—"

"We'll enquire at the hospital," De Villaret informed Madeleine as he turned his back on the Sister Clotilda, and started back up the stairs.

The hospital ward was one hundred and twenty feet long and thirty feet broad. It was supported lengthwise by a row of arches and lit only by small, double-light, round-headed windows set high up in the wall. The patients lay on straw pallets the length of the hall, but De Villaret strode past them with Madeleine in his wake. As grand hospitaller, he had assumed over-all responsibility for the hospital here and it was here that all the wounded from Acre had been brought when the city fell. He knew that Rachel was not here, but he hoped that the chief infirmarer might have some information.

The chief infirmarer was in one of the chambers carved into the wall of the ward. Here patients with infectious diseases or requiring special care were segregated from the others. Leaving Madeleine in the ward, De Villaret ducked through the door leading to the chamber and Madeleine could only hear the low murmur of their voices while they conversed.

As they consulted, she let her eyes wander along the lines of sick and wounded. Most of the patients dozed but some stared at the ceiling, gossiped with their neighbours or even played dice in the space between their pallets. Unconsciously she searched for faces from Acre, but she recognised no one. For the first time she thought it might be possible to find a convent here in Cyprus where no one knew her or her past. If Jules de Villaret vouched for her, surely she could find admittance... But she would have to admit that she came from Acre. They would make enquiries...

De Villaret stood before her looking grave. "You'd best come with me," he advised, taking her elbow again.

"Have you found Rachel?" she asked, surprised.

"Not exactly, but the Infirmarer says he remembers her. Sister Clotilda was not quite so shameless as I thought. The Infirmarer diagnosed leprosy – still in an early stage, to be sure, but leprosy nevertheless. He sent her to the leper colony outside the city."

Madeleine just stared at De Villaret. She had wanted to do Jean a service. She had hoped to please him. But how could she possibly take this news to him? He would hate her even more.

"If you are afraid to go there, I will send one of our sergeants—"

"No!" Madeleine hardly knew herself why she reacted so sharply. "No. I will go myself," she added more calmly, the decision ripening as she spoke. She could not go to Jean and say that she had found where Rachel was but had not bothered to visit her there. "Where... how... Do I need a horse to go there?" she asked hesitantly.

De Villaret considered her intently and did not answer at once. He had lost more than an hour with her already, and he had other pressing duties. He should delegate a serving brother or sergeant to escort her to the leper colony, and loan her a horse. But to do so was to dismiss not only her but Jean de Preuthune. And Jean was like a fractured mirror, showing him the other road – the truly Christian road – he had not chosen.

Jean could have made a career in the Temple as brilliant as De Villaret's own in the Hospital – if he hadn't constantly done unorthodox things like favour Jewish children with gifts, employ a runaway squire, defend a murderous Brother, squander Templar funds on freeing slaves and even interfere with the Inquisition! De Villaret had chosen the rewarding path to power, but sometimes he felt guilty about it. Sometimes he remembered the idealism of his youth, and wondered if he had really done what God intended.

He drew a deep breath. "I will take you there, Sister. Come with me to the commandery and let me take care of a few things. Then we can go this afternoon."

*

The leper colony was nothing more than a cluster of crude mud structures crouching around an ancient well beside the road. Some awnings of tattered canvas were stretched upon sticks to provide shelter from the sun between the hovels. A ditch behind the colony provided an open latrine, and beyond was a graveyard of shallow graves marked only by wooden crosses. Dogs and cats scavenged at the edges of the colony, and a lone, bony donkey was tethered under the only tree – a gnarled pine. The stench that emanated from the cluster of hovels was almost insufferable and Madeleine tried to swallow her nausea. De Villaret's face grew rigid.

The arrival of strangers – much less an Hospitaller in the robes of his order on a massive destrier – brought the inhabitants from their dwellings. They stood on crutches or crawled footless on to the stoops of their houses. Filthy rags hid the corrupted hands, the stumps of arms and swathed the faces. Here and there creatures of indefinable age stared from burning eyes past a wasteland of discoloured and distended flesh, and others followed only the sound of the horses, staring with sightless eyes. All held out their hands – or what was left of them – and called out for alms.

"The lepers live exclusively on alms," De Villaret reminded Madeleine as she shrank back from the cacophony of begging, and he reached for his purse.

"It's not that," Madeleine whispered. "It's that... I... I have nothing to give." The sight of the lepers filled her not so much with revulsion as guilt. She, who felt herself unclean and rejected, was confronted here by creatures more afflicted than she herself. It made her feel ashamed of her self-pity.

De Villaret had emptied his purse into his left hand and selected all the small change he had. He then distributed the coins with rigid fairness, sternly shaking his head when someone tried to get more than their share. Madeleine noted that he worked with grim efficiency but

– so it seemed to her – without compassion. He was performing a duty but a distasteful one.

When he had finished distributing his coins, there remained a cluster of lepers who had not received any alms. They clamoured all the more insistently when they saw that his hand was empty.

"*Monsieur le Chevalier de St Jean!*" a cultivated voice called out from one of the hovels. "How will you answer before Our Lord for the meanness of your alms! You ride a stallion worth a hundred gold bezants and vowed your life to the service of the sick – but scorn to give all you have in your purse? God have mercy on your soul!" And then the man added something in Arabic.

Madeleine felt a chill go down her spine and the hair stand on the back of her neck. She had heard the voice before, in the same ringing accusatory tone, but she did not know where.

De Villaret had turned to study the figure in the doorway of the hovel. It was an old man – bony and bent – with a long white beard and a weathered face. Though his clothes were filthy and ragged, there were no bandages covering missing limbs and the skin of his face was splotched with age marks but not the putrefaction of leprosy.

"Who are you, Monsieur?" De Villaret demanded with controlled anger, adding the 'monsieur' automatically. The voice had been too educated and too self-assured to belong to anyone of lower class.

"I am your conscience, *Monsieur le Chevalier de St Jean.*"

"No – and it is presumptuous to make such a claim. Who are you and what are you doing here – since you are not afflicted with leprosy?"

"That is my affair, Monsieur, and the question can be turned on you no less than I. You did not ride such a distance on such good horseflesh to cast such a ludicrous pittance among us!" the voice scoffed.

Madeleine's subconscious called to mind the slave market at Nazareth, and she started to remember the last slave – the man who had once been a Christian priest but had converted to Islam.

"We are looking for an orphan girl from Acre by the name of Rachel. She has a hare lip and is about fourteen years old."

"You surprise me, *Monsieur le Chevalier!* You concern yourself with a Jew?"

"Is she here?"

The old man nodded vaguely to his left. "She is in that house there – but she is demented."

"I'll be the judge of that," De Villaret retorted, springing down from his stallion and turning to offer Madeleine his hand. "Or would you rather remain here?" he asked her softly.

"No. I'll come," Madeleine told him, though her knees were shaking and she was afraid. De Villaret took both horses and tethered them beside the donkey while Madeleine stood in the circle of still unsatisfied lepers, helplessly smiling at one after another.

It was a woman who spoke to her first, and again the voice was incongruously cultivated, if touched with an Italian accent. "Is this your first trip to us?"

"Yes." She mouthed the answer more than spoke it. She was too weak to speak loudly.

"Horrible, isn't it? When I was rich and unafflicted, I never visited such places either. I preferred to flit from banquet to tournament, and my head was full only of the latest fashions, the best perfumes, the young men. I was pretty. You wouldn't think that now, would you?" The woman had no nose, her eyes were lidless and her lips swollen and contorted, but Madeleine forced herself to look her in the eye.

"And how did you fall ill?" she asked timidly.

"At sea. We left Venice on a pilgrim ship and when we landed in Limassol half of us were afflicted. My husband set me aside at once. He had a mistress anyway. And my lover never came near me again. No man has ever touched me since – not even here." She gestured vaguely toward the colony in general with an arm that ended at the elbow. Although Madeleine could not identify with her longing, she heard the bitterness in the woman's voice and knew that this – more than the poverty or even the leprosy – was her greatest complaint.

De Villaret was back. Taking Madeleine by the elbow, he took her to the hovel which the old man had indicated. They had to crouch to go through the door and found themselves in a circular, windowless chamber with a mud floor strewn with straw. Sitting cross-legged against the wall was a girl wearing a shawl over her head and swaying back and forth. She took no note of the newcomers but continued swaying, staring straight ahead, her lips moving soundlessly.

De Villaret went down on his heels beside her. "Rachel!"

She flinched. She recognised her name. But she would not look at him and now she swayed even more vigorously and they could hear a keening of meaningless words.

De Villaret looked up at Madeleine, but it was the old man who answered his look. "It is Hebrew. She repeats the prayers for the sabbath endlessly."

"Has she said anything else?"

"In the beginning, she asked me in Arabic where a certain 'Monsieur Jean' was. But when I tried to find out who this 'Jean' might be, she covered her eyes with her fists and flung herself into the corner with her face to the wall."

De Villaret turned to Rachel again. "Rachel, listen to me. Jean is alive. He is at Kolossi. He sent us to look for you."

Rachel did not appear to hear him. She continued to sway back and forth and her prayer increased in volume.

"Don't you want to see Monsieur Jean again?" he asked her.

She did not even look at him.

He turned again to the old man in the door. "How long has she been like this?"

"Over a month."

"Is there nothing you can do for her?"

The old man snorted and again Madeleine felt the chill run down her spine. "There are hundreds of things I could do for her and for all the others – if I had money! Look at this filth! The darkness! The stench! Even the well water is muddy and foul! You – a Hospitaller! – must at least be able to guess what the consequences are. Or is Christian medicine still so backward?" he spat.

"What do you know of any kind of medicine?" De Villaret scoffed.

"I am a trained physician, *Monsieur l'Hôpitaller*! I probably know more about medicine than you will ever know! I know – and even you must know – that there is no cure for leprosy. But there is much that can be done to retard or even arrest its advance. And half what you see here is not leprosy at all but scurvy – the results of inadequate diet. These souls live on alms which are never sufficient for a balanced diet. The only fruit they see is what I steal or beg from the surrounding farms. And the filth, the stench of the rotting dead, intensifies the effects of the leprosy itself. If your order were really concerned with the welfare of the sick, Monsieur, it would spend less money on galleys and arms and stallions and spend it instead upon the sick! You could build a hospital for lepers with decent sanitation, baths, orchards of citrus trees and olives – all for less than it costs you to keep a troop of mounted knights! But you are not really interested in the sick, are you, Monsieur?"

De Villaret had had enough. He stood and pushed past the accusing old man. Madeleine, with a last glance at Rachel, followed him. De Villaret was striding toward the horses, but the old man caught Madeleine by the arm and held her back. "And who are you, Sister?" he enquired. "Do you think you can win points in heaven by looking at us piteously and then riding away? Do you feel saintlier for having cast us your insipid smiles? Christ will be watching you as you lie on your feather bed in your comfortable, cool cell and drink deeply of good wine! When the winter rains come and you sit cosy in your warming room gossiping with your sisters, we will still be here, shivering in the rain – and He sees that!"

His words missed their mark. She did not have a feather bed, a cool cell or good wine. She lived on the charity of the Preuthunes and she too was an outcast. Certainly she did not feel in the least saintly. So she met his eyes and replied instead. "Didn't you gain your freedom from slavery in Nazareth?"

The old man started so violently that Madeleine could see it, and she knew she had not been mistaken. "How do you know that?" he demanded.

"You were a Dominican and converted to Islam, didn't you?" she persisted.

He gripped her with his skeletal hand more tightly. "Who are you?"

Still Madeleine refused to answer. "You should have been turned over to the Inquisition – or at least the authorities of your order, but Brother Jean let you escape instead. He was punished for his generosity."

"My centurion?" Father Bernard asked, his eyes lighting up. "An unusual young man. I presumed he died at Acre."

"No, he lost his arm defending Rachel there – and brought her and over a hundred other refugees to safety in an old longboat."

"I'm glad to hear it." The old man broke into a half-toothless smile – an incongruous expression on his sour face. "Send him here, Sister – he would not be so heartless as your Hospitaller!"

"Monsieur de Villaret is not heartless," Madeleine loyally defended the grand hospitaller.

"Merely ambitious," the old man told her with a cynical smile that suited him better. "He would not have risked the displeasure of his superiors by buying freedom for a renegade priest – much less letting him escape."

De Villaret came back leading the two horses and went to hold Madeleine's stirrup for her to mount. She did not dare hesitate any longer and quickly took up her reins and mounted. De Villaret sprang on to his stallion easily despite his robes, and from this superior position gazed down at Father Bernard coldly. "It is unwise to insult those whose charity you seek," he told the old man succinctly.

The old man laughed outright. "You are right, Monsieur. But they say you can't teach an old dog new tricks."

De Villaret put spurs to his stallion and Madeleine's mare followed docilely. They had left the leper colony far behind before she ventured to call to him. "Monsieur de Villaret?"

Only now did he notice that he was setting a hard pace and the hired mare was lagging behind. He drew up a little and let Madeleine catch up to him.

"Monsieur," she repeated. "What the old man said makes sense, doesn't it? That the lepers suffer from deprivation and poor diet, filth and poverty as much as from the disease itself."

"Yes. And he is right that some of the lepers there are suffering from scurvy – on Cyprus! What irony, on this garden of an island! In short, he would appear to know something of medicine in truth." De Villaret was clearly baffled by this fact.

Madeleine hesitated to tell him what she knew about Father Bernard. He might feel compelled to inform the Inquisition, and she had no desire to see Father Bernard arrested – not when Jean had let him go free. She continued with her own thoughts. "The Templars are charitable. If Jean knew—"

"Sister, I beg you, think before you act! The Templars have lost not only all their fortresses in Palestine, they have lost their grand master and every one of their senior officers – except poor Gaudin. The flower of their knights were slaughtered in Acre. A general chapter has been called and must convene in the next few days, and whoever they elect as their next master will have to concentrate on rebuilding the strength of the order. He needs men and he needs every sou he can scrape together for the training, outfitting and mounting those recruits. Do you think he would welcome it if one of the few experienced commanders he has left came to him with a request to build a leper hospital?"

Though he tried to be patient, De Villaret's exasperation was evident. He was regretting the entire escapade. Jean could learn as much from him as he from Jean. Ultimately Jean would achieve more if he attained a position of influence within the powerful Templar order rather than with his spontaneous and undirected acts of charity.

Seeing that Madeleine was looking rebuked and sorrowful, however, De Villaret relented somewhat. "Sister, the military orders have their hands full right now. If you want to do something for the lepers, then try to awake the consciences and open the purses of the wealthy citizens. There are a number of wealthy families on the island which would be in a position to support such a project. The Ibelins, Montforts and Filangieri, for example, could be approached," he suggested.

Madeleine nodded dutifully, but De Villaret feared she would speak to Jean anyway. "You will not be doing Jean a favour telling him the state Rachel is in. He can do nothing for her, but he is sure to feel guilty – feeling that he should have done or should try to do more for her. As if he had not done more than most men would do already!"

Again Madeleine nodded wordlessly. She did not dare tell Jean what had become of Rachel, but this realisation did not make her happier to be returning empty-handed to Limassol. If only she knew someone else who might be able to help. She could return to the colony and live as Father Bernard did. He had not recognised her – and something told her that he would not despise her even if he had. He too had been a slave. He knew what it meant. But it seemed senseless to go to the lepers if the only service she could offer was to share their misery. If she could improve their lot, that would be worth doing, but simply to share it? What good would that do anyone? What was the point of her life, if she didn't return? What was the point of life at all?

"Sister, there is something that you should tell Jean, when you see him," De Villaret interrupted her thoughts and his voice had a curious intensity to it.

She looked over, startled.

De Villaret drew up his stallion and stared her directly in the eye. "You must tell Jean that when *The Falcon* put in yesterday not only the Templar preceptors of Normandy and France were aboard, but Jacques de Molay as well."

Cyprus
October 1291

It was mid-afternoon when Geoffrey and Eleanor finally took their leave of Geoffrey's relatives, and Geoffrey's nerves were strained to the breaking point. He wanted nothing more than to escape as rapidly as possible. To put the entire day behind them and bury the memory forever. He made no effort to disguise his impatience to be gone, and Eleanor felt compelled to soothe the feelings of his offended relatives. Though they could not understand her words, her gestures and her smiles did much to balance Geoffrey's glowering curtness.

At last they left the house of his birth and childhood behind but a mood of animosity lingered between them. Geoffrey's shame had turned to resentment against his wife for having insisted on coming here. For forty years he had kept his family 'hidden' from her. She knew, of course, of his mother's humble birth. It had nearly prevented their marriage because King Louis had been reluctant to give the Najac heiress to a man whose mother had been a lowborn Cypriot woman. But though the King had relented in the face of Geoffrey's qualities and Eleanor's insistence, Geoffrey had never let Eleanor see the fat, stupid, slattern who had borne him.

His mother, to be sure, was long since in the grave, but his brother's brood were very much her descendants. Geoffrey wanted to crawl into a hole and hide: they had spoken only of the price of purchases and the behaviour of the neighbours. They had eaten with their greasy hands, wiped their mouths on their sleeves. They shouted at one another, arguing over old jealousies and screaming enough recriminations at one another to bring down the smoky beams of the roof. They had cuffed and kicked at their children like stray dogs. One of the younger boys, who had tried to ride Geoffrey's stallion secretly and been thrown, had been chased about by his uncle with a whip until Geoffrey intervened. Geoffrey felt as though he would never be able to hold his head up with pride again!

Eleanor could read the hostility in her husband's rigid back as he spurred his stallion forward up the trail, leaving her mare to follow as best she could. Eleanor sighed but did not protest. Geoffrey had his moods, and it was best to leave him undisturbed. Eventually his anger would consume itself. He would be better in the morning at the latest. With a sigh, she prepared for a chilly night of distant politeness mixed with sarcastic barbs.

They topped the crest of the hill behind the farm, but Geoffrey did not give her a chance to enjoy the breathtaking view down to the coast. Instead he pushed his stallion down the far side with a growl about it's being late and the sun low. His eyes fixed on the road, it was Eleanor who – sneaking a glance to the right – saw the rider in white coming along the crest of the hill.

"Geoffrey!"

"We don't have time!" he snapped back, without looking up.

The rider rode slowly because the rocky spine of the mountain was poor footing for a horse, and it bobbed its head unevenly as it scrambled unhappily forward. The rider came from the east and the setting sun bathed his white surcoat in rose-coloured light. But Eleanor sensed more than saw the splayed cross of the Temple.

She drew up and waited with inner tension. The Templar was carrying something in his arms across the pommel of his saddle. In horror, she realised it was a child, a boy, and he lay limp as if unconscious or dead. "Jean!" She recognised her son intuitively, her imagination seeing the youth who had brought his younger brother home the day of Alice's wedding, her fantasy seeing the knight who had carried a Christian slave girl out of captivity. She turned her mare from the road to ride to meet him.

The mare balked at once and no amount of kicking could convince the sensible beast to venture out on to the uneven, rocky surface of the corniche. Geoffrey, already a hundred yards down the slope, at last stopped and looked back.

The sunlight highlighted Jean's features and glinted in his red-blond beard. His chainmail coif seemed made of gold. And then he was almost beside her, and Eleanor recognised that the boy in his arms was the boy who had tried to ride Geoffrey's stallion; his great-nephew.

Geoffrey had swung his stallion around and came clambering back up the slope. "Jean! Where did you come from? What—"

"They told me at the monastery that you had come here." Jean answered simply. "And I saw the boy." He jerked his head in the direction he had come. "He had hanged himself on that tree."

Silhouetted against the skyline of the already darkening eastern sky they could make out a single, tall gnarled tree.

"Jésus Maria!" Eleanor reached out to touch the boy's face, seeing now the bruises and swelling on the boy's neck and behind his ears. He was still warm. "Is he..."

"Unconscious," Jean answered. "His neck isn't broken and, with the clumsy noose he'd made, he could only strangulate slowly. I suspect he was hanging there a quarter of an hour or so."

"Give him here," Geoffrey ordered. He had jumped down and stood beside Jean's stallion. Jean, with one arm, could hardly support the body, little as he was, nor could he take up his reins as long as he held the boy. So Jean willingly surrendered the boy to his father.

The boy stirred as he was let down from the stallion into Geoffrey's arms. He coughed and gagged and moaned. Eleanor jumped down and bent over the boy as Geoffrey lay him on the side of the road. "Shouldn't we take him back down to the farm?"

"No!" Geoffrey told her grimly.

"Take my blanket, Mamá." Jean indicated the blanket rolled behind his saddle, and Eleanor went to Jean's horse and untied the laces holding the blanket to the saddle. Then Jean himself dismounted and together they managed to spread the blanket on a patch of dusty ground between the thorns and the rocks. Jean returned to his saddle and removed his wineskin. Geoffrey held the boy's head on his arm, and Jean held the neck of the wineskin to the boy's lips while Eleanor held his hand.

The boy choked and coughed on the wine, but it also brought him to. He turned his head from side to side and squirmed on the blanket and then his eyes flew wide open. "Master!" He had recognised Geoffrey. "Master!" He tried to sit up, but Eleanor and Jean both reached out to hold him gently still. Speaking in Greek to Geoffrey, he pleaded, "I didn't mean any harm."

"I know. No harm was done - except what you've done to yourself. How could you do such a silly thing!? On account of nothing!" Geoffrey scolded in the same tongue. But he held the boy gently and there was no mistaking his concern.

Tears glinted on the boy's eyes and lashes. "They all hate me. They all wish I were dead. I can't go on. I don't want to ever go back. Can't I come with you, Master? I could look after your horse." No sooner had he said this than he realised that under the circumstances it might not be the best recommendation and he added breathlessly, "I swear I'll never try to ride him again. Never! Please let me come with you!" The self-pity had been transformed to hope so rapidly that Geoffrey had to laugh.

But it was a kind laugh, and the boy broke into a smile. "May I come? Really?"

"I don't know." Geoffrey shook his head, and glanced up at Eleanor and Jean. "He wants us to take him with us. He says they all hate him and wish he were dead."

"Who?" Jean asked somewhat confused.

"His family – my family." Geoffrey indicated the farm over the crest of the hill with a nod of his head.

Jean looked back over his shoulder but the valley was lost in darkness now, the sun sinking rapidly down the sky and losing its strength by the minute. The western sky was orange.

"I'm sure they don't hate him! How could they?" Eleanor protested.

"They think he's cursed." Geoffrey indicated the ugly red birthmark which stretched diagonally across his face. "And you saw the way they treated him. I will not send him back there against his will." Geoffrey was remembering his own flight forty-five years earlier. He might have been a few years older, but his feelings had been much the same.

"We can't take him away from his mother without even asking her!" Eleanor insisted. She suspected the gist of Geoffrey's thoughts, and so she added sincerely, "He's welcome to come with us, but we can't just kidnap him."

"All right, you stay here with Jean and I'll go and enquire." Geoffrey spoke briefly to the boy, and then remounted and rode hastily back the way they'd come.

Jean watched his mother while she brushed the untrimmed black hair out of the boy's eyes and with the hem of her skirt wiped some of the dirt from his face. The boy grinned shyly at her and spoke in

Greek. She smiled and shook her head to indicate that she did not understand, and with the back of her hand she brushed his birthmark. The boy drew back slightly, but her hand communicated her compassion and after a moment he surrendered to her charm and let her caress his blemish without shame.

She was still an attractive woman, Jean noted, especially in this dying light that blurred the wrinkles and the age splotches, leaving only the clean, regular bone structure: her high forehead and cheeks, her deep, wide-set eyes and her fine, straight nose. She looked hardly different, by this light, from the mother who had leaned over his bed in childhood.

Jean felt the bitter bile of jealousy rise up in him again. The corroding hatred for his elder brother, who had been allowed to take a wife and raise a family, welled in him. Louis could watch Eleanor or his bride bending to comfort a sick child any day of the year. Louis could lie in his wife's arms. Louis had a home, a place in the world, a future. Jean felt a choking, blinding rage against God. He lashed out at his mother. "I very nearly joined the boy rather than cutting him down!"

"Jean!" She looked up in horror. Her lips parted, her eyes wide with shock.

"Why not, Mamá? What use am I to anyone? What do I have to live for?"

"Jean!" She pulled herself to her feet and took a step toward him, but he drew back before her. "Have you gone mad? You, of all my children, are the only one who has risen above the mundane! You are the only one who has been more than you were born to be. And to think I tried to stop you! Do you need to hear it from me again? That I am sorry? That I was wrong?"

Jean laughed, but the mirthlessness turned hysterical and he had to grab his pommel to hold himself upright as he laughed. "But you weren't wrong! We've lost it all! The Holy Land is gone – soaked in the blood of better men than me! Jacques de Molay has been elected master, and now I must crawl back to the West and hide my head in shame for having been at least in part to blame – and for not having the self-respect to share the fate of Acre. De Beaujeu was right..." Jean could hear the rasping voice of the dying master ordering them not to take him to the waiting ship.

"You saved a shipload of refugees—"

"I did them a disservice." Jean cut her off. "They would all have been better off dead."

"How do you know that?"

"What life does any penniless widow or orphan have in exile? What life does a disgraced Templar with one arm have?"

"Disgraced? Why are you disgraced? What have you done?" It was Geoffrey's voice. In the heat of their own emotions, they had not heard him approach.

Jean spun about and gazed up at his father, sitting straight in his saddle, his shoulders as broad as a young man's though they sagged a little these days, the colour of his beard indecipherable in the dusk. Jean quailed before him inwardly. He remembered the gist of De Sonnac's dream and letter. He could picture the master's mantle on his father's shoulders, and he imagined that the hilt of De Sonnac's sword glinted once. "I survived," he answered his father's question.

"So did I," Geoffrey pointed out, springing down from his stallion and flinging the reins over the horse's head in a single motion. He led the stallion forward. "Did you curse God the night Acre fell? Could you see the severed heads of your friends and brothers by the light of the burning city, hear the taunting chants of triumph from the Muslims, and not curse God?"

"I was too tired to curse anyone," Jean admitted somewhat shamefacedly.

Geoffrey stood directly before him and they looked each other in the eye. Geoffrey could identify with Jean's pain and confusion. He knew, furthermore, that it had taken Eleanor and Brother Hilarion to inspire him to go on living. And he had been whole of body. The sight of Jean's empty sleeve was like a splinter in his heart.

"Do you know what De Sonnac wrote?" It was Jean who broke the silence.

Geoffrey shook his head. "Does it matter after all these years? You are the better Templar, Jean, the better knight and the better Christian."

Jean had to break his father's gaze. He could not bear the admiration and love that he read in his father's eyes. He did not deserve it. He looked away and forced a laugh. "You think I am a better Templar? If you only knew how often I've broken my vows!"

"I told you from the start you would not find chastity easy."

"I vowed chastity, poverty and obedience, and I've kept none of my vows!"

"Poverty?"

"You know the Temple at Acre! Kings do not live better!"

"Obedience?"

"I did as I pleased." In his mind's eye he saw the slave market at Nazareth, the Templar funds he had spent with the uninhibited generosity of a great lord. "Do you know the reason I was indulged, Father? Because De Sonnac asked his successors to take you into their hearts and household – and prepare you to be master one day. He saw that in a dream."

"He had taken a serious blow to the head," Geoffrey answered hastily, but he was shaken by the revelation nonetheless.

Something sent a cold shiver down his spine and he was afraid to look in Eleanor's direction. Eleanor was already beside him, however. Tense and alert she stood listening. She did not attempt to interfere directly, but her almost palpable feelings were too powerful to ignore.

"You are my heir, Jean," Geoffrey told his son.

"No, damn it! Louis is your heir! Louis, Louis, Louis! Do you know how much I hate him, have always hated him?!" It exploded from Jean with unnecessary violence and he was ashamed of himself almost before the words had disintegrated in the evening air.

"Do you know how jealous Louis is, that I love you more?" It was Eleanor who answered softly.

"You had a strange way of showing it!" Jean retorted almost against his will. He could feel the strength of his parents' love. He knew that his bitterness was hurting them – and they were the only two people in the whole world who did not deserve to be hurt.

Geoffrey put his arm around Eleanor to support her as she took the blow Jean had delivered and he spoke to distract Jean from his mother. "Louis is heir to your mother's estates. You are heir to anything of mine – especially anything due to me as a would-be Templar."

"De Beaujeu is dead – and we burned De Sonnac's letter so it wouldn't fall into Muslim hands. De Molay doesn't even know who you are – but he wants me buried alive! He's sent me to the commandery at Mingary – wherever in God's name that may be."

"As commander." It was unclear if this was a question or a statement.

"As commander of what?" Jean returned. "I can't even train horses in my present state – much less boys whose hearts are filled with visions of rescuing Jerusalem."

"You can do both, if you want to, Jean. The trouble is you don't want to."

"What is the point? What, in God's name, is the point of living at all?"

It was the piping, tear-filled voice of the Greek boy Niki, who answered. The boy, forgotten by the other three, assumed that he was the cause of the argument he could not understand, and he called out in anguish. Only Geoffrey understood his words, and turned to assure the boy that he need not fear.

But Eleanor was quicker to understand his significance.

"That is the reason for living, Jean!" She pointed to the frightened boy. "To give others life and hope and freedom!"

Jean stared at his mother and she met his eyes. She could sense that he was not convinced, could read the resentment and defiance and rebellion in his smouldering eyes.

Jean had dozens of answers to her statement. What worth was Niki? Or Rachel? Or even Madeleine? What made their lives any more valuable than those of De Beaujeu or De Sevrey, Pirenne or even poor Pierre? Did sex and poverty make a soul more valuable? More worth saving? If any living soul in Acre had deserved to survive then it had been De Beaujeu – and the patriarch perhaps, Jean conceded, remembering the old man loading the human rubbish of Acre into his skiff until it capsized and they all drowned. The loyal bandy-legged Paul who had come to the Holy Land to find his missing brother had died under the crushing weight of the collapsing Temple, while his rogue of a brother sold fake relics at the quayside of Limassol. A certain cynical twist marred the line of Jean's lips. He fought with his mother mentally.

Eleanor had thought Jean too good for the futile idiocy of fighting for a Holy Land she knew was lost before he ever set foot in it. Jean's answer had been to give his life more meaning than had he become a peer of France or the Pope in Rome – much less married a spice merchant's daughter or any of the other fates she might have planned for him. Sister Madeleine, De Villaret, Father Etienne,

MacDonald, Lady Melisende – everyone who had known him in Acre – spoke of him with awe. But what good was the admiration – even the adoration – if it did not fill Jean with the warmth and joy and contentment which made it worth living?

"Go to the leper hospital outside Paphos, Jean," Eleanor urged him abruptly.

The remark seemed so totally inapposite that Jean frowned and cocked his head, looking for the relevance. "You think I belong with the lepers? I'd rather be dead."

"No, you aren't a leper yet," Eleanor retorted with a sharpness that made Jean wince involuntarily. "But you owe it to Rachel – before you hang yourself – to pretend at least that you don't blame her for the loss of your arm."

The shock that went through Jean's body was visible. "Rachel? Rachel is at the leper hospital?" Eleanor nodded. "Christ! What have I done to deserve this! Don't you see? She would have been better dead – a hundred times better dead!" His horror was real, the horror that most healthy people felt at the thought of leprosy.

But Eleanor was unimpressed. "You have no right to decide that – not without even visiting her. The girl suffers far less from the disease than from her sense of guilt. She is demented – and all because she thinks you blame her for the loss of your arm."

"I find that hard to believe," Jean told his mother stiffly. He suspected that his mother had some ulterior motive for wanting him to go to the leper hospital even if he couldn't decipher it.

Eleanor shrugged. "Go and see for yourself."

Jean opened his mouth to protest again, but his father cut him off. "Your mother is right, Jean. You owe it to the girl to at least visit her. You saved her life. You cannot wash your hands of her now."

Jean could defy his mother, but not his father. Without thinking he gave the answer he would have owed De Beaujeu. "In God's name, so be it."

Paphos
October 1291

The De Montfort estate outside Paphos had been badly damaged in an earthquake at the start of the century and thereafter had never again been used as a De Montfort residence. The farm buildings, like the grand house, fell into increasing disrepair while the lands were rented out to tenant farmers. Then, two months earlier, Lady Melisende had donated the vacant buildings for use as a leper hospital and ordered the rents from the estate turned over to the leper colony for their upkeep. The news of this grant had reached even Nicosia and Limassol, and although there were voices in Paphos who objected to a concentration of lepers so near their city, most citizens were impressed by the generosity of the widow in making this charitable gesture.

Jean was impressed by the extent of the repairs that had evidently been effected in such a short time. The large stone barn and several of the other sheds had been rethatched extensively so that jarring blond thatch disturbed the harmony of comfortable decay that dominated the complex. The animal pens were also fenced in with rails so newly split that the wood was still white where the axe had cloven the branches. There were new, bright orange tiles scattered liberally across the roof of the house, and whitewash – if somewhat thin – had done much to clean the appearance of the ancient structure. On closer examination it was clear that much of the plaster was cracked and chipped, and it would need to be redone some time soon. Jean supposed, however, that the repairs could wait till the spring when there was no risk of rain and the plaster would dry faster.

In the yard behind the barn, a large iron vat over a fire was seeping steam, and the scent of lye hung heavy in the air. Draped across lines strung between the trees were sheets and linens, garments and bandages. One woman stirred the vat with a long wooden oar while two other women wrung out the laundry and hung it up to dry.

They all wore pale-blue gowns with loose, blue and white striped surcoats and white wimples wrapped almost like a Muslim woman's chador. It was an unusual habit for serving sisters, Jean thought first, and then with horror he realised that the woman stirring the vat had only one hand and a stump wrapped in bandages. These women were lepers, and the veils covered the ulcers or missing features of their faces.

As he registered that the women were themselves patients, he forced himself to stop and look at them again, but they were mature women, too large to be Rachel.

He rode into the courtyard and dismounted from his stallion. A man in a caftan of the same blue and white homemade linen as the sisters hobbled out of the barn on a crutch. *"Bonjour, Monsieur le Templar*! I'll see to your horse. Do you want him watered and fed? Shall I brush him down?" As he spoke he held out his hand for a coin, and after a moment's hesitation Jean gave him the same tip he would have given any stable boy for similar services.

"I am looking for a girl called Rachel, a refugee from Acre," Jean told the man who had taken his horse.

"The loony Jewess?" the man asked in surprise. "What does a Templar want with her? She only mumbles Hebrew and other gibberish."

"Do you know where I can find her?" Jean insisted, with just a touch of hardness in his voice to remind the impertinent man that he had no right to question a knight Templar's business.

"She keeps to the loft most days."

He indicated the rethatched barn and Jean made straight for this spacious building. Entering, he was startled to discover that it had been converted to a dormitory. The effect was startling. It must have been nearly a century since livestock had been housed here and there was no trace of the stench left. The walls were freshly whitewashed. The floor was covered with fresh straw and blankets were rolled neatly along the edge, ready to be rolled out. Light poured down from the windows set under the rafters. At one end, a flimsy wooden partition separated off the last bay, into which the loft had been built. As he advanced toward this part of the barn, he noted that the stone troughs lining the barn held clean, gently flowing water, as in a monastery lavatorium.

Stepping through the opening in the partition he was confronted with a shock of a different kind. Here the patients too ill to move lay side by side and, despite the bundles of herbs hung from the rafters and the clean straw, the stench of rotting flesh dominated the area. Jean gagged and his hand went automatically to cover his nose and mouth. The nun bending over one of the patients looked up in surprise at the unexpected intrusion and her eyes widened in disbelief.

Jean flushed in shame. "Sister Madeleine." He dropped his hand from his face.

"Sir Jean." She too had flushed a violent shade of red, but Jean was too embarrassed to notice.

"My mother said Rachel was here," he managed, thinking that his mother had also known Madeleine was here. His devious, conniving, clever, intuitive, dangerous mother...

"Rachel." Of course, Rachel. "Rachel is in the loft." Sister Madeleine pointed toward the wooden ceiling over their heads. She had elegant long, white fingers and her gesture was graceful – even though her skin was rough and her fingernails clipped short.

"May I go up?" Jean asked.

"Of course. Maybe you can help her. None of the rest of us have been able to."

"The rest of you?" Jean asked, hesitating indecisively. "There are other nuns here?"

"No, just the lepers and Father Bernard."

"Ah. Father Bernard is from the Brothers of Saint Lazarus?" Jean tried to put some coherent, familiar form to this curious institution.

"No, he was once a Dominican and he is now a doctor. You remember him."

"How should I remember him?" Jean countered, irritated. "I've never been here before."

"But in Nazareth, Centurion!" Father Bernard remarked in his echoing voice as he ducked through the partition.

Jean spun about in confusion and found the old man – dressed in the same blue and white caftan as the patients – laughing delightedly at him.

"You! You nearly cost me my mantle!" Jean found that he was angry at the man for not having turned himself over to his order. He remembered that horrible scene in De Beaujeu's chapel and the loss of his command, the months of disgrace.

"Your mantle, Centurion? What does your mantle mean to me? If I had let myself fall into the hands of the Inquisition, I would not be here today, would not be able to help these poor souls. Besides, your order claims not to scorn even the excommunicate, so how dare it scorn the convert returned to the true faith?" He mocked and provoked and meant every word he said.

Jean knew no answer to his question, and he had no patience for a debate. He looked from Father Bernard back to Sister Madeleine. "Let me see Rachel."

Madeleine collected her skirts in her hand and led the way up the narrow flight of stairs that slanted up the loft along the back end of the barn. The loft was filled with bales of fresh, sweet-smelling hay, and strings of various herbs drying out hung from nails in the wall. Jean looked about, bewildered at first before at last he located two bare feet sticking out from between some bales of hay. Madeleine was already advancing toward the feet, speaking gently. "Rachel. There's a visitor come to see you."

Jean followed Madeleine, conscious of the malicious shadow of Father Bernard behind him. The old Dominican was evidently looking forward to the coming encounter. Rachel sat on the floor of the loft between the bales of hay dressed like the other patients in her homespun, blue gown and striped surcoat. She did not wear the wimple, however, only the head covering of a Jewish maiden. She clasped her crossed arms over her chest and swayed back and forth muttering in Hebrew. Her eyes were red and watering and her hands discoloured, but otherwise Jean would not have recognised her as a leper.

"Rachel." He said her name softly, and he saw her flinch. But she did not look up. Madeleine stepped aside so he could approach still nearer and he went down on his heels. "Rachel." He repeated. "It's me. Jean."

The droning of her prayers and her swaying stopped abruptly. She sat like a frightened rabbit, stock-still except for an almost imperceptible quivering.

"Rachel." He reached out his only hand toward her. "Don't you want to come for a ride with me?" It was a silly offer perhaps, but he didn't know what else he should suggest.

The girl lifted her head very slowly, but her gaze never reached his face. Her eyes fixed upon the empty sleeve of his hauberk and she screamed. Then she clamped her hands over her ears as if to block out the sound of her own screaming and flung herself about to crawl back into the hay. She crushed her face against the hay bale with her hands over her ears and shook her head, whimpering.

Jean looked at Madeleine helplessly. He felt completely inadequate. He didn't know if he should try to comfort Rachel or leave her alone. Madeleine resolved his dilemma by going on her knees and putting her arm around Rachel's shoulder. "There's nothing to be afraid of, Rachel. Sir Jean has come to see you. He wants to know how you're faring. He is concerned about you. He wants you to get well."

Jean pulled himself together. He remembered what his mother had said about Rachel feeling guilty about his arm. Certainly it had been the sight of his wound that had set off her screaming. "You've nothing to be upset about, Rachel," he told her, and then flushed as he remembered she was an orphan and a leper with every reason to be distressed. "Not on my account," he amended. "Don't you want to come down and see my new stallion?" She had always loved petting his stallions.

Rachel shook her head and kept her face buried in the straw.

"Let her be now," Father Bernard ordered from the background. "There is no point in harassing her. She is happier alone."

Jean, discomfited by the entire encounter, readily followed Father Bernard's advice and withdrew backwards. Sister Madeleine patted Rachel on the shoulder and murmured a few words of comfort and then followed the two men to the floor below.

Father Bernard took a perverse pleasure in noting the paleness of Jean's face. "What? Have we distressed our brave centurion? Come, come, such sights are common enough in this world."

Jean would have liked to lash back at the man, but Sister Madeleine laid her hand on his arm. "Wouldn't you like to see the rest of our colony, sir?"

"Yes," he replied stiffly, turning his back on Father Bernard, who cackled in delight as Madeleine led him out of the sick chamber. They left the barn and went into the yard where the women were doing the laundry. Madeleine exchanged a few words with them and then continued into the next shed. Here the pens had been cleared away and replaced with crude shelves on which a few, isolated glass phials and bottles stood. "We want to build up our own apothecary," she explained. "We haven't got very far yet, but anything we can grow, grind and prepare ourselves we will collect here, and we will purchase what we cannot produce if and when we can afford it." She led him out of the far door.

"This will be the herb garden," she announced. The fenced-off area was ploughed and furrowed but as yet bare of plants. Whether anything had been planted he could not tell.

They continued through a little gate in the fence and across what had once been a cobbled path to the next shed. Even before entering, Jean could smell the manure and knew that this shed was still in use for livestock. There were two pigs lying contentedly on the muddy floor and a black goat.

Madeleine explained in a flood that their goal was to provide the patients with a properly balanced diet. They wanted to make sure that the patients ate meat at least once a week. The men could shepherd and tend the animals. They also wanted to produce their own cheese. They would start with sheep and goat's cheese, but she hoped that eventually they would be able to afford a dairy cow.

They had olive trees and lemon trees of their own. There were many dead trees and she knew they would have to get some help restoring the productivity of the orchards, but it was a start. Father Bernard said the citrus fruits were particularly important. They would, of course, grow their own carrots, onions, leeks and beans. She gestured to another area which had been cleared but not yet ploughed.

They would have to buy fresh fish at Paphos or one of the other fishing villages, she admitted somewhat regretfully. But they received wheat from the tenants and she wanted to talk to Lady Melisende about seeing that it was delivered as flour. She and Father Bernard had no means of getting to the mill and back, at least not yet. As soon as they had the money together they would buy a wagon and one sturdy cart horse.

But there was so much to be done. In the ruins of the other buildings she painted pictures of women working at looms and spinning wheels. She spoke of a carpentry shop of their own, and a cooperage, since one of the men was a trained cooper. She spoke without prompting and without stopping. Her enthusiasm and her concerns were undisguised.

Jean watched her sidelong more than directly. He looked dutifully at all she pointed to and he asked the occasional question, so as not to appear disinterested. He was impressed as much by the ambition of Sister Madeleine's plans as by what had already been achieved. And he noted to himself that she had never looked so lively or so lovely before. It was not just the comparison with the half-starved, filthy creature of Nazareth, but with the pink and white nun in starched veils at Acre. Here she had let the sun burn her face and her hands were raw with work, but she glowed with inner health and the kind of beauty that cannot be painted on.

They had come full circuit, having toured all the buildings except the manor house itself, and stood again before the entry to the dormitory-barn. "There is no known cure for leprosy," Sister Madeleine was telling him authoritatively. "But by providing proper food and decent hygiene it is possible to keep the victims otherwise healthy. Father Bernard thinks that with time we may even be able to find means of treating the disease. At the very least—"

The crack of thunder drowned out her sentence and made Jean start. The sky had filled with seething black clouds and these were being chased in from the sea by a rising wind. Jean had been conscious of the gathering storm, the first of the autumn rains, as they did their tour, but he had not been particularly distressed by it. He'd often ridden escort duty in weather like this, and was stoical about it. Besides it was not that far to Paphos.

Madeleine, however, had been so absorbed in showing around her guest and explaining her plans that she only now realised the rains were about to break. "Oh, we must get the laundry in!" she cried even as she sprinted away from him.

For a moment, Jean stood where she had left him, and then, feeling ridiculous just standing there, he followed her. The three patients who had been tending the laundry had long since seen the coming storm and were already nearly finished with the task of bringing it in when Madeleine and Jean arrived. Jean took a load of clean linens in his arm and carried them into the future apothecary as directed. Other half-dry to soaking wet garments and bandages were heaped about the room, and behind him the women were chattering and arguing about whether they could hang it all up in the dormitory. Jean dumped his load upon a broad shelf and then started to withdraw.

"You can't ride in this weather!" Sister Madeleine protested, the roar of the rain pelting the roof almost drowning out her voice as the clouds burst open. "You needn't fear infection. We can make up a room for you in the house," she added, seeing the refusal in his eyes even before he opened his mouth.

The three leper women were standing in the doorway watching the storm with the good-natured excitement of people with a good solid roof over their heads. Focusing on their chatter, he heard they were laughing about how dreadful it had been the winter before, when they had had to beg in weather like this and had only their miserable mud huts, soon filled with water. And there had been that one storm that had washed away half the colony! Yes, and so-and-so had drowned in the mud slide! They were enjoying telling of the misery of years passed, and did not mind that the rain smashing on the cobbles of the courtyard was spattering them with spume. They decided to make a dash for the kitchen part of the house, where the evening meal was being prepared and the patients ate at a massive pine table on crude benches.

Sister Madeleine and Jean remained behind. The rain poured from the heavens in sheets and Jean felt no desire to go out into it – much less ride for an hour. Though it was warm, he'd be soaked through before he made the Temple at Paphos and even his well-oiled chainmail would start to rust and need to be sanded and re-oiled. But it could hardly rain this hard forever, he consoled himself. "I'll wait out the storm in the stables," he informed Madeleine.

"Why the stables? You can wait in the house. I can bring you some dinner and wine."

"You don't need to wait on me, Sister."

"You are our first guest other than Lady Melisende – and she's the proprietor. Let me bring you something to eat." Then, collecting her skirts, she led them in a dash across the courtyard to the manor house.

They clattered into the entrance hall, rain dripping from Jean's nose and the empty sleeve of his hauberk. Madeleine snapped her veils off in a sharp, efficient motion and shook off the water with quick flicks of her hand. Her hair, which had been shaved off after her release from slavery so that it could grow back its natural colour, came only to the base of her neck. The sight of her naked head, her hair gleaming and exotically short, sent an unpleasant shock through Jean's body. Was she really as innocent as she pretended or was she intentionally being coquettish? A woman with her past could hardly be called naive, Jean decided with a tightening of his jaw. He looked at her sidelong through narrowed, bitter eyes.

"Here." She indicated the doorway into a long room dim now because of the oppressive overcast sky of the storm. Jean strode past her, consciously scorning looking at her more closely. And was astonished to find that he was standing on an exquisitely tiled floor. The chamber was almost naked of furniture – there was only a single chest between two windows of one wall and a forlorn looking table at the far end of the room with two short benches flanking it. "This is where Father Bernard and I take our meals," Madeleine explained to him. "I realise it is not particularly comfortable, but we don't want to spend money on ourselves – not until our patients have everything they need."

"So why don't you eat and live with them in the kitchen and barn?" Jean asked unkindly.

Madeleine absorbed the blow and her eyes widened slightly with pain, but she answered levelly. "Father Bernard says we must not eat, bathe or sleep near the lepers or we risk infection ourselves. I'll bring you a lamp and something to eat and drink." Already she was refitting her veils in preparation for going out into the rain.

Jean regretted his nastiness. Maybe she really didn't suspect the effect her uncovered head with its exotic short hair had on him...

She was gone into the rain and he wandered across the room, absently tracing the pattern of the mosaics with the toe of his boot. The border was a black and white geometric pattern but in the centre a rider was spearing a lion. He paused and studied the mosaic by the imperfect light. It was a beautiful piece of art – and certainly hundreds of years old. He glanced up at the room around him. It was not as old as the mosaic. No doubt the house had been built upon the foundations of a ruined Roman residence.

In his imagination he substituted sandals for his dusty, leather boots and conjured from the feet up senators, centurions and matrons striding or dawdling across the surface of the floor. The Romans had lost their empire piece by piece, withdrawn and retreated, leaving their colonists to the mercy of the barbarians, leaving the shattered fragments of civilisation to crack and collapse and crumble. They had left their mark in Jerusalem no less than here and in Nîmes and York. But Master De Molay was sending him beyond the reach of Rome, beyond the edge of the civilised world, to Western Scotland. He would take MacDonald with him, he decided. As commander, he had the right to a sergeant, a serving brother and two squires as escort.

Jean was yanked from his reverie by the banging of the door, and, looking up from the mosaic, saw Madeleine carrying a tray laden with food and drink. His good manners prodded him to come to her assistance. He took the tray from her and carried it to the table while she hastened back to close the door against the rain. He set the tray down on the table and she was beside him almost at once, unloading the things she'd brought including an oil lamp and a candle. "It will be dark soon," she said by way of explanation. In fact the storm had already plunged the room into gloom.

"The tiles look Roman," Jean spoke his thoughts aloud rather than responding. "Do you know the history of the house?"

"No. But it was certainly built on Roman foundations. There is a magnificent bath. Do you want to see? Come."

Jean's eyes narrowed suspiciously, but his curiosity was greater than his resentment. He followed her out a door at the end of the chamber, through two naked chambers with cracked and faded frescoes. Suddenly an atrium opened before them surrounded by Corinthian pillars. The rain fell in unbroken sheets upon the broken remnants of a fountain and had long since washed the dust from the thirsty weeds. The rain even blew in under the columns, to soak the shattered pavement of the walkway around the open court. Puddles were already forming and water running with a guilty-gleeful gurgling diagonally across the walkway to empty in one of the rooms beyond. As they walked along beside the courtyard, they were sprinkled liberally with rain and Jean noted that the skirts of Madeleine's habit was now spattered with mud, the hem caked in the slime.

They stepped down two marble steps into a large room lined with a marble bench. The ceiling was made of thin slabs of alabaster that – had the sun been high or the rain less violent – would have lit the room with diffused, natural light. The bath filled nearly the entire room, leaving only a four foot border of once-polished marble. Jean advanced to stare into the bath itself, expecting it to be filthy with the accumulated dirt of centuries, but the tiled bottom stared back up at him distinctly, wiggling slightly. "You cleaned it out?"

"Yes, it was one of the first things Father Bernard did. He said that if we were to spend our days with the lepers, we must be careful to bathe every night before retiring."

Jean was gazing into the water again. The tiles depicted nude nymphs flirting brazenly with muscular men clad only in shinguards and sandals. The scene bordered on the explicitly pornographic.

"You are welcome to bathe if you like," Madeleine offered, misreading the longing in his gaze.

Jean spun about on her angrily. "Are you in Jacques de Molay's pay or my mother's?"

"What are you talking about?" she asked in genuine bafflement, quailing under the viciousness in his eyes. His anger lacerated her, but she could not make the least sense of his remark.

"I'm a monk not a castrate, and you can't mean that you are trying to seduce me for your own sake!" he snapped back. "De Molay would pay a fortune to be justified in locking me in a windowless dungeon for the rest of my life – as if Western Scotland were not itself a sunless prison! And my mother…" Jean could only shake his head in frustration. His mother never gave up. She had seduced one man out of the order and she could not accept that he could not be lured back. Damn her!

"I'm not a whore," Madeleine managed to get out, but she was trembling so violently that she knew she could not stay. She turned and tried to withdraw without running, without breaking into sobs. She failed. She tripped on the steps leading back to the atrium, and the cry that escaped her had as much to do with inner agony as surprise and the hurt of a banged knee.

Jean had his arm around her even as she tried to scramble to her feet. "Forgive me. Please forgive me!" He was trying to pull her to him, to hold her against his chest, but was sorely disadvantaged by having only one arm. She wriggled free of him but fell on her side, sobbing openly now and refusing to look at him.

"Please. Please, forgive me," he begged her desperately. The injustice of his behaviour and his remarks filled him with an inner shame he could not bear. How could he have hurt this vulnerable young woman? Like his parents, she had not earned the blows he had delivered, but unlike his parents she was not strong enough to deflect or absorb them. He had broken something when he hit out at her, and he hadn't meant to. "Madeleine, please, forgive me."

"Just explain why you wanted to hurt me! Why does everyone want to hurt me?" Madeleine demanded in her pain.

"I didn't want to hurt you. Don't you understand? I'm fighting with myself. Oh, Madeleine..." He sank down beside her on the steps and gently, sadly touched her shoulder.

She looked up sharply at him. "Then why imply I would sell myself for money? Why call me whore?" The tears glistened in her eyes and on her cheeks but she was angry too.

Jean was sufficiently ashamed to admit the truth. "Because I was trying to stop myself from wanting you."

She caught her breath and stared at him, but he would not meet her eyes. He looked down at the worn marble, noticing the patterns of black in white, the blood of shame and desire flushing his cheeks and ears.

Madeleine's heart was pounding in her chest enough to deafen her. Oh Christ, she thought, what was she supposed to do? She loved Jean so much she thought she would willingly die for him. And even in the dusk she could see the lines carved by pain on his face, the weariness of his entire body, and she knew that he was miserably unhappy. She did not understand exactly. Was it his missing arm or De Molay's rise to power, Rachel's madness or the loss of his friends at Acre? All of it together, she decided. He was suffering, and she wanted to comfort him.

She swallowed down an inner revulsion and forced herself to accept the fact that men found comfort in sexual intercourse. She had never learned Arabic, only a few hundred isolated words, but she had not needed to understand the language to sense the aggression, contempt and even hatred of the men who had used her. She had sensed curiosity and eagerness and occasionally even pity. There had even been one guest who had gently wrapped her in the silken robes his predecessor had stripped off her and sent her back to the harem without touching her. And there had been one middle-aged man who had borrowed her more than once and taken comfort from the Christian slave who could not complain or nag or place any demands upon him.

After all that, what was one man more? Roger de Flor had used the same reasoning to make her pay her passage to Marseilles with access to her bed. She had no other means of payment and she had been desperate to flee Cyprus. At the end of the voyage, he said she had not yet 'worked off' her passage, and he would have kept her prisoner for God-knew-how-long had not Geoffrey de Preuthune paid the 'outstanding fare' in gold. If she could prostitute herself to a man like De Flor, how could she deny her favours to Jean?

She had removed her veil to shake off the rain in absolute innocence only an hour earlier, but now, when she sat up slowly and shoved her veil off her head, she knew what she intended. Jean recognised the difference and blushed to think that he had misjudged her earlier.

Madeleine was ashamed to meet his eyes. She had never looked any of her rapists in the face, so she stood and walked away from Jean. At the edge of the Roman bath she stopped and removed her shoes. She did not rush, but there was nothing even remotely coquettish about the wooden way she drew her arms inside her habit and then shoved it off, over her head. She folded it and laid it beside her shoes. Under the shabby, white habit, she also wore the blue homespun gown of her patients. She reached up under her skirts, her back still to Jean, and removed her stockings and drawers without exposing any flesh. Fascinated, Jean watched from the entryway. She pulled the blue gown over her head and folded it on top of the habit. "I'll just bathe so there is no risk of infection," she murmured over her shoulder and stepped into the bath still wearing her shift.

Jean did not dare to move and he breathed with difficulty. The sleeveless shift exposed her firm, shapely arms, white as ivory and splendid as a statue in the dimness of the room. The silk of the shift clung to her hips and her gently curving buttocks, the crevice between them sharply defined by shadow until she sank from sight in the water of the bath.

Absently, Jean removed his sword and then leaned forward and unbuckled his spurs. His conscience reproached him, but his fingers hesitated only for an instant. He pulled off his boots, the garters holding his hose and then the hose themselves. It took a long time, fumbling as he did with one hand. He cursed to himself as he struggled to pull the heavy hauberk off over his head and he was left panting and sweating from the effort. His aketon and shirt followed, but he could not bring himself to drop his drawers, so he started forward with his loins covered. Shoving his clothes aside, he noticed in a wall niche that must have once housed a statue a pile of towels and a collection of jars and bowls containing bath oils, scented soaps and creams. He stooped to inspect the collection more closely and selected a bar of scented soap. He was reminded of poor Pierre and felt a wrenching pity for the dead squire. That day in Acre so long ago, Pierre had not wanted anything other than what he wanted now – the comfort of physical love.

Madeleine had swum to the far side of the bath and stood with the water up to her chest, rubbing herself with water, her face to the far wall. Her hair was soaked and plastered to her head. Jean had never seen a woman with short hair before, nor had he ever bathed with a woman. The excitement that possessed him drowned out the last feeble protests of his conscience, but it intimidated him as well. He advanced with hesitant steps into the bath and the thundering of his heart and tightness of his throat reminded him of the moments before battle.

Madeleine had not realised he had entered the water until he was directly behind her. She gasped in surprise and was unable to disguise the fear in her eyes as she glanced over her shoulder.

"Let me..." Jean murmured, lifting the soap to her neck and gently starting to soap her.

The protest on her lips against the use of soap in the bath was not spoken. She went stock-still and waited for what would happen.

Jean massaged her shoulders while he cleaned them, inch by inch, gently shoving the straps of her shift off her shoulders and down her arms. Her tenseness communicated itself to him and made him more gentle still. He caressed more than he cleaned.

The shift was held up only by her breasts, which she pressed against the side of the bath. Jean ran his hand up the back of her neck and into her hair. A shudder went through her and she caught her breath. Jean stopped, waited, his fingers kneading the back of her head gently. She seemed to relax slightly. The shift fell to her waist by its own weight.

Jean returned his attention to soaping her back and then down her backside, pushing the shift before him. He had to dip his head underwater as he worked his way down her body, but he did not mind. Even with his eyes closed, his hand led him down one leg and then, after surfacing for air, down the other.

While he washed her legs, Madeleine stepped out of the useless shift. She did not understand the tension of her body. She did not understand why she could not relax. Once she had learned that resistance and protest aroused her attackers, she had learned how to relax her body so utterly that her response to even the most vulgar and violent assaults upon her had been a passivity that bored if it did not actually repulse her aggressors. She had learned to detach herself utterly from her body during all the tedious and disgusting preliminaries. In the past, even with Roger de Flor, the only moment she had ever actually felt had been that degrading instant of male victory when the words 'Allah Ahkbar' pounded in her brain to the rhythm of the thrusting. Now she felt every nerve and every millimetre of skin he touched. She felt as if his touch set her veins on fire and the burning blood rushed to her heart and head, making her hot despite the coolness of the bath.

Jean bent and whispered in her ear, "Please turn around," and the hair on her head seemed to stand on end. She turned around, slavishly obedient, but she kept her eyes closed. The touch of Jean's hand on her throat sent a ringing through her body that made her try to hold her breath. She could not. His fingers caressed her shoulders and his lips fluttered over her closed eyelids. His beard tickled her nose and cheek. His hand had reached her breasts and his lips touched hers.

Not one of the Arab men who had violated her had ever kissed her on the lips. Roger de Flor had pressed his garlic-smelling mouth over hers and she had gagged, making him angry. But his anger had been useful. Thereafter he had dispensed with the fraud of foreplay and got on with taking what he had come for. Madeleine had been glad to have it over with quickly.

Jean's breath was warm and yet neutrally fresh. His lips were dry, slightly cracked and incredibly gentle. Madeleine lifted her chin just a fraction. An inexplicable hunger for the reverent touch of kind lips overpowered all her memories of abuse. Jean's response was instantaneous. He kissed her again and again – eagerly and joyfully but careful not to become insistent. He kissed not just her lips but her eyes and her ears and her throat. Only later did she realise that he held her breasts in his hand while he kissed her.

His lips to her ear, he murmured, "Madeleine, forgive me." And she could feel his breath burning its way from her ear down her throat to her lungs and her heart.

"Christ!" she prayed inarticulately, aware only that she had lost control of the situation entirely. "Christ!" He had somehow entered her and she felt the burning between her legs and the cramping of her stomach. And she was frightened of what was happening to her because it was utterly unfamiliar. She gasped for breath and lost her footing, winding her feet around Jean's back, locking her ankles together and holding him tightly in her arms.

He had pressed her against the back of the bath, but his kisses found her lips again. "I love you, Madeleine. I love you so much."

The cry that followed shocked her, frightened her, and then, with a drawn-out moan, he begged again, "Forgive me."

She had to hold him tightly with her legs to keep from falling back on to the floor of the bath. She kissed his ear, she stroked his hair with her wet hands still wrapped around his neck. "It's all right, Jean," she told him honestly. "It's more than all right, Jean." She expanded. "I love you. I have loved you since the day in Nazareth when you came like the Archangel Gabriel to raise me out of the filth."

"To drag you back again?" Jean had come to himself. He gently withdrew and took Madeleine in his arms with remorse rather than passion.

"Was that filth?" Madeleine asked, surprised. "I thought it was lovely."

Jean looked at her sharply. "Do you mean that?"

"It is the first time I did not hear a Mameluke grunting 'Allah Ahkbar' in my ear as the man fucking me reached his climax," Madeleine told him bluntly.

She felt the shock that went through his body and at once regretted her candidness. She held him fast as he went to pull away in shame. "It's all right, Jean. You didn't force yourself on me. I invited you – and I have no regrets. Come, let us dry off before we both catch cold." She released him but she took his hand and led him out by the stairs.

Out of the water, she remembered her nakedness and was embarrassed. She reached for her gown, anxious to cover herself, even wet and without a shift, but now Jean stopped her.

"Let me dry you," he urged and grabbed a towel.

Madeleine stood still and let him dab her dry. Her embarrassment was greater than at any time since the very beginning of her slavery, but she sensed an almost equal bashfulness in Jean so she submitted without resentment. When he had finished, she took another towel and rubbed his back and chest, but – despite her past – she could not find the brazenness to dry him below the waist. He took the towel from her hand and hastily dried himself.

She reached again for her pile of clothes.

"Wait." He stopped her with his hand. "Come." He spread fresh towels on the marble flooring and gestured for her to lie down. She obeyed him unquestioningly although she looked into his face anxiously. She did not know what he wanted, only that she trusted him not to hurt her even though her embarrassment was acute.

Jean sniffed at the oils and creams and selected one. Removing the stopper, he up-ended it on to his hand and started to rub her right foot gently. The gesture brought tears to Madeleine's eyes. "You don't need to do that, Jean."

"But I want to," he answered solemnly. His remaining hand was surprisingly strong and his thumb pressed into her aching muscles, releasing pent-up weariness. Madeleine's eye fell on his naked stump. Although their eyes were adjusted to the dark, it was still too dim to see the scars clearly. She could make out only the puckering of skin around the end of the stump.

"Is it very offensive?" he asked, without removing his eyes from her feet.

"No. It's humbling."

He looked up questioningly.

"It was a high price to pay."

"Others gave their lives," he answered harshly, and for the first time since they had made love she heard the bitterness and the anger in his voice.

"Don't you believe in the God you serve? 'I am the resurrection and the life, he who liveth and believeth in Me, though he be dead, yet shall he live.' Surely, Master De Beaujeu and Marshal De Sevrey lived and believed in Christ?"

Jean's hand fell still. He stared into nothingness.

"Jean?"

He looked up and met her eyes. "I was wondering about my squire Pierre who was a sodomite, and Sergeant Pirenne, who killed a cripple and all the others with so many sins on their consciences. Are you sure they are forgiven?" It was a rhetorical question. After a pause he continued. He had finished with her feet and rubbed oil on her legs, working his way upwards. "I made a mistake when I joined the order. I am not fit to be a Templar. I have broken my vows over and over again – all of them, not just the vow of chastity. De Molay is right to ban me, right to scorn and despise me—"

"No!" She sat up abruptly, forgetting her nakedness. "No! De Molay is not half the man you are, Jean. He has no right to judge you, much less despise you."

"I joined the order out of arrogance, because I thought I was better than my brother Louis, because I thought I could save the Holy Land. Christ forgive me! I pictured myself a hero, while my brother was a nameless, nervous little baron of no consequence in Languedoc."

"And isn't that exactly what happened?" Madeleine had met Louis in Najac. He had not impressed her.

Jean shook his head. "No. In case you haven't noticed, the Holy Land is lost. And I have not only violated my own vows but debauched a nun – an unwilling nun at that. I am not fit to wear the mantle of the Knights Templar. I am not fit to wear spurs of any kind." He had intended to shock his mother when he spoke of hanging himself, but now he started to consider the option more seriously.

Madeleine did not answer with words. She reached for the oil and, pouring it into her left hand, she started to oil Jean's feet. A shock went through him. "What are you doing?"

"I am anointing your feet with oil. When I am finished, I will rub the rest of your body with it – especially your left arm."

Jean shook his head. "Madeleine, you mustn't. You are too good to play slave to me."

"Was Mary Magdalene Christ's slave?"

Jean could find no answer and Madeleine had not expected one. She worked methodically at oiling his calloused feet. His toe-nails were ragged, torn off rather than clipped, and she suspected that no one had ever tended to his feet other than himself. Arab men were more vain: they had regular manicures and pedicures and shaved their body hair. Jean's body had been much neglected. His skin was dry in patches, particularly where the hauberk rubbed under his swordbelt. His calf wound had never been treated, much less stitched. His hand was calloused and the fingernails as crudely tended as his toenails. Without noticing it, she had lost her shyness and discovered a contentment in this naked proximity.

"I love you, Madeleine," Jean declared sadly.

She started at his words. She knew that the professions of love gasped out during lovemaking had nothing to do with feelings. How many men who despised her as a worthless infidel had ejaculated declarations of love with their sperm? But this declaration had nothing to do with the confusion of sexual climax. It was said by a rational man in full consciousness. She gazed at him in wonder and met his eyes. He was not lying. She bent and kissed his chest in answer, too overcome to repeat his words. She caressed him with her fingers.

"Yesterday I came upon a boy who had tried to hang himself. I cut him down in time and brought him to my parents. He was ten years old and had hanged himself because he said no one loved him."

Madeleine stopped and looked at Jean alarmed.

"How much more reason to hang oneself when all one ever does is hurt the people who love you."

Madeleine was too shocked to move.

"My mother has been the victim of my stubbornness for thirteen years, and look what I've done to Rachel – and now you."

"You are not to blame for Rachel's condition, and you have given me more than you ever took away."

"Madeleine, don't you see? I've not only wasted my life, I've damaged others by what I've done. I made the wrong decision when I joined the Templars!"

"Possibly," Madeleine conceded, carefully rubbing the oil into his chest with a rhythmic circular motion. Her eyes followed her hands, and Jean fixed his gaze upon her serene face, the strands of wet hair falling on either side. "Certainly, I made a foolish decision when I took my vows so long ago in Poitou. I would laugh if it didn't make me cry! What in the name of God did I think a spoilt girl-child could achieve in Tripoli? Prayer alone was supposed to work miracles!" She shook her head in self-contempt, and then continued simply. "But we can't change what we did then. We can't go back in time and live our lives differently up to this point. The only thing we can do is try to live our lives differently from now on. I have decided to give my life to the lepers here. Maybe in ten years, I'll realise this too was an empty, futile—"

"No. You are doing something very beautiful, very meaningful. I envy you. What the hell am I supposed to do in the Outer Hebrides among the Vikings?"

"Convert them, perhaps, by your example. Or save other boys from hanging themselves in despair. Jean, when I was a slave, I wanted to die. In the slave caravan I ate as little as possible because the trader said he would leave me to die if I kept losing weight. And even after you rescued me, my life had no meaning. It was only after I'd been to the leper colony to find Rachel for you that I had the idea of doing something for them. You can't know now what you can do with your life in the future. All you can do is decide to make the most of it."

Jean stared at her. What was the point in telling her that all he wanted was to wake up beside her every morning? It would only hurt her, and he had to stop hurting the people he loved. She was right. He could not undo what he had done. He could not take off the mantle of the Temple – except to take on the habit of a stricter order. He could not even join the Hospitallers, though he felt it was a better home for him now that De Molay had control of the Temple. And he could not hang himself. De Sevrey had read him rightly. He clung to life, worthless as it seemed. And if he had hanged himself yesterday, he would never have lain here in the dark and seen how beautiful, graceful and loving Sister Madeleine was naked. Who knew what pleasures tomorrow might bring?

Jean raised himself from the towels on which they had lain and walked to the pile of clothes Madeleine had left by the edge of the bath. He took her gown and brought it back to her. Clumsily he tried to help her into her gown, but he was not much use. When she was clad, she helped dress him because he could no longer dress himself without assistance. Only then did he take her into his arm again and kiss the top of her head.

"If I once raised you from the gutter of slavery, you have raised me up from the dead – Mary Magdalene."